Sheryl Lister has enjoyed reading and writing for as long as she can remember. When she's not reading, writing or playing chauffeur, Sheryl can be found on a date with her husband or in the kitchen creating appetisers and bite-sized desserts. She holds a BS in Occupational Therapy and post-professional MS in Occupational Therapy from San Jose State University. She resides in California and is a wife, mother of three and works as a pediatric occupational therapist.

Amy Andrews is a multi-award winning, *USA Today* bestselling author who has written over forty contemporary romances for several Mills & Boon series. She's an Aussie who loves good books, fab food, great wine and frequent travel – preferably all four together. She lives by the ocean with her husband of twenty-nine years. To keep up with her latest releases and giveaways, find her website at amyandrews.com.au

USA Today bestselling author **Catherine Mann** has over a hundred books in print in more than twenty countries with Mills & Boon True Love, Heroes, and other imprints. A six-time *RITA* finalist, she has won both a *RITA* and Romantic Times Reviewer's Choice Award. Mother of four, Catherine lives in South Carolina with her husband where they enjoy kayaking, camping with their dogs, and volunteering at a service dog training organisation. For more information, visit: catherinemann.com

Sports Romance

Sports Romance:
In The End Zone

SHERYL LISTER

AMY ANDREWS

CATHERINE MANN

MILLS & BOON

First Published in Great Britain 2025
by Mills & Boon, an imprint of HarperCollins*Publishers* Ltd
1 London Bridge Street, London, SE1 9GF

www.harpercollins.co.uk

HarperCollins*Publishers*
Macken House, 39/40 Mayor Street Upper,
Dublin 1, D01 C9W8, Ireland

Sports Romance: In The End Zone © 2025 Harlequin Enterprises ULC.

Still Loving You © 2018 Sheryl Lister
Girl Least Likely to Marry © 2013 Amy Andrews
Reunited with the Rebel Billionaire © 2016 Catherine Mann

ISBN: 978-0-263-39783-3

This book contains FSC™ certified paper and other controlled sources to ensure responsible forest management.

For more information visit: www.harpercollins.co.uk/green

Printed and Bound in the UK using 100% Renewable Electricity at CPI Group (UK) Ltd, Croydon, CR0 4YY

STILL LOVING YOU

SHERYL LISTER

For all those experiencing love
the second time around.

Chapter 1

"Are you out of your *freaking* mind?"

Lauren Emerson paused in her packing and glanced over at her best friend sitting on the other side of the bed. "What? I just think it's time to move back home. I miss my family." She had moved to Phoenix from LA eight years ago to complete her master's in nutrition at Arizona State and stayed after being offered a job at the hospital where she had worked as an intern. Now she had a chance to go back to LA, and with a job that most people could only dream about.

Valencia Flores snorted. "Moving back home because 'I miss my family' is getting a nice job at a hospital or some other health center, *not* taking a job with the LA Cobras football team." She jumped up. "This is like…like *crazy*."

"Maybe so, but I can't pass up this opportunity."

"What do you think he's going to say when he walks in and sees you?"

Lauren resumed folding her shirts and placing them in

the open suitcase. "I don't know. It's been a long time, and I'm sure Malcolm has forgotten all about me."

Valencia stared at Lauren as if she had lost her mind. "A man does *not* forget the woman who broke his heart. Malcolm Gray loved you and you loved him. Everybody knew it. We were all just waiting for the wedding bells."

Lauren tossed the top in and blew out a long breath. She had been waiting for the same thing—until she made a foolish mistake. By the time she realized it, Lauren had ruined the best thing in she had going. "I'm sure there may be a few tense moments, but we're both adults and professionals. I plan to do my job and that's all. Not many people get the chance to be a nutritionist for a professional football team. And this will go a long way in giving me the credibility I need to write the book on nutrition for athletes."

Valencia folded her arms and angled her head thoughtfully. "Are you sure that's the only reason you're going?"

"Of course." Lauren had asked herself the same question several times over the three weeks since she'd accepted the position. Only yesterday had she finally admitted that a small part of her wanted to see Malcolm again. As a football fan, she had followed his career, and she was happy he'd been able to live the life they had talked about all those years ago. Back then, they would lie together laughing, talking and sharing their hopes and dreams.

"I hope you know what you're doing."

She glanced up to see Valencia still frowning. "I do. I'm taking advantage of an opportunity of a lifetime, and I'll be near my family. It's a win-win situation for me. How can that be a bad thing?" She had found a condo in Carson, a twenty-minute drive from her parents' house, which was far enough to maintain her privacy. The modern two-bedroom end unit had an open floor plan, granite countertops in the kitchen, hardwood flooring, a separate dining room, a two-car garage with direct access to the home, a balcony and a spacious master bedroom. And although it wasn't gated, there was twenty-four-hour security. A bonus was that the Cobras' practice facility was only about thirty minutes away.

Valencia viewed Lauren skeptically. "Okay, if you say so. Since you follow football, do you know if Malcolm is married or dating someone?"

Lauren walked over to her dresser, opened a drawer and grabbed another armful of clothing. "I follow *football*, not his personal life, so I have no idea." Malcolm had always been a private person when it came to his relationships, even when they dated. As a popular athlete at UCLA, he had been interviewed on a number of occasions. Whenever questions came up about his relationship with Lauren, Malcolm would give the standard "no comment" and shift the conversation back to football. Lauren did remember seeing a picture of him with a beautiful actress floating around on social media a year or two ago, with speculation about whether the two were headed to the altar. However, she never heard anything more, so she assumed it hadn't happened. She'd seen notices of his siblings' weddings, including that of his twin sister, Morgan. Lauren hadn't been the least bit surprised that Morgan had married a football star and had a successful career as a sports agent. The woman was a bigger fan of the game than Lauren. "So, you are coming to visit me soon, right?"

"Heck, yeah. I've only been to LA twice, so get ready to party." Valencia snapped her fingers and did a little dance step. "I'm going to be putting in for some time off as soon as I get in to work on Monday. Do you think the team needs another nutritionist? I mean…there's, like, how many on the team?"

"Usually about fifty-three."

"See, that's plenty for two people." She wiggled her eyebrows. "With all those fine muscular men in one place, I might learn to like football a little more."

Lauren laughed. "You're a hot mess." But her friend was

right. The LA Cobras were an impressive team. In more ways than one. She zipped the full suitcase and dragged it off the bed until it stood upright on its wheels. She set it next to the other two and glanced around the room at all the luggage and boxes stacked against the walls. It was a good thing she had ended her job two days ago. No way she would have finished packing everything otherwise. She hated moving. Somehow she had accumulated enough stuff over the past eight years to open her own variety shop. Clearly, she would have to go through her things after getting settled in her new place. "I really appreciate you taking today off to help me."

"You know I couldn't let you do all this alone. Besides, I haven't taken off one day this year, and we're already at the halfway mark." Valencia taped a box closed. "What time is the moving truck coming tomorrow?"

"Five in the morning," she answered with a groan. "The drive is supposed to be close to six hours, but with traffic, who knows?"

"Are you sure you don't want me to drive with you? I could stay overnight and hop a flight back on Sunday."

She stared at her best friend and seriously considered her offer. Lauren hated driving, and having someone with her would make the time go by faster. "Truthfully, I'd rather not drive by myself. You sure you wouldn't mind?"

Valencia rolled her eyes. "Of course I wouldn't mind. That's why I offered two weeks ago when you first told me."

Lauren chuckled. "I appreciate you, girl. It'll be easier if you just stay here tonight."

"I agree." Valencia finished taping another box. "Let me tape up these last two boxes and I'll run home, pack a bag and be back. Do you want me to stop and pick up something for dinner?"

"Seeing as how I've packed up all the dishes and cleaned

out the refrigerator, that might be a good idea. Maybe pizza? That's quick and doesn't require utensils."

"That works." The other woman picked up her purse and dug her keys out of her pocket. "Are you sure this is what you want to do, Lauren?"

Lauren knew Valencia wasn't asking about the job. "Yes." At best, she and Malcolm could come to some sort of truce—she'd do her job and he'd do his. At worst, he could still hate her guts and make her dream job a living nightmare.

Malcolm Gray finished his last set on the bench press, then moved so his brother-in-law Omar Drummond and another teammate, Marcus Dupree, could take their turns. All three men played for the LA Cobras, and although training camp didn't start until next month, everyone had been summoned for a Monday morning meeting. They decided to make good use of the time by arriving early and getting in a workout.

"I think I might be done when my contract is up," Marcus said, lying on the bench and starting his repetitions. "This body is getting too old for all those hits."

Omar nodded his head in agreement. "No lie."

Malcolm chuckled. "I hear you. Sometimes I feel like I'm going on sixty instead of thirty." While both Marcus and Omar started at the wide receiver position, Malcolm was the team's running back, and the punishment his body took week after week could be grueling. "My contract is up at the end of the season, and my agent is trying to get me to go for four more. I'm drawing the line at two, if that."

Marcus pushed the bar up and grunted. "You'll be what? Thirty?"

"Thirty-two by then." When he retired, he planned to join his brother Khalil's business. Maximum Burn Fitness Center had two locations that were currently doing well. They had discussed opening a third one within the next two years if the centers continued to run successfully. Though Malcolm had never imagined doing anything other than football, he was realistic enough to know he wouldn't be able to play forever. His family owned a home-safety company that manufactured everything from bath rails and specialized mattresses to in-home alert systems that let a person know if a door had been left open or a stove left on and detected human movement and sent the information to a smartphone. But the idea of wearing a suit and sitting behind a desk for the rest of his life like his brother Brandon and sister Siobhan held no appeal. Instead, he'd followed in Khalil's footsteps and earned a degree in kinesiology, which would give him options other than a desk.

Omar did a final set and moved to another machine. "You know I'm done when my contract is up. School is kicking my butt." He was halfway through his doctoral study program in clinical psychology and planned to join the staff of the veterans' mental health center he had cofounded. "What about you, Dupree? What are your plans?"

"Most likely physical therapy, since that's what my degree is in. I haven't decided whether I want to jump into academia or work in the field." He had completed his clinical doctorate in physical therapy two years ago.

They moved from machine to machine, perfectly executing the movements while continuing the conversation about their postfootball plans.

As they finished, another player approached. "Hey, you guys might want to hurry up and get to the auditorium. I heard the new nutritionist is a woman and she's *fine*! I'll be sitting front and center. Gotta get my eating program together." He hurried off.

Malcolm, Omar and Marcus shook their heads. The previous nutritionist had been fired at the end of last season when management got wind of him fudging the numbers on players who were in danger of losing their starting positions because they were overweight. Two players had been released during the controversy as well.

By the time they showered and made it to the auditorium, the room was abuzz with speculation.

"I'm so glad to be out of the dating game," Omar said with a chuckle. He and Malcolm's twin sister, Morgan, had married two years ago. "But you two…"

Marcus shook his head. "Nah, bro. I'm good."

"Me, too." Malcolm dated when it suited him and planned to remain a bachelor for life. He'd been down the road of heartbreak and would not do it again.

Once the head coach entered, the talk died down to a murmur as everyone slid into the leather theater-style seats.

"I want to thank you all for taking time out of your busy schedules to come in." His statement was met with laughter. He followed up with some general announcements, and then said, "We want to take a moment to honor Joe Marshall. He's been with the organization for twenty-five years and we're sad to see him retire, but he'll always be family. We wish you and Nancy all the best." Applause, whistles and shouts of approval sounded throughout the room.

Joe stood, nodded and waved. Joe's wife, Nancy, was battling breast cancer, and the special teams coach wanted to be there for her full-time.

"The next thing is we have a new dietitian on board. Please welcome Lauren Emerson."

Malcolm didn't hear the rest of the introduction. He struggled to draw in a breath, and his heart beat so loud in his ears it drowned out every other sound. He closed his eyes, hoping there was some mistake, but when he opened them again, she still stood at the front of the room.

Lauren moved to the center and shared some details about herself—background, previous employment and experience working with athletes.

Many of the younger players seemed to be spellbound by her presence. Malcolm heard Marcus whisper, "I think there's going to be more than a few guys camped outside her office."

Omar chuckled.

Malcolm said nothing. Her honey-brown face was as beautiful as he remembered, her smile still bright enough to light up a room and her curves sexy enough to stop traffic. Nothing had changed. Including his feelings. He'd never wanted to see her again.

Chapter 2

Lauren stared out at the room full of football players, her nerves a jumbled mess. Some sent flirtatious winks her way, while others' gazes held skepticism. But one pair of piercing light brown eyes bored through her. She didn't need a PhD to know that Malcolm wasn't happy about seeing her.

She ignored him for the moment and smiled. "Thank you for the welcome. I'm looking forward to working with all of you. I previously worked as a nutritionist and dietitian at a hospital in Phoenix and as a consultant with Arizona State's athletic department. I'll be working closely with you and the coaches. We'll schedule appointments with each of you to establish baselines, set goals and individual programs, as needed. Are there any questions?"

"Are you going to cook, too?" a player called out.

"No, but I'll be consulting with the staff chef."

Another player asked, "Are you married?"

Lauren laughed. "No." The question had nothing to do

with her credentials, but she figured the more they knew about her, hopefully, the more they'd come to trust her. She was under no illusions that the job would be easy, but she planned to be the best nutritionist the team had ever had. Lauren answered a few more questions then stood to the side as the general manager spoke. She surveyed the large meeting room that looked more like a movie theater, with its leather seats and a huge video screen that covered the front wall. The owners had spared no expense.

Her gaze shifted to Malcolm, who sat off to one side. His expression hadn't changed—it held about as much warmth as a blizzard. She discreetly studied the man she had intended to marry. The handsome face that had haunted her dreams so many nights had matured into one that she was sure had women drooling wherever he went and gave new meaning to *good-looking*. His athletic body looked even more toned, and the muscles of his chest and upper arms bunched with every movement. An image of her running her hands over his smooth, hard frame rose unbidden in her mind. She quickly dismissed it. With the way he kept frowning her way, she would be lucky if he even said hello, let alone came in for a scheduled appointment. The general manager's voice filtered through her thoughts.

"Before we end, I'd like to congratulate Malcolm Gray on being named one of the city's humanitarians of the year. He and his brothers and sisters will be honored for their work with the homeless community." Deafening applause broke out. Once it faded, he gave the date, time and place of the gala. "I'd like as many of us as possible to show our support." The meeting ended shortly after.

Lauren had no idea Malcolm's family held such prominent roles in the community. She turned and was immediately surrounded by several football players, who introduced themselves and cited all the reasons why they should have the first appointment. Though the big men towered over her like mountains, she caught a glimpse of Malcolm leaving out of a side door. Their eyes locked briefly, his so cold she shivered. Then he pivoted and strode out of the room without a backward glance.

She refocused her attention on the men in front of her and assured them she would be meeting with all of them as soon as she set up her schedule. Finally, they dispersed, except for one. He had to be at least six eight, and by his size, she guessed he might be a linebacker. He had dark skin and equally dark eyes.

He gave her a shy smile. "Ms. Emerson, I'm Darren Butler." He stuck out his hand.

His large hand engulfed her small one. "It's nice to meet you."

"Um… I know you're still working on your schedule, but if possible, can you give me one of your earliest appointments?"

The sincerity in his eyes tugged at Lauren. "Is there something specific you want to discuss?"

Darren glanced around, seemingly uncomfortable. "Yeah, but not here."

"I'll probably start having meetings by the end of the week. Can it wait until then?"

He nodded.

"I'll make sure to put you at the top of my list."

Relief flooded his face. "Thank you. I'll see you then." He inclined his head and made his way to the exit.

She hoped it wasn't anything serious, healthwise, and made a mental note to schedule Darren as one of her first appointments.

"You handled yourself well, Ms. Emerson."

Lauren turned at the sound of the GM's voice. "Thank you, Mr. Green."

"Have you had a chance to see your office?"

"Not yet." It had taken her a minute to find her way around the massive facility when she arrived earlier. By the time she'd somewhat figured out the layout, the meeting had been ready to start.

He smiled. "Then come on. Let me show you your new digs."

She returned his smile. They walked down a series of hallways, their footsteps echoing on the highly polished marble floors. He pointed out the locker room, weight room, training room, hot and cold spas, a few other meeting rooms, and a door that led to the practice field.

Mr. Green stopped at the dining hall. "Training camp doesn't start until next month, but the chef will be here later this week to meet with you. Nigel is a great guy to work with."

"I'm looking forward to working with him." She really wanted to ask what had happened to the previous nutritionist, since these positions weren't readily available, but kept the question to herself. Lauren surveyed the room. It was far from the cafeteria-style area with long tables and hard, narrow benches she had envisioned. It resembled an upscale restaurant—dark wood tables for four and six with matching cushioned chairs and half a dozen buffet stations.

They continued the tour until he stopped and opened a door. "Wow," she said softly when he gestured her into a spacious office easily three times the size of the one she'd had at the hospital. She walked across the plush carpeting to a huge mahogany desk on one side of the room that had an oversize chair tucked neatly behind it. Behind her, a half wall of windows overlooked a beautiful grassy area and walking trail. A small conference table took up space on the opposite side of the room.

"There should be information on all the players from last year in that file cabinet, and I'm sure you'll find some on the computer, as well."

Lauren glanced over to where he gestured.

"But, this is your show now, so you can set up a system that works best for you. It may take a few weeks for the players to get on board." He smiled. "Or maybe not, judging from the way they cornered you earlier."

She felt her cheeks warm.

"I'll leave you to settle in. If you need anything, let my assistant know."

"Thank you, I will."

Mr. Green gave her one last smile and departed.

Alone, her thoughts went back to his previous comment. Lauren had never had that much male attention in her life, even from the last man she'd dated. That relationship had ended six months ago. Her ex had been all for them climbing the corporate ladder together—as long as he stayed a rung above hers. He hadn't been happy when her salary topped his by a thousand dollars a year, and their easygoing, idyllic romance turned agitated and contentious. In the end, she tossed his ring and assurances of forever back and walked away, much like she'd done with the promise ring Malcolm had given her. She thought she had loved Jeffrey, but the moment she'd locked eyes with Malcolm, every memory and emotion she'd kept buried sprang to life. She realized she wasn't over Malcolm. Not by a long shot.

As soon as Malcolm parked his motorcycle in the garage, his cell buzzed. Without looking, he knew he'd see Morgan's name on the display. His stripped off his riding gloves, dug into his pocket for the phone and smiled. "What's up, sis?" He pressed the button to lower the door and entered the house through the garage.

"That's what I want to know, so I'll be over in an hour." Morgan hung up.

He released a deep sigh. He and Morgan always had that twin thing where they could sense when the other was bothered or upset. Based on his morning, he suspected she'd felt his emotional turmoil. He'd never expected to see Lauren again, especially since she moved to Arizona years ago for what she'd called a "better opportunity." Now he would be forced to see her damn near every day. To make matters worse, she looked even better than he remembered. As he'd noted during the meeting, the beautiful girl he had been in love with had grown into an even more beautiful woman. The curves he used to enjoy caressing were fuller and...

Malcolm cursed under his breath and ran a hand over his head. He stilled, remembering that he'd cut his hair a week ago, replacing the locs he had sported for over a decade with a scalp-hugging style that would take time to get used to. He climbed the stairs, took the short hallway to his bedroom, dropped his duffel on a bench at the foot of his bed and stepped out onto the balcony overlooking his large backyard. The June temperatures had warmed, and in anticipation of the annual barbecue he held for his teammates before the new season started, he had pulled out the deck and lawn furniture. He would need to cut the grass, but otherwise, the yard was ready for entertaining.

His thoughts shifted back to Lauren. He had to figure out a way to get out of any consultation with her. Malcolm's diet was just fine and his weight perfect, so he had no real need to see her. And that's what he would tell her. He glanced down at his watch. Knowing that his sister would be arriving soon and that she'd most likely want to eat, he headed down to the kitchen to prepare a late lunch.

Morgan rang his doorbell just as he removed the chicken breasts from the stove-top grill. He placed them on a plate and went to let her in.

"Hey," Morgan said. "Something smells good."

Malcolm chuckled and kissed her temple. "Come on in. I knew you'd want to eat."

She followed him to the kitchen and took a seat at the table. "Hey, you know I've never liked cooking. Nothing has changed. Lucky for me, my wonderful husband is an ace in the kitchen, and so is my favorite brother." She gave him a bright smile.

"So I'm your favorite, huh?" They'd been joined at the

hip since birth and there wasn't anything he wouldn't do for her. She was his baby sister by five minutes, and he took his charge as big brother seriously. It had been hard relinquishing the reins to her husband, even if Omar was his friend and teammate. He pulled out a bowl of mixed greens, sliced the chicken into bite-size pieces and added them. "How've you been feeling?"

Morgan ran a gentle hand over her rounded belly. "Pretty good. The only thing is whenever I sit for more than five minutes, this kid starts moving around so much, I swear there's a full-fledged game of tackle football going on."

"Well, you only have two more months to go. Did you and Omar change your minds about finding out the baby's sex?" Malcolm placed the bowl on the table, along with plates, utensils and a smaller bowl of salad dressing.

"Nope. We're going to wait. Of course, Vonnie and Faith are trying to get me to change my mind, talking about they need to know what to shop for." Siobhan, whom they affectionately called Vonnie, was the oldest of the five siblings. She and her husband, Justin, had a daughter who'd just celebrated her first birthday.

He smiled, got two glasses of iced mint tea and brought them to the table. "Faith isn't expecting, is she?" Faith and their oldest brother, Brandon, were trying for a baby, and Malcolm hoped they had good news soon.

She shook her head as she filled her plate.

Their mother was beside herself with being a grandmother and with all of her children getting married. The only problem was that her attention had now shifted solely to Malcolm, the only single one. But he wasn't biting. As he had told his family countless times, he planned to be a bachelor for life. He loved the freedom to come and go as he pleased, and the ability to decide when he wanted to date. No hassle, no fuss. He would gladly accept the role of uncle and spoil his nieces and nephews.

After reciting a short blessing, he and Morgan started in on the meal.

"What kind of dressing is this?" She sniffed. "Lemon what?"

"It's lemon basil. Something I ran across at a restaurant where I had dinner. This is my attempt to recreate it. I used light sour cream to cut some of the calories, fresh basil, lemon juice and a little salt and garlic pepper. What do you think?"

Morgan ate a bite, angled her head thoughtfully and groaned. "It's really good. And that's why I come over here to eat when Omar isn't home."

Malcolm shook his head. "Did he go over to the center?"

"Yes. Rashad is finally going to talk to one of the psychologists, but he said he'd only go if Omar went with him. He's gone to a few of the group sessions, but that's it." Omar and a group of organizers had opened a mental health center geared toward veterans two years ago. Omar's older brother, Rashad, suffered from PTSD, and Omar wanted a place for Rashad and others like him to seek treatment that didn't center wholly around medication.

"I'm glad. I know how much he's been hoping Rashad would go." They ate in silence for a few minutes.

"What's going on?"

He glanced up from his plate. "Nothing. Why?"

Morgan stared at him a long moment. "So you're okay with Lauren being the nutritionist? I assume it's the same Lauren responsible for breaking your heart in college."

Malcolm set the fork down and pushed the plate aside. He blew out a long breath. "Yeah, it's her." Just the mention of her name conjured up an image of her standing in the center of the room earlier.

"I still owe her for that, so I hope I don't run into her while I'm at the practice facility."

"Let it go, Morgan." When Morgan found out what happened, she had stormed over to Lauren's dorm room, and he'd had to carry Morgan out to keep her from kicking Lauren's butt. In their family, the rule had always been mess with one, mess with all. It was even truer for him and Morgan. "She doesn't matter. I've been over her a long time." At least he thought so. Malcolm had been in several relationships since their breakup and hadn't thought of her once after the sting had died down. But his reaction to Lauren today told him he still had some lingering feelings that he'd buried.

Morgan took a sip of her tea. "What are you going to do about having to consult with her?"

"Nothing. I eat clean eighty percent of the time, work out four or five times a week, sometimes more, and my weight is fine. I have no need to see her." Malcolm knew Lauren would be sending out emails to all the players to schedule the preseason consultation—the same routine every year—but he intended to send her the same information he had just mentioned to his sister, with the numbers, and ignore her for as long as possible. He had to stay far away from her. His sanity depended on it.

Chapter 3

Thursday morning, Lauren made it to the Cobras' training facility at seven thirty. After three days on the job, she considered it a major accomplishment that she went straight to her office without taking a wrong turn. She powered up her computer, checked her schedule and read through her emails. She had sent a message to all the players and had three scheduled for today, including one with linebacker Darren Butler. So far, a little over half had responded, but not Malcolm. Not that she expected him to. A knock sounded, and her head came up.

"Morning. May I come in?"

Though the man wore athletic pants and shirt, she didn't remember seeing his face on the roster. He stood close to six feet with a trim, toned body, military-short dark hair and deep brown eyes set in a handsome olive-toned face. "Certainly."

"I'm Nigel West, the chef."

Lauren smiled and stood to shake his hand. "It's a pleasure to meet you, Nigel. I'm Lauren."

"The pleasure is all mine."

"Please have a seat." She gestured to the small table and joined him there. "How long have you been the team chef?"

"Going on six years. For the most part, it's been a blast, but there have been a few hiccups along the way," Nigel added with a chuckle.

"Tell me a little about the meal setup. I want to see what you already have before making any changes."

"Sure." He leaned back in the chair and crossed his ankle over his knee. "There used to be a variety of approved snacks available at all times and a good amount of fruits and vegetables. But over the last year, let's just say things weren't as tight."

"There were fewer healthy options."

"You got it."

Lauren wondered if that was what had led to the former dietitian being let go.

As if reading her mind, Nigel said, "When a few players weighed in at fifteen or twenty pounds over what had been reported, it was bye-bye, Stan. To make matters worse, he had taken money from two players who'd bribed him to lie."

"Are they still on the team?" If they were, she needed to know up front. In no uncertain terms would she be party to any of those schemes.

"Nope. They were sent packing with Stan."

It must have been kept hush-hush, because she didn't recall reading anything about a scandal or seeing it mentioned on the sports news. "Well, you won't have to worry about any of that with me."

He smiled. "I believe we're going to work well together. Let's talk menus."

For the next forty-five minutes, Lauren shared her plans, including color-coding stations based on the category of food, having a fresh vegetable and fruit station at every meal, and going back to providing the healthy snack options. "During training camp and practices, did Stan ever have your team make recovery shakes for the players after they worked out?"

"I mentioned it to him a couple of times after talking with a friend of mine who works with another team, but…" Nigel shrugged.

"Okay. I'm thinking a smoothie station might be something to add." Lauren added it to her list. They talked awhile longer, and by the time he left, she felt more confident. Not that she couldn't do the job, but working with elite athletes whose very livelihoods depended on them being in peak performance condition could be intimidating initially. And with her being a woman, she also had to endure the flirting, but she knew that would die down soon enough.

Her first two clients were team veterans and had a good handle on their dietary needs. They would only require check-ins unless something changed. Her third client, a rookie offensive lineman, was a different story. As she'd seen with most college students, athletes included, their diets consisted mainly of high-fat and processed foods— pizza, burgers, sodas and an array of sugary desserts. Trying to teach him to eat differently would be a challenge, and she had already made an appointment to go grocery shopping with him. She made a mental note to talk to Mr. Green's assistant about holding a diet and nutrition session for the rookies.

She was still chuckling at the player's disgruntled expression as he shuffled out of her office. Her cell rang, and she smiled upon seeing Valencia's name on the display. "Hey, girl."

"Hey, yourself. How's LA?"

"So far, so good. For the first time, I didn't get lost coming to my office this morning. It's only taken me four days. That's progress."

Valencia laughed.

"It's not funny," Lauren said, fighting her own laughter. "This place is *huge* and could double as a maze."

"I can't wait to see it when I come down." There was a pause on the line. "Have you talked to Malcolm yet?"

She'd known that would be the first thing her friend asked after hello. "No, but I saw him on Monday when I was introduced to the team. There wasn't an opportunity for chatting—not like he'd say anything to me anyway." A vision of the hostile glare he'd sent her way surfaced in her mind, and she involuntarily shuddered.

"You never know. Like you said, it's been a long time and you've both moved on. Is he still fine as all get-out?"

She laughed. "He is. The only difference is that he cut his locs."

"Really? I used to think they made him look so sexy."

So did she, and she remembered holding on to them as he thrust… Lauren jerked upright in her chair and shook the vision off. "Hey, girl, can I call you when I get home? I need to get ready for my next appointment."

"I should be home around seven, so any time after that is fine. Later, girlfriend."

Lauren disconnected and rubbed her temples. "What have I gotten myself into?" she muttered.

"Ms. Emerson?"

Her head snapped up, and she rose swiftly from her chair. "Come in, Darren. And call me Lauren." They took seats at the conference table and she turned the page on her notepad. "You mentioned needing to talk to me about something." She had read that the young man was in his third year as a defensive lineman.

Darren expelled a long breath. "Yeah. I lost my starting position because I'm twenty pounds overweight. Coach said if I didn't lose the weight by the time the season starts, I'd be benched." He looked at Lauren with sad eyes. "Can you help me?"

"Absolutely. But you'll have to commit to following the program."

"I'll do anything you ask," he said emotionally. "I worked hard to get that position, and I don't want to lose it." He threw up his hands. "And my girlfriend told me yesterday that she wasn't going to accept my marriage proposal unless I did something. Said she wasn't going to marry somebody just to become a widow when I die early."

Lauren didn't know how to respond to such a blunt statement. "Obviously, she cares a lot about you and your health," she said carefully. "And I'll be happy to help you. Training camp starts in a little over three weeks." She wrote down some notes.

"Right."

"Then we have work to do." For the next hour, they went over his current eating habits and the changes he needed to make. He grumbled and whined like a big kid at times, but in the end accepted her plan. "I want you to check in with me at least once a week."

Darren nodded. "Thanks, Lauren." He rose to his feet. "I'll see you next week."

"Call me if you have any questions."

"Okay." He left and closed the door softly behind him.

Lauren smiled as she shut down her computer and packed up to leave. All in all, it had been a good day. She slung her purse on her shoulder and made sure she had everything. Satisfied, she opened the door and hit a warm mass. She gasped sharply.

Mr. Green's blue eyes widened and he grinned sheepishly, his face turning a deep shade of red. "Sorry." He lifted a hand to steady her.

"No problem," she said, willing her heart rate back to normal.

"I just wanted to give you your invitation to the awards banquet I mentioned at the team meeting on Monday. It'll give you a chance to meet more of the management team and the owner."

His request sent her heart rate right back through the roof. She hadn't planned to attend the event. He stared at her expectantly, and she took the invitation from his outstretched hand. "Thanks, I'll be there."

"Wonderful. Have a good evening."

"You do the same." It was bad enough having to see Malcolm. She wasn't looking forward to being in the same room with the rest of siblings, especially Morgan. After her breakup with Malcolm, the woman had wanted to rip Lauren's head off, and Lauren didn't think time would have changed Morgan's stance. *So much for having a good evening.*

Malcolm had avoided Lauren for over a week. He'd ignored the first two messages and then responded to her latest email yesterday informing her that he wouldn't need her services. Now, as he sat waiting for his brother, he read a message from the running back coach indicating an appointment had been set up for Malcolm with Lauren this afternoon. This wasn't how he wanted to start his week.

"What's up, little brother?" Khalil rounded his desk, dropped a folder on top and sat. "You just returned from a three-week vacation in Brazil a little over a week ago, training camp doesn't start for another couple of weeks and, while everyone else is working on a Monday, you're off. I can't imagine one reason why you have that frown on your face."

"I was thinking about retiring at the end of the season, instead of having my agent ask for two more years."

"Is that right?" He studied Malcolm, no doubt reading him like he did everybody else in the family. Khalil had lost his hearing last year in an explosion and had had a rough time adjusting. Thankfully, he had regained his hearing fully in one ear, but even after surgery, he still had to wear a hearing aid in the other. At third oldest, Khalil tended to be the most easygoing and perceptive of the bunch, and Malcolm was glad to see him back to his old self...just not at this moment.

"You know a running back's lifespan is pretty short with all the punishment our bodies take. I'm just thinking it might be better to get out while I'm still healthy. Besides, with the second gym doing so well, it would be a good time to capitalize on the success."

Khalil leaned forward and clasped his hands together on the desk. "That was a great spiel. Now, are you ready to tell me the real reason you're in my office with this nonsense?"

Malcolm muttered a curse. He'd known his brother would see right through him. He hesitated a beat. "Lauren."

Khalil's eyes widened and he slowly sat up straight. "Your old girlfriend from college?"

"Yeah. Her."

Khalil frowned. "I'm not following. What does she have to do with your decision to retire early?"

"She's been hired as the team's new dietitian."

There was silence for a full minute before Khalil burst out laughing. "I can't believe it. I mean, the odds of that happening are, like, what...one in a million? Wow."

"Right. Wow. Not funny."

"I take it this is the first time you've talked to her or seen her in the eight years since the breakup." When Malcolm nodded, he asked, "While it's a shock, it shouldn't be a problem. You've moved on and I assume she's done the same, so..."

Of course he'd moved on. Malcolm had an active dating life and enjoyed women on his terms. Besides, Lauren hadn't exactly given him a choice about *moving on* after she'd accused him of seeing another girl on campus and broken things off without bothering to listen to his explanation. He felt nothing for her now. *That's not what your body said the other day.* Malcolm immediately dismissed the mocking voice in his head as not knowing what the hell it was talking about.

"Or maybe not. Look, Malcolm, you have a job to do. I've never seen you let anything, much less a woman, interfere with that job. You're both professional enough to deal with whatever issues you have."

He sighed wearily. "I know. I just didn't expect to see her, that's all. I'm fine."

Khalil checked his watch. "I have a client in ten minutes, but if you want to talk more, you can come by the house later."

A smile curled Malcolm's lips. "Lexia won't mind?"

At the mention of his wife's name, Khalil's face lit up. The two had gotten married nine months ago. "Nah. She's gotten used to all the impromptu visits and phone calls at all hours of the night." The siblings were all close, and it wasn't unusual for one to show up at another's home unannounced. However, now that all but Malcolm were married, the visits occurred less often.

He stood. "I'll see." Lately, he had begun to feel like the odd man out, especially every time his mother tried to tell him he would be happier if he found a nice young lady and settled down. Except he didn't see any reason to settle down at the moment, not when he enjoyed his single life. He had plenty of time to think about marriage and kids.

Khalil came to where Malcolm stood, and the two shared a one-arm hug. "See you later."

Malcolm took the stairs down to the main level and pushed through the doors leading to the parking lot. In his car moments later, he toyed with going home but decided to go directly to the facility. "Might as well get it over with," he muttered and started the car.

When he arrived forty minutes later, he sat in his car contemplating how he wanted to handle this first encounter. A riot of emotions swirled in his gut, most of them not good—anger, irritation and, somewhere deep down, a hint of desire. Finally, he got out and entered the building. He stopped to talk to a couple of the staff members then continued toward the offices. The closer he got, the harder his heart pounded.

Malcolm heard Lauren's laughter before he saw her. The same laughter he used to love.

"Thanks for your help," he heard her say. A moment later, she rounded the corner. "Oh, Malcolm. Hey."

He mumbled something he thought passed for a greeting.

They stood in awkward silence for several tense seconds before she said, "Um... I was just making...copies... We can talk in my office."

He gestured her forward but didn't comment. They stopped halfway down the hall at her door, and he followed her in. She had a pretty nice setup—spacious, expensive furniture, great view. Malcolm sat at the conference table and waited. As she walked past, he was treated to a view of her shapely backside in a pair of navy slacks that clung enticingly to her curves. The familiar scent of the soft citrusy fragrance she always wore wafted across his nose, and he closed his eyes briefly to block out the unwanted memories.

"Are you okay?"

Malcolm opened his eyes and met her concerned gaze. "Fine," he said tersely.

Lauren regarded him thoughtfully. "It's good to see you, Malcolm. I'm happy you've been able to live your dream."

"Thanks." Too bad he couldn't say the same about her. "Let's get this over with."

Lauren sighed softly. "Malcolm, I—" She squared her shoulders and opened a file folder. "They've already done the DEXA scan, and your bone, muscle and fat percentages are all excellent. For your diet—"

"I already emailed you that information, so we don't need to repeat it. My goals are to maintain where I am.

Simple. This is my eighth season, so it's not as if I don't know the drill." Malcolm didn't know how much longer he would be able to sit in this confined space with Lauren. He was torn between wanting to lash out at her for what she'd put him through all those years ago and kissing her senseless. He prided himself on having a good amount of control, but felt it slipping as the minutes ticked off.

Her pen stilled, and she looked up from the pad where she had been writing notes. "You did." She rose and retrieved a sheet of paper from her desk. "Height, six one, and weight, two hundred fifteen pounds. Diet consists of fish, chicken, lean beef and a variety of vegetables and fruits." She tossed the paper aside. "Look, Malcolm, I know this is awkward for both of us."

"Awkward? Is that what this is?" Malcolm leaped to his feet, and she instinctively took a step back. "Awkward doesn't begin to define what this is. Why are you here?"

Lauren frowned and folded her arms. "I don't know what you mean."

"You could've taken a job anywhere. Why *here*?" he asked through clenched teeth. "I don't want you here."

She placed her hands on her hips and leaned up in his face, her dark brown eyes flashing with anger. "Because this is where I wanted to work. I was offered an opportunity few get, and taking it meant being closer to my family. What was I supposed to do, check with you first? News flash, Malcolm Gray, I don't need *your* permission for *my* job choice, and whether you like it or not, I plan to be here for a long time!"

Something within him snapped and before his action registered in his brain, he hauled her into his arms and crushed his mouth against hers in a hungry and demanding kiss. Malcolm expected Lauren to push him away, slap him or make some kind of protest…anything, but she didn't. She kissed him back. And in the way that drove him crazy, like only she could.

"Malcolm," Lauren whispered.

Finally, sanity returned, and he jumped away from her as if he had been burned. *What the hell am I doing?* His breath came in short gasps, and his heart thumped erratically in his chest. His gaze was drawn to Lauren's lips, still moist from his kiss, and the rapidly beating pulse in her neck, which didn't help matters. He needed to leave *now*. Malcolm stepped around her, crossed the office in three strides and snatched open the door. He paused and turned back. "This changes nothing. I still don't want you here."

He strode out and didn't stop until he reached his car. He couldn't be around her for the next three years, especially not now. Not when he still wanted her.

Chapter 4

Several minutes later, Lauren still stood in the middle of her office, body pulsing, heart racing and mind reeling from Malcolm's kiss. Why hadn't she stopped him? And why had she kissed him back?

Memories of their relationship sprang up with such clarity she closed her eyes to block out the images. It didn't help. Lauren recalled every moment of the two years they had dated. But she couldn't let herself get caught up. She startled at the knock on her door. She glanced down at her watch. It was time for her next client. As she crossed the office to open the door, Lauren told herself she had a job to do, and that was the only thing she planned to focus on. She beckoned her next client in and, putting Malcolm out of her mind, sat and focused her attention where it needed to be—on her work.

Lauren didn't leave her office until after seven that evening and was back in the office at six Friday morning. She had her rookie training session at nine and wanted to make sure she had everything ready. At eight thirty, she met one of the office staff members in the room she'd be using, which happened to be a smaller version of the auditorium she had been in the first day. The woman gave Lauren instructions on how to work the video and audio equipment and departed. Lauren had just finished laying out the materials she wanted each player to take on his way out and making sure her presentation was on the correct page when the players started drifting in. At precisely nine, she began with an overview of nutrition and how it impacted performance.

"How many of you eat vegetables at least three times a day? No one? How about twice?" Lauren glanced around the room. Only two of the ten men in the room raised their hands. "Once?" Another three hands went up. She had her work cut out for her.

"I'm a defensive lineman and need these pounds. I can't tackle anybody if I'm all skinny and half-starved," a young man she hadn't met with called out.

"What's your name?"

"Brent Carroll."

"Well, Brent, you won't be able to tackle anyone if you're winded after five minutes or you can't move around fluidly and catch your opponent because your body is weighed down by all the useless high-fat calories you've consumed."

Low murmuring and deep chuckles sounded in the room.

"The goal here is to still meet your caloric needs, but with foods that will truly make you a beast on the field." A deafening roar went up, and she laughed. "Okay, so I guess that means you're ready to—" Lauren froze at the sight of Malcolm standing in the door. She promptly lost her train of thought. She turned to gather herself and, when she looked up, he was gone. Silently cursing herself for letting him rattle her, she turned her attention back to the waiting group and continued with her presentation. She heard a few grumbles and then gradually saw some nods. "Nigel and I have come up with some menus that incorporate more whole grains, vegetables and fresh fruits earlier in the day, along with the proteins to fuel your workouts. I'm going to add pre- and postworkout snacks, as well. For dinner, the emphasis will be on proteins and vegetables and lighter on the carbs, since you won't need them while you sleep. Any questions?" She acknowledged a blond-haired young man who looked to be barely out of high school.

"At first, I thought you were going to be putting us on a diet, but you're not, huh?"

Lauren smiled. "Well, not in the way you're thinking. No. The team and your fans are counting on you to get the job done on the field. I'm going to make sure you get it done off the field. And even when you're done playing football, you'll still be healthy." She took a few more questions, passed out the materials and scheduled each of those she hadn't seen for appointments. She had included sample meal plans and suggested shopping guidelines in the pamphlet, as well as her contact information should they have questions.

She had two clients to see after the session, including Omar Drummond, Malcolm's brother-in-law. Lauren found the gorgeous receiver far more pleasant than she expected, knowing how much Morgan disliked Lauren. Afterward, she spent the remainder of the day consulting with Nigel. She mentioned her earlier session with the rookies, to which he responded, "Hallelujah! Finally, someone who gets it."

At five thirty, she locked her desk and files, packed up her tote and slung it, along with her purse, on her shoulder and headed out to her car.

"Lauren, you have a minute?"

Lauren groaned inwardly and turned. "Sure, Mr. Green."

The general manager quickened his steps to reach her. "This will only take a moment. I know you're anxious to get out of here." He smiled. "I just wanted to hear how the rookie nutrition session went this morning."

"It went pretty well, actually." She shared what she'd told them, as well as their initial reluctance and the measure of acceptance. "I don't expect them to fall perfectly in line, but if I can change their eating habits now, they'll be better off in the long run. And so will the team."

"I agree. We did the right thing bringing you on board. Thanks, Lauren. I won't hold you. Enjoy your evening, and I'll see you tomorrow night."

"Tomorrow?"

"Yes. The award ceremony I mentioned last week. You'll be there, right?"

Great. "Oh, yes. I remember. I'll be there." Lauren couldn't very well tell her employer she couldn't attend because she wanted to avoid their star running back. "Have a nice evening." She continued out to the parking lot, tossed her bag onto the back seat of the car and slid in on the driver's side. She leaned against the headrest. Why hadn't she told him she'd be busy? "It can't be that bad," she rationalized. There would be a room full of people and, if her path crossed with Malcolm's, it would only be long enough for a polite nod. She started the engine. "I can do this. No problem."

When she got home, she called Valencia, hoping her friend could offer some advice about how Lauren should handle any further contact with Malcolm outside work. Part of her felt their relationship should be strictly business, but the parts of her that had responded to his kiss wanted a repeat performance. Valencia's cell went straight to voice mail, so Lauren would have to deal with her own emotions.

Her bravado held up all night and into the next morning. By Saturday afternoon, all of Lauren's boasting had been reduced to a mass of butterflies dancing in her belly. While she searched for a suitable dress in her closet, she wished she had begged off yesterday when she had the chance. Surely Mr. Green would have understood if she'd told him she couldn't make it. After all, she was still getting situated in her new place. She picked one dress after another but put them back. Finally, she settled on an off-the-shoulder black sheath dress that skimmed her curves, stopped just above the knee and had a modest side slit. Setting it aside, she went to shower.

Lauren dried off, wrapped the towel around her and hurried out of the bathroom to catch her ringing phone. "Hey, Valencia," she said, walking back to the bathroom.

"Hey. Sorry I missed your call last night. My cousin asked me to go to the movies with her at the last minute."

She activated the speakerphone and placed the cell on the bathroom counter. "No problem." She smoothed lotion on her arms and legs.

"What did you want? Is it about Malcolm?"

"Yeah. I never got around to telling you about what happened when he finally came in for his appointment. Well, he asked me why I took this job when I could've gone anywhere else."

"Seriously? Sounds like he's still angry."

Lauren recalled the confrontation. "Something like that. We kind of argued a little, but then…"

"But then *what*? Please tell me he didn't put his hands on you."

"No! Malcolm isn't that kind of man. He would *never* do anything remotely close to hitting a woman, no matter how angry he got." A memory of a girl in college who'd been upset by him shunning her unwanted attention surfaced in Lauren's mind. The crazy girl had gone so far as to shove Malcolm and throw water in his face. Malcolm had calmly told her, once again, that he wasn't interested and walked away. If anyone deserved his wrath, that girl had. Yet he'd done nothing. "He kissed me." Valencia was silent for so long, Lauren said, "Lyn, you still there?"

"Um…yeah. Okay, that was not what I expected you to say."

"I didn't expect it, either."

"And, so… I mean…what happened after that? Did you throw him out of your office?"

"Worse. I kissed him back." She slipped into her underwear, picked up the phone and went back to the bedroom.

Valencia burst out laughing.

"Not funny." Lauren placed the phone on her nightstand, picked up the dress and stepped into it.

"Oh yes, girl, it is. How was it? As good as you remember?"

"Better," she admitted grudgingly. "But he told me as he left that the kiss didn't change anything. He still doesn't want me there."

Lyn snorted. "I hope you told him that's too bad."

"I didn't get a chance to tell him anything, because he walked out. Now tonight the GM is expecting me to attend an awards ceremony for Malcolm and his siblings. They're getting some humanitarian award for work with the homeless. I really don't want to go, but I've only been on the job two weeks."

"True. And when your boss asks you to be someplace, you go."

"Exactly." Lauren examined herself in the full-length mirror in the corner of the room. "I keep telling myself that I'll be in a room full of people and, even if our paths cross, it'll just be a polite hello and keep it moving."

"Lauren?"

"Huh?"

"I know you've dated since then and your relationship with Jeffrey was pretty serious, but are you truly over Malcolm? Could you honestly say you felt nothing when he kissed you?"

She dropped down on the side of the bed and blew out a long breath. How she wished she could lie and say she'd felt nothing. That the kiss didn't make a blip on her heart meter. But it would be a lie. He'd had her heart beating at a pace that could be considered dangerous and sensations flowing through her body that should be outlawed. "No, I can't," she mumbled. "I told myself I was over Malcolm, and I am."

"Are you sure, sweetie?" Valencia asked. "What you and Malcolm shared was pretty deep. And it's hard to forget the first man you truly loved. Hell, if my first love showed up and kissed me, I'd probably succumb right then and there."

Lauren stuck her feet into a pair of black sandals with four-inch heels, fastened the ankle straps and chuckled. "You are crazy."

"Did you or did you not just tell me you kissed the man back? I rest my case," she added with a laugh before Lauren could respond.

"Shut up."

"Anyway, what are you going to do?"

"My job. It'll be easier for both of us."

"And if he wants more?"

"He doesn't."

"So you say."

"The man told me he didn't want me working there, so if that's not a clear sign that he doesn't want anything to do with me, I don't know what is." Hearing herself say the words, she knew this would be the best way, no matter how well Malcolm kissed. "I need to finish getting ready. Thanks for listening to my rant."

"Hey, you've done the same for me countless times. Let me know how it goes."

"I will." They talked a moment longer, then Lauren hung up. She applied light makeup, took one last glance in the mirror and, satisfied, left.

The gala was in full swing when Lauren arrived at the popular chain hotel. The grand ballroom was elegantly decorated, large chandeliers hung from the ceiling and a rose brocade pattern adorned the walls. She spotted several players, the GM and, on the far side of the room, Malcolm and one of his brothers. She couldn't remember which one.

"You made it."

Lauren turned at the sound of Mr. Green's greeting.

"Hi, Mr. Green."

He escorted her over to a small knot of people and introduced her to his wife, the team owner and his wife, and two more of the front office staff. "I was telling Mr. Lawler how much you've accomplished with the players in two short weeks."

The team owner, Mr. Lawler, nodded in agreement. "I'm impressed, Ms. Emerson, and I'm looking forward to having healthier players this year."

She smiled. "Thank you, Mr. Green and Mr. Lawler. I appreciate your confidence."

Soon they took their seats for dinner and the awards portion of the program. Lauren listened as Malcolm and his brothers gave short speeches. However, it was the one given by a man she didn't know—Cameron Hughes—that pulled at her emotional strings. He spoke of losing his wife and children in an accident and, unable to bear the pain, ending up homeless. But he also expressed gratefulness to his wife's best friend, who happened to be Khalil's wife, for not giving up on him.

Afterward, the music started and couples took to the floor, including Mr. Lawler and his wife. Lauren stood, intending to use this opportunity to go to the bathroom.

Mr. Green stood and helped her with her chair and waved at someone. "I know you're still meeting with players, but have you had a chance to meet Malcolm Gray yet?"

The hairs stood up on the back of her neck. Before she could respond, she felt the heat and, without turning around, knew it was Malcolm.

"Congratulations, Malcolm," Mr. Green said, shaking

Malcolm's hand. "Have you met Lauren Emerson? She's going to be a great asset to the team."

Malcolm stared down into Lauren's eyes. "Thanks, and yes, we've met. Hello, Lauren."

That's one way to describe it. "Hi, Malcolm." She had only seen photos of him wearing a tuxedo, and those pictures hadn't come close to capturing the raw magnetism he exuded standing next to her. She couldn't decide whether she liked him better with his locs or the close-cropped look he now sported.

"Well, my wife is going to have my head if we don't get at least one dance in, so I'll see you two later. Malcolm, can you make sure Lauren gets acquainted with everyone?"

Lauren's eyes widened. "Oh, I'll be fine. I'm sure Malcolm has some other people to see." She looked to Malcolm, expecting him to agree. To her amazement, he extended his arm.

"Shall we?"

With Mr. Green and his wife staring at her with huge smiles, she couldn't very well say what she wanted. Instead, she took his arm and let him lead her out to the dance floor. She regretted it the moment he wrapped his arm around her. Malcolm kept a respectable distance, but it didn't matter. His closeness caused an involuntary shiver to pass through her. And why did he have to smell so good? The fragrance had a perfect balance of citrus and earth that was as comforting as it was sensual. How was she going to make it through the next five minutes?

Malcolm must have sensed her nervousness. "Relax, Lauren. We've danced closer than this, so what's the problem?"

Lauren didn't need any reminders of how close they'd been in the past. "I'm fine," she mumbled.

A minute went by and Malcolm said, "Smile. You don't want everyone to think you're not enjoying my company."

She glared up at him. "You're enjoying this, aren't you?"

He grinned. "I'm holding a beautiful woman in my arms. What's not to enjoy?"

Mr. Green and his wife smiled Lauren's way, and she smiled back. As soon as they turned away, she dropped her smile. "I can't play these games with you, Malcolm," she whispered harshly.

"This is no game." Their eyes locked for a lengthy moment, then he pulled her closer and kept up the slow sway.

Lauren fell silent and tried to maintain her composure. The softness she saw reflected in his eyes gave her pause, given that it had only been a few days since their confrontation. She figured he was just being polite because they were in a room full of people, but deep inside, a small piece of her wondered if it was something else. Common sense said to let it go, but she couldn't. "Why are you doing this?"

Malcolm's brows knit. "Doing what? I'm just dancing."

She let out an exasperated sigh. "You know what I mean. Five days ago you wanted me gone. Now, tonight, you're acting like you don't hate me…almost like you care or something."

"I don't hate you, Lauren. At least not anymore."

She gasped softly.

"I won't lie. For about six months afterward…let's just say you weren't at the top of my favorite-persons list." He shrugged. "Now…" He let the sentence hang.

"A lot of time has passed, and we're not the same. I've changed and so have you."

He didn't say anything for a moment. "That's true. But there are some things that are still the same."

The last notes of the song faded, and he led her off the dance floor. "What are you talking about?"

Malcolm stopped near her table. "Your kiss." He pivoted and walked off.

Lauren stood stunned and unconsciously brought her hand to her lips. Realizing what she'd done, she snatched it down. She turned and saw Morgan glaring at her from across the room and hoped to escape a confrontation. She didn't need one more thing tonight. After locating upper management and a few of the players and saying goodbye, she left the ballroom. If Lauren were lucky, she'd make it out of the hotel and to her car without any problems.

When she took the job, Lauren had known she would have to deal with Malcolm, but she hadn't counted on this.

Chapter 5

Monday afternoon, Malcolm tossed another pass to the rookie running back who'd just been signed. He'd been more than surprised when Christopher Long asked him to help with some drills and laughingly said he wanted to be ready when Malcolm retired. Many of the younger players were hesitant to ask for help from the veterans, so it pleased Malcolm that Chris felt comfortable enough to seek him out. If the twenty-two-year-old continued to display the skills Malcolm had seen today, he'd be more than ready.

"Bring it in, Chris." Chris jogged over to where Malcolm was placing cones on the field. Malcolm gestured for the ball. "Now we'll work on the three-step cut." The drill helped a player develop lateral movement and cutting speed, both of which were necessary for eluding tacklers. It also helped improve ball-handling skills. "Let me see what you've got."

Chris nodded, assumed the position and started the drill. After he finished, Malcolm said, "Not bad. A little repositioning will help with your agility and speed. Place your feet shoulder-width apart, bend your knees slightly and keep your toes pointed straight ahead." He demonstrated the technique in slow motion and at full speed, then had Chris repeat the motion. They started at ten yards and increased the distance by five yards until reaching twenty-five. After the last round, they crossed the field and went inside to the cafeteria. Nigel was seated at a table with some papers in front of him, but he glanced up at their approach.

"Hey, Nigel."

"Hey, Malcolm." He extended his hand to Chris. "I'm Nigel West, the chef."

"Christopher Long."

"Camp doesn't start until next week, so what are you two doing here?"

"I asked Malcolm to help me with a few drills," Chris said.

Nigel stood. "How about I make you two one of the recovery shakes Lauren is implementing? You can be the test subjects. Chris, if you haven't seen her yet, make sure you schedule an appointment."

"I meet with her on Wednesday."

"Good. Have a seat and I'll be right back with the shakes."

Chris sat at the nearest table. "Thanks."

Malcolm followed suit. The mention of Lauren's name conjured up memories of their dance on Saturday night and the way her soft curves had felt pressed against his body. Just the thought spiked his arousal. He had done a good job putting her out of his mind for the past two hours, knowing she would be at the facility, but now she was front and center again. He just hoped to leave without running into her. Visions of how she looked in that body-hugging black dress that had left her shoulders bare had played havoc with his mind all weekend. He wasn't supposed to want her.

Chris's voice pulled him out of his reverie.

"I want to thank you for working with me today, Malcolm. My boys thought I was crazy for asking. Said no veteran would groom a rookie to take his position."

He chuckled. "Most wouldn't. But I'm not worried about you taking my position. Two years from now, it'll be all yours."

Chris laughed. "What else do I need to know to make it on this team? I know I won't be starting and most likely won't play but a few downs all season, but I don't want to get cut."

Nigel returned with the drinks. "Let me know what you think."

Malcolm waited until Nigel went back over to his table and resumed whatever task he'd been doing before speaking. "The first thing is you can't miss practice and expect to make the squad or be part of the game plan. Everybody takes bumps and bruises, but you work through them." He took a sip of the drink and grudgingly admitted that it tasted good, something like the ones he made for himself.

"What if I get hurt?"

"If you're seriously injured, that's a different story. You've been playing long enough to know that your legs will get heavy and muscles will ache, but the coaching staff needs to be able to trust in your ability to find a way to push through the day and answer the call if need be."

"Got it. I plan to be ready." Chris lifted the drink. "This is really good. Is this the kind of stuff Lauren will make me drink all the time? And is she going to put me on a strict diet?"

"The shakes are good for muscle recovery after a workout, so I assume they'll be available after practices. As far as a diet, Lauren will give you the tools you need to play your best game. You just have to follow her plan." They finished their drinks and headed for the showers. Malcolm took a moment to tell Nigel he thought the shakes would be a good addition. Obviously, Lauren knew her stuff.

Afterward, Malcolm slid behind the wheel of his black Camaro, started the engine and cranked up the air. The temperature had reached the upper eighties, typical for July, but once practice started, it would feel at least ten degrees warmer. He backed out of the parking lot and started down the two-lane highway. The facility was located four miles outside Buena Park and there was nothing but open space and a few trees along that stretch of the road. Halfway to the city limit, he spotted a car parked on the side of the road. A woman stepped out with a phone to her ear. Lauren. As he got closer, he was treated to the sweet curve of her backside in the gray slacks. Malcolm could see irritation on her face. He pulled up behind her and got out. He leaned against her car and waited until she disconnected. "What happened?"

"When I left work a few minutes ago, nothing was wrong. All of a sudden, the stupid car started losing speed and all it would do when I stepped on the pedal was rev up, so I pulled over and called the emergency road service."

From what she said, Malcolm suspected it might be her transmission. "How long did they say you'd have to wait?"

"Two and a half *freaking* hours," she said, scrubbing a hand across her forehead. "I don't have time for this." Lauren paced back and forth and then threw up her hands. "I don't even know where to tell them to take it."

He straightened from the car, intercepted her when she passed him and placed his hands on her shoulders. "Relax. I know a good mechanic. I'll call the shop and have them tow your car there, okay? You can call and cancel yours."

She let out a frustrated breath. "Okay. Thanks."

He pulled out his cell, made the call and arranged to have her car picked up. "It'll be about an hour."

"That's much better. Now I don't have to wait as long in this heat."

"You won't be waiting at all, because I'm taking you home," Malcolm said without thinking.

"Um…you don't have to do that." Lauren waved him off. "The wait won't be that long."

"No matter what has happened between us, you know

I'd never leave you here alone, Lauren. And it's too hot to sit out here."

Lauren stared up at him, apparently considering his offer. Finally, she nodded.

"Why don't you grab your stuff and lock up."

She reached into the back seat and took out a purse and large tote, closed the door, and locked it by remote.

At his car, helped her in then got in on the driver's side and pulled off.

"Still like muscle cars, huh?"

"Yep," he said with a smile. "And I have my motorcycle, too."

"I should've known you'd make good on it. That's all you used to talk about in col—"

The mention of college seemed to raise the tension and an uncomfortable silence ensued, but Malcolm didn't want to ruin the light mood. "I bought it after I got my first paycheck, just like I said." They shared a smile. He'd also promised to buy her an engagement ring with that check. One out of two wasn't bad. "So, where do you live?"

"Carson. I wanted to be close to my parents, but far enough to discourage surprise visits."

Malcolm laughed. "I totally understand. But my mother doesn't let that stop her. She doesn't think anything about the thirty to forty-five minutes it takes to get to any of our houses."

She turned in the seat to face him and groaned. "Are you serious? I hope my mother doesn't start doing that."

"Very serious." He told her stories of times when his mother had camped out at each of her children's homes and laughed as Lauren shared some of her own parent woes. He realized that he still enjoyed talking to her and wanted more time. "How about we have some dinner?" He took his eyes off the road briefly to gauge her reaction.

Lauren leaned back against the seat and stared out the window. "I don't know if that's a good idea, Malcolm," she said quietly.

She was probably right, but he ignored the warning bells in his head telling him to keep his distance. He didn't know why, but he wanted more time with her. "Think of it as an apology for my behavior last week."

"What are we doing, Malcolm?"

"We aren't doing anything. Just two people having dinner. Nothing more." Except maybe kissing again. The last time he had been angry, but it didn't change the fact that the passion still burned between them—or that she had kissed him back.

"All right. But what about my car?"

"When we get to the restaurant, I'll call and give him your number." Malcolm glanced at the clock on the dashboard, which read four forty-five. "The shop doesn't close until six thirty, and I doubt they'll close up before checking out your car and letting you know what's wrong. Since it's pretty early, I'm hoping we'll miss the dinner crowd. We can stop by afterward, if it'll make you feel better."

"It would. Thank you."

They rode the rest of the way in companionable silence, the only sounds coming from the hum of the air conditioner and the soft beat of the music playing.

"Ruth's Chris?" Lauren asked when he parked in the lot across the street from the restaurant.

"Yes. You don't like the food here?" Malcolm shut off the engine and regarded her thoughtfully. He probably should have asked where she wanted to eat, but the women he'd taken out in the past typically didn't care where he took them, only that he paid the bill.

"No, that's not it. Actually, I've never been to the restaurant."

"Good. I think you'll enjoy the food." He hopped out of the car, went around to her side and helped her out. She still wore a slight frown. "What?"

"I figured we were going somewhere less...elegant... and cheaper." She glanced down at herself.

He followed her gaze and took in the slacks and sleeveless blouse. "You look great, so stop worrying. We won't be put out," he added with a chuckle.

"Fine. But I'm paying for my own food."

Malcolm glared. "Nah, baby. I don't think so." Belatedly, he realized what he'd said. The endearment slipped out as if there hadn't been eight years of separation. He reached for her hand and escorted her over. Due to the early hour, they only had to wait ten minutes for a table. Fortunately, they were seated in a booth near the back.

"Tom will be taking care of you and your guest tonight, Mr. Gray." The hostess handed them menus. "Enjoy your meal."

"Thanks, Ms. Virginia."

Virginia smiled and departed.

"I take it you're a regular," Lauren said.

He shrugged. "I come here enough."

She shook her head and opened the menu. "Mmm-hmm."

Minutes later, Tom came to take their drink order, but both opted for water. With the season starting, Malcolm wanted to limit his intake of sugary and alcoholic drinks. He'd probably have a beer on Saturday at his barbecue, but that would be the limit.

Lauren closed her menu. "Malcolm?"

He lifted his head.

She seemed to struggle with her words. "I know it probably doesn't matter and is far too late, but I'm sorry for hurting you."

Malcolm slowly set the menu aside. For the past eight years, it hadn't mattered, but tonight, for some reason, hearing her apologize made him feel different. "It matters, Lauren, and I accept your apology. But I have to know why. Why didn't you give us a chance?"

"I don't know. I was young, insecure."

"Insecure?"

"Very much so. I was dating the school's star running

back, and more than one girl made sure I knew that I wouldn't be able to hold your attention for long."

His eyes widened in shock. "Lauren—"

She held up a hand. "Please let me finish. It was nothing you did or said. In fact, you made me believe that we could have forever." She took a deep breath. "One of my friends was dating an athlete at the time, as well, and the moment he had a shot at going pro, he walked away. He told her that he needed to be with someone who would run in the same circles."

Malcolm felt his anger rise. "That had nothing to do with us."

Lauren looked at him with sad eyes. "You're right. But seeing her misery and listening to her tell me over and over to get out before the same thing happened to me... I bought in."

He wanted to hold it over her head, but he couldn't. They'd both been twenty-one, and he didn't know a twenty-one-year-old who hadn't made a mistake, him included. And strangely, he understood her point. He'd seen a few of his teammates do exactly as she had described, and they'd ended up being linked to paternity suits, baby-mama drama or some other spectacle. Malcolm had never been a party to that scene, because his parents would have killed him— if his older siblings didn't do it first.

"If I could go back, I'd do things differently."

"I think that could be said for a lot of situations." Malcolm lifted his glass of water. "We can't go back, but we can start again. To the beginning of a new and mature friendship."

Lauren smiled and touched her glass to the side of his. "To new beginnings." She took a sip and set it down. "No matter what you think, Malcolm, I didn't come here to intrude on your life. But I appreciate your friendship."

Friendship. The word left a bitter taste in his mouth. After all they had shared, he didn't know if he could think of her as just a friend. Not when the first thing he'd wanted to do when he saw her on the side of the road was take her in his arms and reacquaint himself with the smell and taste of her. Before he could delve further into areas where he had no business, the server came with hot French bread and butter and to take their orders. When he left, Malcolm asked, "Why sports nutrition?"

"Actually, I have you to thank for that. During one of our conversations about me going to grad school and having to write a thesis, I complained that I didn't want to do the same subjects that everyone always did. You suggested doing something related to correlating improved nutrition to performance, and that's what I did. It worked so well that I was offered a consultation position at the junior college where I conducted the study. It was only a few hours a week, so I got a job at the hospital where I interned and did that on the side."

That she had taken his suggestion filled Malcolm with a weird sense of pride. "I'm really happy it worked out for you, and I think you're going to do well with the team."

"That means a lot coming from you. Thank you."

Over dinner, he told her about his plans to join Khalil in business and listened while she told him about wanting to write a book on nutrition for athletes. As she spoke, he couldn't help staring at her lips and remembering all the ways they'd kissed—and all the places. He thought back to the friendship toast earlier. Just friends? He didn't see it lasting that way for long. Hell, he didn't see it lasting when he took her home.

Lauren listened to the mechanic and felt a headache coming on. "But the car is less than ten years old. How did the transmission go out?" When she purchased the used Maxima four years ago, she'd had it thoroughly checked out and nothing came up.

He shrugged and handed her an estimate.

Her eyes widened at the cost. At this rate, she would

be better off purchasing a new one. "I'd like to check out some other options first before deciding whether to fix it. Can I call you late tomorrow morning?" She had too much to do to go looking for a new car. Fortunately, her first appointment wasn't until noon, but she needed a rental in the meantime so she could get to work tomorrow. She didn't want to impose on Malcolm any more than she already had, but outside of Uber or Lyft, she had no other way to get to the rental place. Her gaze caught Malcolm's. He gave her a sympathetic look.

"Sure thing." The man walked over to the other side of the long counter, retrieved a business card, wrote his name on it and handed it to her. "I'll just make a note that you'll call before we start any work on the car."

Lauren accepted the card. "Thanks." She followed Malcolm back to his car. "Thank you for everything."

Holding the door open, he asked, "You're welcome."

"I didn't mean to monopolize your entire evening. I know you're probably anxious to get home. Do you have to go far?" He'd been driving her all across town. Luckily, the repair shop had only been a short ten-minute drive from the restaurant.

A slow grin made its way across his handsome face. "Actually, I live about five minutes from here."

She faced him. "Oh, no. I can just call Uber or Lyft to take me home."

Malcolm's smile faded, and he shook his head. "Get in."

"Malcolm..." She trailed off when he folded his arms. He gestured with his head, and she sank into the leather seat.

Malcolm closed the door with a solid thud and then got in on his side. He leveled her with a look. "You do not need to spend money for that when I'm right here."

"But you'll be driving almost half an hour in the opposite direction, only to turn around and come right back here."

He ignored her and pulled onto the street. "So, are you thinking it might be cheaper to buy a new car?"

"I am. For now, though, I need to find a rental."

"I'll pick you up in the morning. Just tell me what time."

"I'm sure you have other things to do. I can just call—"

"Yeah, I know... Uber or Lyft. I'm taking you home now and I'm picking you up tomorrow. What's your address?"

Lauren refused to acknowledge how his possessiveness made her feel. Knowing she'd never win the argument, she rattled off her address. They discussed her options for the car and confirmed a pickup time for the morning. When he turned in to her complex, she directed him to a spot near her unit. "I appreciate your help, Malcolm. See you tomorrow at nine." She placed her hand on the doorknob.

Malcolm shook his head and chuckled.

She paused. "Now what?"

"You know I'm not letting you walk to the door alone."

She pointed to her unit less than fifty feet from where they sat. "Malcolm, I live right here. There's no reason for you to get out of the car. You can see me, and I'll wave when I get to the door."

"Stay there until I come around to your side." Without waiting for her response, he got out of the car and went to open her door. He extended his hand.

Lauren glanced at his hand, up at him and down again. She slapped her palm into his.

"You can glare at me all you want. I opened car doors and walked you to your dorm or your parents' house from day one, and that won't ever change."

She laughed and let him lead her to the condo. He had made it clear the first time they went out that he would treat her like a princess, and he always had. She used her key to let them in and turned to face him. "Safe and sound, okay?"

For a moment, he stood there staring at her with an intensity that made her heart race.

Malcolm lifted his hand and slowly caressed her cheek. "I know I said we'd work on being friends again, but…"

"Malcolm," she whispered. He lowered his head and covered her mouth in an all-consuming kiss. Unlike the kiss in her office, this one held no trace of anger, only passion. He slid an arm around her waist and pulled her against his hard body, making her senses spiral. She ran her hands up and down his back and heard him moan. Each stroke of his tongue conjured up flashes of their past relationship until the memories came back in a flood. Lauren felt herself losing control and broke off the kiss. "We shouldn't be doing this."

"Maybe not," he murmured, brushing his lips across hers once more. "I told myself that we needed to get along for the job, and friendship should be the only thing we should focus on." He held her gaze. "Am I wrong?"

She hesitated briefly. "No."

He smiled faintly. "Good. Lock up and I'll see you in the morning."

She watched his long strides cover the short distance to his car and then closed the door. This wasn't supposed to happen again. Sure, she had hoped they would declare a truce of sorts, but this? And what had he meant by *good*? This attraction seemed to be out of their control, but she couldn't see anything good coming from them starting up again.

Chapter 6

Wednesday morning, Lauren sat with Nigel discussing food placement and labeling the stations. She decided on a stoplight-type system to keep it simple—red for high-fat, high-calorie foods that should be very limited; yellow for foods that had nutritional value but still should be eaten in limited quantities; and green for fruits, vegetables, lean proteins and low-fat options. The goal would be to encourage players to eat from the green list most often. She had also decided to set up a smoothie bar with greens, fruits, yogurt, milks and protein powders, all labeled to assist players in understanding what each food provided for their bodies.

Nigel sat back in his chair and folded his arms. "Lauren, I know I've said it before, but you're a great fit for this team."

"Thanks." His words brought back what Malcolm had said over dinner two nights ago. Automatically, her mind shifted to the kiss they'd shared in the door of her condo. She hadn't been able to forget it or his words. When he picked her up yesterday, he'd placed a quick kiss on her lips, but nothing more. The parts of her that loved his kisses were disappointed, but the saner parts of her knew she should try to stop whatever was developing. Nigel's voice pulled her back into the conversation.

"And I know for a fact that those recovery shakes are going to be a huge hit."

Her brow lifted. "Oh? Practice hasn't started."

"No, but Malcolm Gray was here on Monday working with a rookie, so I made them the one with strawberries, pineapple, vanilla protein powder and orange juice."

So that was why Malcolm had been at the facility. Yet he hadn't mentioned anything about the smoothie over dinner. "They liked it?"

"Better than that. Malcolm mentioned it being similar to ones he made for himself. If the star running back is on board, it'll be easy to bring everyone else along."

"I'm glad to hear it. I hope they don't think I'm trying to be the food police. I don't expect them to eat healthy one hundred percent of the time, but if they do it close to eighty, I'll take it."

He laughed. "The food police? I think it'll be fine, but between me and you, a few of these players *need* someone to police them."

Lauren smiled. "I'll have the color-coded signs done by the end of the week, as well as the diagram for the station layout we discussed." She glanced down at her watch. "I need to get going." She gathered her notes and stood.

Nigel followed suit. "Showtime next week and we'll be ready. We can get together next Monday to go over the grocery list. Training camp starts on that Saturday, so I'll have my two assistants do the shopping on Thursday. I want to give us time just in case we overlook something."

She pulled up her calendar on her iPad. "I have some free time between eleven thirty and one—will that work?"

He picked up his phone and pushed a few buttons. "Let's make it twelve."

"Got it." She powered the device off and put it and a folder into her tote bag. "See you later." She made a quick stop at her office to pick up the shopping list for Terrell on her way out. She would be going shopping with the player to help him make better selections. Her cell rang as soon as she got to her rental. Lauren smiled upon seeing her father's name on the display.

"Hi, Daddy."

"Hey, baby. Sorry about not getting back to you last night. I didn't realize the phone was off until this morning. Did I catch you at a bad time?"

"No. I have an appointment in half an hour, but it won't take long to get there. I know you probably listened to my message, so do you think I should get the transmission fixed or buy a new car?"

"With the price they quoted, you'd be better off buying a new one. I checked around at a couple more repair shops, and the cost was about the same."

She opened the door, tossed the tote and her purse onto the back seat, and released a deep sigh. "I was afraid of that. I just paid that car off a few months ago, and I don't want to start up again."

"I checked into one of those pick-and-pull places, and you can get a couple thousand for the Maxima. Your mother and I can help you."

"I can't ask you guys to do that."

"I don't recall you asking at all. Now, when do you want to go looking?"

Lauren smiled and shook her head. She loved her daddy. "Saturday, if you're available."

"Got nothing to do but mow the yard."

Her father usually got up with the chickens and she figured he'd be done before ten. "If I came at eleven, would that give you enough time to finish?"

"Plenty."

"Thanks, Dad." They spoke a moment longer; she sent love to her mom and hung up. Lauren couldn't ask for better parents.

"Any news on your car?"

She gasped and spun around. "Malcolm. You scared me half to death. What are you doing here?" He had come up behind her without making a sound. She searched and saw his car parked several spaces over. She hadn't even heard him drive up.

"Sorry. I'm here for a meeting."

"Oh. My dad is going car shopping with me on Saturday. It's cheaper to buy a new one."

Malcolm nodded. "Are you done for today?"

"No. Going grocery shopping with one of your teammates."

He unleashed that sexy smile. "So, if I needed you to help me with food selection, you'd be available to go shopping with me?"

"*If* you needed help, yes. But you don't, so the point is moot." He moved close enough for her to feel the heat emanating from his muscular frame. She took a step, then remembered where they were and what she should not be doing. "I… I have to go."

He looked like he wanted to say something else, but he stepped back. "See you later."

Lauren quickly got into her car, started it and drove off. "You have a job to do," she muttered under her breath. "And that does *not* include dating a player three weeks after you start your new job." *But he's not just any player. He's the first man you fell in love with*, an annoying inner voice reminded her. Not that she needed any reminders. Her memory worked just fine. And that was the crux of her problem.

Malcolm stared after Lauren's car. After kissing her again, he'd told himself he needed to slow down and not get caught up. No reason to travel the same road, especially when he suspected the end result would be the same. When he had asked her to stay and work things out, she'd told him the move would be better for her career. With her just starting with the Cobras, he could see her choosing the job over their relationship once more.

"Hey, Malcolm."

He turned at the sound of Chris's voice. "What's up? You ready to work?"

"Let's do it."

They worked out for over two hours, repeating the previous drills and adding two additional ones that focused on agility and speed. If Chris kept the same work ethic and avoided injury, he would be more than ready to step into Malcolm's shoes when the time came. Now that the coaches used a Mobile Virtual Player during practice, injuries had decreased. The robotic dummies could mimic many football cuts and moves, and were used for tackling, chase drills and even as stand-ins for defensive players.

After showering, Malcolm planned to stop by the two transitional living facilities scheduled to open in two weeks. This would be the final piece of the project he, his siblings and Cameron started. The mobile grocery and shower had turned out to be so successful that they'd received donations to add two new buses equipped with showers and one more for fresh groceries. The buses traveled through areas with a high population of the homeless on a rotating basis. The hope was this small token would restore some dignity to the homeless population until they could get back on their feet.

His cell rang as soon as he got into the car. He smiled, started the engine and connected through the Bluetooth system. "Well, if it isn't the laziest engineer in Sacramento. What's up, cuzzo?"

Lorenzo Hunter's laughter came through the speaker. "Lazy, my ass. I'm not the one who only works six months out of the year." Lorenzo worked as a civil engineer at his family's construction company. "Since you're still slumming, you available for dinner tonight?"

"You're in my neighborhood?"

"Yep. Attending a conference. It should be over at four thirty."

"Cool. Come on over and I'll throw something on the grill. I'll text you the address."

"All right. Later."

Malcolm disconnected. He hadn't seen his cousin since Khalil's wedding last year, and he looked forward to catching up. Good thing he had driven his car instead of the motorcycle, because he needed to make a grocery run on his way home.

With some traffic, it took nearly an hour for him to get across town to the central Los Angeles neighborhood where the two side-by-side hotels that had been renovated as apartments stood waiting for their new occupants. They would house up to fifty men, women and families. It would have been more, but because the Grays had wanted to include families, some of the units needed to be larger.

The foreman turned, waved and started in Malcolm's direction. Malcolm met him halfway and extended his hand. "It's looking good, Mr. McIntyre." Though he knew the man to be in his fifties, he was in as good shape as Malcolm.

A smile creased his dark brown face. "They turned out better than I thought. Would you like to see inside?"

"I would." They passed landscapers, painters and other construction workers putting on finishing touches and entered a one-bedroom ground-floor apartment. The smell of fresh paint greeted Malcolm as he crossed the navy-carpeted floor. All would be furnished with appliances, furniture and basic supplies like towels, bed linens and toiletries; once the person or family moved in, groceries would be added to give them a head start. Malcolm took a few pictures to show his siblings. The place could easily fit two to three people. Next, Mr. McIntyre led Malcolm into one of the three-bedroom family units, where he took more pictures. "Your company did a great job."

"All we did was bring your vision to life, son. And I have to tell you, Cameron's suggestion of hiring some of the people who will be living here turned out to be a good one."

"I'm glad." Cameron had explained that allowing the residents to invest time and work in their new place would go a long way in restoring some of their self-respect and give them a deeper sense of pride, all while providing a wage. "I won't keep you. I just wanted to see the finished product."

"Will you be at the grand opening?" he asked, walking back out to Malcolm's car.

"Depends on the practice schedule."

The foreman's eyes lit up. The first time Malcolm had met Mr. McIntyre, the other man had quickly let it be known that he was an avid football fan with season tickets to the Cobras. "Oh, yeah. Training camp starts next weekend. I'll be waiting for that championship trophy again."

Malcolm grinned. "We'll do our best."

Someone called out to the foreman. "Let me get on back. I'll see you on the field." He shook Malcolm's hand once more and departed with a smile.

Malcolm chuckled as he drove off, scanning the buildings one last time and wishing they could have funded a few more.

He made it home twenty minutes before his doorbell rang. To his surprise, not only had Lorenzo come, but their cousin Cedric Hunter was with him. Their fathers, who were Malcolm's mother's twin brothers, owned Hunter Construction. "What's up? Zo, you didn't tell me this bum was tagging along." All three men laughed. After a round of one-arm hugs, Malcolm waved them in. "You both came for the conference?"

"Yeah," Cedric answered, taking a seat on the sofa in the family room.

Lorenzo sat on the opposite side of the sofa and leaned his head back. "Three days away from fourteen-hour days is heaven."

Malcolm dropped down in his favorite recliner. "You guys have a big project?" The company built everything from residential and commercial buildings to roads and bridges. Cedric, with his construction engineering degree, headed up the real estate division, while Lorenzo focused more on the larger-scale civil projects.

"That and the fact that Dad and Uncle Reuben are talking about retiring."

Cedric shook his head. "Ever since Uncle Nolan turned over the company to Brandon, that's all they've talked about."

Malcolm burst out laughing. "I thought you wanted to be in charge, Ced."

"I *am* in charge. I just don't know if I'm ready to be stuck in an office for eight hours a day. Hell, we're only thirty-three. Being co-CEOs will cut into my social life even more." Both Cedric and Lorenzo were one year younger than Brandon.

"Social life? You dating someone seriously?"

Cedric slanted him an amused glance. "Of course not. I like to keep my dating life fluid."

"Don't even look over here," Lorenzo said. "I need a break from women right now. And before you ask, she was into stuff that could have cost me my freedom."

Malcolm lifted a brow. "Illegal?"

"Yeah, man."

It sounded similar to what Khalil had recently shared had happened to him during his modeling days, except it had cost Khalil thirty-six hours in a Mexican prison.

"What about you, Malcolm? The women still trying to follow you when you're on the road?"

"No, thank goodness." His first year in the pros, Malcolm had been flattered by all the attention. But after seeing all the trouble some of his teammates had gotten into, he'd distanced himself from the madness and just focused on his game. Any woman he dated knew up front that if they shared any photos or personal information not already public knowledge, they would have trouble on their hands. He pushed to his feet. "I'm going to put the steaks on the grill. There's beer in the fridge if you want." In the kitchen, he preheated his stove-top grill.

Cedric followed Malcolm to the kitchen. "You know, you still didn't answer the question."

"What question?"

"The one about dating."

"I…no." He didn't know how to describe what was going on between him and Lauren. He couldn't call it dating.

Cedric burst out laughing. "Yo, Zo. Malcolm's going to be taking that marriage plunge with the rest of his siblings."

Lorenzo appeared in the kitchen. He and Cedric sat at the bar. "Really? Congrats."

Malcolm shot Cedric a glare. "Shut up, Cedric. I'm not dating anybody *or* getting married."

"I don't know. You should've seen the look on his face when he tried to answer, and then there was all the stuttering going on."

"Keep talking and you're going to find yourself starving tonight."

Still chuckling, Cedric held up his hands in mock surrender. "The only reason I'm backing off is because I'm hungry enough to eat two cows."

Lorenzo smiled. "So what's the deal, Malcolm?"

He paused in seasoning the steaks. "Lauren is back."

"From college?" they asked in unison.

"Yeah, from college." Malcolm shared the details surrounding her return, her work with the team and their first encounter—minus the kiss.

"Have you kissed her yet?"

He glanced at Lorenzo. "Why?"

"Never mind. You did. And you still want her, right?"

He didn't know what he wanted, so he remained silent. Instead, he placed the steaks on the grill. When he turned back, Lorenzo and Cedric were staring at him with wide grins. "Since you both think this is so funny, you can work for your supper." Malcolm pointed to the three potatoes and salad fixings resting on the other side of the counter.

Lorenzo shifted to face Cedric. "See, I told you we should've just gone to the restaurant in the hotel."

"I know, right? We could be chillin' instead of cooking."

"Whatever," Malcolm said, grabbing a bowl for the salad and shoving it at Cedric, who had come around the bar. They worked together until the meal was done, then carried their filled plates to the kitchen table. While his cousins drank beer, Malcolm opted for water. For the first few minutes, the only sounds were from forks scraping against plates.

Cedric lifted his beer in salute. "This is the best steak I've had in a while."

"Thanks."

"So, what are you going to do about Lauren?"

Malcolm paused in cutting his steak. "I have no idea."

"You'd better figure out pretty quick. The last thing you need is a woman crowding your head space like that, especially with the new season starting up."

He knew Cedric was right. He had to decide one way or another how to handle the rekindled attraction between him and Lauren. Common sense said to just let it go, but he wasn't sure if he could. Not wanting to dwell on it, he steered the conversation toward his cousins' families. They spent the remainder of the meal catching up on one another's families and talking sports. When it came time for them to leave, Malcolm offered to let them stay overnight, but they declined. With a promise to return for at least one of Malcolm's home games, the two men said goodbye.

As he cleaned up the remainder of the food and loaded

the dishwasher, his thoughts went back to Cedric's comment about Lauren. *No time like the present.* He checked the time—only seven thirty. He added detergent, started the machine and grabbed his keys.

Less than half an hour later, he knocked on Lauren's door.

Surprised filled her eyes when she saw him standing there. "Malcolm! What are you doing here? Is something wrong?"

"We need to talk."

Lauren moved aside for him to enter, closed the door and leaned against it. She folded her arms.

He had been so focused on what to say that he just noticed the skimpy tank and shorts she had on. The curves he'd felt the night they danced and when they'd kissed were on full display. Her folded arms emphasized the sweet swell of her breasts visible above the low-cut top. His gaze roamed lazily down her body to her toned legs and bare feet. His arousal was swift.

"You said you wanted to talk."

Malcolm took the two steps to where she stood, letting his body touch hers and wanting her to feel just what she was doing to him. He heard her breath hitch. "I don't know what to do about this dilemma. On the one hand, I should be keeping my distance. On the other..." He brushed his lips over hers. "I never want to let you go."

She closed her eyes briefly. "I didn't come here to complicate your life or mine, Malcolm. Only to do my job."

"Maybe not, but you're complicating it just the same. And as much as I want to deny it, there's still something between us." Lauren stared at him as if she didn't know what he meant. She opened her mouth and he added, "If you lie, lightning will strike you right now."

Lauren sighed. "We could ignore it."

Malcolm studied her. Less than three weeks ago, she'd blown into his life, forcing him to remember everything good about what they'd shared. And heaven help him, but he wanted to experience it again. "True, we could. But I don't want to, and your kiss says neither do you." Before she could refute him, he kissed her, slowly, provocatively, until all of her protests melted away. He banded his arms around her, lifted her off her feet and carried her into the living room. He lowered himself to the sofa and shifted her until she sat across his lap. "You were going to say?"

She punched him in the shoulder. "You know you're not playing fair."

"I'm not playing at all, baby." He captured her mouth again, slid his hand up her thigh and caressed her hip. Her hand moved across his chest, up and around his neck, sending heat straight to his groin and causing him to groan. He trailed kisses along her jaw and exposed throat, her faint citrus scent filling his nostrils and making him even harder.

"I…*oh*. I missed you, Malcolm," she whispered.

Malcolm went still. Her eyes snapped open, and he saw a look of panic, as if she hadn't meant to say it.

Lauren sat up and tried to leave his lap. "I—"

He tightened his hold. "I missed you, too, Lauren. More than you know." She relaxed. He had spent the last seven and a half years playing football, dating when it suited him and generally living life on his own terms. True, long-term commitments weren't on his radar, and he had been fine with that. And now she was back, invading his mind and his space. From the first, he had always found her easy to talk to—no pretense, no drama. She had been the first and only woman who respected his need for privacy. And ever since they'd had dinner, he'd realized he missed the easy rapport they always shared.

"So what does this mean?"

"I have no idea, but I do know that I want you. Maybe we can keep finding out, taking each day as it comes." Malcolm hoped it would be enough. Right now, he couldn't commit to more.

Chapter 7

"How did the barbecue go?" Khalil asked Malcolm Sunday afternoon, as they stood around the pool table at their parents' house talking with their brother and brothers-in-law.

"Fine. I didn't cook as much this year so I'd have less to clean up and put away. But I still have some grilled salmon left if you want it."

"Lexia and I will stop by on the way home tonight." He and Malcolm lived ten minutes from each other.

Malcolm grinned, knowing he'd say that. Khalil ate even healthier than Malcolm. He'd been a model for close to a decade before studying for his kinesiology and business degrees and opening up a fitness center. "Speaking of Lexia, when is her book signing?" Khalil's wife had written a cookbook geared toward college students.

"Two Saturdays from now. She's excited, but a little nervous with it being her first book. She's worried no one will show up and no one will buy the book." He lined up his shot and just missed the pocket.

"The way she cooks, I don't think she'll have any problems with people buying her book," Brandon said. "We'll all be there to support her."

Justin took his turn at the table and sank his shot. "And with this brood, she won't have to worry about the bookstore being empty."

They all laughed. All of Malcolm's siblings had gotten married in a space of less than four years, and if everyone's parents and extended family were in attendance, Justin's assessment would be correct. Only Malcolm and Omar would possibly miss it, due to the start of training camp.

"I haven't checked the practice schedule, so I don't know whether I'll be able to attend," Omar said.

Malcolm nodded in agreement. "Oh, Lorenzo and Cedric were here this week."

Brandon paused with a water bottle halfway to his lips. "Really? Why didn't you invite them over?"

"I did, but they had to get back to Sac. They said they'd be back during the season."

Morgan stuck her head in the door. "Dinner, guys."

Khalil and Justin replaced the pool sticks, and they all filed out and took seats at the large dining room table that his mother insisted she needed to accommodate the growing family. She was ecstatic about her granddaughter, Nyla, and the pending birth of Morgan and Omar's first child. Along with Nyla, Siobhan and Justin were going through the process of adopting a four-year-old boy named Christian. Though the little boy had spent time with Siobhan and Justin, today was his first time meeting the rest of the family. It hadn't taken him long to become comfortable and Malcolm had distinctively heard him call Malcolm's mother Grandma. In order to allow for the extra time, the social worker had agreed to pick him up from here later.

Once everyone had a seat, Malcolm's father blessed the

food, and conversation commenced as plates were filled. Malcolm watched Siobhan's relaxed features as she smiled and fed her daughter. For years, she had blamed herself for Malcolm getting hurt during one of his daredevil stunts after she had gone out with friends as a teen instead of staying home while their parents were out. Marriage and motherhood had mellowed her a great deal, and Malcolm couldn't have been happier.

Malcolm forked up some of the macaroni and cheese and stifled a groan. No one could hold a candle to his mama's version, and he'd be working out extra hard tomorrow because he planned to have another helping.

"How is Lauren working out with the team?"

He stared at Brandon. Somehow, he'd known he wouldn't be able to get through dinner without someone asking.

"Specifically, how are things working out between you two with her being there?"

Confused. Complicated. Unsettling. Pick one. Keeping his voice neutral, he said casually, "Fine. She's doing her job and I'm doing mine."

Khalil leaned back and studied Malcolm. "Is that right? Because you two looked *real* cozy on the dance floor last Saturday night."

"It was nothing."

Morgan pointed her fork Malcolm's way. "Whatever. Cozy or not, she'd better not hurt you again."

Malcolm lifted a brow and shook his head at his twin. "Morgan, I think I can handle my life just fine. Oh, I stopped by the transitional housing the other day, and it looks great," he said, changing the subject.

"I'm just so proud of you all," his father said. "Your mother and I will be at the grand opening. Thad said he'd be there as well." Thaddeus Whitcomb, whom they affectionately called Uncle Thad, was his father's best friend and business partner. Malcolm and his siblings had been shocked to find out Uncle Thad had a daughter, who he'd found after several years of searching. Malcolm chuckled inwardly remembering all the fireworks that sparked between Brandon and Faith when he found out she was that daughter and stood to inherit part of the company Brandon had thought he would be running solo. They were now happily married.

"How many families will they house again?" Justin asked.

"Up to fifty for each building."

"And that's one hundred less on the streets." His mother sighed. "I just wish the city would do more. It doesn't make sense to have all these vacant buildings sitting around when they can be put to good use."

Siobhan laughed. "Uh-oh, y'all got Mom started."

"Hey, she does have a point," Lexia said.

Faith held up her hand and high-fived Lexia. "Agreed."

Laughter flowed around the table, and they continued eating and conversing until plates were clean. Afterward, everyone shuffled to the family room and relaxed, too full to do anything else for the time being. However, an hour later, no one turned down the peach cobbler and homemade vanilla ice cream served for dessert.

Christian devoured his portion in a matter of minutes, then held his empty bowl out. "Grandma, can I have more ice cream?"

Malcolm's mother beamed. "Of course, baby." She set her bowl aside, stood and took his hand. "Come on and let's get you some."

Justin shook his head. "Two hours and he's got your mom wrapped around his finger."

Siobhan playfully elbowed him. "And he doesn't have you wrapped, too?"

Christian came back wearing a huge smile and sat on the floor next to Malcolm.

Malcolm ruffled his head. "You're going to have to do a lot of exercising to work off all this dessert, little man."

The boy just smiled around a huge spoonful of ice cream.

They were just finishing when the social worker arrived. No one wanted Christian to leave, especially Malcolm's mother and Siobhan. Christian's little sad face moved Malcolm in a way he hadn't anticipated. He had no idea how many more trial weekends were necessary, but he hoped not many, because Christian had captured all their hearts.

After several rounds of goodbyes, Christian ran over and wrapped his arms around Siobhan's waist. "Mama, *no*! I want to stay with you," he cried.

Malcolm heard Siobhan's sharp gasp and saw her fighting for control. His mother and Morgan looked stricken, as did Faith and Lexia.

Justin rushed over and gently scooped up Christian. "Malcolm, take Siobhan out of here!" He strode toward the door with the screaming little boy.

"No! Mama!"

Malcolm picked his sister up, carried her to one of the extra bedrooms and placed her on the bed.

"My baby, my baby. He's never called me Mama before." Siobhan jumped up from the bed and started toward the door, but Malcolm blocked her way. "Tell Justin he can't let her take him," Siobhan pleaded as she wept.

Seeing his sister, always the strong one, who never lost control, crying this way broke Malcolm's heart. "Everything's going to be okay, Vonnie. This is only temporary. Christian will be with you before you know it." Not knowing what else to say, he just held her. She was still crying when Justin came in a few minutes later. He kissed his sister on her forehead. "How's Christian?"

Justin's pain was reflected in his face. He shook his head. "He's never done this before. It nearly killed me to put him in that car. She said we'd probably be able to have him for good in two or three weeks. I hope so, because I can't go through this again." He gathered Siobhan in his arms and led her back to the bed. "Thanks, Malcolm."

Malcolm nodded and left quietly. He found everyone still subdued when he entered the family room. He, Brandon and Omar put away the food and loaded the dishwasher, then everyone said their goodbyes.

Hours later, long after Khalil and Lexia had come and gone, Malcolm sat on the balcony off his bedroom, unable to get the sound of Christian's screams out of his head. Back when they were dreaming, he and Lauren had talked about having children, but he hadn't thought about it since then. Tonight, however, those imaginings came back full force and, for the first time in eight years, he contemplated what it would be like to have children of his own. The realization startled him and he quickly shoved it aside. He needed to keep his focus on the upcoming season and not the crazy musings of two kids who had fancied themselves in love. He could handle that. He hoped.

Monday morning, Lauren had her hands full with the third day of training camp. Fortunately, she eased into the transition, somewhat, since only the twenty-seven rookies started for the first two days. But by Friday, the entire fifty-three-man lineup and an additional ten reserve players had descended on the facility. When she arrived at six thirty, she passed several players in the gym and in the various meeting areas.

"Man, by the time the season starts, I'd better be a lean, mean blocking machine, eating all this healthy stuff."

Lauren cut a look at Brent. He'd complained their entire session. She leaned over to see what he had on his breakfast plate.

"See, Lauren, a six-egg omelet with spinach, mushrooms and red peppers, salmon cakes, whole-wheat bagel, two bananas, yogurt, and milk."

She patted his arm. "Nice job. You'll be energized for

practice instead of moving like a slug." She wanted the lineman to keep the mass and protein levels higher because of the constant contact he'd have during games. For the players who ran more, increased carbohydrates and good hydration were the key.

Brent laughed. "You're cool people, Lauren."

She couldn't help but smile. "Thanks. So are you." She went over to where Darren stood scooping eggs. He'd lost nine pounds already and needed to lose eleven more. Even so, he still needed a little over five thousand calories a day.

"Hey, Lauren. What else is on the list? I have the four scrambled eggs and I added the spinach and mushrooms to get in some veggies."

"Oatmeal, turkey sausage and a smoothie made with two scoops of protein powder, low-fat milk, peanut butter and a banana." She had one of the guys from Nigel's team make the smoothie. This was going better than she had hoped. Lauren turned and went still at the sight of Malcolm making his way over to the buffet. He glanced her way, smiled faintly and picked up a plate. Moments later, she sensed him behind her.

"I like the signs." Malcolm filled his plate.

"Thanks." He reached for a bagel and his arm brushed hers, the contact sending heat spiraling through her.

"What made you decide to do this?"

"I thought it would be a good way to bring attention to what everyone is eating. When it's in your face, it's hard to miss."

He studied her. "Good point. It is hard to miss something when it's right in your face."

The way he looked at her and the softness in his voice told her he meant something else altogether. "I…need to get going. Have a good practice." Without waiting for a reply, Lauren made a beeline for the kitchen area. Just seeing Malcolm conjured up visions of his mouth and hands on her last week. Standing next to him pretending that nothing was going on between them and that she barely knew him tested her in ways she couldn't begin to describe.

She shook herself and continued to make her rounds in the dining room, stopping to talk to players and answering any questions. However, she felt Malcolm's gaze whenever she passed him. She was relieved when the dining area emptied out.

"You did well in all this chaos," Nigel said, coming her way. "I couldn't believe how many players asked for the added veggies in their eggs or omelets. Then again, with someone so pretty asking, they'd probably eat a bowl of castor oil to please you."

Lauren made a face. "I hope not. Do you need me for anything else before lunch? If not, I'll be in my office."

"Nope. My guys can handle the smoothies or the players themselves, so we'll see you later."

She spent the next two hours updating player profiles and answering emails. Then, curious about the practice, she made her way outside, stood at the edge of the tunnel leading to the practice field and watched them run plays. She searched until she saw Malcolm at the far end of the field, marveling at his agility, speed and the way the muscles in his legs flexed with every movement. He was at the top of his game, and she couldn't imagine a time when he'd have to give up the game he loved.

Lauren took a quick peek at her watch and headed back. Practice would end in the next hour, and she wanted to make sure the staff laid out lunch to her satisfaction. She figured she wouldn't need to be too involved in the kitchen in a couple of weeks and could spend her time individually with the players and coaches. Today's lunch consisted of grilled chicken breasts, top sirloin steak, brown rice, sweet potatoes, a variety of green vegetables and salad and fruit bars.

After lunch ended, Lauren collapsed in her office chair and let out a long breath, but she had a smile on her face.

All in all, it had been a good day. The last meeting ended at four thirty and Nigel would be preparing dinner, but Lauren didn't feel she needed to stay around for that. *I'm loving this job.* She allowed herself a few minutes of quiet—being around over fifty giants could get pretty loud—then got to work.

She was so engrossed in the figures on her computer screen that she jumped at the sound of a knock on the partially opened door. "Come in."

"Hey."

"Hey, Malcolm. What are you doing here? Practice is over?" He had showered and changed into a pair of basketball shorts and fitted tee.

"It's almost six. What are *you* still doing here?"

"I guess I lost track of time." She stood and stretched. "You didn't answer my question."

Malcolm hesitated a beat. "I wanted to know if you had any plans tonight."

"Um…no, not really. Why?"

"I wanted you to come to my place so we can talk. I know you haven't had dinner. I can fix something."

Lauren's mind screamed, *don't do it!* Malcolm had readily admitted that he didn't want to let their attraction die down, but she continued to have reservations about starting up with him again. However, curiosity about where he lived got the best of her, and she agreed before fully considering the ramifications of her choice. "I should be ready to leave in about ten minutes. Um…" She didn't want them to walk out together, giving anyone reasons to speculate.

"I'll wait for you in the parking lot."

His expression told her he wasn't too fond of the idea, but she had to protect her reputation. "Thank you."

"See you in a few."

As soon as he was gone, Lauren dropped her head in her hands. "What am I doing?"

Chapter 8

Lauren discreetly scanned the parking lot as she walked to her car. A few players stood around talking, while others leaving passed her with a wave. She spotted Malcolm about ten spaces away getting into his car. Her phone rang as she opened the door, and she hurriedly got in and dug it out of her purse. Seeing Malcolm's name on the display, she glanced around again. "Hey."

"No one can tell who you're talking to on the phone, Lauren, so you can stop looking like you're about to do something wrong," Malcolm said with a laugh. "And before you say anything, there aren't any rules or policies against us dating."

"I'm not thinking about that," she lied. A guilty expression crossed her face. He had voiced her exact concerns. She knew about the no-fraternization policy between players and cheerleaders and had wondered if it extended to all staff.

"If you say so. Anyway, I'll meet you on the road."

"Okay." She disconnected, started the car and backed out. She noticed him waiting a few hundred feet ahead. When he saw her approach, he pulled off in front of her. During the entire drive, Lauren questioned her sanity. While there were no written rules, surely this would be frowned upon. "What are you thinking, agreeing to go to his house?" she muttered. Two miles onto the freeway, traffic slowed to a crawl. This was the one thing she didn't miss about home, and it seemed to have gotten worse over the years. It finally picked up several minutes later, and she began to have second thoughts. It would be really easy to keep going to her place. As if he read her mind, she caught his gaze in his rearview mirror, probably checking to see if she was still following. He'd said he wanted to talk, but he'd said the same thing when he showed up at her place last week. Somehow, his definition of *talking* differed from that of the rest of society. *Not that you minded*, an inner voice argued.

She drew in a deep, calming breath. He'd mentioned cooking. They'd talk over dinner and she would leave right after. There. A good, solid plan that didn't involve kisses. Now, if she could just follow through.

The traffic finally lightened up and they made the rest of the drive in fifteen minutes. Lauren expected Malcolm to live in a gated community. Instead he drove into an upscale neighborhood with large, stately homes. His was located in the center of a cul-de-sac that held only five houses. Malcolm stopped in the driveway, and one of the three garage doors lifted. He gestured for her to pull into the driveway behind him.

With daylight savings time, the sun hadn't yet set, and she had a clear view of his magnificent Mediterranean-style home—red tile roof, archways and tile walkway. Inside the garage, she could see his motorcycle and smiled.

Malcolm parked in the garage, got out and came toward her. "What are you smiling about?"

"The motorcycle."

He glimpsed over his shoulder. "We can take a ride if you want."

"That's okay." Lauren shouldn't have cared, but she wondered how many other women he had taken for a ride. *When I get my bike, you'll get the first ride.* The memory rose unbidden and shocked her. He had made the promise years ago, but she doubted he remembered.

"You sure? I have an extra helmet that I kept for Morgan until Omar bought her one of her own."

"Positive." He made it sound as if no other woman had used it, and she felt a measure of relief. *Get it together, girl!* "Your home is beautiful," she told him, needing to change the subject.

Malcolm smiled. "Thanks. Come on in and I'll give you a quick tour before dinner."

She followed him up the walk to the wooden double doors and waited for him to unlock it. He moved aside for her enter. She stopped inside the door with wide eyes and stared at the winding twin staircases that showcased an expansive second story. The highly polished wood floor in the short foyer led into a formal living room with expensive furniture and plush carpeting. A formal step-up dining area with the same wood flooring sat slightly behind the living room. He had a chef's kitchen—equipped with every modern appliance known to man—that opened into a breakfast nook and large family room. Each space flowed into the next and was separated by huge columns. "You must do a lot of entertaining."

He spun around. "Why would you say that?"

She waved her hand around. "The floor plan is so open, and it's the perfect kind of house for lots of gatherings. How long have you lived here?"

"Four years. And the only gatherings I have are the ones where my family comes over and the barbecue I host for a few of my teammates every year before the season starts. I don't like a lot of people in my space."

Lauren smiled. "I guess you haven't changed."

He met her smile with one of his own. "You know better than most how much I value my privacy. That won't ever change." He reached for her hand and started up one set of stairs.

"How many bedrooms do you have?"

"Five."

"Five?"

"My brothers and sisters and I usually hang out at each other's houses and stay overnight, so whoever stays has a place to sleep. But since they've all gotten married, we don't do it as much."

"You have a library, too." An open nook at the top of the stairs had been outfitted with two comfortable chairs, a small table and three filled bookshelves. They both enjoyed reading and it hadn't been uncommon for them to spend hours on the weekend reading together. He showed her three tastefully decorated guest bedrooms, each with en suite bathrooms. The master bedroom occupied the entire opposite side of the floor. Lauren shook her head. "I think you're taking this whole privacy thing a little far."

Malcolm laughed and shrugged. "Hey, I didn't build the house."

"But I bet it was the thing that sealed the deal for you."

He gestured her forward. "I plead the Fifth."

She rolled her eyes as she entered the room. "Mmm-hmm." Just like the rest of the house, he'd spared no expense. Dark, heavy furniture accentuated the space, but the big bed remained the focal point. A television had been mounted on the wall, a sophisticated sound system took up a portion of the far wall and a sitting room connected via an archway. He had a private deck, a bathroom with a spa tub and marble shower, both of which could easily fit two people, and an extensive walk-in closet. "This is beautiful, Malcolm. I thought you said you have five bedrooms."

"Thanks. And the other one is downstairs off the family room." He stood there a moment just looking at her.

"Something wrong?"

He closed the distance between them. "No. I just…"

"Why did you invite me here?"

He tilted her chin until their eyes met. "Because the first thing I wanted to do when I saw you today was kiss you."

She opened her mouth to protest, and he kissed the words right off her lips. He drew her closer, his tongue twirling with hers and sending waves of pleasure through her. He lifted her until she felt the hard ridge of his erection pressed against her center and she moaned.

Malcolm walked over to the nearest wall and held her in place. He gripped her buttocks and brushed kisses along the shell of her ear. "Why are you doing this to me? Do you feel how much I want you, baby?"

"I…" Her breath came in short gasps and she found it impossible to form words. But, truth be told, she wanted him, too.

His hand feathered up her torso to her breast. "I want to touch you and watch you come apart in my arms," he murmured.

He captured her mouth again, and the sensations were so staggering she was three-quarters of the way to orgasm already. A *kissgasm* was the only way she could describe it. "Malcolm."

He eased back, his breathing just as ragged as hers. "I know what you're going to say. Tell me you don't feel this and I'll stop."

Lauren stared into the eyes that had sucked her in the first day she saw him sitting in a biology class and that held her captive even now. "You know I do, but what about my job?" She wanted to call the words back as soon as they left her mouth when she saw the split second of pain that crossed his handsome face. "I'm not choosing my job over you, if that's what you're thinking."

Malcolm didn't respond immediately. Finally he said, "I know what you meant. What if we keep this between us until we can figure it out?"

"Okay." She kissed him softly, appreciating him seeing her point of view.

He gently lowered her to her feet. "Let's go get some dinner. I'm back on the clock now and can't be out too late."

"How are you breaking curfew if you're at home?" she asked as they descended the stairs.

"I have to follow you home."

"No, you don't."

"I'm not going to argue with you and I *am* following you home, so let it go."

"Fine."

Later, while eating, Lauren thought about their agreement, and it should have made her happy. But somewhere in the back of her mind, she was afraid they would end up just as they had eight years ago.

After following Lauren home, Malcolm stood beneath the warm stream flowing from his shower thinking about her and his agreement to a secret relationship. He admitted to himself that she had been right about where his thoughts had gone when she mentioned her job. A part of him still questioned whether she'd make the same choice and whether he would get the short end of the stick again. But he could no more stop his growing feelings than he could turn day to night. He finished his shower, made sure he'd turned on the alarm and slid beneath the cool, crisp sheets on his bed. The clock only read ten—early by most thirty-year-olds' standards—but football was his life, and his longevity depended on him doing the right things.

When he first started in the league, two of the veteran players had come to him and asked about his career aspirations. When Malcolm had voiced his desire to play for at least ten years, they immediately told him that meant eating right, cutting out all the partying and going to bed at eight thirty during the season. He'd laughed at the time, but within two months he began to see the wisdom of their advice. He'd never had a big problem when it came to eating, but he did occasionally hang out on the weekends and stay up late with some friends from college. Practices were much more grueling with no rest, so he'd known he had to make some changes or risk losing everything he had worked for since age eight.

Malcolm still went out, but he didn't drink alcohol and left early. And he started going to bed no later than ten. His game improved dramatically, and he'd kept the practice up until now. Several of the players who started their professional careers at the same time as Malcolm had washed out of the league in less than three years because their on-the-field performance had been negatively impacted by all of bad habits they'd adopted—partying and drinking, not eating properly, and consistently breaking curfew—landing them in trouble no team wanted to deal with. Although Cobras management didn't check, he rarely broke curfew. The few times he had had been for family emergencies.

He turned over and closed his eyes, but images of Lauren earlier with her head thrown back, eyes closed in an expression of pure ecstasy, wouldn't leave him alone. As a result, he tossed and turned all night and, when the alarm went off at five forty-five the next morning, he felt no more rested than he did when he'd lain down the night before.

Malcolm made his usual preworkout smoothie, and by the time he entered the gym, his energy level had climbed a notch or two. He hadn't been this sluggish while working out since the time he'd pulled an all-nighter to study for a kinesiology exam in college. The twenty reps at 225 pounds he normally bench-pressed felt like twice the weight.

"You know, you wouldn't be this tired if you stopped fighting your feelings for a certain dietitian."

He almost dropped the weight. He glared up at Omar. "I don't know what you're talking about." He lifted the weight once more.

Omar waited until Malcolm completed the set. "I'm assuming you're trying to keep you two a secret like Morgan and I did at the beginning of our relationship." Omar had been Morgan's first client when she left her job as an attorney for their family's home safety company and entered the field of sports management. She'd feared that she wouldn't be taken seriously if word got out that she was dating a client.

Malcolm didn't respond.

"If that's the case, you're going to have to do a better job."

He sat up on the bench. "Meaning?"

"Meaning you can't look at her like she's your favorite dessert."

"She just might be," he muttered.

Omar laughed. "That's *exactly* what I told your sister when she said that to me. And you see where we ended up."

He jumped up from the bench and stalked across the gym with Omar's laughter following him. The wide receiver caught up to Malcolm. "Let me know if you want to use my cabin for a short getaway."

Malcolm leaned against the next machine and folded his arms. "I don't even know what I'm doing, Drummond. I shouldn't want to *talk* to her, much less be with her."

"You've been feeling that way since the breakup?"

"No. I'm not going to lie, when it first happened I never wanted to see her again. But it's not like I've spent the last eight years waiting for her or wishing we could get back together." He'd dated, had relationships that lasted for several months and had enjoyed his life. "I didn't feel that anger again until I saw her."

Omar sat and did a set of leg extensions then switched places with Malcolm. He chuckled. "You seemed to have gotten over it pretty easy."

"I don't know about that," he said, gritting his teeth as he lifted the weight.

"In all seriousness, Malcolm, you can't go back. If you want her, you need to let go of the past."

And that was the crux of his problem. He didn't know if he could.

It was easier to keep his feelings and thoughts on lockdown during the weekend practices, when Lauren wasn't at the facility. But Monday morning, she was back with her sensual curves and enticing smile, and Malcolm had to work hard to stay in control. He did a good job keeping his distance for the first half of the week. Other than polite conversation if he passed her in the hallway or the dining room, they had no other contact. By Thursday afternoon, he'd reached his limit. After practice ended, he made his way to her office, praying she didn't have a client. As he rounded the corner, one of his teammates called out to him.

"Hey, Gray. You headed to see Lauren?"

Malcolm glanced over his shoulder at Carlos Jenkins, an offensive lineman. "Yeah. Just need to check in, then I'm headed home. You?"

"Actually, I was going to do the same as you."

He muttered a curse under his breath.

Before the man took a step, his phone rang. He pulled it out and glanced at the display. "Guess I'll talk to Lauren tomorrow. My agent." Carlos answered, nodded Malcolm's way and went in the opposite direction.

Thank goodness. Malcolm reached her open door and stood just outside it watching Lauren for a moment. She sat behind her desk scribbling furiously on a notepad. Her hair partially covered her face, and he couldn't recall seeing anything more alluring. He knocked on the door.

Lauren's head came up and she smiled. "Hey, Malcolm."

Her smile sent a jolt to his midsection. "Got a minute?"

She stood and came around the desk. "Sure. Come on in."

He closed the door and discreetly turned the lock.

"What are you doing?" she asked with a nervous laugh.

"Making sure no one interrupts us." Malcolm crossed the office in three strides, hauled her into his arms and slanted his mouth over hers. What started as a sweet kiss turned hot and demanding in a nanosecond. Lauren slid her hands beneath his shirt, moving them up his abs and chest and driving him insane. She pressed her body closer and he groaned. He was quickly losing control and broke off the kiss.

"I'm not done." Lauren grasped the back of his head and pulled him down for another kiss.

Malcolm was two seconds away from stripping her naked, laying her down on the conference table and burying himself deep inside her until she begged him to stop. "Baby, if you don't want everybody in our business, we need to stop, because I'm about a minute away from taking you on that table over there."

Lauren gasped and nearly jumped out of his arms. "Oh my goodness."

"Hold up a minute," he said, tightening his grip.

She rested her head on his chest. "Somebody could've come in."

He chuckled. "Not unless they can open locked doors."

Her head came up sharply. "What?" She glanced around his shoulder and stared up at him. "You locked the door?"

"I told you I didn't want anyone interrupting us."

She backed out of his hold. "I'm going to have to ban you from my office."

With the erotic fantasies running through his mind at the moment, Malcolm was inclined to agree. Omar's words came back. With his schedule, he wouldn't have time to take a trip up to the cabin, but he needed to figure out a way to get her alone. He didn't have a day off until Sunday. It wasn't soon enough for his tastes, but it would have to do. "What are you doing Sunday afternoon?"

"My friend will be visiting from Phoenix this weekend, but she leaves on Sunday around noon. Why?"

"Just want to spend some time with you. If I pick you up at four, will that give you enough time to do what you need to do for the day?"

Lauren nodded. "It should."

"Good." He leaned down and kissed her softly, being careful not to touch her. It wouldn't take much to send him over the edge. "I'll see you on Sunday."

She reached up and cupped his cheek. "Okay."

The smile she gave him had his heart beating double time. He didn't understand why this one woman affected him so, but his brother-in-law was right about one thing. Malcolm and Lauren couldn't go back, but they could start again, and he knew the perfect way.

Chapter 9

Friday evening, Lauren greeted her parents with strong hugs. "Sorry I'm late. My last appointment ran longer than expected." Christopher Long, the rookie she'd seen with Malcolm, had asked her every question under the sun related to diet, nutrition and the best foods to keep him in peak condition. She appreciated his zeal but thought he could relax a bit.

Her mother waved her off. "Don't worry about it, honey. Come on and get washed up. Dinner is ready."

She hurriedly washed her hands then joined her parents at the table. The aroma from the food made her stomach growl. Lauren tried to practice what she preached when it came to diet and nutrition, but she hadn't eaten her mother's cooking in almost a year and tonight she planned to go all out.

"By the sound of your belly, I guess you're hungry." Her father's deep rumble made her smile.

"Dad, you have no idea. Mom, this smells *so* good. I'm going to try not to hurt myself."

Delores smiled. "I fixed all your favorites, so eat up."

After her father said the blessing, Lauren helped herself to the barbecued chicken, sautéed corn, broccoli with cheese sauce and roasted potatoes. She groaned with every bite. "You outdid yourself, Mom."

"She sure did," Walter said around a mouthful of chicken. They ate in silence for a few minutes. "How are you liking the new job?"

"I love it. Everyone has been so nice, and even though a few of the players complain, I haven't had much trouble. Now that training camp has started, I'm a lot busier."

Her mother reached over and patted her hand. "That's wonderful, sweetheart." She paused. "And Malcolm? I'm sure you've seen him by now."

Lauren had known that would be among the first questions they asked. They understood better than anyone else how devastated she had been over the breakup, particularly since she'd been to blame. Instead of her listening to his explanation and trying to make things right—and Malcolm had made several attempts to talk to her—she'd allowed fear and other people to mess up a beautiful relationship. She speared a piece of broccoli and popped it into her mouth. "Yes, I've seen him."

"And?" her father prompted with his fork. When Lauren didn't answer, he frowned. "Did something happen between you two already?"

Happen? She couldn't begin to describe what was *happening* with her and Malcolm. She had never been so out of control with a man before in her life. *Yes, you have*, that annoying inner voice corrected her. Okay, so she had. Only once. And it was the same man. But she had never done anything so reckless as coming close to having sex at her office. She didn't think it was a good time to share that piece of information.

"No, Daddy. We actually went to dinner the night my car broke down—he was the one who found me on the road—

and we talked. Both of us have grown up, and we're leaving all the rest in the past."

"I'm glad to hear it. You and Malcolm were like two peas in a pod. It's good to see him doing so well in his football career, but the thing that impressed me about him most was that no matter how much sports demanded of him, he never hesitated to leave football on the field and give time to the things that mattered most."

Lauren gave a little laugh. "Wow, Mom. I didn't realize you paid that much attention when he and I were dating."

She smiled knowingly. "I realize more than you're letting on." She lifted her glass of lemonade and took a sip.

What the heck does that mean?

"Finish your food. Didn't you say you had to pick up Valencia from the airport later?"

"Yes." Had Lauren given something away? Mothers always seemed to discern the truth beneath a story, and Delores Emerson was no exception. Lauren went back to eating but pondered her mother's statement for the rest of the visit.

When it came time to leave, her father engulfed her in a comforting hug that let her know he'd be there if and when she needed him. No one gave out hugs like Walter Emerson, and she counted herself blessed to have him in her life. "I love you, Daddy."

"I love you, too. Is the car working out okay?"

She nodded. "It rides like a dream." Despite her protests, he and her mother had gifted her with a new black Acura and told her to think of it as a belated graduation gift to celebrate her master's degree and a congratulations on the new job. Lauren hugged her mom. "Love you, Mom."

"Ditto, baby. And tell Valencia I said hello. If you two aren't too busy tomorrow, I'd love to see her."

"We'll try to stop by after I take her on a tour of the Cobras' practice facility tomorrow."

"All right. You be careful."

"I will." Lauren waved as she got into the car. Before

driving off, she checked to make sure Lyn's plane was on schedule.

She'd forgotten how crazy LAX could be, and all the construction made it worse. She circled twice, had one driver yell and accuse her of driving slowly and another one cut her off and nearly take off the front end of her new car. She finally spotted her friend on the fourth go-around and sent up a silent thank-you. She signaled and eased to the curb.

Valencia threw her bag in the back and got in the front seat. They shared a quick hug. "Hey, girl. It's so good to see you. Nice car."

"You, too, and thanks. The transmission went out on the Maxima and it was cheaper to buy a new one." Lauren checked the traffic before merging. "How was the flight?"

"It was fine. Oh, guess who asked about you today as I was leaving?"

"Who?"

"Jeffrey."

Lauren gave a quick roll of her eyes at the mention of her ex. "Why is he asking about me? He didn't say two words to me the last three months I was there."

"I have no idea. He said he hadn't seen you around and wanted to know if you were okay. I think he was fishing for information. Information I didn't give him," she added with a laugh. "All he knows is that you don't work there anymore."

"And that's all he needs to know." Aside from her supervisor and Lyn, Lauren hadn't told anyone else where she would be working—just that she had a dream opportunity. She wasn't naive enough to believe people wouldn't find out sooner or later. A woman entering a male-dominated field most always made the news. She just wanted to fly under the radar for as long as possible, especially now that she had agreed to date Malcolm. The media would have a field day with that piece of news.

"You're still taking me to tour the Cobras' practice facility tomorrow, right?"

Lauren chuckled. "It's either that or you'll bug me to death."

"Please, *please* tell me the team will be practicing."

She slanted her friend an amused glance. "Yeah, they'll be practicing."

Valencia pumped her fists in the air. "Yes, baby! I have to make sure my phone is fully charged. I don't want to miss one photo op." She bounced in her seat. "Wait. Do you think any of them will pose for pictures?"

"I have no idea, but you can ask."

"I think it'll be better coming from you," she said sweetly.

"Mmm-hmm."

After they got to Lauren's condo, the two spent the rest of the evening laughing, eating their favorite cookies-and-cream ice cream, and catching up.

Valencia yawned. "I am so tired. I worked ten hours today and went straight to the airport from the hospital."

"Were you covering for someone?"

"Yep. The new dietitian was out sick, so I saw three of her patients after I finished with mine."

Lauren stood. "Well, let me show you where everything is so you can go to bed."

Valencia slowly got to her feet and trudged down the hallway behind Lauren. "I really like your place."

"Thanks." Lauren pointed out the cabinet holding the towels. "If you need anything else, I'll be in my room. Otherwise, I'll see you in the morning." They shared another hug. "I'm so glad you're here."

"Me, too. You get a pass for the night on Malcolm, because I'm too tired and I need to be fully alert for this update. But I expect *all* the details tomorrow."

Lauren smiled and shook her head. "Figured as much. Good night."

"'Night."

Lauren had planned to sleep in until at least ten, but Valencia was up at nine the next morning, standing in Lauren's bedroom door asking when they'd be leaving. They got to the facility at ten, instead of at eleven thirty, like she had intended.

They stopped at the security desk to get a visitor's badge before beginning the tour, and Valencia's eyes were wide as she followed Lauren around the facility.

"This is *fantastic*! I see why you got lost. You've turned down so many hallways, I have no idea which way is which."

"I told you." She stopped at her office, unlocked the door and gestured her in with a flourish. "My office."

"Wow. You have moved up, girlfriend. Don't you need help? I'm more than willing to relocate." She walked over to the large window. "And look at this view. Those gardens are beautiful."

Lauren came to stand next to Valencia. "They are. I try to go walking on the path as often as I can, which hasn't been much since training camp started."

"Speaking of…"

"Yeah, I know. You want to go watch practice. You are way too excited."

"You got that right. Who wouldn't be excited about seeing a bunch of sexy guys in those tight-fitting athletic outfits with muscles flexing and all glistening from sweat…?"

"You are truly crazy, girl. Come on. I want to introduce you to Nigel, who's the chef, and then we'll head out to the practice field."

Valencia did a little shimmy and rubbed her hands together with glee.

They found Nigel in the kitchen with his team, deep into the lunch prep. The fruit and salad stations had been filled and the warmers turned on and awaiting whatever selections were on the day's menu. Two of the kitchen staff had blenders going, making the recovery smoothies for players to have when practice ended in half an hour. They'd have about an hour to consume the drink and shower before heading to their respective team meetings.

"Hey, Lauren," Nigel said, his eyes widening in surprise. "What are you doing here?"

"Hi, Nigel. My friend Valencia is visiting from Phoenix, and I'm showing her around."

"Nice to meet you, Valencia. I'd shake your hand, but as you can see, mine are a little messy right now." He had on a pair of gloves and was seasoning a tub of chicken breasts.

Valencia laughed. "It's no problem, and it's nice to meet you, as well."

Not wanting to interrupt his flow, Lauren said, "We'll get out of your hair. See you on Monday."

"Enjoy your weekend, ladies. Wish I could be enjoying it with you," he added with a smile.

They both laughed and left him to his work. Lauren led Valencia down two hallways and out a back door and tunnel that led to the field.

Valencia stood as if starstruck. "Lord, have mercy. Have you ever seen such a glorious sight?" she whispered in awe.

Lauren had to agree. The men were impressive. There were several drills going on in various areas, but she only had eyes for one player. She observed Malcolm practicing taking handoffs from the quarterback and running various patterns.

"You are in so much trouble, Lauren."

She shifted her gaze to Lyn. "What do you mean?"

"Malcolm is even finer than he was in college, and his body…my, my, my."

Yeah, she was in trouble. Big trouble.

"I think I'm ready for the 411 now. And by the look on your face, a whole lot more has happened."

"You don't know the half of it." Lauren told her about Malcolm coming to her rescue the day her car broke down, the dinner where they cleared the air and the subsequent kisses. "The other day, he came to my office, and I was this close to having sex with him right there." She held her thumb and index finger together.

Valencia's eyes went wide. "Are you *serious*?" she squealed, then slapped a hand over her mouth. She repeated the question, but this time quieter.

Lauren ran a hand over her forehead. "There's more. He wants us to see each other again."

"And you said?"

"Definitely not what I should have." She'd been wrestling with her decision for the past few days but couldn't force herself to walk away.

"Which means yes."

Lauren nodded. "And he asked me to spend the day with him tomorrow after you leave." A wide smile spread across Valencia's face, and warning bells sounded in Lauren's head. "What are you thinking?"

"That after I get my pictures, we're going shopping to get you something cute to wear tomorrow." Valencia winked and turned her attention back to the field. "Who are those two brothers that just ran by?"

"They're the wide receivers. Marcus Dupree, and the one with the locs is Omar Drummond. And he's married... to Malcolm's twin sister."

"I'm guessing they hooked up because of her brother?"

"Nope. From what I understand, their relationship started after he asked her to be his agent. She worked as an attorney for the Gray family's company, initially."

"I am *so* in the wrong field. Maybe I need to check out the requirements to be an agent."

Lauren burst out laughing. A few minutes later, practice ended. Several of the guys called out greetings to Lauren and were more than willing to pose for photos.

"Hey, Lauren," Malcolm said, stopping in front of them. His eyes held hers for the briefest moment, but long enough to send heat flowing through her body. "Hey. I don't know if you remember my friend from school."

"I do. Good to see you, Valencia."

"Same here." She held up her phone. "You mind?"

"Not at all." He stood next to Valencia and smiled as she snapped the photo.

"Thanks, Malcolm."

"You're welcome. I'll see you later." He spoke to Valencia, but his gaze was focused on Lauren.

As soon as he was out of earshot, Valencia said, "I predict that the two of you will be engaged before the football season is over." She pointed a finger Lauren's way. "And this time, neither one of you better mess it up."

Lauren whipped her head around, praying no one else had heard. "Let's go, Miss Trouble."

"Yes, let's. We have some shopping to do. A lovely sundress that shows off your curves and a little leg will be perfect." She grabbed Lauren's arm and ushered her back the way they'd come.

She tried to ignore her friend's outrageous prediction, but the words stayed with Lauren for the rest of the day. And as crazy as it sounded, secretly the thought thrilled her.

Saturday evening, Malcolm lay on the floor in Siobhan and Justin's family room tossing his niece into the air and listening to her delighted squeals. He had been worried about his sister since the episode at their parents' house the previous week. Although he had called to check on her, he needed to see for himself how she was doing.

"How's work?" Siobhan worked as the PR director for their family's company.

Siobhan chuckled. "It's work. I've had to stay late a couple of days because we're getting ready to launch Justin's in-home alert system, and you know I have to make sure my baby gets maximum exposure." Justin had partnered with the company to manufacture his new product.

With the use of sensors placed around the home, real-time data could be sent directly to a smartphone from a wireless hub—whether a door had been left open, a stove left on, or if a person hadn't moved in hours—that allowed elderly relatives to remain at home and gave caregivers peace of mind.

Malcolm glanced over at her. "Yeah, I bet." He hesitated asking, but he wanted to know. "Any word on when Christian can come to stay permanently?"

She brightened. "The social worker called yesterday and said we could bring him home in two weeks, tops. Justin and I are going to take off that first week so we can get him enrolled in preschool and generally try to make the transition easy for him. He's been bounced around so much since his parents died two years ago it makes my heart hurt."

He sat up, cradled Nyla in his arms and handed her a book. "What happened to them?"

"From what we were told, they died when the party yacht they were on was struck by another boat," Justin said. "The guys on the other boat had been drinking and lost control."

Malcolm shook his head. "I don't know what I'd do if we lost Mom and Dad now, so I can't even imagine how it is for Christian." He instinctively held Nyla closer.

Siobhan nodded. "He doesn't remember them, really, just that they were gone and not coming back. And that's why Justin and I are going to make sure he gets all the love he deserves. He's such a sweet little boy."

Nyla decided she'd had enough of being held and squirmed until Malcolm set her on her feet. She smiled at him and opened and closed her hand repeatedly. When he didn't move, she started to whine and did it again. Malcolm's brows knit in confusion. "Sorry, baby girl, Uncle Malcolm doesn't know what that means. Vonnie?"

She chuckled. "She wants some milk. Lexia taught us

some baby signs so Nyla can communicate with us instead of crying every time she wants something."

Because her best friend had lost her hearing as a teen, Lexia had learned sign language. Malcolm would always be grateful to his sister-in-law for helping Khalil through his ordeal. "That is so cool. What else does she know?"

"More, all done and eat," Justin said with a laugh.

"Hey, well, she's got all the important ones." When Nyla made the sign again, Siobhan stood, picked up her daughter and went into the kitchen.

"Justin, how is Vonnie really doing?" he asked quietly.

Justin leaned forward. "Sunday and Monday were rough, man. You know how strong she always is, but this time…" He trailed off, and Malcolm could see the agony reflected in his face. "Hearing her cry felt like my heart was being ripped from my chest, and I couldn't do anything about it. I felt so damn helpless. But she's handling it better now, and knowing we only have a week or so before Christian will be here permanently has helped."

He felt his own emotions rising. "I hope the time passes quickly." Though Siobhan was six years older, Malcolm was still very close to his sister. All of his siblings maintained a rare bond that had grown stronger as they gotten older. It had been hard for him and his brothers to relinquish responsibility for Siobhan and Morgan's well-being to their husbands, but both couldn't have found better partners. He checked the time. "I need to get going."

On the heels of his words, Siobhan came back with Nyla and her sippy cup filled with milk. "Since you're off tomorrow, you're welcome to come by for dinner."

"Sounds good, but I already have plans."

"Plans that no doubt include Lauren, correct?" she asked pointedly.

"Yes."

"Well, you might not want to hear what I have to say, but I'm going to say it anyway."

He rolled his eyes and steeled himself for her speech about how he needed to be careful and not get too caught up.

"I know she messed up things between you two years ago. We all made stupid mistakes when we were young. I also know that, although you've moved on, you still have feelings for her. I believe she's the one for you, Malcolm."

For a moment, Malcolm sat stunned. When he finally found his voice, he asked, "And why do you think that?"

"Simple. She's the only woman who has ever owned your heart." Siobhan waved a hand. "Yeah, yeah, you've dated other women, and I'm not saying you weren't happy with them. You were. But none of them could make your eyes light up the way they do when you're around Lauren. I saw you two dancing at the awards dinner."

He divided his gaze between his sister and brother-in-law.

Justin smiled. "Big sister has spoken."

Malcolm pushed to his feet. "On that note, I'm outta here." He kissed Nyla, and she stopped drinking her milk long enough to give him a wet one of her own. He pressed a kiss to Siobhan's temple. "See you later, sis."

Justin walked him to the door. "Since we're passing out unwanted advice, I'll just add if you plan to pursue Lauren, be ready to go the distance, no matter what."

"Thanks." He didn't know if he was ready to go the distance, only that he wanted her now.

Chapter 10

Lauren opened the door to Malcolm Sunday afternoon a few minutes before four. He was dressed casually in shorts and a pullover tee. "Hi. Come in." Malcolm didn't move. His gaze made a slow tour from her sandaled feet to her face. She would have to be blind not to see the naked desire in his eyes. The appreciative gleam in his eyes let her know that the purple halter sundress was a good choice.

"Um…you never said where we're going, so I didn't know what to wear. Is this okay?"

"It's better than okay." He kissed her lightly. "And I don't think I should come in. If I do, we aren't leaving."

Her breath caught. She had no problem interpreting his meaning. And she wouldn't protest if they didn't. "Let me get my purse."

Once on the road, he said, "I really like the dress."

"Thank you."

"Did Lyn get home okay?"

She smiled at his use of Valencia's nickname. "Yes. She

sent me a text. I want to thank you and the guys for being so gracious yesterday. She was beside herself with excitement."

"I could tell."

"You never said where we're going."

"My place."

Lauren didn't know where she'd expected them to go—a movie, early dinner or something—but his house? After what happened in her office, he'd only have to suggest going farther and she'd agree. It was only a matter of time before they had sex, and she didn't know if she would be able to separate her emotions from the physical aspects. She never had. Not with him.

"Are you okay with it?"

She rotated in his direction. "Yes."

"I hope you don't mind starting so early."

"Not at all. I know you have a curfew, even if they don't enforce it. I think it says a lot about your integrity and commitment." She'd read lots of stories of athletes hanging out late and getting into trouble and respected Malcolm even more, because not once in all the years that he'd been playing football had she read or seen one bad thing about him. "Besides, I have to go to work tomorrow, too."

"Speaking of work, it seems like you're settling in well. The guys all speak highly of you. The veterans are glad to have someone there who's about helping the players be better instead of trying to make a profit."

"I'm glad to hear it. Of course, there are a few who aren't too happy with the changes I'm suggesting, but I knew it wouldn't be an easy road. And I'm hoping this will help with the book I'm writing."

"If you need any help or information, let me know."

"Seriously?"

"Of course," he chuckled.

If she could get a testimonial from Malcolm attesting to the fact that her methods were sound, or even a quote, it would be a huge boost. "I hope you know that I will be taking you up on that offer."

"I hope you do."

When they arrived at his house, he parked in the garage and took her in through the door that connected to his laundry room. She hadn't seen it her first time here, but just like everything else, the washer and dryer were state-of-the-art. The room had plenty of cabinet space and a counter, which she assumed could be used for folding clothes.

"Go on into the family room and I'll be there in a minute," he said.

Lauren went through the kitchen and stopped in her tracks upon seeing a large blanket spread out on the family room floor. Something about it seemed familiar. She moved closer and brought her hand to her mouth. It was same blanket they'd picnicked on in his apartment nearly ten years ago. They had planned to go to a park but had to alter their plans due to a surprise spring storm. She couldn't believe he'd kept it all this time. Her gaze went to the deck of cards in the center. She recalled with vivid clarity what happened the last time they'd played, and just the thought made her nipples harden and the space between her thighs throb.

"I thought we'd have a picnic," Malcolm said, entering with a basket similar to the one they had used before.

"What are you...why the picnic?"

He placed the basket on the edge of the blanket and framed her face in his hands. "You said we couldn't go back, and I agree. But we can start over. And this was the start of everything good between us. I want it to be better this time." He touched his mouth to hers.

"I want it to be better, too."

"Then we're in agreement, sunshine."

He kissed her with a tenderness that almost melted her on the spot, and the long-forgotten endearment went straight to her heart. When she had asked why he called her that the first time, he said her smile was like pure sunshine.

Malcolm kicked off his shoes and gestured for her to take a seat.

She sat, removed her sandals, tucked her legs beneath her to one side and smoothed her dress down.

He lowered himself next to her and unearthed two plates, two coasters and two champagne glasses. "I figure this time we can have a little champagne to celebrate," he said wryly, opening a bottle.

Lauren chuckled. The first time, they'd had sparkling cider because both of them were just shy of their twenty-first birthdays. "Yeah, I think we could pass for legal." She held up the glasses, and he filled them.

He set the bottle aside, accepted his glass from her and held it up. "To starting over and doing it better."

"To starting over and doing it better." She touched his glass and took a sip. "So, what are we having?"

A secretive smile curved his lips. "A little of this and a little of that."

"What are you up to?"

Malcolm reached inside the basket and took out three containers. "Open them."

Lauren removed the tops of the containers and gasped. Her gaze flew to his. He had recreated the meal—fried chicken wings, raw carrots and celery, and strawberries, mangoes and grapes. "You remembered what we ate."

"It's not something I've ever forgotten."

She searched his face, trying to figure out what he meant.

"You go first." He handed her a plate and napkin. "And this isn't going to get me into trouble with the team dietitian, is it?"

"I'll talk to her, but I'm sure she won't mind one splurge meal." They shared a smile. She filled her plate and waited while he did his own. He grasped her hand and recited a short blessing. She decided to start with the chicken wing.

"I haven't fried chicken in I don't know how long, so I hope it tastes okay."

"I remember how well you cook, so I'm not worried at all." Lauren moaned with the first bite. It tasted even better than she remembered. "This is so good! I could eat these every day."

Malcolm chuckled. "That's what you used to say. And then you said if you gained weight, it would be my fault."

"Yeah, well... I have gained a few pounds over the years," she said, smiling.

"And they're in all the right places, trust me. The guys on the team can't seem to take their eyes off you every time you enter the room."

The tone in his voice gave her pause. "You almost sound like you're jealous or something."

All playfulness fled. "Do I need to be?"

She met his serious eyes. "No." Since that kiss in her office, she hadn't thought of any other man.

Malcolm dipped a carrot in ranch dressing and popped into his mouth. "Good to know."

They ate in silence for a few minutes, but every time Lauren glanced his way, she found him staring. "Is something wrong?"

"Not at all. Everything's perfect." He leaned over and pressed a soft kiss behind her ear.

When they finished eating, she pointed to the cards. "You still have the same deck."

He shrugged. "No need to throw them away. I pull them out every now and again to play solitaire when I'm trying to clear my head. You want anything else?"

"No, thanks."

"We'll have dessert later." He repacked the basket and moved it aside. "But right now," he said, picking up the cards and shuffling them, "we're going to play."

Lauren grinned. "And as I recall, I wiped the floor with you in gin rummy."

He wiggled his eyebrows. "At first."

Her heart rate spiked. The last time they'd played, the bet started with pennies, but when she won nearly every hand, he'd upped the ante to articles of clothing. Lauren had done well and had him almost naked—until the last two hands. He took sweet revenge, and it turned out to be the most erotic game of cards she had ever played. Today, she had on only three things—her dress, bra and panties—which meant she couldn't afford to lose even one hand. "Um… Malcolm, we're not going to bet… I don't think—"

"Nope. We're not betting articles of clothing."

She relaxed.

"Something better."

"What?"

Malcolm scooted closer until they were only a breath apart. "Kisses," he murmured against her lips. "Every spread counts as one kiss, and we pay up at the end of each game. Deal?"

Confident in her skill and the fact that it was only kisses, she stuck out her hand. "Deal." In the recesses of her mind, that little caution signal reminded her about the effects his kisses had on her and that, more than likely, the end result would be the same. *Kissgasm.* He dealt the first hand, and Lauren smiled inwardly at her cards. He wouldn't be getting one kiss.

"Let's see whatcha got, sunshine."

She drew a card. "Oh, you'll see, angel eyes." The name tumbled out before she could stop it. She took a wary glance his way to gauge his reaction.

He smiled. "Haven't heard that in a while. Just make sure you don't say it when we're at the office," he added with a wink.

"Shut up," she said, rolling her eyes and spreading three matches.

"Oh, the girl thinks she still got a little game, huh?"

"A little? Baby, I got more game than you know."

Malcolm's hand paused on the deck. "Is that right? Hmm… I'm definitely up for that."

His expression said he was talking about more than a card game. She had slipped back into their old banter without missing a beat. In the past, she wouldn't have hesitated to play these sensual games, but tonight the sexual tension between them was so thick that they'd be in his bed if she gave the slightest hint she was ready to take the next step. Her mind said it might be too soon, but her body disagreed. And to prove its point, a sweet ache spread between her legs.

Malcolm threw out a card.

Two rounds later, Lauren laid out two more spreads. "Gin." She smiled serenely. "Well, I guess that means five kisses for me and…" She spread her hands. "None for you."

He leaned back on his elbows. "Then I'm at your mercy."

She hesitantly rose to her knees, braced one hand on the blanket next to him and kissed his temple. He raised an eyebrow, but she ignored it. "One." She kissed his cheek, and then his lips briefly, twice.

"I thought you said you had game."

She put her hand on her hips. "What? You saying you don't like my kisses?"

"When you kiss me, I'll let you know. I think you have one more," he said with a challenge in his eyes.

Lauren had never backed down from a challenge and leaned forward. She nibbled his bottom lip and slid her tongue inside, capturing his and taking her time reacquainting herself with the taste that was uniquely him. He reached up to cup the back of her head to hold her in place, and she broke off the kiss. "Five. How's that?"

His eyes remained closed for a moment. "Not bad, but I think we need to play another game to be sure." Malcolm gathered up the cards and placed them in front of her. "Your deal."

That last kiss had tested her resolve and she was tempted to toss the cards, knock him backward and straddle him then and there. She shuffled the deck and dealt another hand. Turning over her cards, Lauren noted that it wouldn't be as easy this game. She only hoped Malcolm's hand was as bad as hers. If he ended up winning, she could call it a wrap on her control.

His face was unreadable as he drew the first card. He studied his hand for a moment, then discarded another one. "Problems?" he asked with amusement.

"Nope." She took her turn. Midway through the game, she was up four to two and felt confident in winning and in her ability to control the rising heat.

Malcolm took his turn, smiled then counted, including the two he already had, "One, two, three, four, five, six…gin."

Lauren's mouth dropped. "How did you do that?"

"Skill, baby. Now…" A wicked smile spread across his face. "I believe it's time to show you *my* game."

Uh-oh.

He rose on all fours and came to her slowly, as if sizing up his prey, his smile still in place. "Mmm…where to start…"

"What do—" The feel of his mouth on her bare shoulder stole the rest of her words.

"One." He eased back a fraction. "I think I like this game a lot better than strip gin rummy. What about you?"

"When you kiss me, I'll let you know," she said, repeating his earlier words.

Malcolm angled his head thoughtfully. "Oh, I'm going to kiss you, all right." He moved over her until she was lying flat on her back. "Baby, I'm going to kiss you in ways and in places you've never been kissed," he said in a heated rush, holding her gaze.

His words shattered what little control she had left. She wanted this man, plain and simple. "Then kiss me, Malcolm." Without waiting, she grabbed his head and crushed her mouth against his. He wasted no time taking over the kiss and making her senses spin.

At length, he raised his head. "Are you trying to steal my kisses?"

"Can't steal something you haven't given."

Surprise lit his eyes. "Well, I'd better remedy that right now. And that one didn't count as one of mine." He slid down her body and pushed her dress up to her waist, caressing from the ankle to the upper thigh of one leg, then the other.

Lauren could barely breathe. He snaked his tongue up her inner thigh, stopping mere inches from her center, and placed a lingering kiss there. She had no doubt he knew how wet she was. When he kissed the other thigh, her legs began to shake.

"Three more to go. Hmm...where should I go next?"

She didn't care, as long as he didn't stop. He grazed her core as he made his way up to her belly button and swirled his tongue around, eliciting a loud moan.

"I take that to mean my kisses are getting better. What about this one?" Malcolm asked, releasing the tie on her dress and freeing her breasts. He pushed them together and suckled both nipples.

Her breath came in short gasps. "Mal... Malcolm..."

He dragged his body along hers until they were face-to-face and braced himself on his forearms. "What is it, sweetheart?"

Lauren was so on fire, one more touch and she'd go up in flames. He reclaimed her mouth in a slow, drugging kiss. Then he changed the tempo. His tongue thrust deeply, plunging in and out as if he were making love to her and sending shock waves straight to her core. She tore her mouth away and screamed his name as a blinding orgasm ripped through her. She shuddered and sucked in a deep breath, trying to force air into her lungs. Malcolm had always been attentive to her needs when they had sex, but never in her life had she come just from kissing. She opened her eyes and saw him above her with a pleased male smile.

"Like I said…in places and ways you've never been kissed. And we're just getting started." Malcolm scooped her into his arms, stood, carried her up to his bedroom and placed her in the center of his bed.

Chapter 11

Malcolm stared at the alluring picture Lauren made lying in his bed with her dress half-on—her bra pulled down, dress up around her waist. He didn't think he could get any harder. He never brought women to his home, because he always worried that his address would end up being blasted through social media or he'd find groupies camped out in his yard later.

His last relationship had ended at the beginning of the year—the woman had taken exception to the fact that she wouldn't be accompanying him on his monthlong vacation—and he'd been content not to date. Until now. He found it ironic that Lauren would be the first woman he brought to his house. And regardless of how this turned out, he trusted that she would never divulge any of his personal information.

Lauren sat up on her elbows. "Are you going to stand there all evening? It's almost eight o'clock, and you do have a curfew."

He laughed softly and climbed onto the bed. "We have

plenty of time." He lowered himself half on top of her, being careful not to place his full weight on her, and locked his mouth on hers. Sensations he'd tried to keep at bay came back full force. He'd spent the last two weeks wanting Lauren this way, and no amount of reasoning had taken away the longing. He stripped off her dress and laid it on the bench at the foot of the bed. Next came the strapless deep purple bra and matching bikini panties. "I like these." He remembered that she had always liked matching her underwear. He liked them, too. So much so that he had accompanied her to Victoria's Secret on more than one occasion, picked out and paid for his favorites.

"I know. That's why I wore them."

"And you knew we'd end up here."

"Without a doubt," Lauren said, leaning up to kiss him. She grabbed the hem of his shirt and pulled it up and over his head. She ran her palms over his chest and arms. "Mmm, even better than I remember."

Malcolm sucked in a sharp breath when he felt her warm tongue circling around his nipples. Her hands went to his belt buckle and, with deft fingers, undid it and his pants in a matter of seconds. He raised himself up to facilitate their removal. He sat up and let his gaze roam over her nakedness, noting the slight changes. She had maintained her slender frame, but her breasts were slightly fuller and her hips wider. Malcolm closed his eyes and used his hands to chart a path from her feet, up her toned, honey-brown legs and thighs, and over her hips. He paused a moment to stroke her wet center, then continued his journey upward to her breasts. Lauren's soft moans filled his ears and aroused him to a level he hadn't experienced in a long time, if ever.

She reached between them, grasped his engorged shaft and slid her hand up and down his length. "Stop teasing me."

He clamped down on her hand almost immediately. The pressure of her hand on him, coupled with the fact that he hadn't had sex in almost five months, had him just this side of exploding. "Don't do that," he gritted out.

"Do what?" she asked sultrily, still rubbing her thumb under the head.

Trying to maintain control, Malcolm carefully disengaged her hand and left briefly to don a condom, then came back to the bed. "You were never this playful before."

Lauren shifted beneath him until he fit snugly at her center. "Like I said before, I've changed."

"Let's see how much." Using his knee, he spread her legs and eased his way inside. She was so tight he glanced up questioningly.

A faint smile touched her lips. "It's been a while."

As irrational as it might seem to expect that she hadn't slept with another man in eight years, he felt a quick flash of jealousy. Determined to make her forget every other man except him, he met her eyes and started with slow, deep thrusts. A familiar emotion welled up, but he pushed it down and concentrated only on drawing out as much pleasure as he could from this interlude.

She locked her legs around his back and tilted her hips to meet his strokes, while her hands reached for his head. "I miss your locs," she murmured.

A vision of her gripping his hair as she came surfaced and made him increase the tempo. Her walls clamped down on him, and he gritted his teeth to keep from coming. "Damn, baby. You feel so good."

"Mmm, so do you."

Automatically, Malcolm tilted her hips higher, knowing it would increase the sensations.

Lauren arched and let out a long moan. "Malcolm, *Malcolm!*"

"Right here, sunshine," he murmured against her ear, pumping faster. He felt her tiny contractions, signaling her release was near, and slowed his movements. "Look at me, sweetheart. I want to see your eyes when you come." He rotated his hips in a circular motion, plunging with deep, measured strokes. Her expression of sheer ecstasy mirrored what he felt. Malcolm was close, and he wanted them to come together. "Come for me, Lauren." He pulled back and drove inside with one hard thrust, and she screamed. His orgasm roared through him with such force, it left him gasping for air. Their bodies shook and shuddered for what seemed like forever before their breathing slowed. He placed a gentle kiss on her lips and rolled to his side, taking her with him.

She lay facing him with her leg thrown over his and her head on his chest. "So, who won?"

"Technically I did, since I had six to your five, but I'm willing to call it a draw," he said with a chuckle. "I do think my kisses were better than yours, though."

Her head popped up, and she punched him playfully. "I beg your pardon."

He angled his head and raised a brow. "You can beg all you like, but weren't you the one who had an orgasm downstairs?"

Lauren dropped her head. "That's never happened before."

"And I've never done it to anyone before."

He felt her smile. "Then we can keep the kissgasm between us."

Malcolm laughed. "*Kissgasm?* That's not even a word."

"It is now. Next time, we'll see if I can't give you one. I'm certain there are a few places I can kiss that will produce the desired effects."

He grew hard again with just the thought.

She stroked a finger down his chest to his abdomen. "Like somewhere along here, or—" she skimmed a hand over his rising erection "—here, maybe. What do you think?"

His stomach clenched. "I think if you keep that up, you're going to be in trouble." Malcolm glimpsed at the clock on his nightstand. As much as he wanted to go a second round, it would have to wait. They still had to shower and he had to drive Lauren home. "Unfortunately, we'll have to take a rain check." He kissed her forehead, sighed deeply and swung his legs over the side of the bed. "Come on, let's go take a shower."

"Together?" she asked warily.

"Yeah. I'll behave, even though I don't want to."

Afterward, he drove her home and walked her to the door. "I gotta tell you, baby, I'm going to have a hard time ignoring you tomorrow."

Lauren came up on tiptoe and kissed him. "You don't have to ignore me. You can say hello."

He swatted her playfully on the butt. "Sassy woman. You know what I mean."

"I do, and I'm going to have a hard time, too," she confessed.

He opened his mouth to tell her they didn't have to pretend, but closed it. He knew how hard it was to land this type of job and wanted her to succeed, so he respected her enough to wait. Besides, the first preseason game would be next weekend, and he needed to keep his head clear. He couldn't afford a distraction this late in his career.

Lauren had a much harder time masking her feelings for Malcolm than she'd anticipated. By Wednesday, she had taken to avoiding him, because each time she saw him, it took every ounce of control she possessed not to plant her lips on his. He seemed to have an easier time, barely acknowledging her when their paths crossed. But this was what she'd asked for, so she had to deal with it.

Turning to her computer, she logged on to her Twitter account. She followed a number of the players and found many of their tweets hilarious. Her hand paused on the track pad when she saw a tweet from Brent. He'd posted before and after photos of his previous night's dinner. The former showed a large sub sandwich, a whole pizza loaded with toppings, a family-size bag of barbecue chips and a two-liter of Coke. The latter showed empty packaging and bottle, with the words Best dinner ever!

Lauren replied to his tweet with I guess I'll be seeing you in my office this week, along with a frowning emoji and photos of lean meats, fruits and vegetables. She knew he'd seen her reply when she passed him on his way to the dining room after practice and he wouldn't meet her eyes. She sent him an email with an appointment for Friday after practice.

She spent the remainder of the day compiling information on those players whose body composition measurements had been done recently and comparing them with the previous tests. All of the players would have their testing done over the course of the next week, and she would adjust eating plans accordingly, if necessary.

Friday afternoon, Brent sat across from her desk sulking. He had weighed in three pounds heavier than the last time.

"I can't even get a cheat meal?" he complained.

"Of course you can, Brent. But the fact that you've gained weight despite the heavy workout schedule tells me you're cheating more often than not." She sighed. "Look, I'm not going to police your eating habits, but know that I also will *not* report anything to management but the truth. You're just starting in the league, and you've worked hard to get here. I'm sure you don't want to jeopardize any chance you have to stay here."

Brent slumped down in the chair. "No, I don't. I just like to eat."

Lauren smiled. "I understand. Let's see if we can't incorporate a few lower-fat versions of your favorite foods so that you're staying within your daily caloric limits... say, maybe once or twice a week."

A smile blossomed on his handsome tanned face. "Like brownies and chips?"

"Yes. I'm sure we can find a few recipes or ready-made options." An hour later, they'd come up with a workable meal plan. He stood, and she followed suit. "I'll see you in two weeks to check your progress, but if you have any questions or problems, call or email me."

"I will. Thanks, Lauren."

Before she could blink, he wrapped her in a hug that lifted her off her feet. "Whoa."

A tinge of red colored his cheeks, and he offered up an embarrassed smile. "Sorry."

"No apology necessary. I'll see you later."

He nodded and left.

Lauren was still standing in the same spot with a smile on her face when Darren knocked. "Come on in, Darren. How's it going?"

Darren grinned. "It's going great. Have you seen my latest numbers?" By the perspiration dotting his forehead and damp clothing, he had obviously come straight from practice.

"I have, and you're down fifteen pounds in five weeks."

"So, if I keep doing what I'm doing, I should be able to make my weight goals, right?"

"I think so."

"I talked to Coach, and he said I have a good chance. Oh, my girlfriend is really proud of me and said it's helping her eat healthier, too. On my days off, I eat a little bit less but still go running."

"Sounds like you've got a good handle on things, Darren."

"I couldn't have done it without your help."

"I appreciate that, but you're the one who did all the work." His praise was one more reason why taking this job had been a good idea. The preseason started next weekend, and she had no doubts that Darren would be back to his ideal weight well before the regular season.

"I won't hold you. I need to shower before dinner."

"Okay. Why don't you check in with me in a couple of weeks?"

"Will do." He departed with a smile.

Lauren made a few more notes, including some she planned to use in her book, and packed up to leave.

"Hey, baby."

She whirled around at the sound of Malcolm's voice. Her heart rate kicked up. Because of their schedules, they hadn't spoken other than a few text messages and two brief phone calls, and she had missed him. He stood leaning against the closed door dressed in basketball shorts and a sleeveless fitness tee. "Hey yourself." She crossed the floor, wrapped her arms around his waist and laid her head on his chest. She heard the strong, rhythmic sound of his heartbeat beneath her ear. "It's been a busy week."

Malcolm gathered her closer and dropped a kiss on her temple. "It has, and we have a late night tonight—watching films after dinner."

A twinge of disappointment hit her. She had hoped they would be able to spend a couple of hours together tonight.

He must have sensed it, because he said, "I'm disappointed, too, but I'll make up for it."

She lifted her eyes to meet his. "It's okay. I understand." And she did. It had been the same when they were in college, and she couldn't fault him for doing his job.

"We're done at three tomorrow, but my sister-in-law is having a book signing, and I promised to attend. I have next Tuesday off, so maybe we can sneak in a few hours after you get off."

"That would be great. What kind of book did she write?"

"A cookbook for teens and college students."

Lauren smiled. "With the way college students eat, her book should fly off the shelves."

He buried his face in her neck and kissed her. "She's hoping so. What are you going to be doing?"

"I'm going to spend time working on my book."

"I know you said it was going to be about nutrition for athletes, but what kinds of things are you including?"

"Some basic nutrition guidelines, the science behind it and then, more specifically, how nutrition impacts performance. I'm hoping a couple of the guys on the team will allow me to use a quote or two."

"I'm sure they will, and I'll do one, too, if it'll help."

"Aw, thank you, baby. But don't you think people will say you're biased?"

He shrugged. "I won't be lying, so…"

He slanted his mouth over hers, and Lauren gave herself up to the sensations flowing through her. It felt like ages since he'd last kissed her, and although they probably shouldn't be doing this in her office, she wanted every second of what he gave her.

At length, Malcolm lifted his head. "I need to get out of here while I still can. Be careful going home and text me when you get there."

"Okay."

"I'll call you tomorrow night."

She leaned up and kissed him once more. "Talk to you tomorrow."

He opened the door, smiled and gave her hand a gentle squeeze.

A moment later she heard him talking to someone and eased to the door. She didn't recognize the other man's voice but distinctly heard him ask about Malcolm being in her office.

"Just doing my check-in. Have you done yours?" she heard Malcolm ask.

Lauren's eyes widened. But then, she had contact with all the players, so it would be expected that Malcolm checked in with her. Had someone seen something? She racked her brain for any improprieties, but they had been careful about their public dealings. She couldn't mess up, not now. But she didn't want to lose Malcolm, either.

Chapter 12

Malcolm and Omar drove to the bookstore after practice. The Grays believed in supporting family and Omar's held a similar principle, so both men had no problems being in attendance. Morgan had dropped Omar off at practice, and they would meet up and drive home together after the signing.

"How are things progressing with you and Lauren?"

"I don't know."

"Ah…okay. What don't you know? You either want her or you don't."

Malcolm sighed in frustration. "I want her. I just don't want to want her as much as I do."

Omar's laughter filled the car's interior. "If that was the case, you shouldn't have touched her."

He slanted Omar a look. "What are you talking about?"

"You know exactly what I'm talking about. And don't bother denying it."

"I had only planned to…we weren't supposed to…hell,

I don't know. One moment we're kissing, the next we're in my bed. The thing that scares me the most is that I'm setting myself up for her to do the same thing again."

Omar shook his head. "Who says she's going to do the same thing? Did she give you any hints that she's thinking of bailing?"

"No. She said she's not choosing the job over me." Malcolm related the conversation he and Lauren had had.

"Sounds to me like you're the one on the fence, not her."

"I'm not on the fence." He wasn't anywhere near the fence, not when he was the one who'd set the pieces in place. He'd jumped clear over the thing like a professional hurdler. He'd known where they'd end up after that card game—intense, passionate sex. He just hadn't counted on the emotional pull he would feel.

"Things didn't go as planned, I take it."

"No. It was supposed to be just sex."

"And it wasn't." It was more statement than question. "You and Lauren have history, and from what Morgan told me, you were planning to marry her."

"Morgan talks too damn much," Malcolm muttered.

"That's the same thing she says about you. With that kind of history, I'm not surprised by the emotional connection. You dated her for two years and were practically engaged. Strong feelings like that can easily be rekindled under the right circumstances, and maybe these are the right ones."

He didn't know if the timing was right or not, but somehow his emotions didn't care. Malcolm hadn't been able to stop thinking about Lauren, and that kiss in her office yesterday had done nothing to satisfy the craving he had developed for her. The feelings he now experienced seemed deeper and more intense. "How do I make it stop?"

"Sorry, bro, but there's no cure. Believe me, I tried. The only thing you can do is surrender and pray things work out this time."

"We'll see."

The signing had already begun when they arrived, and he and Omar took up a position in the back. Lexia looked quite comfortable reading from the book in front of a group of about fifty people. Of course, Malcolm's family had shown up in force to support her. He spotted Lexia's parents, her staff from the café she owned and a good number from the college-age crowd. He tuned back in as she shared a recipe from the book and took questions from the audience.

She ended the signing by providing a sample of the recipe she had shared. Malcolm finally made his way to the front, where she sat signing books. "Congratulations, sis." He kissed her cheek.

Lexia threw her arms around him. "Oh, I'm so glad you made it. How's training camp going?"

"Grueling," he answered with a smile, handing her his copy of the book to sign.

She passed the book back. "You're coming by the house afterward, right?"

"I'll be there."

"Good."

Malcolm went to greet his parents. "Hey, Mom, Dad." He kissed his mother's cheek and shook his father's hand.

"How are you, son?" his father asked.

"A little tired, but good."

His mother patted his cheek. "Make sure you get some rest tonight. Are you planning to stop by Khalil and Lexia's afterward?"

"For a while." He glanced around at the mass of people still surrounding Lexia. "If she ever gets out of here," he said with a chuckle.

"I know. Isn't it fabulous?"

"It is. I'm going to talk to the Gray clan. I'll see you at the house." Malcolm spoke to Lexia's parents and sought out his siblings. They all stood with their spouses, and the

possessive hold each man had on his wife was a stark reminder that he was the last single one standing, something
that hadn't bothered him in the past.

As always, Morgan hugged him first. "Hey, big brother."

"How are you feeling?"

"Good." She took his hand and, smiling, placed it on
her belly.

Malcolm had no words to describe the emotions that
grabbed him when he felt the baby move. The little girl he
had been attached to at the hip from birth had grown up and
would become a mother soon. "He's an active little one."

Omar slung an arm around Morgan and cradled her
belly. "He definitely is, especially at night."

Justin and Siobhan laughed, and Siobhan said, *"For
real."*

Malcolm glanced Brandon and Faith's way.

Brandon held up his hand. "We don't know anything
about that. I get good sleep every night. Well, maybe not
every night…" He smiled at his wife.

Faith elbowed him. "Brandon!"

"What? Everybody here knows what we're doing at
night, and they're doing it, too."

Morgan shook her head. "I see he still has that speaking-
without-thinking thing."

"He's getting better, but I do have to remind him about it
every now and again," Faith said, rubbing Brandon's arm.

Brandon placed his hand over his heart, as if wounded.
"Hey."

"I said you were getting better."

They all laughed and launched into a discussion of one
another's spouses' missteps. A pang of jealousy hit Malcolm, and he immediately shook it off. *What the hell is
wrong with me?*

He scanned the room and noticed Khalil stood not too
far from Lexia with an expression of pride Malcolm had
never seen, even during Khalil's modeling days, when he

had received several accolades. An image of Lauren standing in front of a room with her book floated across Malcolm's mind. Would he be standing by her side? Would their relationship even last that long?

Omar had said Malcolm should surrender and pray things worked out. But to Malcolm, that was akin to playing Russian roulette with his heart, and he had no intentions of coming away with it blown to pieces again. The best thing for him would be to step back for a while, but he couldn't see that happening any time soon. Just the opposite—he was as anxious for Tuesday to come as a kid waiting for Christmas.

Lauren sat cross-legged on her bed, so engrossed in her typing it took a moment to hear her cell ringing. She hit the save button and snatched up the phone. "Hey, Malcolm."

"Hey. Did I catch you at a bad time?"

"Nope. Just typing. I can use a break. How was the signing?"

"It turned out well. She had a full house."

If Lauren ever got her book published, she hoped to have the same success. "That's wonderful. Do you know whether she published the book herself or had a publisher?"

"I have no idea, but I can ask. She'd probably be happy to talk to you. Do you want me to give her your number?"

Lauren didn't know if that would be a good idea. If she and Malcolm broke up, would his sister-in-law still talk to her, or would things become awkward? "Um…not yet. I'll let you know when I'm ready."

"Fair enough. That kiss in your office Friday wasn't nearly enough."

She paused at the abrupt change in topic. "Oh? So what would have been enough?"

"Nothing, until I heard you scream my name. And the next time we're together, I'm going to make you scream loud enough to be heard back in Phoenix."

She gasped.

"I'm going to kiss every part of your body, starting at your eyelids, and work my way down to your nose and your cheeks. I'll spend some time at that little spot on your neck right below your ear, using my tongue, branding you. You remember that spot, don't you, sweetheart? As I recall, it's a sensitive area. Do you think if I stayed there long enough, it would produce a kissgasm?"

Lauren couldn't answer. She closed her eyes as her nipples tightened and her pulse spiked.

"I think your breasts will be my next stop. They fit so perfectly in my hands. Mmm… I can feel them now as I massage and rub my thumbs over your nipples. Can you feel me touching you, baby?"

She could more than feel it. "Malcolm," she whispered, her hand going to her belly.

"What, sunshine? You want more? Okay, I'll give you more. What about when I take them into my mouth? I love how hard they get when I suck and circle my tongue all around them."

Her breathing increased, and she slid down on the bed, her body on fire.

"I can't forget how you squirm when I trail my tongue down your belly and to your sweet center. I want to make you wet for me."

No problems there. She was more than wet, and the throbbing in her core increased. She squeezed her thighs together and clenched her teeth. "I'm—"

"Not yet. You can't come yet. Not until I taste you. One long stroke, a short one, another long one… I don't want to miss one drop of that honey."

Lauren couldn't take it. She came in a rush of pleasure that left her shaking. A deep moan escaped her, and she gripped the phone tighter.

"I see your kissgasm and raise you a *phone*gasm. Sleep well and I'll see you on Tuesday, sweetheart."

She dropped the phone on the bed and lay there panting,

still trying to catch her breath. "I can't believe he made me come by talking on the phone." She'd just had *phone sex*! The man was *good*. Clearly some things had changed about Malcolm, and she speculated on how many other women had he done that with. She told herself it didn't matter— they'd been apart for eight years and of course he'd dated other women—but right now she had a hard time convincing herself. Things like this made it difficult for her to keep things moving slowly between them. If she were being honest with herself, Lauren would have to admit that she was falling for him all over again…and hard.

When her body finally calmed, she dragged herself off the bed and ran a bubble bath. She stepped in, rested her head against the edge and closed her eyes. She and Malcolm had only been officially dating less than a month, and she'd already slept with him and tonight…tonight… Just the memory sent her arousal through the roof again. A part of her wanted to call him back and do the same thing to him, but she knew he'd already gone to bed. A smile curved her lips. He wanted to play games? Fine. Come Tuesday, she'd give him a taste—pun intended—of his own medicine.

After her bath, Lauren went back to working on her book, but she had a hard time concentrating. Flashes of that erotic phone call kept intruding on her progress. She gave up forty-five minutes later, powered off the laptop and went to bed.

Lauren woke up the next morning determined to get some work done. She pushed thoughts of her sexy lover out of her mind and, after a breakfast of two boiled eggs and yogurt, settled in with her laptop and starting typing. She spread several books and articles across the table to reference. She also had her graduate thesis, which offered a direct link to the impact of eating habits on performance.

She typed and made notes until her fingers cramped, then reread what she'd written. She made a few changes and, satisfied, decided to pay a visit to her parents.

"Lauren, what a surprise." Her mother engulfed her in a hug and moved aside for Lauren to enter. "Why didn't you tell me you were coming by? We would've waited for you to eat dinner."

"You didn't need to wait." On Sundays, her parents tended to eat dinner around three o'clock, instead of their normal weekday time of six. "Where's Daddy?"

"He's in the family room reading some article on optometry." Her father had worked as an optometrist for almost thirty years, fifteen in his own practice.

"Well, I'll wait to say hello. I know how he gets when he's reading." Lauren smiled. "And I bet you were reading up on the latest in MRI technology, huh?"

"Well, with all these young folks coming in, I have to stay up on what's happening to make sure I have job security."

"Mama, you know they aren't going to replace you. No one can make someone feel at ease going into that little tube as well as you can." She followed her mother to the kitchen and sat at the table.

Her mother took the seat next to Lauren and waved her off. "You're just biased because I'm your mama."

"No, I'm not. I've seen you in action, remember?" Her high school had participated in the Take Your Daughter to Work program, and Lauren had seen firsthand how comforting her mother could be with a frightened patient.

"Enough about that. What brings you by?"

"Nothing really. I just wanted to see you."

"I see."

Her mother's penetrating stare almost made Lauren squirm in her chair.

"Are you sure it's not related to you and Malcolm?"

Why are mothers so perceptive? "Maybe," she mumbled and slumped in the chair.

"I take it the two of you are back together."

"How did you know?"

"It was clear as glass the last time you were here. I figured you'd share when you were ready."

"Things are going so fast, and I'm scared the same thing is going happen again."

"Lauren, sweetheart," her mother said, grasping Lauren's hand, "you can't move forward if you're holding on to the past. As for things moving quickly, I'm not surprised. You and Malcolm were very close in college and I'd venture to say that a lot of those feelings are still there."

Lauren had acknowledged that she still cared about Malcolm the moment she locked eyes with him her first day on the job, but her emotions had taken on a life of their own and she had no idea how to control them. "But what about my job?"

"What about it? Malcolm playing for the team has no bearing on you doing your job. Are there any rules against you dating a player?"

"No."

"Then just take it one day at a time. Honestly, I thought you two would be married by now and I'd have a couple of grandchildren."

Her shocked expression met her mother's amused one.

"I don't know why you're so surprised. I think Malcolm is a very special young man. He always treated you with the utmost respect, and that made him a keeper in my book."

"Gee, thanks, Mom," she said with a chuckle. "That makes me feel even worse." She'd always known her mother liked Malcolm, but her mother had never mentioned anything about the whole marriage-and-kids thing. "You may have liked him, but I'm not too sure about Daddy."

Her mother laughed. "Honey, your father felt the same way. And he was looking forward to season tickets to whatever pro football team picked Malcolm up."

Lauren burst out laughing. "Are you serious?"

"I thought I heard your voice in here," her father said, entering and kissing Lauren's temple.

"Hi, Daddy."

Her father placed his hands on her shoulders. "Job still going well?"

"It's going better than I hoped."

"And how's Malcolm?"

She felt her cheeks warm. "He's fine."

He peered into her face. "That good, huh? Maybe this time I'll get those tickets."

Lauren spun around. "Daddy!"

"I told you," her mother said.

"What? You know that's my team. Well, unless *you* can get me some good tickets."

She shook her head. "I don't think so."

"Well, I need you to put in a good word with Malcolm then."

Her mother stood. "You want some dinner, Lauren?"

"Yes. It's much safer than this conversation." She took in her parents' pleased expressions, and her anxiety over the relationship jumped up a notch. They would be devastated if the relationship didn't work out. And so would she.

Chapter 13

Tuesday, Malcolm had originally planned to hang out with Lauren at his place, but after that phone call on Saturday, felt it best they stayed far away from either of their homes. He had no idea what had possessed him to engage in phone sex with her. He'd never in his life done that with another woman. As a result, he'd been grumpy and horny for the past three nights. She was becoming a distraction he couldn't afford, and he didn't know how to deal with it.

In the past, he'd just tell the woman he needed some distance to focus on the game, and they hadn't balked. For those who complained about the lack of time he had for them during the season, he'd swiftly ended the relationships. But he didn't want to end his relationship with Lauren. And when she opened the door to him wearing another one of those sexy sundresses and a smile that made his heart skip, he knew making any kind of decision would be that much harder.

"Hey."

He kissed her. "How'd the day go?"

"It went okay. Did you sleep in today?"

"Nope. I rarely sleep in these days." And he'd been up at the crack of dawn for the past three mornings taking a cold shower. "Hazard of the job, I guess." He led her to his car and drove them to the marina, where they had dinner before taking a walk.

"I think you have a couple of fans over there," Lauren said, gesturing with her head to two teen boys staring their way.

Malcolm called out a hello and the teens took that to mean they could approach. He shook hands, answered questions and took pictures with them but made sure none included Lauren. After a few minutes, the excited guys ran off, and he and Lauren continued their walk.

"That was nice of you to stop."

He shrugged. "I don't mind. You never know what you might say that could affect someone's life. I remember when I was young and my dad took my brothers and me to a basketball game. I saw one of my favorite players and wanted an autograph. Not only did he refuse, he rudely shoved me aside. I was crushed. It changed my perception of him, and I vowed that no matter what job I had, I would always treat people with respect."

Lauren reached up and kissed his cheek. "And that's one of the reasons I like you."

He liked her, too. A lot. "Come on, let's head down near the water." He waited while she took off her sandals then reached for her hand, lacing their fingers together. Closer to the water, he sat and pulled her down onto his lap. The level of comfort he experienced with her didn't surprise him. It had always been that way. They also didn't need to fill every second with conversation and were content to just sit quietly and enjoy the gentle waves and setting sun.

Malcolm wanted to kiss her badly but held himself in check. Neither of them needed a photo of her across his lap and his mouth planted on hers hitting the front page of some newspaper. Just being out this way was risk enough.

At length, Lauren asked, "Would you be willing to give me a quote for my book when I'm done? After you've read it, of course."

"I'd be honored. How long do you think it'll take for you to write it?"

"I don't know. Some days the information flows well, others…not so much. Hopefully, no more than six to nine months."

Six to nine months meant she expected them to still be dating. Malcolm hadn't had a relationship that lasted longer than six months in the past six years. He'd gotten used to his solitary life and didn't know how to be with one woman for an extended time anymore. The two years with Lauren had been his longest relationship. "Let me know when."

"Thanks." She snuggled closer and shivered.

"Cold?"

"A little."

"We can go." They'd seen a good portion of the sunset.

"I forget how fast the temperatures drop in the evening sometimes. Next time, give me some warning so I can be prepared. I love watching sunsets."

Malcolm kissed the top of her head. "I'll remember that." He helped her to her feet, stood and brushed the sand off his shorts. They reversed their course, leisurely strolling to the car.

Once inside the car, Lauren rubbed her hands up and down her arms.

"Do you want me to turn up the heat?"

"No. I'll be fine in a minute. It's already warm in here. When do you leave for the game?"

"Friday," he answered, merging onto the road. She'd given him the perfect opening to ask for distance, but he couldn't do it. He sighed inwardly. He turned up the music and heard Lauren humming quietly to the latest Jill Scott song. He smiled. "You can go ahead and sing. I know you want to."

She returned his smile. "You know I love singing in the car. And the sound system in my new car is so good, I can blast my music and sing at the top of my lungs."

Malcolm laughed. Flashbacks of her singing with her hands raised in the air popped in his head. "It's a good thing you have a decent voice, otherwise…"

Lauren snapped her head around, and her mouth dropped open. She punched him in the shoulder. "I beg your pardon. I'll have you know I sang in the church junior choir and my high school chamber choir, which was audition only." She pointed a finger his way. "My voice is *better* than decent."

He merely smiled. *That's my girl.* He'd always loved her confidence and take-no-prisoners attitude. He was certain it played a large role in her landing the dietitian position with the team. While there were a few women filling the role for other teams, her gender and age might have made a less self-assured person think twice about applying.

When they got to her house, Malcolm hesitated getting out, not ready to end the evening on one hand and contemplating running away forever on the other.

He walked her to the door.

"I enjoyed myself tonight, Malcolm," Lauren said, looping her arms around his neck.

"So did I." So much so that he wanted to back her into the house and bury himself deep inside her. But he settled for kissing her with a hunger that astounded him. He had to leave. Now. He'd gotten in too deep, too fast. "The next few weeks are going to be pretty intense and I need to stay focused, so—"

She cut him a look and slowly removed her arms. "So you need some space."

"Yes. No…" He sighed deeply. "That's not what I'm trying to say. It's just…" He didn't know what he was trying to say, but his words and his heart were running toward opposite ends of the field.

"I get it. No problem," she said curtly. "You still don't really trust me, do you?"

"I never said I didn't trust you. Don't put words in my mouth." How she had seen into that small corner of his heart that still harbored the hurt of the past, he didn't know.

Lauren scrutinized him a long moment.

"I trust you." As much as he could for the time being.

"You probably should get going. I don't want to be responsible for you missing curfew." She stepped through the door. "Good night, Malcolm."

"Lauren…" She folded her arms, hurt and confusion lining her features. He'd already stuck his foot into his mouth once and decided he should leave well enough alone for tonight. "Good night." She closed the door softly, and Malcolm felt as if she'd closed the door on them.

He loped back down the walk to his car. His mind said he'd done the right thing—they needed to slow down—but his heart said just the opposite.

Lauren spent Wednesday and Thursday compiling all the body compositions and weights of the players, along with the goals from the coaches, and sending them to the players with her recommended dietary changes. The information would also be sent to management by the end of the day. There were a few players who had gained weight, and she wondered how that would affect their status on the field.

She didn't have to wonder long, because Thursday afternoon one of the players burst into her office, angry about his numbers.

"You just cost me my position!"

Inside Lauren was shaking like a leaf, but she refused to let him intimidate her. "I don't know what you're talking about, Carlos. I have nothing to do with who does or doesn't play." Carlos Jenkins, an offensive lineman, stood six eight, weighed 280 pounds and had dark, piercing eyes and a handsome coffee-with-cream face that was contorted with anger.

"You're the one who's going to tell Coach I'm over my weight limit by eight pounds."

"All I do is report the information. I sent it to you with a few recommended changes that would get you back to your goal weight pretty quickly." Because of all the physical activity, it didn't take football players long to drop the pounds, whereas most other people would struggle for weeks.

"I know you haven't sent the information to the coaches yet, so I need you to change those numbers."

Lauren stared at him incredulously. "Excuse me? You're asking me to lie?"

"No, I'm asking you to keep my secret, and I'll keep yours."

What secret? The hairs on the back of her neck stood up. His was the voice she'd heard talking to Malcolm outside her office that day. "So, blackmail. I'm sorry, Carlos, but I will not alter any numbers."

Carlos braced his hands on her desk and leaned down. He smiled coldly. "You sure about that? I wonder what management would say if they found out their new dietitian is knocking boots with the star running back."

Her heart nearly stopped. She and Malcolm had been very careful while at the office. "I'm not sure what you're getting at."

"I saw Malcolm Gray leaving your office last Friday pretty late. And the door was closed…" He let the sentence hang.

Lauren slowly pushed to her feet. "Two other players were in my office right before that, *with the door closed.* Are you accusing me of sleeping with them, too?"

"I know what I saw. Like I said, you do this one thing and no one has to know."

She met his glare with one of her own. "Then do what you think you need to do, because I'm not changing those numbers." They engaged in a stare down, and Lauren didn't flinch.

Carlos threw her one more hostile stare, let out an animalistic growl and stormed out, slamming the door.

Lauren collapsed in her chair and dropped her head in her trembling hands. She couldn't decide which emotion had the upper hand at the moment—fear or anger. She voted for anger. She jumped up and paced the office. The man must be out of his mind to try to blackmail her. No way would she mess up the best job she'd ever had over some stupid threat. Not like she needed to, anyway. She stopped pacing and sighed heavily. Malcolm wanted space...or *something*. So she'd give it to him. He still didn't trust her. He said he'd let go of the past, but clearly he still held on to some things. As much as it pained her, she had to. She just wished she could shut off her feelings in the process.

Right now, she had to determine what to do about Carlos. Should she go directly to Mr. Green and let him know about the confrontation or let it go? Lauren didn't want to be that tattletale who always ran to tell the teacher, but she also didn't want anything to come back on her. She paused with her hand on the doorknob. No, she'd wait to see how things played out. Whatever the coaches decided had no bearing on her job.

Rounding her desk, she finished the rest of the reports, sent them to the respective coaches and packed up to leave. Since the team would be gone tomorrow, she really didn't need to be on-site, so she planned to work from home in her pajamas.

Lauren opened the door, glanced over her shoulder and surveyed her desk and conference table one last time to make sure she had everything. She hit the light switch, turned back and ran into a solid mass. She let out a small squeal and jerked away, almost losing her balance.

Strong hands banded around her waist to steady her. "You okay?"

She clutched her chest. "Malcolm, you scared me half to death." Ignoring how being in his arms made her feel, she asked, "What are you doing here?" She took a deep breath and released it gradually, trying to slow her runaway heartbeat.

"I wanted to see you."

Her gaze darted up and down the hall, and she moved out of his embrace, praying no one had seen them. She already had one person threatening her and didn't want to give anyone else something to talk about. "Why? I thought you wanted some space."

Malcolm reached for her again, and she pushed his hand away. He sighed. "Those were your words, not mine."

"But it amounts to the same thing. I have to go. Have a safe flight tomorrow and good luck with the game." Lauren tried to move around him, but he blocked the doorway.

"Can I just have five minutes, please?"

"No. We don't want to give anyone else something to talk—" She cut herself off and wanted to slap a hand over her big mouth. *Great! Just great.*

He frowned. "What the hell does that mean? Did someone say something?"

She waved him off. "Nothing. I'll see you later." She pushed past him and rushed down the hallway. She didn't stop until she got to her car. Her cell phone rang as soon as she closed the door. Seeing Malcolm's name on the display, she tossed it on the seat next to her and let it go to voice mail. If she gave him those five minutes, one look in his eyes and he'd have her weak and agreeing to any and everything he had to offer.

Instead of going straight home, Lauren took a detour and went shopping. A little retail therapy would improve her mood.

An hour later, Lauren emerged from the Del Amo

Fashion Center with a deep-blue bra and matching pair of panties from Victoria's Secret's Dream Angels Wicked collection, aromatherapy body wash from Bath & Body Works, two milk-chocolate truffles from Godiva, and a new tube of her favorite MAC Oh Baby lip gloss. The golden-bronze color worked well for casual or dressy. She'd also picked up a Santa Fe salad from BJ's Restaurant and Brewhouse.

When she arrived home, she unloaded her haul and curled up on the sofa to eat her dinner. She turned on the television and surfed until she found a rerun of *Major Crimes*. Of course it had to be the episode focusing on the relationship between Detective Sykes and Lieutenant Cooper, bringing to mind her own relationship woes.

Maybe she should have listened to Malcolm's explanation, but she was afraid to put herself all the way out there again. Her growing feelings were stronger than before and, truthfully, they frightened her. She refused to settle for a one-sided relationship similar to the one she'd had in Phoenix, where she gave everything and he gave whenever it happened to be convenient. Putting Malcolm out of her mind, she focused her attention on the show and her food.

Later, Lauren ran a bath and added some of the foam bath she'd just purchased, deciding on the stress relief fragrance. While the tub filled with the scent of eucalyptus and mint, she checked the messages on her phone. She read a text from Valencia lamenting about an issue at work. "Join the club." She sent a reply detailing what happened with Carlos. One minute later, her phone rang. "I knew you would call," she said with a laugh.

"Girl, did you report his behind?" Valencia asked.

"No. I sent the report to the coaches, and now the only thing I can do is wait to see what he does. Now, you said you're still covering for the new dietitian?" She turned off the water.

Valencia's heavy sigh came through the line. "This

woman was hired less than three months ago, but she's always got some issue as to why she has to be off. First, it was her back. Next, it was her wrist and now her hip. And she takes off three or four days each time."

"I can't see them keeping her on much longer if she keeps this up."

"Me, either. But I wish they'd decide one way or another, because this is wearing on the rest of us. Now back to you. Did you tell Malcolm?"

Lauren didn't answer.

"You didn't, did you?"

"I don't want him interfering in my job, just like he wouldn't want me to with his." She could imagine Malcolm's reaction and didn't want to cause him any trouble.

"I get that, but what if this guy outs you two? Malcolm doesn't deserve to be blindsided."

She flopped back on the sofa. "I hadn't thought of that. But I know Malcolm. He'd march right up to the guy, and all hell would break loose. I'll think about it, though. Anyway, girl, my bubble bath is getting cold. I'll call you tomorrow."

"Okay. Keep me posted."

"I will, and you do the same. Talk to you later." Lauren disconnected and noticed she had a voice mail from Malcolm. She hesitated briefly, not sure she wanted to hear what he had to say. But curiosity propelled her to dial the number and listen.

"Lauren, I know you think I don't want to see you, but that's not the case. I also know that I'm taking a risk of losing my man card by telling you this, but honestly, this thing between us seems to be moving at a pace that scares the hell out of me. So, yeah, though I feel like I need some space, I want you in my life more. I'm not giving you up. I'll talk to you when I get back, sweetheart. Oh, and I haven't forgotten about that comment."

Lauren held the phone against her heart. She was fighting a losing battle. And, somehow, she didn't care.

Chapter 14

Malcolm missed a second pass during the walkthrough Friday morning. He cursed under his breath. He'd never been this distracted, and he attributed it to Lauren, but not in the way he'd originally considered. In the past few weeks that he'd been seeing her, never once had he had difficulty putting thoughts of her aside while on the field. Now, with things unsettled, he couldn't stop thinking about her and, as a result, had dropped two easy passes he should have been able to catch with his eyes closed.

Marcus passed him. "You okay, Malcolm?"

"Yeah, fine," he gritted out. Frustrated and angry with himself, he took a deep breath, recentered and went out for the next play. Thankfully, his focus held for the next hour and he didn't embarrass himself further.

Afterward, the team showered, went through the TSA check set up at the practice facility—something that teams had started to make the flight process quicker—and then rode the bus to the airport for their trip to Houston. He lay back against the seat and stared out the window as the rest of the team and staff boarded. They used the same chartered plane from a national airline chain and the same flight crew every time. The layout offered each player the equivalent of one and a half seats, with first class reserved for the bigger linemen. Malcolm turned on his cell and was disappointed to find that Lauren hadn't responded to his message. He was honest enough to admit that he did have some lingering trust issues, but he felt they could overcome them with time. Had she decided not to give them a chance? If she had, he planned to do everything in his power to change her mind. His finger hovered over the call button for a few seconds, wanting to hear her voice and clear the air, before he decided against it. He'd told her what he wanted her to know for now. The rest could wait until he saw her.

"Thinking about your situation?"

He rotated his head in Omar's direction. "Is it that obvious?"

Sitting across the aisle, Omar stretched out one long leg. "About as obvious as it was when you missed those two passes earlier."

Malcolm chuckled wryly. "Sounds like your game in the season opener two years ago." At the time, Omar and Morgan had been going through a rough patch in their relationship, and Omar's concentration had taken a nosedive.

"That was the worst week of my life. My suggestion is you get whatever it is straightened out before the regular season starts."

He appreciated Omar not using Lauren's name. Anyone who might be listening wouldn't know what the conversation entailed. "Yeah, I know." It also brought to mind the question of how long he and Lauren would have to hide, and he decided that would be another topic for them to discuss.

Malcolm put the phone in airplane mode, closed his eyes and made himself comfortable for the three-and-a-half-hour trip. Unlike on normal flights, lunch consisted of a three-course meal that fell in line with the players' dietary needs, as outlined by Lauren.

After landing, they traveled by bus to the hotel. To minimize public contact, several measures had been put in place—separate entrances, key-controlled elevators, private floors and a dedicated security staff. Not even employees were exempt. They couldn't ask for autographs and pictures or post on social media without consequences. All of which ensured players were rested and left undisturbed. Malcolm dropped his bag on the chair in the hotel room that would be the first of many for the season and stretched out on the bed. His veteran status afforded him a room to himself, but players in their first or second years had to double up. A quick glance at the nightstand clock showed the time to be just after five, which left him two hours to rest before dinner. He would have preferred to order room service, however, team rules prohibited its use, along with accessing the room's minibar or going to the hotel's bar.

He had just dozed off when his cell buzzed in his pocket. Groaning, he fished it out and checked the display, then smiled and sat up. Siobhan had sent him photos and videos of the transitional housing's grand opening, and he immediately saw her PR skills at work. Malcolm's heart swelled at the video of a single mother and her two children seeing their home for the first time. The two girls, who looked to be between six and eight, ran from room to room, their happy squeals filling the air, while their mother dropped to her knees and said a prayer of thanksgiving. It made him take stock of how blessed he was, and he vowed to always do what he could to help others.

Malcolm clicked on the final message and smiled at the attachment. Instead of replying, he activated his video messaging and called.

"Hey, baby brother," Siobhan said when she answered.

"Hey, sis. Thanks for sending the pics. Looks like everything went well."

"Oh my goodness, Malcolm. It was *awesome*! I've cried so much today, they sent out a memo saying the drought in California is over."

Malcolm laughed. Though his sister's eyes were slightly red, they were also sparkling with joy. "Congratulations, mama. I thought you guys had another week or so before Christian came to stay permanently."

"I have no idea what happened. All I know is Justin and I got a call while we were at the opening from his social worker saying we could take him home."

"And I bet you were there before she could complete the call."

"Just about," she said with a laugh. "You should see Nyla. She's been following him around since we got home. And Christian is just as happy about being a big brother. We're going to have dinner here Sunday afternoon, sort of a welcome party. I know you and Omar will be getting in late tomorrow, but I hope you guys can pop in for a few minutes."

"Tired or not, you know I'll be there. Where is he?" Siobhan walked into a bedroom, and he heard laughter and his niece's happy giggles.

"Here they are. Christian and Nyla, Uncle Malcolm is on the phone." She turned the phone so he could see the children.

"Hey, Christian. How's your new room? Hey, Nyla."

Christian's face lit up. "It's good." He turned around and tried to point out everything in the room. "And see my bed? It has *PAW Patrol* on it."

Malcolm had no idea who or what a *PAW Patrol* was, but he nodded. "That's pretty cool. Well, I'll see you in a couple of days, okay?"

"'Bye." And he was gone.

Siobhan laughed. "So, I guess the conversation is over."

She held the phone toward Nyla. "Say hi to Uncle Malcolm."

He waved. "Hey, Nyla. How's my baby girl?"

Nyla babbled something, tried to eat the phone, then got upset when Siobhan wrestled it out of her hands.

"That's it for the phone, little girl. Here's your book." That seemed to satisfy her. Siobhan came back to the phone. "I see you're all reclined on your bed. Are you in for the night?"

Malcolm yawned. "Nope. Dinner is in an hour, then we have a chapel service and pregame meeting."

"Oh. Okay. How are things with you and Lauren?"

Malcolm had figured that with everything going on, his sister would have forgotten about his love life, but he should have known better.

He obviously hesitated too long, because she said, "What did you do?"

He told her about him wanting space. "I didn't say those words exactly, but in Lauren's mind, it meant the same thing."

"You're afraid history's going to repeat itself. I totally get that, Malcolm, because I did the same thing with Justin… more than once. Thank goodness my husband is a patient man." She chuckled. "Otherwise I might have missed out on the best thing that has ever happened to me. Stop fighting your feelings for Lauren. Take it from me—all it does is make things worse."

"I don't recall asking for any advice. Don't you have enough to worry about?"

Siobhan rolled her eyes. "Like that's going to stop me from giving it. And I'll never have so much to worry about that I can't be there for you. Remember I changed your stinky diapers. That gives me privileges."

Malcolm laughed. "Really, Vonnie? Why are you bringing up old stuff? It's definitely time for this conversation to end."

She blew him a kiss. "Love you. Be careful tomorrow, and have a safe trip home."

"Love you, too. I will, although I probably won't play more than a few downs."

Justin appeared in the picture with Christian on his shoulders and Nyla in his arms. "What's up, Malcolm?"

"Hey, Justin. I see you're busy."

"Yeah, but I'm loving it." His smile matched Siobhan's. "Later, bro."

"All right. Gotta go. See you Sunday."

"'Bye, sis." Malcolm disconnected, his smile still in place. He tossed the phone on the bed and resumed his position. He adjusted the pillow under his head and stared up at the ceiling, thinking about his sister's unsolicited advice. He'd never imagined having feelings for Lauren again and didn't know how to stop fighting against the fear that had a grip on his heart. But one thing Siobhan had said rang true. He felt worse now than he had three days ago.

Lauren pulled the grocery cart up the steps leading to her condo and into the house. Valencia had teased her about looking like an old lady, but Lauren didn't care. She could carry all her bags in one trip instead of two or three. And today she had more than usual. She'd put off shopping last week and had to replenish just about everything, including the basics like flour, salt, eggs and milk. It took her longer than necessary to unload because she was hungry and kept stopping to snack.

She put everything away, except for the items she planned to use for cooking. Lauren usually spent her Sundays doing meal prep for the week. With it being summer, she opted for light menus that included salads with shrimp or chicken and one-dish dinners—combined vegetables, meat and occasionally pasta—that took less than thirty minutes to prepare. She started with the shrimp and made enough to include in a shrimp-avocado salad and to sauté with asparagus. It would have been much easier to make or grab a sandwich daily, but Lauren tried hard to stay away from eating too much bread, so she learned to be creative with her meals. Bread topped the list of her most favorite foods and she had, once or twice, inhaled an entire loaf of warm French bread covered in butter over the course of one night.

Lauren removed the shrimp from the pan and added a small amount of butter and the asparagus. She cooked it just until it was tender and spooned it onto a plate to cool. Just as she lined up the bowls on the counter, her doorbell rang. She hoped it wasn't her new neighbor who had moved in earlier in the week. The woman had come over three times asking to borrow first a screwdriver and a hammer, then later, after returning the tools, she'd asked if Lauren had a blanket she could have because she'd misplaced hers in the move and didn't feel like going shopping for one. Lauren had been so outdone that it took her moment to respond. Using all the home training her parents had raised her with, she told the woman she didn't have a spare one.

She snatched open the door, ready to say no to whatever the woman wanted but went still upon seeing Malcolm.

"Hey, baby."

It took her a moment to find her voice. She hadn't returned his call or replied to his voice mail. "Um…hey. Come on in. I'm in the kitchen."

Malcolm followed her inside and closed the door. "Smells good. Is this for the week?"

She divided shrimp and asparagus into two containers. "Pretty much. I just do enough to take care of a few days, in case I don't feel like cooking when I get home." He watched her silently for a few moments. "I didn't expect to see you, with you just getting back and all."

"I know, but you didn't call me back and I wanted to make sure we were clear on a few things."

"I didn't call you back because you needed to be focused for your game," she said, not looking in his direction.

Malcolm gently turned her to face him. "You didn't call me back because you were upset," he countered. He pulled her into his arms. "I meant what I said, Lauren. I'm not giving you up. Not without a fight. That first day you showed up at the training facility, I was angry and hurt all over again, and I never thought we'd be here. I'm still scared as hell that we'll end up like before, but I can't stop what I'm feeling. And I think you're feeling the same thing."

His intense gaze dared her to lie. "I am, and I'm just as afraid as you are, Malcolm." Truthfully, she'd fallen in love with him all over again, but now wasn't the appropriate time to tell him. What if he didn't feel the same? The chemistry between them had always been strong, and she could see him reacting to it and viewing their connection as nothing more than lust. Lauren stepped away and continued putting away her food.

He leaned against the counter and folded his arms. "So what do you want to do about it?"

She gathered her haul and placed it in the refrigerator. "We could continue as we are…if that's what you want to do." She moved the dirty dishes to the sink to wash later, wiped down the counters and hazarded a glance his way.

Malcolm angled his head and studied her. "Yeah. But that's not all I want."

Her pulse spiked. "What do you mean?"

"Are you done in here?"

"Yes. I'll wash up everything later."

Malcolm reached for her hand, led her into the living room and gestured her to the sofa. "For starters," he said, sitting next to her, "I think we need to slow things down. Not sure how that's going to work out, since all I want to do every time is see you is strip you naked and make you scream."

Lauren blinked.

"But as you pointed out that night on the dance floor, we've both changed, and I want us to take time to get to know each other all over again."

She hadn't expected him to say that. "I think that's a good idea. So, that means no more kissing and…"

He cut her a look. "Oh, I didn't say all that. I will be kissing you just as soon as we're done with this conversation. As far as the sex, we'll see how it goes."

"But you just said…"

"Yes," he said slowly. "But I'm also a man who's very attracted to you and who remembers with vivid clarity how it feels to be inside you." He shrugged. "I'll do my best, but that's all I can promise. Hell, I'm having a hard time resisting carrying you to your bed right now."

Lauren's body came alive with his declaration, and it took all she had not to drag him there herself.

Malcolm placed a soft kiss on her lips. "Lucky for you, I can't stay long. Otherwise…"

She smiled as a wicked thought crossed her mind. "You did say we would still kiss, right?"

"Yes."

"And if I kissed you right now, you wouldn't resist?"

"Hell, no."

"That's all I needed to know." She pushed him down on the sofa and straddled him.

Malcolm's eyes widened. "Lauren, what are you doing?"

"I'm going to kiss you, that's all." Lauren just hadn't said where. She leaned down and kissed him with a thoroughness that had him groaning. She slid down and moved her hands under his shirt, taking it higher and higher as she kissed her way from his rock-hard abs to his well-defined chest and back down again.

"You're going to get yourself in trouble," he said through clenched teeth.

She silenced him with another kiss and continued her journey down his body. She grasped the waistband of his basketball shorts and rid him of them and his briefs. He tried to sit up and shift his body, but she held tight.

"Baby, no!" He cursed and jerked upright as she took him into her mouth.

But she didn't stop. And she didn't plan to until he screamed *her* name. His stomach muscles contracted beneath her hands and his legs shook. She swirled her tongue from base to tip and sucked him in deep, eliciting another guttural moan. He'd taught her how to please him, and she wanted to show him that she remembered every lesson and had picked up a few tricks on her own.

"Lauren, baby," he panted, gripping the back of her head and keeping her in place. She increased the pace, and he went rigid and exploded. *"Lauren!"*

Lauren didn't stop until the last spasm left his body. She lifted her head. He lay sprawled with his eyes closed, hands fisted and his breathing ragged. "Should I take that to mean you're liking my kisses a little more now?"

Malcolm opened his eyes but made no comment.

She sat back, a satisfied grin covering her mouth. "I see your phonegasm…"

He chuckled. "Girl, you ain't nothing nice."

"That's not what you were screaming a minute ago."

He sat up and braced his hands on his thighs. "I thought we agreed to go slow."

She smiled serenely. "We can go as slow as you like now. Oh, and your man card is safe with me."

He shook his head. "I need to clean up."

"I'll get you a towel." While he cleaned up in the half bath, Lauren did the same in her master bathroom and met him back in the living room.

"Do you have any plans for the rest of the afternoon?"

"Not really. Why?"

"Wanna take a ride with me?"

"Sure." She glanced down at her shorts and sleeveless blouse. "Do I need to change?"

"Nope," he said with a smile. "You're fine."

"Where are we going?"

"You'll see."

Lauren eyed him for a lengthy minute and went to get her shoes and purse. Half an hour later, he drove them into an upscale residential area and stopped at a house that had several cars parked in the circular driveway and in front of it. "Whose house is this?"

"Justin and Siobhan's."

She went still. "Malcolm, I don't think this is a good idea." She knew how Morgan felt about her and could imagine what the rest of the family thought.

"I think it is. If you hadn't interrupted our conversation, I would have told you the rest."

"What rest?"

"That we're done hiding our relationship."

"We can't… I mean…what if—" Her head was spinning. Carlos's threat came back to her.

Malcolm grasped her hand and brought it to his lips. "Sweetheart, there are no rules against us dating. I don't plan to go all out when we're at work, but I'm not going to avoid you or not say anything when our paths cross. As far as my family, they already know."

Lauren rubbed her temples and groaned. "Your family hates me. I can't go in there."

"My family does not hate you."

She skewered him with a look. "Morgan?"

"She'll be fine." He got out, came around to her side and extended his hand. "It'll be okay. I promise."

She sighed and placed her hand in his. If this didn't go well—and she didn't see how it could—she would never speak to him again.

Chapter 15

Lauren let Malcolm lead her up the walkway to a large house with a meticulously manicured lawn. She expected him to ring the doorbell, but he just opened the unlocked door and gestured her in. "Shouldn't you ring the bell or something? We can't just walk in," she whispered.

"Whenever we get together, we always leave the door unlocked. Go on in."

As soon as she crossed the threshold, she heard laughter coming from somewhere in the back. Her gaze was drawn to the glossy natural maple hardwood floor. As followed the sounds, she surveyed the house's open layout, with each room flowing seamlessly into the next one. Her steps slowed as they reached what she figured was the family room. When they noticed her and Malcolm, every eye turned their way and all laughter stopped abruptly.

Malcolm shook his head. "Hey. You all remember Lauren."

His mother seemed to recover from shock first and

rushed over. "Hello, Lauren. It's so good to see you again." She gave her a warm hug.

His father followed suit.

"Hi, Mr. and Mrs. Gray. It's nice to see you, too."

"Congratulations on your new job. That's quite a feat. We're going to bring these men into the twenty-first century yet," Mrs. Gray added with a wink.

Lauren smiled, feeling slightly better. "Thank you." While everyone else wore shorts and tees or tanks with flip-flops or sneakers, Mrs. Gray had on a pair of navy slacks and a navy-and-white printed short-sleeved blouse with dressy two-inch heeled sandals. Her face looked as if it had been expertly made up and not a strand of her cropped salt-and-pepper layers was out of place.

"Welcome to our home, Lauren," Siobhan said, embracing her. "This is my husband, Justin, our daughter, Nyla, and the newest member of our family and the reason for this celebration, Christian."

Lauren smiled at the little girl and boy staring her way. The fact that Christian was older than Nyla and had been referred to as the newest member had her thinking that they'd adopted him. "Hi, Siobhan. They're adorable." She didn't remember Siobhan being so open and relaxed and wondered if it had to do with the handsome man at her side and her children.

Justin placed a kiss on her cheek. "Nice to finally meet you, Lauren. I've heard a lot about you."

Lauren glanced at Malcolm over her shoulder. What had he told his family? "Same here. You guys have a lovely home."

"Thank you," he said. "Make yourself comfortable."

She noted the curious gazes of two women she had yet to meet, but guessed they were Brandon and Khalil's wives. They came toward her with smiles, introducing themselves—Faith was married to Brandon and Lexia to Khalil—then steered Lauren over to where they had been seated. Brandon and Khalil greeted Lauren with hugs.

"What's up, Lauren?" Omar asked.

"Hey, Omar."

He glared at Morgan, and she reluctantly mumbled a greeting.

Trying to remain friendly, Lauren asked, "When's your baby due?"

"Next month."

"Congratulations. I hope all goes well."

"Thank you."

Omar kissed Morgan on her temple and smiled. "Thanks, Lauren."

She made small talk with Lexia and Faith and found out that Lexia owned a café and Faith was the vice president of the Grays' home safety company and worked as a website designer. Both women suggested they meet for lunch sometime, but Lauren didn't commit because she had no idea how her relationship with Malcolm would play out. Still weighing heavily on her mind was the bombshell he'd dropped about them going public.

After playing with his niece and nephew, Malcolm finally made his way to where she sat and handed her a bottle of green tea. "See, I told you it would be okay."

Lauren accepted the bottle, mumbled a thank-you and rolled her eyes.

"What?" he asked with a little laugh.

"You should've warned me…and them that you were bringing me."

Malcolm regarded her thoughtfully. "You're right. I'm sorry."

She met his sincere gaze. "Why didn't you tell me?"

"Because I didn't think you'd come, and I really wanted you here." He ran a gentle finger down her cheek and kissed her.

Why is he doing this? she wailed inwardly. Before she could question him further, Khalil came over.

"Okay, you lovebirds. Y'all save all that for later."

Lauren felt her face warm.

Malcolm snorted. "I know you're not talking, as many times as I caught you and Lex—"

Lexia jumped up. "It's time to eat. I'm going to start setting everything out." She grabbed Khalil's hand. "Come help me."

"And make sure that's *all* you two are doing," Malcolm called out.

Khalil turned back and smiled. "No promises." He tossed Lauren a bold wink and followed his wife into the kitchen.

For the first time, she saw that he wore a hearing aid and vowed to ask Malcolm about it later.

Once the food had been laid out, everyone gathered around and held hands while Mr. Gray blessed the food and offered a prayer of thanksgiving for Christian coming into their lives. After a rousing *amen*, everyone filled their plates and sat around eating and talking.

Lauren watched the men interact with their wives and felt a twinge of envy. Anyone would be able to see the love flowing between the couples. She tried to concentrate on her food and not worry about the possibility of her and Malcolm never having the same thing.

"What's on your mind, sweetheart?" Malcolm whispered.

"Nothing. Your brothers really love their wives."

He scanned the room. "Yeah, they do. But none of them had an easy path to get to this point. They put in the work, and even though they messed up a few times, they stuck it out."

Did that mean he wanted the same for them, and were his feelings deeper than he'd let on? She really wanted to find out, but this wasn't the time or place. When she finished, Lauren rose to take her empty plate to the trash. Morgan was in the kitchen, and Lauren braced herself for a confrontation.

"I don't want you to hurt my brother again."

She sighed. "Morgan, I don't plan to hurt your brother. I didn't plan to the last time, either, but youth and listening to friends caused me to lose a good man."

Surprise lit Morgan's eyes. "What do you mean?"

"Let's just say I was already insecure, and all it took was hearing a couple of horror stories from my friends who'd dated athletes. Don't tell me you've never made a mistake before."

"Yeah, I have." She paused as if remembering. "How do you feel about my brother?"

"I love Malcolm. I don't think I never stopped," she said wryly.

"Have you told him?"

"No, and please don't say anything."

Morgan folded her arms and narrowed her eyes. "You don't want me to say anything to him, yet you're admitting it to me. Why?"

"Because you're the only one who's convinced I have ulterior motives...and I don't." Lauren held Morgan's gaze unflinchingly.

"Morgan, Lauren...what's going on? Morgan, you aren't..." Malcolm divided a wary gaze between them.

Morgan waved him off. "We're fine. Stop worrying." She rounded the bar and kissed his cheek. Giving Lauren a nod, she departed.

"Are you sure nothing happened?" he asked, searching Lauren's face.

"Positive." She grabbed his hand and dragged him back into the family room. She only hoped he hadn't heard any of her conversation with Morgan. Especially the part about her loving him.

Malcolm kept an eye on Lauren for the rest of the afternoon. He didn't believe for one minute that nothing had transpired between her and Morgan. His twin had made it clear on several occasions how she felt about Lauren, and he didn't think she had changed her mind overnight. But he was pleased by how the rest of his family treated her. He hadn't intended to ask her to accompany him because, in his mother's eyes, it would be tantamount to an announcement of permanency, but he'd wanted her with him. Maybe the thought of being the only single person had prompted the invitation. As Lauren had pointed out, it was hard to miss the love between all the couples, and today, for reasons he couldn't explain, he didn't want to be the odd man out.

He studied Lauren as she talked to Faith. She took a sip from her water bottle and licked her lips. The sight instantly conjured up images of that little impromptu session at her house earlier. His groin stirred, and Malcolm tried to shift his thoughts to something else, otherwise every person in the room would get an eyeful. He couldn't believe what she'd done. And that little thing she did—sucking him deep into her mouth while her tongue made circles around his shaft—always drove him out of his mind. He had no idea how she did it, but no other woman had come close to making him feel the way she did.

Brandon came to where Malcolm stood. "Those must be some thoughts, baby bro."

"I don't know what you're talking about."

"Sure you do. It's the same look I have when I want to make love to my wife. Just ask Khalil, Omar or Justin. They know. Seems like your feelings for Lauren are a little stronger than what you want us to believe."

Malcolm eyed him. "What makes you think that?"

Brandon chuckled. "The fact that you brought her to a *family* gathering, for one. And, for another, your emotions are all over your face. Better hope Mom hasn't seen it." He started humming the wedding march quietly.

A wave of panic hit him, and he searched out his mother.

He relaxed upon seeing her playing with her grandchildren. He met Brandon's smug gaze and wanted to punch him.

Still chuckling, Brandon clapped him on the shoulder. "Let me know if you want to talk about it. I'll be more than happy to help you out with this thing called love. Although, since you've been there before with Lauren…"

Malcolm shrugged Brandon's hand off. "Get the hell away from me." He refused to acknowledge the truth in his brother's statement. He wasn't in love. Yes, he liked Lauren. Yes, he wanted to be with her, but that didn't mean he was in love with her. His heart started pounding in his chest, and the panic came back. He had to get out. He went through the kitchen and stood out on the deck, waiting for his heart to get back to a normal pace. He wasn't supposed to fall in love with her this fast. They had agreed to go slow, and this would complicate everything.

He heard the sliding door open and turned. "Hey, Dad."

His father stepped out and closed the door. "Everything okay?"

"Yes, I'm fine."

"You sure you're not running scared because you just realized you love Lauren?"

Malcolm couldn't very well tell his father the same thing he'd said to Brandon—not and live to tell about it—so he kept his mouth shut.

"Son, we've all been down the road you're on, and though it seems frightening sometimes, being able to find that special one to share your life with is worth it all. When I first realized I loved your mother, I was running so fast, I could've broken Usain Bolt's record in the one hundred."

He met his father's smile. "I never thought about that. You and Mom seem to always be in sync."

"Oh, we are…now. I almost let her get away with my foolishness." He shook his head and chuckled. "I want you to remember something. We men are quick to run off, but we come back just as quickly. A woman hangs in there for a long time deciding what to do, but once she decides to leave, she's gone for good. Don't ever let her get to that point if you love her."

Malcolm stared out into the yard, processing his father's words. The thought of Lauren closing the door on them for good made his stomach churn. "Thanks, Dad."

"Any time, Malcolm. Now, let's go get some of this cake Lexia made."

Inside, Siobhan was helping Christian cut pieces of cake and pass them out. Lexia had done the *PAW Patrol* theme—Malcolm still had no idea who or what that was. By the looks of the cake, he assumed it had to be some comic or book character and made a mental note to ask Siobhan about it.

"Is everything okay?"

He slid an arm around Lauren's waist. "Yeah, baby. Everything's good." When she smiled up at him, it took all his control not to blurt out that he loved her. He promised they'd go slow, and he would try to stick to that agreement, even if it killed him.

After the cake, Christian opened the mound of presents his new family had bought, from clothes and room decorations to puzzles and a motorized car. Malcolm and Omar had purchased football jerseys in the Cobras team colors of purple and silver—a white one with the accent colors for home and purple with silver for away—with his first name on the back and a football, also with Christian's name on it.

By the time the family gathered to leave, Christian had fallen asleep in the middle of the floor with the football tucked under one arm and a puzzle under the other. Nyla had lost the battle to sleep an hour ago. Malcolm stood off to the side observing his family saying goodbye to Lauren. He saw her exchange numbers with Faith and Lexia and hug Siobhan and his mother. Though Morgan didn't offer any type of affection, she did say goodbye, and that gave him hope. If Malcolm could leave the past behind, so could Morgan.

Once they made it to the car, Lauren let out a long breath and leaned back against the headrest. "You're lucky it didn't turn out bad, because if it had, I was never speaking to you again." She rolled her head in his direction. "After I punched your lights out."

Malcolm threw his head back and roared with laughter. When he finally calmed down, he drove off and said, "That's a serious punishment, baby. But I was never in any danger."

"Why's that?"

"I know my family. And I knew they'd treat you just like they always have. Well, except Morgan."

"Yep. Except Morgan."

"I know you said nothing went down between you two in the kitchen, but somehow I don't believe that."

She didn't reply for a moment. "She just warned me not to hurt you again. I told her I didn't plan to. After that, it was fine."

He still didn't believe her, knowing his sister, and he intended to call Morgan later.

"I noticed that Khalil has a hearing aid. I don't remember him having one."

"There was a gas explosion across the street from the building where my family's company is located, and Khalil just happened to be outside talking on the phone. A few people were killed and several others injured. Khalil was thrown several feet, had broken ribs and a sprained wrist and lost his hearing for several weeks." The memory of that time rose to the surface, and he thanked God every day that his brother hadn't been one of the casualties. "If it wasn't for Lexia, I don't think he would have made it through the ordeal. He'd basically shut all of us out."

"Oh my goodness. He was fortunate."

"Very. He regained full hearing in one ear after almost

two months and had surgery to repair the eardrum on the other. He only has about fifty percent hearing in that ear."

"Wow. Lexia is very nice, but I thought she owned a café. You said she helped him?"

He laughed. "Her café is on the first floor of the building, and she was there with him until help arrived. Brandon talked her into visiting him in the hospital. Khalil wouldn't eat, yelled at any of us if we tried to help in any way…he was in a bad place. But he loves Lexia's low-fat coffee cake, so she brought a piece. I wish I'd seen it, but apparently when he said he couldn't eat, she told him his hand was fine—and so was his mouth with all the yelling and fussing she could hear out in the hallway—handed him a fork and said 'eat.'"

Lauren burst out laughing. "She seems so sweet and quiet. I can't imagine her doing something like that."

"Ha! Don't let that little pint size fool you. She doesn't take any mess. Neither does Faith, for that matter. They fit right in with my sisters." And so did Lauren. She didn't hesitate getting into his face during their confrontations.

"Sounds like they do." Silence rose between them. "When we left, you mentioned not hiding our relationship anymore. You meant just around your family, right?"

"No. Like I told you earlier, there's nothing that says we can't date and I'm not going to jeopardize your job in any way, but I'm not going to avoid you or barely say two words when I do see you. And if I want to walk you to your car when you leave when I'm not practicing or in a meeting, then I want to be able to do that. There's nothing to worry about, sweetheart."

"I'm not so sure about that," she mumbled.

Malcolm frowned, recalling her comment in her office on Thursday. "Wait. Has somebody said something? When I came to talk to you last week, you said mentioned not giving someone something else to talk about. What did you mean?" She didn't respond. His eyes left the road briefly and he saw her tight features. "Talk to me, Lauren."

"It's nothing."

"If it's nothing, then you can tell me about it. Do I need to pull over so we can talk?"

"No," Lauren answered quickly.

"Then let's hear it."

"First you have to promise me you won't say anything or do anything."

"Why do I need to—"

"Promise me, Malcolm."

He blew out a long breath. "Fine. I promise."

"Well, one of your teammates gained a few pounds, and you know how I send out the weight and testing results with any suggestions to the players and the coaches?"

"Yeah. I like that. It helps us stay on track."

"Which is why I implemented it. But the guy who came in accused me of costing him his starting position and asked me to change his weight before sending the information to the coach. Then he said…"

"Said what?" he prompted when she didn't continue.

"He said he'd keep my secret if I made the change."

"What secret?"

"Us."

Malcolm whipped his head in her direction. *"What?"*

"Eyes on the road, Malcolm."

He jerked back into his lane. He didn't understand. They'd been very careful in their dealings. "What did he see?"

"Nothing. He just said he saw you leaving my office late one afternoon and the door had been closed. I told him that two other players had been in my office right before and asked if he was accusing me of sleeping with them, too. That was after I refused to change those numbers."

Malcolm clenched his teeth and bit back the acerbic comment poised on the tip of his tongue. He never should have made that promise. "Who was it?"

"I'm not going to say. He got my message loud and clear. I just didn't want you to be blindsided if he told other players and they asked you about it."

"Then it's even better that we're going public. It won't matter who he tells." He still wanted to know who had tried to blackmail her, but he understood she wouldn't say. "Still worried about it?" he asked, trying hard to keep the anger out of his voice.

"A little, I guess."

"You don't need to. If he does anything to hurt you, he'll answer to me."

"Malcolm, you promised you wouldn't do anything."

"I know." But promise or no promise, if the coward got in her face again—teammate or not—he would find out how Malcolm felt about him threatening Lauren.

Chapter 16

Every time someone knocked on her office door Monday, Lauren jumped and her stomach lurched, thinking it was Carlos. Or worse, Malcolm coming to camp out just in case. By lunchtime her nerves were shot, and she decided to eat outside on one of the benches on the walking path. She found one positioned beneath a shade tree and hurried over. For the time being, she didn't have to worry about Carlos since practice didn't end for another hour.

While eating her shrimp and avocado salad, she thought about her time with Malcolm's family. Aside from the tension between her and Morgan, everyone else had been as nice as she remembered. His parents seemed to still be very much in love, and she'd noticed them sharing a kiss or an intimate touch on more than one occasion. The same could be said for all the couples in attendance, and she found herself feeling a little envy. She and Malcolm were progressing, but Lauren longed for the relaxed contentment she had seen on all their faces.

Although he hadn't said so, she knew he still didn't trust her completely. Not that she blamed him. But it made her speculate on whether the relationship would crumble with the slightest test. If she could go back in time, she would definitely do things differently, starting with not listening to her friend back in college. She and Malcolm still might have broken up eventually, but it wouldn't have been because of her.

Lauren forked up another portion of the salad and realized how much she liked it. She'd found the recipe on the internet while looking for some lighter summer dishes. Thinking about recipes reminded her that Nigel had asked her to stop by. She finished her lunch, drained the green tea and headed back to her office to drop off the containers and pick up the large gift bag.

She found Nigel seated on a stool at the back of the kitchen making a list. She placed the bag on the counter next to her.

He glanced up at her entry. "Hey, Lauren."

"Hi, Nigel. It always smells so good in here." She didn't know what he and his staff were cooking for lunch, but it made her mouth water, despite the fact that she'd just eaten.

Nigel smiled. "You're welcome to grab a plate. We cook for the staff, too."

"Maybe next time. I just ate. You said you wanted to see me."

"Yes. I'm making the grocery list and I remember you mentioning a couple of new snack recipes you wanted to try."

"Oh, yes. I've had several of the guys—mostly the rookies and first-year players—complain about having to cut back on their sweets, so I wanted to try out a couple of lower-fat and low-sugar treats."

"What did you have in mind?"

Lauren pulled out her phone and clicked on her memos where she had noted the recipes. "One is a brownie recipe that uses dates and dark chocolate and doesn't need to be baked. It's just over one hundred calories per serving and has less than four grams of sugar."

"Anything without sugar *can't* be labeled a dessert," he teased. "Hey, that's the number one requirement for me."

She laughed. "True, but since we have this regimen to consider..." She shrugged.

Nigel waved a hand. "Yeah, yeah. What else you got?"

"The other one is an apple-peach crisp." She passed him her phone so he could see the recipe. "It's about two hundred fifty calories, and we can even add a little light ice cream on top."

He shook his head. "No butter, no sugar. This is just sacrilegious, Lauren."

Lauren burst out laughing. She pointed to a line on the recipe. "There's honey."

He slanted her a glance. "Three tablespoons...in the crumb topping." Still shaking his head, Nigel said, "Okay, but if I get any complaints, I'm throwing you under the bus."

"Whatever."

He chuckled. "I'm just giving you a hard time. These sound really good." He checked several cabinets. "I have most of the ingredients. Just need to get the fruit." He wrote the items on his list. "Anything else you want to try?"

"Actually, I made some cookies."

He gestured toward the bag. "Is that what you have in the bag?"

"Yep." She had found a recipe that called for a small amount of coconut sugar, dark chocolate chips and peanut butter. Thankfully, no one on the roster had a peanut allergy. She dug out a Ziploc bag and opened it. "Here, try one."

Nigel took one, bit into it and chewed thoughtfully. "I hate to admit it, but these are good. I hope you have enough."

"I hope so, too." Lauren had made several dozen cookies that were about three and a half or four inches in diameter. "I'll leave them here and you can add them to the buffet. How are the morning recovery shakes working out?"

"Very well. My staff has taken to making a few extra because the coaches seem to enjoy them."

The news made Lauren smile. Having the coaching staff buy in to her recipes and suggestions meant the possibility of longevity in the position. A couple of staff members passed her with large bowls filled with fruit and salad mix. "Glad to hear it. I'll get out of your way." The team would be descending on the dining room shortly, and she wanted to be gone so as not to run into Carlos or Malcolm.

"I'll probably try out the brownies tomorrow. Feel free to pop in."

Now that her plan had been implemented, Lauren didn't really need to be in the dining room during meals too often. She stopped in briefly a couple times a week just to answer questions or check on her more problem athletes. But she did want to find out how well the new dessert was received. "I may do that."

Nigel picked up the bag. "Thanks, Lauren."

With a wave, she departed. She made it halfway down the hall before she heard male voices. *Great.* Several guys passed her and spoke. She returned their greetings but didn't break stride.

"It's too bad you didn't take my offer."

The soft, menacing voice stopped her. She met Carlos's dark, cold eyes. She quickly scanned the hallway, praying Malcolm was nowhere in sight. However, since Carlos, like most of the players, loomed over her like a mountain, she couldn't see anything. Carlos stood waiting for her to respond, but rather than get into a confrontation, she chose to ignore him. Lauren turned away from his glare only to lock eyes with Malcolm.

"I need to talk to you for a minute."

"Malcolm—"

Malcolm leaned closer and said for her ears only, "If you

don't want me to pick you up and carry you out of here, then you should start walking."

Not wanting to cause a scene, she said, "Sure, I have a couple of minutes." He followed her to her office and closed the door. Lauren rounded on him. "I thought you said you weren't going to go all out and…and…whatever." She threw up her hands.

He folded his arms. "I didn't. I only said I wanted to talk to you. If I were going all out, I would've kissed you like I did when we were playing gin."

She stared.

"What? No comeback?" He laughed softly.

No, she didn't have a comeback. "You said you wanted to talk to me."

"What did Carlos say to you?" He held up a hand. "I saw your expression, Lauren, and I know he said something to upset you."

"It was nothing I can't handle." She went over to her desk and straightened a stack of folders.

Malcolm came around the desk and rotated her to face him. "He's the one who threatened you, isn't he?"

She opened her mouth to lie, but the scowl on his face stopped her. "Yes," she said resignedly.

He released her and stalked toward the door muttering, "When I get done with him…"

Lauren rushed around the desk, stepped into his path and blocked the door. "*No!* You promised me you wouldn't say anything to him."

"The man is three times your size, Lauren," Malcolm snapped. "I'm not going to stand by and let him bully you."

She placed her hands on his chest. "Malcolm, please don't. I don't want you to get into trouble, and I already handled it."

His jaw tightened. "That doesn't mean he won't try to do something to hurt you. I will *not* allow that to happen. Don't fight me on this, baby."

She would never forgive herself if Malcolm got suspended or worse, fired, and had to get him to see reason. "Listen to me. He's not going to hurt me. He can't. If no one knew about us before, they do now. You didn't leave much room for question whispering in my ear," she added wryly. "Baby, I couldn't take it if you ruined your career for me. This is my job and I won't let him or anyone else bully me into doing something wrong or illegal. You have to let me deal with it my way."

He let out a frustrated breath, brought his hands up to frame her face and rested his forehead against hers. "You're killing me, baby. All I want to do is protect you."

Her heart skipped. She loved this man. "If I need you, I'll let you know. I promise."

Malcolm kissed her softly and nodded. "I need to go shower."

She wrinkled her nose. "Yes, you do."

He smiled for the first time. "You're a cold woman."

"No, I'm a truthful one."

He gazed down at her. "I... I'm glad you're back in my life, Lauren." He gave her one more kiss that nearly melted her to the floor and slipped out.

Lauren leaned against the closed door and smiled. Maybe they would make it this time.

Omar slid into the chair across from Malcolm in the dining room. "So, that's the new definition of discreet?"

Malcolm glanced up from his plate. "I told her yesterday we weren't hiding anymore."

"Feel better now?" he teased.

He smiled. "Shut up." He didn't know if *better* was the right word. Their time together would be limited now that the season was in full swing. The schedule didn't allow another weekend off until two months from now, when the team had a bye week. They typically had a day off during the week, usually Tuesdays when the regular season started, but Lauren didn't have the same schedule. And Malcolm typically still came in for a short workout. That only left the evening, and those two or three hours wouldn't be nearly enough to satisfy him.

Marcus set his plate on the table, went back for something to drink and came back. He leveled Malcolm with a stare. "So, what's up with you and Lauren?"

Omar chuckled and kept eating.

"We're dating."

"Ah, moving kind of fast, aren't you? You just met the woman. She's only been here, what, two months or so?"

He cut a piece of his chicken and ate it before responding. "I didn't just meet her."

"Malcolm and Lauren go way back," Omar tossed out nonchalantly.

Marcus divided a questioning glance between Malcolm and Omar. "Like how far back?"

"College," Malcolm said. "We dated for almost two years."

"Well, I'll be damned. I know a couple of players whose feelings are going to be hurt," he said with a laugh, gesturing across the room.

Malcolm turned in the direction Marcus indicated and saw Lauren smiling and talking to Darren. For a split second, he felt a surge of jealousy. Then he calmed down. This was her job. She had to talk to the players. He shrugged. "Not my problem. She's mine."

"So, what happened the first time?"

Malcolm didn't like rehashing the story, but he relented. "A couple of my buddies went to a party, and one of them got drunk. The other one called me and asked me to come help get him back to the dorm." Malcolm had lived off campus, but his friends had known he'd be studying at the library that night for a kinesiology exam. He told how he went to the party, searched for his friend and convinced him to call it a night. "We got him outside and two girls

followed, trying to persuade us to stay. Both had had a little too much to drink." He paused as the painful memory
came back. "Lauren and her roommate happened to be
passing just as the girl plastered herself all over me and
tried to kiss me."

Marcus shook his head. "No need to say more. I hope
it works out this time."

So did Malcolm. He finished eating and stood to leave.
The running backs' meeting wouldn't start for another
twenty minutes, but he had something he needed to do
first. "I need to go talk to Coach for a few minutes." Both
men looked at him with concern. Knowing he could confide in them, Malcolm braced his hands on the table and
quietly told them what Carlos had done.

"So do we kick his ass now or later?" Omar asked.

Marcus made a move to stand.

"I promised Lauren I wouldn't say anything to him, but
I never said I wouldn't mention it to the coach or management," Malcolm said.

Slow grins spread across Marcus and Omar's faces, and
Marcus said, "Okay, but if he threatens her again, all bets
are off. I'll leave Jaedon to pick up Carlos's remains." His
attorney brother was ruthless in the courtroom and had
been instrumental in taking down Omar's former agent,
who had tried to ruin Omar and Morgan's reputations.

Malcolm nodded. "We think alike. I'll see you later."
He passed Carlos on the way out, and it took a great deal
of control to keep that promise he'd made.

He knocked on Coach Smith's open door. Martin Smith
had been head coach of the Cobras since the beginning of
Malcolm's career, had taken the team to the playoffs seven
of those eight years and brought home the championship
trophy three times. He reminded Malcolm of retired coach
Tony Dungy because of his uncanny way of connecting
with the players and his calm demeanor. The two even

favored one another slightly, with the exception of Coach Smith's darker skin. "Hey, Coach. You have a minute?"

Coach Smith waved Malcolm in. "Sure, Malcolm." He set aside his papers and clasped his hands together on the desk. "What can I do for you?"

He reached for the door. "You mind if I close this?"

"Not at all." He frowned. "Is everything all right? You're not coming in here to tell me you're retiring?"

Malcolm smiled. "I still have a couple good years left in me, so I'm not retiring yet."

Relief flooded the other man's face. "Thank goodness."

"I wanted you to hear it from me first that Lauren Emerson and I are dating."

His eyebrows shot up. "Really?"

"Yes. She and I have...history. I assure you this won't affect either of our jobs."

"Well, there aren't any policies against it, so I'm not following why you needed to make an announcement."

"There's something else." He paused a beat. "She's been threatened by one of the players who wasn't happy about her reporting his weight stats."

Coach leaned forward, concerned. "Exactly what do you mean by threatened...physically?"

"No." Malcolm shared the details of the threat. "He wanted her to do the same thing Stan did last year."

Coach scrubbed a hand down his face and rose to his feet. "I thought we handled all of that."

Malcolm wondered if Carlos had been part of the original scheme and had somehow slipped through the cracks. It could be why the man had felt bold enough to approach Lauren the way he had.

"Who is it?"

"Jenkins."

"Carlos?"

"Yes."

Coach Smith shook his head. "I'll talk to Green."

"I'd appreciate it if you didn't mention me talking to you to Lauren."

A smile broke out on his face. "Don't want her to know you're interfering in her business."

"No." If Lauren found out, she'd be livid. Malcolm's feelings for her now were stronger than they'd been in college, and he couldn't risk losing her again.

He clapped Malcolm on the shoulder. "You don't have to worry about her finding out."

"Thanks, Coach." Malcolm left feeling much better. If management dealt with Carlos, he wouldn't have to.

Malcolm didn't get home until after eight. He was tired but wanted to talk to Lauren. He trudged up the stairs to his bedroom, tossed his keys on the dresser and removed his shoes and shirt. He stretched out on his bed and called the number that topped his frequent-caller list.

"Hey, Malcolm," Lauren said when she answered.

"Hey."

"You sound tired. Are you just getting home?"

"Yep. How'd the rest of your day go? You didn't have any more problems, did you?"

"It was fine, and no. You should probably go to bed."

"What? You don't want to talk to me? I think my feelings are hurt."

She laughed. "Silly man, your feelings are fine. I'd love to talk to you all night, but I know how exhausting your day can get."

Malcolm had always appreciated that about her. She never hassled him about the long hours he put into football. "Would you really?"

"Really what?"

"Talk to me all night."

"Yes."

"Then talk to me, baby."

"What do you want to talk about?"

"I don't know. Everything. Nothing." The sound of her

voice seemed to ease the weariness steeped in his bones, and he wondered if this was what his brothers meant by coming home to that special one. "You said you've changed. Tell me what's changed about you."

"Okay. Hmm…let's see. I'm not insecure anymore, and I go after what I want."

Malcolm's heart rate kicked up a notch. What was she telling him?

"But I still like to eat my Baskin-Robbins chocolate-chip ice cream in two cones."

He laughed so hard he started to choke. "I can't believe you still do that." The first time they'd gone to the ice cream shop, she asked for a second cone, and when they got back to his apartment, she'd divided the one scoop between the two cones, saying she liked a little ice cream with her cone. "And you still only get the one scoop?"

"Yes, I do."

"I thought by now you would have at least graduated to two scoops."

"Whatever, Malcolm Gray. I bet you haven't changed much, either."

"And you would be right." He liked keeping his things a certain way, and when he was younger he'd often gotten into fights with Khalil and Brandon because they would always rearrange his books or his collection of miniature cars just to get a rise out of him.

"Do you still have your Hot Wheels?"

"You'd better believe it."

"I don't recall seeing them when I was there."

"That's because I have them stored in my shed."

"What?" she asked with mock surprise. "I can't believe you just tossed them in a box somewhere."

"You must be out of your mind, woman. I did *not* just toss them in a box. Each one is wrapped and boxed individually and stacked *neatly* in the storage container." Lauren's laughter came through the line. They continued to talk and tease each other, and when he checked the time, over two hours had passed. He had enjoyed their conversation and was reluctant to end it, but tomorrow promised to be another long day with practice, meetings and watching film.

"It's getting late."

"I want to talk to you longer, though."

"Mmm…me, too. I missed talking to you this way, Malcolm."

"I missed this, too, sunshine." He never remembered wanting to spend hours on the phone talking to the women he dated. Lauren was the only one. They'd been friends first, and maybe that made the difference. "But I need to go to bed."

"Can we do this again?"

"Any time you want."

"Sleep well, angel eyes."

Malcolm laughed softly. "'Night, sweetheart." He swung his legs over the bed and plugged the phone into the charger on his nightstand. His thoughts went back to what she'd revealed. *I'm not insecure anymore, and I go after what I want.* Good, because so did he. And he wanted her.

Chapter 17

Lauren stood in the tunnel watching practice. It had been almost three weeks since she and Malcolm had spent time together. While she enjoyed their nightly phone calls, she wanted to feel his lips on hers and run her hands over every inch of his hard body. Training camp had ended two weeks ago, and this Sunday would be the first game of the regular season. Malcolm had asked her to go with him early and wait for him after the game. Her eyes were glued to him as he executed a movement with the power, speed and agility of a cheetah. "Mmm, mmm, mmm…that body," she murmured. And he belonged to her.

There were fewer players on the field, and she learned some had not made the cut. She also didn't see Carlos and wondered if he'd been benched because of his weight gain. She shook her head. Had he followed her suggestions, he would have most likely already lost the excess pounds. Lauren was proud of Darren, however. He had shed every one of his twenty pounds, plus five more, and she looked forward to seeing him in the starting lineup Sunday.

Lauren stood there a moment longer then went back to her office. Two hours later, she looked up and saw Malcolm standing in her doorway.

"Hey, beautiful."

"Hey yourself, handsome. Are you coming to give me one of the hundreds of kisses you owe me?"

Malcolm closed the door and came toward her. "Hundreds?"

"Hundreds," she reiterated.

"Since I only have five minutes, I'd better make it count." He pulled her flush against him and crushed his mouth against hers in a long, drugging kiss. "It feels like it's been forever since we've had time together."

His hands roamed up and down her body as he reclaimed her mouth. She held on as his tongue made sweeping, swirling motions, driving her out of her mind with desire. Lauren's hands found their way under his shirt, and he promptly captured them.

"Don't do that," he said, his breathing as ragged as hers. "I have to go. I'll call you tonight."

She groaned.

"I know. I'll make it up to you. Talk to you later."

Lauren dropped down in her chair and closed her eyes. Her body pulsed everywhere. It was only Wednesday, and she had to wait four days. She had agreed to take things slow, but she didn't know how much more of *slow* she could take. Right now she wanted it hard and fast. Groaning again, she sat up. She still had two more hours to go before her day ended.

As she packed up to leave later, remnants of the kiss played around the edges of her mind. It would only take a minute to stop in the dining room and seek out Malcolm for just one more. *Do not go to the dining room. Keep walking, girl. You're a professional.* She hated that annoying voice in her head, but this time she grudgingly agreed. Her steps slowed as she pushed through the front door and she saw Malcolm leaning against the column. He gently removed her tote from her shoulder and threaded his fingers through hers.

"I decided I wanted to walk you to your car today. Objections?"

Lauren smiled up at him. "Not one." Once they reached her car, he pinned her against the door and gave her a kiss so achingly tender it melted her heart.

"I don't know how much longer I can go without seeing you, Lauren," Malcolm whispered as he trailed kisses along the shell of her ear. "Feel how much I want you."

She felt the solid ridge of his erection pressed into her belly. "I want you, too." She reached down to stroke him, and he shuddered.

He stilled her hand. "You're about two seconds away from me straddling you on this hood and not caring about everybody and their mama seeing me make love to you. Get in your car and go home before you get us both in trouble."

"Oh, I don't know. Right now I might be okay with getting into trouble," she said with a sultry smile, tracing a path from his chest to his abs.

He chuckled. "You were never this forward back then, but I think I like this new, bold you." He held the door open. "This weekend. You and me."

Lauren slid into the driver's seat, and he closed the door. She started the engine, waved and drove off. She glanced in her rearview mirror and saw him drag his hand down his face. *At least I'm not the only one struggling for control.* Between the kiss in her office and this last encounter, he had every molecule in her body screaming for release, and she didn't think she'd make it until the weekend. She couldn't believe she'd been so reckless as to not care whether someone saw them making out in the parking lot. "Good grief," she muttered.

Two hours after she arrived home, Malcolm was still on her mind. He typically called around nine, and for the past couple of nights they had talked until almost midnight. Tonight, Lauren decided to shower first so all she had to do was slide under the covers after their conversation.

Her cell rang as soon as she slipped a short tank sleep shirt on. "Hello."

"Hey, girl," Valencia said.

"Hey, Lyn."

"Did I catch you at a bad time? You sound weird."

"No. I just got out of the shower. I'm fine." Other than needing to release some sexual tension. "How's it going at work?"

"Miss Thang finally got fired, thankfully, and they just hired someone else. I've been home at my regular time for a week and it's glorious."

Lauren laughed. "Good for you. It's about time. I can't believe they took so long to let her go."

"Me, either. Anyway, I called to see how things are going with you and Malcolm. I'm like two weeks overdue for an update. Oh, and whatever happened with that football player who was threatening you? Did you tell Malcolm about him?"

She shook her head. "You want to let me answer one thing at a time?"

"My bad," Valencia said with a little giggle. "Let's start with the football player and save the juicy stuff for last."

"I don't know what I'm going to do with you, girl. Anyway, I have no idea what happened to him. I didn't see him practicing today, so he could have been benched or something. I did tell Malcolm about him, and I had to make him promise to not confront the man."

"Aw, that's so sweet." She let out a whoop. "Go, Malcolm. Protect your woman."

"Yeah, that's what he said."

"That's because he still loves you."

"He hasn't said anything about love." But everything about the way he had been behaving of late reminded her of when he did. Did she dare hope? Her phone beeped with another call. "Hold on, Lyn. That's Malcolm."

"Go talk to your man. Call me tomorrow."

"Okay. 'Night." Lauren switched over. "Hey, sexy."

Malcolm's deep rumble came through the line. "My thoughts exactly. What are you doing?"

"Sitting here wishing you were here."

"Is that right? And if I were?"

A wicked thought crossed her mind. She still owed him for that phone sex call. "If you were here, I'd start with kissing you until I was drunk with your taste. Then I'd strip you naked and take my time skating my tongue across your chest, lingering a bit on each nipple."

"And?" he said, his voice sounding strained.

"Oh, I have to touch you. Mmm… I want to feel your abs quiver beneath my hands as I continue my taste and touch quest. I love your smooth caramel skin, and it tastes as sweet. And your hard, strong thighs…just what I need to hold me up when we… Oh, wait. We're not there yet. I want you to be hard for me. Are you hard yet, Malcolm?" She heard his labored breathing through the line, but he didn't answer. "You have to be so I can take you deep into my mouth, slide you in and out and use my mouth and tongue at the same time…"

Lauren heard a beep and looked at the display. The call had dropped. She smiled and called back, but he didn't answer. She frowned, waited a few minutes and tried again. The call went straight to voice mail. "What the…?"

Why wasn't he answering? Puzzled, she sighed heavily and flopped down on the bed. Playing that little game had her so aroused it wouldn't take much to push her over the edge. She got up to turn on the ceiling fan, needing to cool off. She sprawled across the bed directly under the flow of air and waited for it to take down the blaze. The ringing doorbell startled her. Who would...? Her eyes widened.

Lauren scrambled off the bed, went out front and glanced through the peephole. *Malcolm?* She undid the locks and opened the door. "Malcolm. What are you—" He hauled her into his arms, kicked the door shut and captured her mouth with an urgency that stunned them both. He placed her against the door and drew her legs around his waist.

"Are you trying to send me to prison?" he murmured huskily, pressing hot kisses along her jaw and exposed throat and grinding his erection in subtle circles against her center.

"I...what... I don't know what you mean." She couldn't think, much less talk.

"I broke every speed limit to get to you." He moved her panties to the side and slid a finger inside her. "So wet."

She whimpered, already on the verge of an orgasm.

"I can't wait, baby."

He entered her on one deep thrust, snatching her breath. "Malcolm, we can't...protection?"

"Already in place. You asked me if I'm hard for you. The answer is hell yeah, I am. Can you feel how hard you make me?" he asked, retreating to the tip and pushing back in inch by incredible inch until he was buried to the hilt. "How do you want it, baby?"

"Hard and fast."

A wolfish gleam leaped into his eyes. "Then that's how I'm gonna give it." Malcolm palmed her bottom and held her firmly against the door.

Lauren wrapped her arms around his neck and locked her legs around his broad back as he set a hard, driving rhythm that rattled the door. She arched and writhed against him as he pumped faster, delving deeper with each thrust. He whispered a mixture of tender endearments and erotic promises that made her desire climb even higher. Their breathing grew louder as he gripped her tighter and drove into her harder. The pressure built inside her with an intensity she'd never felt, and she convulsed and screamed his name as waves of ecstasy crashed through her so violently she thought she might pass out.

"Look at me, sweetheart."

She met his gaze, and what she saw took her breath away.

A moment later, he threw his head back and erupted, shouting her name hoarsely. "You're mine, Lauren. I love you, baby."

Lauren collapsed against his shoulder. She didn't know how long they stayed there, gasping for air and shuddering with the aftershocks of their lovemaking.

Her head popped up. "What did you say?"

"I said I love you, Lauren Emerson."

His words brought tears to her eyes. "I love you, too, Malcolm Gray."

A smile curved his lips. He carried her down the hallway to her bedroom and placed her in the center of her bed. He undressed them both, climbed in and gathered her in his embrace.

"What are you doing? Don't you have a curfew?"

"I'm in for the night. They never said I had to sleep at my house," he added with a wink.

Lauren lifted her head and burst out laughing. "Well, I can't say how much *sleep* you're going to get, and I owe you for hanging up on me."

Malcolm rolled on his back. "Then punish me, baby."

She grabbed hold of his growing erection. "With pleasure." She wanted this to be a night he'd never forget and planned to show him how much she loved him. How much she *still* loved him.

Malcolm woke up disoriented for a moment, then remembered. He stared at Lauren cuddled into his side, her head on his chest. He hadn't woken up next to a woman in years, but he wanted to wake up next to her every day for the rest of his life. The admission was freeing in a way. He'd told Lauren he loved her last night, but what he hadn't said was that he had never stopped. All those years he'd thought he'd been over her, but she'd remained somewhere in the dark recesses of his heart, occupying a space that no other woman could ever claim. He leaned up to see the time. Five fifteen. As much as he wanted to lay her on her back and awaken her with his kiss, they both had to work. Fortunately, he didn't have to lift weights this morning, so he had a little leeway.

Carefully shifting Lauren, he eased out of the bed and went into the bathroom to dress. When he came back, she was awake. "Morning, beautiful."

"Good morning," Lauren murmured. "What time is it?"

"Five thirty. I'm going to head out. I'll see you tonight." She smiled sleepily. "Are you coming over?"

He nodded. "I want to talk to you about something." He kissed her. "Go back to sleep. I'll lock the door."

"Mmm-hmm." She closed her eyes.

Malcolm stepped out into the cool early-morning breeze and walked the short distance to where he'd parked his car. He got in, turned on the headlights to cut the darkness and backed out of the space.

At this early hour, traffic was sparse, and he made it back to his house in under twenty minutes. He tossed the duffel bag on a chair in his room and went to his large walk-in closet. He searched for a minute until he found the box he wanted. Taking a seat on his bed, he took a deep breath. He'd packed the box away eight years ago, and this was the first time he had thought about opening it. He picked up the first item and removed the bubble wrap to reveal a framed photo of him and Lauren that had been taken at the beach. Malcolm laid it aside and reached for the black Camaro Hot Wheels car she'd given him as a reminder to never give up on his dream of owning the real thing. He dug deeper until he found what he was looking for. The small navy velvet box still held the promise ring he'd given her. And that she'd returned. He was ready to make another promise. A promise of forever.

Chapter 18

Despite getting only three hours of sleep, Lauren breezed into work Thursday morning feeling more energized than she had been in a long time. Malcolm's declaration of love still resonated in her heart. After that second round of love-making, he had gone out to his car to bring in the overnight bag he'd packed. Their shower together had turned into another passionate session, with him taking her from behind while she braced her hands on the wall. Her core pulsed with the memory of his slow, hypnotic thrusts.

"Morning, Lauren."

She whipped her head around. "Good morning, Charlotte." She'd been so lost in her fantasy that she hadn't even heard Mr. Green's assistant behind her. Shaking her head to clear it, she unlocked her office, unloaded her tote and powered up her laptop.

Lauren needed to get her mind in work mode. She had check-ins this morning with three of the rookies who'd made the cut, including Brent and Chris. Each would stop in between their morning meetings or workouts. Breakfast ran from six until nine, allowing players, coaches and support staff time to eat at their convenience, depending on their meeting and weight-lifting schedule. Players also had access to the training room, where they could seek information from medical staff or, if injured, receive treatment.

She pulled their files, penned a few notes and set them aside. Rotating in her chair, she checked her email. She read one from Nigel telling her he'd be adding the brownies to the day's menu and asking her to stop by some time that morning. "Now's as good a time as any." On the way, she ran into Darren.

"Hey, Lauren."

"How's it going, Darren?"

Darren grinned. "Great! Did you see my numbers?"

"I did. Congratulations."

"Coach said I'd probably be able to start. I don't know how to thank you."

They spoke to a couple of players as they entered the dining room. "All I did was set the program. You put in all the work, and it shows." The lineman's large frame looked more defined, especially around his midsection.

"You going to be around this afternoon?"

"Yes."

"Can I stop by? There's something I want to show you."

Lauren mentally went through her schedule. She wanted to leave a little early, because she planned to cook dinner for her and Malcolm and she had to pick up a few ingredients. "What time are you free?"

"I can make it between three and three thirty."

"Perfect. I'll see you then."

He gave her arm an affectionate squeeze. "Thanks."

She smiled up at the gentle giant. "You're welcome." When he walked away, she turned and saw Malcolm watching with an unreadable expression. She waved, and he relaxed and smiled. Rather than approach him like she wanted, she reminded herself that she'd see him later and went to speak with Nigel.

Lauren made it back to the office just as Chris showed up and spent the rest of the morning with several other players popping in. She had planned to eat outside, but an impromptu early-afternoon meeting with the coaches left her with fifteen minutes to wolf down her pasta with chicken and asparagus before heading down to one of the smaller conference rooms. When she'd first explained how she wanted to collaborate with them on each player's needs and goals, they'd seemed excited by the idea and wasted no time implementing it. She wanted to build a program for the long haul.

Darren came by as promised a little after three. He had a smile so bright, Lauren asked, "What are you so happy about? I mean, besides reclaiming your starting position."

Darren came and stood in front of her. "My girlfriend said I'm marriage material now and I'm going to ask her to marry me."

"Oh my goodness! That's wonderful." Without thinking, she reached up to hug him.

He returned the hug. "I can't tell you how much I appreciate everything you've done. Look." He took out a small ring box. "Do you think she'll like it?"

Lauren brought her hands to her mouth. "Wow. It's absolutely beautiful." A row of smaller diamonds surrounded a round-cut solitaire that had to be at least two carats. "I know she's going to love it. Congratulations."

"Well, isn't this cozy?"

She and Darren turned to see Malcolm standing in the doorway, his eyes cold.

Darren divided a glance between them, then asked Lauren, "You and Gray?"

She nodded tightly.

"Thanks again, Lauren. I'll let you two talk." He beat a hasty exit.

Malcolm didn't waste any time. "So I guess you were looking for a bigger ring."

"I beg your pardon?"

"Don't try to play me, Lauren. I know what I saw."

Lauren put a hand on her hip. Was he insinuating she had something going on with Darren? "Do you?"

"The hug, the ring, the smiles, the way he was touching you in the dining room the other day… I just don't know what to think." He pivoted and started to walk out.

She stormed across the room and got in his face. "Are you *kidding* me? You think that I could tell you I love you one day and be with another man the next?" She shook her head wearily. "After everything you've said, you still don't trust me, do you?" She wasn't going to bother explaining her conversation with Darren, because Malcolm should know better.

"It's kind of hard to when I walk in and see my woman hugging another man holding a ring in his hand. You're going to tell me I'm wrong?"

"No. I'm not going to tell you anything. You should know me."

He didn't comment.

Angry tears burned her eyes. "See, you won't even deny it. This isn't going to work, Malcolm."

"Then tell me I'm wrong," he said through clenched teeth. He reached out for her, and she pushed him away.

"I shouldn't have to!" Lauren should have left well enough alone—friendship and nothing more—because it was now clear to her that he'd never let go of the past. "After everything we've been through, I can't believe you'd think I'd turn around and cheat on you, especially with someone you work with. You need to leave my office." She stepped around him and kept her back to him.

"Lauren, I—"

She turned and held up a hand. "Just go. I guess that

makes us even now. I broke your heart, and now you've broken mine."

Something like regret flickered across Malcolm's features, and he reached for her again.

She shook her head, trying to keep the tears from falling. His jaw tightened, but he did as she asked.

Once he was gone, she closed the door and let the tears flow. She didn't have any other appointments, so she sent an email asking Mr. Green if she could leave early to take care of some things. He replied favorably, and she was packed and striding down the hall a moment later.

"Lauren, are you okay?" Omar asked as she exited the building, gently taking hold of her arm.

If she opened her mouth to say one thing, the floodgates would open, and she couldn't do that here.

"Malcolm?"

Lauren nodded.

He seemed to understand and gave her a reassuring hug. "It'll all turn out okay. Just hang in there."

She really wanted to believe him, but her world had just gone to hell in a handbasket in a matter of seconds. She couldn't see anything past the pain in her heart.

Malcolm paused in pacing the locker room when Omar entered wearing a deep scowl on his face. "What's wrong? Is Morgan okay?"

"What the hell did you do to Lauren? I just met her damn near running out of the building and crying."

His heart constricted. "I walked in on her and Darren in her office. He had his arms wrapped around her and a huge ring in his hand."

Omar shook his head. "You didn't learn anything from my mistake with your sister, did you? I can guarantee that whatever you *thought* you saw wasn't the truth."

Omar had jumped to conclusions when he thought Morgan had leaked her negotiating plans to the media. Had

Malcolm done the same thing? He closed his eyes and tried to conjure up the scene in Lauren's office, but the only image that he could see was Lauren in the arms of another man. After that, he'd lost all rational thought. "Why are you so sure?"

"Because I saw her at Siobhan and Justin's that night. She's in love with you." He hesitated, as if he were going to say more. "I promised Morgan I wouldn't say anything, but because you chose to act a complete idiot, I'm going to tell you. And if you breathe one word of it, I will kick your ass. Though I should do it anyway."

"Tell me what?" Malcolm asked impatiently.

"Lauren told Morgan that she loved you when they were in the kitchen."

"Why would she... Morgan doesn't even like Lauren, so I can't see Lauren her telling her the time of day."

"Morgan asked the same question. Lauren admitted it to Morgan because Morgan was the only one who believed she had ulterior motives where you were concerned. Basically, she wanted Morgan to know that she didn't."

Malcolm slowly lowered himself to a bench and buried his head in his hands. "She accused me of still not being able to trust her completely, of not letting go of the past." *And of breaking her heart.*

"And have you?"

"I don't know... I thought I had." What had he done?

"If you don't know, you'd better find out quick and decide whether you can live the rest of your life without her." A couple of players came in from the showers and dressed, their gazes straying to Malcolm and Omar across the room. Omar sat and the two continued their conversation quietly. "If you need to talk, you know where to find me."

Malcolm didn't want to talk to anyone except Lauren, but he had a team meeting in five minutes that wouldn't be over for the next two hours. He pushed to his feet.

Omar went to his locker and retrieved a duffel bag.

He frowned. "Where are you going?"

"Coach is letting me leave early. I want to go home and check on Morgan. She had a few contractions last night and two today, and I'm worried about her."

Malcolm's heart rate kicked up. "Call me if you end up taking her to the hospital." Granted, Morgan was a married woman now, but Malcolm didn't care. She would always be his baby sister, his twin.

"I will."

Malcolm went one way and Omar the other. It took all of his concentration to remain focused on the running back coach's voice. The only voice in his head was Lauren's. He had been angry that she'd assumed the worst without giving him the benefit of the doubt eight years ago, and it had taken him less than two minutes to do the same thing to her. He didn't have an excuse, aside from jealousy. From the first time Marcus had mentioned that a couple of guys were interested in Lauren, Malcolm had been scrutinizing every player's interaction with her. The fact that he'd seen Darren with his hands on Lauren more than once sent his mind to a place it never should have gone. And he couldn't very well ask her what her conversations with the players were about. Some players have personal health and diet issues that they would confide in Lauren about and it would be a breach of confidentiality on her part to discuss them with Malcolm.

He pulled out his phone and sent her a text asking if he could still come by after practice.

It took twenty minutes for her to reply with a one-word answer: No!

His chest felt like a three-hundred-pound linebacker was standing on it and he could barely breathe. He started to send another text but changed his mind. Meanings easily got lost in transmission, so he needed to talk to face-to-face. But when? If he went to her office tomorrow, she would probably throw him out, and he didn't want to risk someone hearing something and reporting it back to management. Saturday after the walk-through, he would only have a few hours before he had to report to the hotel. All players were required to stay at a hotel the night before a home game. Truth be told, he should probably delay the confrontation until after Sunday's game. He would be expected to be in full game mode and couldn't afford the slightest distraction.

But he didn't want to wait that long. His father's words rang in his ears: *A woman hangs in there for a long time deciding what to do, but once she decides to leave, she's gone for good. Don't ever let her get to that point if you love her.* His heart almost stopped. He couldn't take the chance that Lauren might close the door on them forever. *That* he wouldn't be able to handle.

Chapter 19

Sunday morning, Lauren checked in with the staff at the stadium to make sure the pregame, halftime and postgame meals, as well as refueling snacks, were prepped and ready to go. There was a bevy of activity in the locker room as the players took advantage of the spread Nigel and his team had laid out. The variety of fish and lean meats, brown rice, pasta, and vegetables would be instrumental in keeping their energy up. There were also sports drinks, pretzels, bananas and the like for halftime and throughout the game. She wished the players good luck and made her way through the crowd.

Lauren spotted Malcolm on the far side of the room. After the text he'd sent her on Thursday, they'd had no contact. He followed her movements but made no attempt to approach, which suited her fine. She was angry and hurt but would never do anything to interfere with his ability to focus. Doing so could get him injured, and despite everything, that would break her heart further.

Omar came to where she stood. "How are you holding up, Lauren?" he asked quietly.

She tried to put up a good front, but it was useless.

"Well, the good news is Malcolm is just as broken up."

She didn't know how that qualified for good news. "Oh?"

"Yep. Gotta go."

Lauren hazarded a glance Malcolm's way and found him still watching her with an intensity that heated her insides. Cursing her body's reaction, she spun around and left.

"Hey, Lauren. Wait up."

Her steps slowed as Darren jogged to meet her. "Hey, Darren. Ready for your big game?"

"You'd better believe it. I just wanted to let you know my girl said yes. We're getting married."

"Congratulations," she said sincerely. "I wish you two all the happiness in the world."

"Thanks. Are you and Malcolm okay?"

They were nowhere near fine, but she waved him off. "Everything's fine. You just focus on winning this game," she added with a little laugh.

Darren nodded. Someone called his name. He held up a hand, signaling him to wait, then told Lauren, "See you around."

Lauren gave him a wave and continued to her seat. It was the longest three hours of her life. The only thing that kept her from going completely insane was the fact that she had to monitor the players' hydration and energy levels throughout the game. The Cobras easily defeated their opponent, but on more than one occasion, she found herself ensnared in those piercing light brown eyes. How Malcolm spotted her in a crowd of seventy thousand people, she would never know. Not wanting to get caught in the mass of people at the end, she opted to leave with five minutes left on the clock. She'd already made sure the postgame shakes were ready, and they would be served by Nigel's staff.

Back in the safety of her home, she curled up on the sofa and cradled a small pillow in her arms. This was so much harder than last time. The love she'd had for Malcolm in college in no way compared to the deep grown-up emotions she experienced now. She'd held off telling her parents and calling Valencia, because she didn't want to tell them she'd failed again. But she needed to talk to someone.

As if on cue, her doorbell rang, and she froze. *Please don't let it be Malcolm.* She slowly made her way to the door and checked the peephole. Lauren frowned. What was Siobhan doing here and how had she gotten Lauren's address? She opened the door and found not only Siobhan, but also Faith and Lexia standing there with wide smiles. "Um…hi."

"Hey, Lauren. We heard my brother made an ass of himself, so we came to check on you," Siobhan said bluntly.

Faith held up a bottle. "We brought wine."

"And food," Lexia said, producing a medium-size gift bag.

Smiling for the first time in three days, she moved back and waved them in. "How did you find out where I live?"

Siobhan dropped down onto the sofa. "I have my ways."

Lexia laughed. "Honey, this woman can talk her way into anything. You don't even realize you've given up information until she's gone."

"Ain't that the truth." Faith lifted her hand, and she and Lexia did a high five.

Siobhan rolled her eyes, but she was smiling.

"Well, since you all went to the trouble to bring food and wine, we might as well dig in." The women followed Lauren into the kitchen. She filled glasses with the wine while Lexia laid out shrimp tacos with a cilantro cream sauce on homemade corn tortillas. "Lexia, you made the tortillas?"

"Yes. They taste so much better."

"And that sauce is to die for." Siobhan placed three tacos on her plate and spooned on a generous helping of the sauce. "Girl, I'm so glad you added this to the menu at the café." She turned to Lauren. "In case you don't already know, Lexia owns the café on the first floor of the building where our company is located. Before she took over, the only thing safe to have in that place was the coffee... *maybe*."

They all burst out laughing and took their food into the living room.

"So, what did Malcolm do?" Faith asked.

Lauren took a sip of her wine and then told them about what he'd walked in on. "The guy was thanking me for helping him with his weight-loss goals, which is my job, and showing me the ring he planned to give his girlfriend."

"Did you tell him that?" Lexia asked around a mouth full of food.

"No, because I shouldn't have had to. We had just spent the entire night together, and for him to think I'd turn around and do something like that..." She released a deep sigh. She noticed they were all staring at her. "What?"

"He spent the night here? During football season?" Siobhan had a stunned look on her face.

"Um...yeah." To Lauren's surprise, Siobhan burst out laughing. "What?"

"Girl, he'll be back. That boy has never, and I mean *never*, spent a night with a woman during the season. Most times he ends up breaking up with whoever he's dating before the preseason is over because he claims the woman is too clingy and he needs to keep his head clear."

"I found that all the Gray brothers are alike, Lauren," Lexia said. "They may mess up, but they're fiercely loyal to those they love and will make it up in the end. Khalil swore that he would remain a bachelor forever, too." She smiled knowingly. "You see how that turned out."

Faith chuckled. "And Brandon is worse. My baby has a bad habit of sticking his foot in his mouth, but I love him. And he's doing much better keeping both feet on the ground. Just like his brothers, all Malcolm needs is a good woman, and he's found that in you."

Siobhan undoubtedly knew her brother well, and Faith and Lexia seemed to believe he'd come around, but Lauren wasn't so sure. Not when he couldn't get past his trust issues. Her heart clenched with the thought of not laughing with him, playing their special card game or indulging in a *kissgasm*. But she didn't want to spend the rest of her life on eggshells with him every time something came up, wondering if he saw her talking to another of his teammates, or some other athlete if she decided to branch out. No, the best thing would be for them to end it now.

Malcolm had no desire to stand through the postgame interviews on the field, in the locker room and at the podium, but he stood there and answered question after question almost by rote.

Just when he thought it was over, he heard a reporter call out, "One last question."

He zeroed in on the familiar face of a man who wrote for a local newspaper.

"Rumor has it that you're dating the team's new dietitian. Can you confirm that?"

"Mr. Duvall, the only thing I can tell you about Lauren Emerson is that she is a team player and she brings a wealth of knowledge and experience that has already transformed our dining room. You saw our performance on the field today. We eat to win." With nothing else to say, he stepped down, and the quarterback took his place.

Malcolm kept going until he reached his car. For the first time in his life, he needed to get away from the football field. When he saw Lauren in the locker room earlier, he'd had a hard time not rushing across the room, hauling her into his arms and kissing her until they both reached a kissgasm, as she'd termed it. But the hurt reflected in her eyes had rooted him to the spot and nearly torn him apart.

It didn't help that he'd heard murmurings in the locker room about Darren proposing to his longtime girlfriend, making him feel even worse.

He had no idea how to go about apologizing and asking for her forgiveness, but he had to find a way. Omar had asked him whether he could live the rest of his life without Lauren, and the answer was a resounding no.

It was after five when Malcolm pulled into his driveway. His cell buzzed. He put the car in Park and dug the phone out of his pocket to read the text from Omar.

Need ur help. Morgan in labor. Won't go to hospital until she finishes Madden.

He replied: On my way.

Malcolm parked the car in the garage and hopped on his motorcycle. It would be easier to maneuver through the traffic and keep him from losing his mind with worry. That, as well as taking the surface streets, turned out to be a smart move, and he made it to his sister's home in less than twenty minutes. He'd barely stopped the bike and turned it off before he jumped off and rushed up the walk.

Omar answered the door less than ten seconds after Malcolm took his finger off the button. "Thank God," he muttered. "Please come talk to your sister. I'm about to pull my hair out."

Morgan yelled from the back of the house, "Hurry up so you don't mess up my game."

Malcolm shook his head and followed Omar inside. Morgan was seated on the edge of the sofa, her fingers moving deftly on the controller and eyes focusing on the large screen. "Hey, sis."

Her gaze left the game briefly to glower at Omar. "I'm still not going until we finish this game. And don't even think about trying to let me win. If you do, we're playing again." She groaned and sucked in a sharp breath as another pain hit.

"Baby, we can play as many games as you want when you get home," Omar pleaded. "Please, let's go to the hospital."

"Not until the game is over," she said through clenched teeth, breathing harshly.

Malcolm turned to Omar. "How far apart are the contractions?"

"About seven minutes."

Malcolm noticed that they were playing at the all-Madden level—the top and most difficult level, where the player could control all aspects of the game. He'd taught his twin how to play the game and was probably the only one who could still beat her most times. He hunkered down next to her. "Morgan, I need you to listen to Omar. Neither one of us knows anything about delivering a baby, and I'm not having my nephew born on the floor." He predicted the baby would be a boy.

"We could be almost done by now if the two of you would stop talking and play the game."

He gestured for Omar's controller. "You mind if I take Omar's place?"

She snorted. "No. You're still not going to beat me."

He laughed. "Girl, I can beat you with my eyes closed." They still had two minutes left in the third quarter and the five-minute fourth quarter to finish. "I tell you what, if I can score two touchdowns in the next two minutes, you go to the hospital."

Morgan paused the game. "And if not?"

"Then we finish it."

"You're on."

Malcolm took a moment to sub out two players then directed his full attention to the television. Within forty seconds, he'd scored a touchdown.

"Lucky," she mumbled.

He just smiled. Her team made it down the field to the

twenty-yard line. When her quarterback took the snap, his defensive end was on him before the quarterback's arm went forward, stripping the ball. Another one of his players picked up the ball and ran it in for a touchdown. Malcolm tossed his controller on the sofa. "Let's go."

They got her into the car, and Omar gave Malcolm a grateful smile. "Thanks."

"I'm right behind you." He donned his helmet, started up his bike and pulled out behind Omar's silver BMW. He worried the entire drive, especially when he saw Morgan slump over on the seat through the window. They couldn't get to the hospital fast enough for him. When they arrived, Omar stopped in the circular driveway in front of the emergency room entrance, hopped out and went around to Morgan's side. "I'll park it. Just get her in."

Omar tossed Malcolm his keys. "Thanks."

Malcolm watched Omar ease Morgan out of the car and slowly lead her toward the entrance. After finding a nearby spot for his bike, he came back, moved Omar's car and nearly sprinted back to the entrance. Inside, his steps quickened down the hallway. He entered the room just as Morgan was being lowered into a wheelchair. He hurried over. It killed him to see her in pain, and as much as he wanted to go back with her, that responsibility belonged to Omar now. It must have shown on his face, because Omar asked if he wanted to accompany them. "No. Just keep me posted. Do you want me to call the family?"

"Please. My parents are probably at the restaurant." They owned a family-style restaurant named after Omar's mother in Buena Park.

He had his phone out and was already dialing. He started with his parents, then called the restaurant and spoke to Omar's mother. Next, he sent a mass text to his siblings. He figured they'd all be descending on the hospital within the hour. Malcolm found a seat in the corner and rested his head against the wall. His heart still beat at an erratic pace, and he regretted not taking Omar up on his offer. He checked his watch again for fifth time. He resumed his position and prayed it didn't take too long.

After what seemed like an hour, he checked the time. Only thirty minutes had gone by. Malcolm didn't realize he'd been drumming his fingers on the arm of the chair until he met the frown of a woman sitting opposite him.

Malcolm clasped his hands together and drew in a deep breath in an effort to calm his nerves. If he reacted this way with his sister, he'd be a basket case when it came to his own wife and child. His own. Immediately, his thoughts shifted to Lauren. He missed his sunshine. And that's what she'd always been to him, lighting the dark areas of his heart with her love. He'd give up everything to be able to hold her in his arms again.

"Malcolm." His mother hurried over to where he sat, and he came to his feet. "Any word?"

He hugged her and kissed her cheek. "Not yet. They've only been back there about forty-five minutes. Hey, Dad." They embraced.

"How are you holding up?"

Malcolm's entire family knew how close he and Morgan were, and it didn't surprise him that his dad had asked the question. "I'd like to say I'm okay, but my stomach is in knots."

His father chuckled. "Wait until it's your turn."

The knot in his stomach tightened.

His mother studied him. She reached up and palmed his face. "Things aren't well with you and Lauren, sweetheart?" she asked knowingly.

He covered her hand with his own. "No. I messed up and I don't know how to fix it," he confessed.

She smiled gently. "I'm sure it'll come to you when you let go of all your past hurts."

Malcolm just shook his head. He never understood how

mothers always knew everything. But she had a point. He had to let go. He just needed to figure out how.

Minutes later, Omar's parents, Brandon and Faith, Khalil and Lexia, and Siobhan entered. The grandparents huddled together while Malcolm's siblings surrounded him.

After a round of greetings, Siobhan asked, "How did you get here so fast? You had a game today."

"Omar texted me right when I got home because Morgan wouldn't let him take her to the hospital until they finished their *Madden* game." He relayed how they'd been able to get Morgan out of the house. His brothers laughed.

"That girl," Siobhan huffed.

Everyone found seats, and conversation flowed intermixed with periods of silence. Three hours passed with no word, and Malcolm could feel his control slipping. He had to know how Morgan was doing. He jumped up and began pacing, then sat back down. His mother told him to relax because babies came on their own timetable. He tried, but his anxiety levels climbed as the hours passed.

At 2:30 a.m., Omar burst into the waiting room with a wide grin, and they all rushed over, clamoring for information. He held up a hand and waited until they quieted. "We have a healthy seven-pound, two-ounce baby boy. Mom and baby are doing fine."

Malcolm breathed a sigh of relief.

"Can we see them?" Omar's mother asked.

"She's asking to see Malcolm first, then we can visit a couple at a time."

Malcolm's family wasn't surprised by the request, knowing the bond between the twins. He could hardly contain himself as rushed down the hall. He stuck his head in the door of her room. "Hey, little mama."

Morgan rolled her head in his direction and smiled tiredly. "Hey. Come see your nephew."

He took slow steps to her side and stared in awe at the tiny baby snuggled in her arms. She lifted her son and Malcolm carefully cradled him in his arms. A rush of emotions engulfed him. "He's a handsome little dude. Looks just like his uncle Malcolm."

She laughed softly. "Mmm-hmm."

"What's his name?"

"We're naming him after Omar."

He wondered how it would feel to have a son who carried his name.

"Omar told me how you messed up with Lauren. Fix it, Malcolm. She loves you."

He stared into the eyes that were mirrors of his own. Even after several hours of labor and delivering a baby, she was still worried about him. "I'm not sure how."

Morgan gave him another small smile. "It's easy. Tell her what's in your heart. Don't be afraid, big brother. It's worth it."

"I love you, sis." Malcolm bent and placed a soft kiss on her forehead, his emotions rising.

"I know. Now give me my baby and get out of here. You need to get some sleep so you figure out how to get my new sister to the altar."

He chuckled and handed the baby back. She gave his hand a reassuring squeeze and closed her eyes. He quietly tiptoed out. He still didn't know how to fix the mess that was now his life, but he'd figure it out. Or die trying.

Chapter 20

It took Malcolm three days to get the courage to approach Lauren. Though he preferred to talk to her away from the practice facility, he guessed his best chance of her not sending him packing or not even bothering to open the door would be to start the conversation at work. He ate a quick lunch then sought her out.

Her office door was open, but she wasn't there. Sighing with frustration, he walked over to her desk to leave a note. He stared out the window for a moment, contemplating what to write. Then he saw her. She was sitting on one of the benches near the walking trail. He remembered her telling him how much she enjoyed the peacefulness of the area. For a moment, Malcolm observed her. The love he felt for her filled his heart and nearly overwhelmed him. When she'd wanted to keep them a secret and he hadn't, she'd risked her career to show him her love. She had been acknowledging her mistakes and trying to rebuild the trust between them little by little since the first day he'd seen her. Another wave of guilt assailed him. Steeling himself, he pivoted and strode out. It was now or never.

Outside, Malcolm slowly approached. The late summer temperatures were still near ninety, but the tree-lined trail provided some shade and relief from the heat. The closer he came, the faster his heart beat. When Lauren noticed him, she stopped eating whatever she had in the bowl and waited. He fully expected her to bolt, but she held his gaze fearlessly. "Hi."

"Hi."

He gestured to the bench. "May I?"

Lauren hesitated briefly before saying, "Sure."

He lowered himself next to her but said nothing for the first few minutes, taking time to savor her nearness. Malcolm leaned forward, braced his forearms on his thighs and clasped his hands. "You were right."

"About?"

"Me still holding on to the past. I honestly thought I'd let go, but seeing Darren touching you in the dining hall and then the hug and ring…it made me lose my mind for a minute. Jealousy, plain and simple. It's not an excuse, but it's the truth."

He glanced over his shoulder and found her watching him intently. He straightened. "I'm sorry for hurting you, Lauren. For not trusting you." Malcolm shifted to face her. He turned her face toward his, and the tears standing in her eyes caused his heart rate to speed up. "I love you, Lauren. I always have, and I trust you with my life, baby." He wiped the tear coursing down her cheek with the pad of his thumb. "Can we talk tonight? I need you in my life, and you'll never have a reason to doubt me if you give me another chance."

He opened her hand and placed the familiar ring box in the center. "I promise. Text me and let me know if it's okay for me to come over tonight." Malcolm leaned over and kissed her, and the sweetness poured into his soul. Rising, he went back the way he'd come.

He slipped into a seat in the conference room as the lights dimmed and the film started. An hour later, the lights came back on and the coaches spent the next while discussing what had gone well, what could have been done better and what changes would be implemented for the upcoming game.

On the way out, Malcolm called out to Darren and asked him to wait a moment. It was something he should have done before now, but pride had stopped him.

"What's up, man?" Darren asked when Malcolm reached him.

"First I want to congratulate you on your engagement. I wish you all the best."

The younger man smiled. "I appreciate that."

"And I want to apologize for my behavior last week in Lauren's office."

He waved him off. "It's all good. I didn't know you and Lauren were tight like that. Are y'all all right?"

Malcolm wished he could say yes, but it had been two and a half hours and she had yet to text him. "I don't know."

Darren clapped him on the shoulder. "It will be. Just wait. Lauren is good people and so are you." He extended his hand.

Malcolm smiled and shook the proffered hand. "And so are you. Thanks, man." He watched Darren saunter off, feeling a load being lifted off his shoulders. He left to go to the running back meeting. Now, if only things could go as smoothly with Lauren.

Lauren clutched the box in her hand, afraid to open it. It couldn't be. Yet when she lifted the lid, it was the same promise ring he'd given her in college. And the same one she'd tossed back. That he'd kept it all these years surprised her. She'd thought for sure he would have returned it for a refund, but he hadn't. She held it against her heart, closed her eyes and let the tears fall. She loved him and had been miserable without him the past week.

Her eyes snapped open. *I love you, Lauren. I always have...* His words came back to her in a rush. He'd never stopped loving her, even when she'd stopped believing in them. The ring was proof of that.

Lauren wiped her face, packed up the remains of her lunch and went back to her office, taking a side trip to the bathroom to check her appearance. For the balance of the afternoon, she read articles on the newest health and fitness developments that might benefit the players, but her thoughts were never far from Malcolm. After having to read the same paragraph three times, she set the iPad on her desk and rotated her chair toward the window.

Malcolm's confession played over in her mind, as did her Sunday afternoon conversation with Siobhan, Faith and Lexia. Aside from Valencia—whom Lauren had finally talked to and who had encouraged her to listen to Malcolm if he attempted to talk to her—she didn't have any other close girlfriends. And she could see herself becoming good friends with them. She opened the side drawer on her desk and took out the ring box. Opening it, she ran her hand over the small solitaire sitting atop a thin white gold band.

"I know it's not very big, but it's my promise to you. When I get my first NFL check, I'll replace it with a real engagement ring."

"It's beautiful, Malcolm, and I don't care about the size. Just you."

Malcolm kissed her passionately. "I promise to love you forever."

"And I'll love you forever."

And she would. Lauren picked up her phone to text him but changed her mind. She had a better idea. She packed up and went to wait for him.

When Malcolm saw her leaning against his bike, his steps slowed.

"I thought I could say it better than a text."

The corner of his mouth kicked up in a smile. "And what are you saying?"

"I'm saying I want you to follow me home." Before she could blink, he banded an arm around her waist, lifted her off her feet and slanted his mouth over hers. The kiss was one they both had been seeking—healing, restoration and renewed commitment. "Does that mean you're coming?"

Malcolm lifted a brow.

Lauren realized what she'd said and shook her head. "You know what I mean."

His eyes glittered with passion. "You sure? I'm down for both."

Sparks of desire shot through her veins. "I'm going to my car." She turned on her heel and strode to her car, his joyful laughter trailing her. She couldn't stop the smile curving her lips.

With traffic, it took almost forty-five minutes to get to her condo. Once inside, Malcolm stood with his back braced against the door staring at her.

"Why are you looking at me like that?"

"Do you have any idea how much I missed you?" He straightened and came toward her. "How much I missed talking to you, laughing with you?" He touched his lips to hers. "Kissing you? I need to hold you for a while. Can I do that?"

"Yes," she whispered. When he wrapped his arms around her and held her close, she laid her head on his chest and listened to the sound of his strong heart beating in her ear. In his arms, she felt sheltered and loved, and she couldn't imagine being any place else. They stood in the middle of her living room for the longest time, neither of them speaking. No words were needed.

Finally, Malcolm released her and, taking her hand, led

her over to the sofa. He stretched out and pulled her on top of him. He idly ran a hand up and down her back. "I don't think I've ever been so afraid in my life. Even when I was waiting for my name to be called in the draft, I didn't have this fear. I'm never letting you go, Lauren."

Lauren lifted her head and met his eyes. "That's good, because I'm never letting you go, either, angel eyes." They shared a smile. They fell silent for a short while, then Lauren asked a question that had been on her mind. "What happened to Carlos? I haven't seen him around."

"He was released."

"Do you know why?"

"The coaches don't let us in on their decisions. There were others who got cut, as well."

"Oh."

"I have a bye in two weeks. Will you go away with me for the weekend?"

"Where are we going?"

A mysterious smile curved his lips. "It'll be a surprise. Will you trust me?"

She knew he was asking about more than just the trip. "Absolutely." She resumed her position with a smile. Lexia had been right. Although Malcolm had messed up, Lauren believed he would more than make up for it.

"You're still not going to tell me where we're going?" Lauren fussed, sitting next to Malcolm in one of the airport cafés. She'd been anticipating the getaway since he mentioned it two weeks ago. Apparently, all of the players were looking forward to having the few days off, if the way they'd practically run out of the practice facility yesterday after their Wednesday morning practice was any indication. She'd heard a few players mention that they planned to spend time with family, but a good number were doing the same thing she and Malcolm were doing.

Malcolm sipped from his bottle of water and smiled.

"You can't hide it forever. We've been sitting here for almost an hour. What if we miss the plane? Shouldn't we sit near the gate?" He had already printed the boarding passes but wouldn't let her see them. And because they only had carry-ons, they'd had no need to check anything.

He reached over and silenced her with a kiss. "Relax, sunshine. You know I've got you." He glanced down at his watch and stood. "Let's go."

She hopped up, listening for the flight calls. She heard three different ones and frowned.

He laughed and stroked a finger across her lips. "This is supposed to be a vacation, so stop pouting."

He held her hand as they passed one gate after another. He changed directions abruptly and pushed through a crowd. There were too many people for her to see the sign as he handed their boarding passes to the man at the gate and started down the Jetway. The Delta logo was the only thing she saw. "You can't just cut in front of all these people in line," she whispered, taking furtive glances over her shoulder.

"I'm not cutting in front of anyone, sweetheart. It's our time to board." Malcolm gestured for her to go in front of him.

Lauren took one step onto the plane, then stopped so abruptly he almost plowed into her. "Wait. That means we're sitting in first class?"

"Yes. You're first-class, baby. Where else would I have you sit?"

"You are such a wonderful sugar daddy."

He laughed. "Get on the plane, woman."

The flight attendant who had been viewing the exchange with mild amusement said as they passed, "Honey, I wish I had a sugar daddy like him."

Lauren smiled. She'd never flown first-class, but as she settled into the large, comfortable leather seat, she mused she could get used to it.

Once everyone boarded and the safety information was given, the flight attendant said, "Sit back, relax and enjoy the one-hour-and-fifteen-minute trip to San Jose."

Lauren whipped her head in Malcolm's direction. "San Jose?" She'd only been to the city once. "The last time we came…"

"I thought it only fitting that we go back to the place where we first made a commitment to each other."

She threw her arms around him and kissed him with an intensity that left him breathing hard. "I love you."

"I love you, too." Malcolm leaned close to her ear. "But if you kiss me like that again, no matter where we are, we aren't going to stop until I make you—"

She clapped a hand over his mouth and hastily glanced around, hoping no one heard. "You are outrageous."

"*Me?* I'm not the one making up words like *kissgasm*."

"*Shh!* Somebody's going to hear you."

He chuckled. "You started it with that kiss."

Thankfully, the flight attendant came to offer drinks at that moment. They spent the remainder of the short flight talking. She told him about the visit she'd had from Siobhan, Lexia and Faith, and he shared pictures of Morgan and Omar's new baby boy.

When the flight landed, they deplaned, picked up the rental Malcolm had reserved and made the one-hour drive to Monterey. Despite check-in not being until four, the reservation clerk at the hotel recognized Malcolm and allowed them to move into their room an hour early.

Lauren went straight for the balcony that overlooked the water. Malcolm came up behind her a short time later and held her. She leaned against him and covered his hands with hers. "Thank you for this."

"Thank you for giving me another chance to get it right."

Lauren had never been more content. They only had three nights, and she wanted to make each one count. The first night they ate at one of the hotel's restaurants. When they got back to the room, Malcolm helped her work on her book and, afterward, they played another one of their special card games.

Friday, he took her to the Monterey Bay Aquarium. She couldn't believe that they spent over three hours looking at all manner of sea life. Her favorite, by far, were the jellyfish. They drove to a park and walked around for a while. Then bought soft-serve ice cream cones, found a bench and sat by the water to enjoy them. The sun shone high in the sky, and the early October temperatures were in the low seventies, a ten-degree drop from LA.

Lauren leaned her head on his shoulder. "Can we stay here forever?"

Malcolm placed her arm around her. "I wish. This is going to have to hold us until the season is over. Though you'll still be working."

"Not as much. I can most likely do most of it by phone or email."

"How long is the lease on your condo?"

"A year. Why?"

He shrugged. "Curious."

She studied him, but his expression gave nothing away. Was he planning to ask her to move in with him? The only way she would do that was if they married, and he hadn't said anything that gave her any indication he was leaning toward that end. "What else do you have planned for this evening?"

"Nothing, besides dinner in about an hour and maybe another walk. Is there something you want to do?"

"No. I'm content just being here with you."

"Then we'll have to figure out a way to do this as often as possible."

After another few minutes, they went back to the hotel. She changed into the pink dress Valencia had talked her into getting when they had gone shopping. Malcolm changed into a pair of dark slacks and white dress shirt. They dined at Domenico's on the Wharf while watching the sun start its descent over the water. Lauren didn't think the night could get any better. She needed that second walk after eating so much. The crab-stuffed prawns were to die for.

Malcolm stopped the car at another stretch of beach, got out and came around to her side. "Are you okay to walk in your sandals?"

"If we're going to be on the sand, I'll take them off. It's not too cold."

"Okay." He took her hand, and they set off.

Halfway down the beach, she spotted what looked like a small house but realized as they came closer that it was a building where visitors could sit and enjoy the water. People could stand outside at the railing or sit inside when it was cooler. She climbed the steps and stood at the railing. The sky was an explosion of blues, oranges and reds, and palm trees swayed with the gentle breeze. Lauren turned and noticed that Malcolm still stood at the bottom. She walked over to the steps. "Are you going to join me?" Instead of answering, he took the steps two at a time until he stood on the one below her. He wore such a serious expression she started to worry. "Is something wrong?"

He lowered himself to one knee.

"Malcolm."

"Lauren, I have loved you since the first day you crossed my path in college. And even though we spent eight years apart, you've always had my heart. From this moment until I take my last breath, know that I will still be loving you, and only you. I promised you eight years ago that I would replace the promise with the real thing, and I'm here to make good on that promise, if you'll have me. Be my wife, baby, and complete my dreams."

He produced a black velvet box holding an emerald-cut solitaire—far bigger than the first one—with two rows of smaller emerald-cut diamonds flowing beneath it. Emotions clogged Lauren's throat for a moment, and she couldn't utter a word. She finally found her voice. "I would be honored to be your wife."

He removed the promise ring and replaced it with the engagement ring.

"Thank you for completing my dreams, too." There under the setting sun, they sealed their love with a kiss that promised forever. She couldn't wait to tell Valencia and her parents. Her dad was finally going to get those tickets.

Epilogue

Malcolm watched his beautiful wife of ten minutes smile and mingle with their guests and couldn't wait to get her alone. They had decided to get married right after the football season ended, when the Cobras had won the championship for the second time in three years. His mind went back the moment he'd spotted her while waiting in the gazebo that overlooked the mountains. She'd come to him on her father's arm in a sexy, strapless white creation that hugged the curves he loved so much. Her beauty had nearly knocked him to his knees.

"I can't believe all my babies are finally married. You and Lauren have made me so happy today. The family circle is complete. How long do I have to wait for grandbabies?"

Malcolm shook his head and chuckled. "Mom, you already have three, and with Lexia *and* Faith expecting, that'll be five. That's not enough to keep you busy for a while?" Even now as Malcolm stood listening to his mother, his eyes were following his stunning wife.

"Oh, I guess. And didn't Christian look so handsome and serious as the ring bearer?"

"He did." Christian fit in so well that it was as if he'd been born into the family. "I'm going to find my wife. Thanks for everything, Mom."

"Okay. I'm so proud of you." She patted his cheek and strutted off.

He made his way through the guests standing around talking while nibbling on the predinner appetizers and stopped to talk to his brothers and four cousins from Sacramento.

Cedric clapped him on the back. "I'm glad things worked out with you and Lauren, but now my mom is hounding me and Jeremy."

Jeremy took up the tale. "Yeah, she said, 'DeAnna has five children, and if they all can find spouses, surely the two of you can,'" he mimicked in falsetto.

Brandon and Khalil burst out laughing.

"Exactly," Lorenzo added.

Lorenzo's younger sister, Alicia, who had a two-year-old son and was eight months pregnant, shook her head. "Been there, done that. I'm done."

Malcolm wondered if something had happened, because she'd come to the wedding without her husband.

"Anyway," she said, coming up on tiptoe to kiss his cheek, "this is your day. Go find your beautiful wife."

He smiled. "I think I'll do that. Later." He spotted her talking to Valencia and made his way to her side. "Do you mind if I steal my lovely wife away for a minute, Lyn?"

Valencia smiled. "Not at all."

Lauren looked up at him, smiled and hooked her arm in his.

He led her to a secluded part of the garden. He'd been waiting all day to get her alone.

"What are you doing? We have guests."

"I needed a private place to kiss my wife."

Lauren's gaze flew to his. "I know you're not thinking…"

"Yep, that's exactly what I'm thinking."

"We can *not* do that here."

She started backing away, deeper into the garden, which was exactly where he wanted her. He closed the distance between them and kissed her possessively, his tongue sliding in and out of her mouth in a way that he knew would only have one result. He slowly gathered the material of her dress, lifting it higher and higher until he had it above her hips. He moved her skimpy lace panties to the side and pushed two fingers deep inside her, keeping rhythm with his tongue. Moments later, she flew apart in his arms, and a deep wave of satisfaction washed over him.

"I love you, angel eyes," she said, her body still trembling.

"I love you, sunshine." She was his first love. His last love. His only love. And from now until eternity, he'd still be loving her.

* * * * *

GIRL LEAST LIKELY
TO MARRY

AMY ANDREWS

To Aimee Carson, Heidi Rice and Kimberly Lang.

Thanks for the laughs, ladies – it was an absolute pleasure. Let's do it again some time!

PROLOGUE

*Ten years ago, Hillbrook University campus,
upstate New York...*

CASSIOPEIA BARCLAY TAPPED the rim of her wine glass to the other three. 'Of course it's not the end,' she said, looking around at her fellow flatmates. 'Of course it's just the beginning. Tonight may be our last night together but not for long. We've got the road trip coming up soon, remember?'

The women all nodded in agreement although trust fund princess Reese looked quickly away, throwing back a hefty slug of her champagne. Gina, the Brit, followed suit, knocking her drink back with practised gusto. Southern Belle Marnie sipped regally, her good manners always on display.

Denying her Australian roots, Cassie also sipped her drink. Not because of good manners, or in deference to the expensive Dom Perignon that Reese and her Park Avenue pay cheque gave them access to—Cassie couldn't care less if she was drinking Dom or Dr Pepper—but because everything she did was calm and measured and logical.

Why down champagne, posh or otherwise, when it only led to a hangover?

Her first ever hangover had been here in this house, with these three women, and she had no desire to repeat the experience. That was the ultimate definition of stupidity.

And Cassiopeia Barclay was far from stupid.

In fact with an IQ of one hundred and sixty-three she was officially a genius.

Their attention was returned to the nearby athletic field, in plain view of their deckchairs. The sky was starting its slow slide into evening but Hillbrook's male track team could still easily be made out as they went through a training drill. It was a regular ritual for the 'Awesome Foursome', as they'd been dubbed, and Cassie joined in because these three women had been her family, accepting her social inadequacies without question, and they enjoyed it.

But, try as she might, she didn't get the fascination with either sport or the men who played it. Most of them were no doubt here on some trumped-up scholarship and Cassie found that pretty annoying. Why was it that there was no money to support scientific research but somehow there was always cash for another track field?

Gina sighed as a particularly buff guy leaned over, touching his toes, exposing the backs of his legs, his shorts riding up to reveal a peek at one taut buttock. 'Now, *that* is a well put together arse,' she murmured, her British accent even more pronounced in this very American setting.

Marnie rolled her eyes. The blonde from the Deep South was as different from the Englishwoman as was possible. She was petite and perky, with an innocence about her that stuck out like a sore thumb next to Gina's brash sexuality. But Cassie had seen Marnie come out of her shell over the course of the year, much like her, and a lot of that was owed to Gina and Reese's differing but vibrant influences.

Reese smiled at Gina indulgently. She'd been doing that a lot this last week, Cassie realised belatedly. Smiling. Gina's assertion earlier that it had something to do with a certain Marine had been confirmed by Reese's startling confession that said Marine was *the one*.

Imagine that! After a week!

Sometimes Cassie felt like an alien in their midst, and it was nothing to do with her Australian accent. Even at nineteen they all seemed sophisticated women of the world next to her, introverted geek girl—Marnie included.

Reese had just dropped the bombshell that she'd fallen in love at first sight, Gina was slowly working her way through the entire eligible—and not so eligible—male population of the United States, and Marnie was sighing over her friend's big white virginal wedding.

It was utterly perplexing, but also interesting—from a behavioural science perspective. How much more could her friends achieve if they locked up their hormones and concentrated on their chosen careers like she had? Still, these three women had opened her up to a whole world that she hadn't been aware of before, and all new experiences were beneficial.

Back home in Australia she'd led a largely solitary existence. Either at home with her parents, shut in her room and absorbed in some research or other, or at university doing the same thing.

There'd been no girlfriends. *No boyfriends.* No late-night drinking or ogling track teams.

But here at Hillbrook her 'gal pals'—yes, according to Gina they *were* gal pals—hadn't taken her social awkwardness, lack of fashion sense or inept dancing as an excuse. They'd dragged her to nightclubs and frat parties, and to bars where they served cocktails by the jug and Karaoke was King. They'd loaned her dresses and shoes, done her makeup and styled her hair and, most importantly, they hadn't taken no for an answer.

She had a lot to thank them for. She would look back on her year in the US as a social experiment, with her as the subject, from which she had collected some very useful data.

'One day, Gina,' Reese said, interrupting Cassie's train of thought, 'you are going to fall hard and fast for some guy, and I hope I'm going to be there to tell you I told you so!'

Marnie raised her glass. 'Cheers to that,' she said.

Gina scoffed in her very English way with a toss of her glossy dark hair. 'To hell with that.'

The others laughed as they returned to their regularly scheduled programming—the track team. Cassie followed suit, smiling at Gina's running commentary but perplexed by it at the same time. She was deeply thankful that jocks did nothing for her and that she was far too rational to be swayed by hormones.

Sure, as a scientist she understood that human beings were under the influence of their biological imperative to mate, but she also believed in head over heart. Certainly Gina wouldn't be in the quandary she was now if she'd been thinking with her brain instead of her ovaries.

Sleeping with Marnie's brother Carter last week had really rattled Gina. Cassie was generally fairly oblivious to nuances, but she'd have had to be deaf, dumb and blind to miss Gina's edginess. Quite why Gina was edgy Cassie had no idea. What was done was done. And it wasn't Gina who was engaged to be married, was it?

Which was exactly what she'd told Gina when she'd confessed the transgression to her last week and Gina had sworn her to secrecy.

It was at times like this that Cassie was glad she'd vowed never to fall victim to love. How could she when she simply didn't believe in it? And, even if she did, she didn't have time for the messy, illogical minefield of it all. Not while there was a big universe to study which was infinitely more fascinating than any man.

A shout of triumph from the track brought Cassie back into the conversation flowing around her.

'Mmm, that's right, my lovely blond Adonis.' Gina's commentary continued. 'Give your mate a hug, then.' The men complied, as if Gina had yanked their strings. 'Ding-dong,' she cooed on a happy sigh, and Marnie and Reese laughed.

Cassie watched the display of male camaraderie, rolling her eyes as they high-fived and man-hugged. They reminded her of gorillas. Next they'd be beating their chests and picking nits off each other. One thing was for sure: should she ever drop a hundred IQ points and end up with some man he would never be of the jock variety.

'Tell us about the stars, Cassie.'

Cassie glanced over at Marnie, whose head was dropped over the back of her chair as she pointed to the first star just visible in the sky. 'That's Venus, right...evening star?'

Cassie smiled. Marnie was forever talking about the night skies over Savannah and had loved having her own personal astronomer at her beck and call. 'Yep,' she confirmed, looking at the pinprick of light in the velvet sky.

'Will we be able to see Cassiopeia tonight?' she asked.

Cassie shook her head. 'It's too light here. When we're on our road trip we'll stop at the Barringer Crater in Arizona. We'll sleep under the stars and I'll show you then.'

It was the main reason Cassie was going on the trip. Time with her gal pals would be great, but she'd always wanted to see the crater site formed when a meteorite had ploughed into the earth fifty thousand years ago, and that was her priority.

'You speak for yourself,' Gina butted in. 'The only stars the Park Avenue Princess and I are sleeping under are of the five-star variety. Isn't that right, Reese?'

Reese nodded. 'Er...yes,' she said, looking quickly away and taking another decent slug of her champers.

'Carter proposed to Missy under the stars at the Grand Canyon. Isn't that romantic?' she said, her voice dreamy. 'Our families were on holiday together. Missy and I stayed up all night talking about how wonderful it was.'

'Bless their hearts,' Gina said, mimicking Marnie's Southern drawl.

It had taken Cassie a few months of Gina teasing Marnie over the quaint Southern phrase to realise it could be used to mock as well as to sweeten. Glancing at Gina's tense profile, she guessed this was one of the mocking times.

'Missy wants a star theme running through the reception,' Marnie continued ignoring Gina's sarcasm. 'She's spending a small fortune on this gorgeous black drapery that billows from the ceiling and twinkles with thousands of tiny lights…'

Cassie didn't really understand why you'd spend good money on creating the illusion of a starry sky when the real thing was up there for free. It certainly didn't seem to be very effective budgeting. But weddings were as much a mystery to her as the notion of love, so she gave up trying to figure it out.

She was just going to lounge here with her friends and watch the stars come out.

One last time.

CHAPTER ONE

A decade on...

CASSIOPEIA WATCHED TUCK...whatever his last name was...of quarterback fame swagger in the general direction of their table with his long, loose-limbed gait. Somehow his big, blond athleticism seemed to dominate the vast expanse of the open tent, with its delicate swathes of royal blue draped across the ceilings and trailing gently to the deck. But then she had a feeling he'd probably dominate any setting.

He made slow progress. Men stopped him to slap him on the back and shake his hand. Women stopped him to bat their eyelashes and put their hands on him. He took both in his stride, shrugging off their adoration with a wide, easy *Shucks, I ain't nuthin'* grin. The man was so laid-back Cassie was surprised he managed to stay vertical.

Very different from the man she'd watched only yesterday playing a very physical game of one-on-one basketball with Reese's ex-Marine ex-husband Mason.

Reese had left the party that had originally been intended to be her wedding to Dylan to go after Mason, but her instructions to the remaining members of the Awesome Foursome had been clear—make sure no one gets into a fight.

Reese had deliberately sat Tuck, the jilted groom's best

man, next to her—away from Gina—to prevent such a calamity.

With Tuck firmly on Team Dylan and Gina, whose favourite pastime was baiting people, on Team Reese, Cassie could already tell it was going to be a long night.

'He sure is pretty,' Gina murmured with relish as she tracked his progress.

A very long night.

Cassie didn't really see the attraction. But then she'd never been a slave to her hormones. She just wasn't programmed that way.

Sure, Tuck Whats-his-name had all the features that the female of the species looked for in a mate. He was tall, broad-shouldered, narrow-hipped. She couldn't see the delineation of the muscles in his chest tonight, although they were obviously there beneath his charcoal suit. She knew from his shirtless one-on-one yesterday that they were plentiful and very well developed.

And, in the animal world, muscles equalled strength.

Another biological tick in his favour.

There was also the symmetry of his face. Square jaw, prominent cheekbones, nose, chin and forehead all proportional. Eyes evenly spaced. Lips perfectly aligned. Facial symmetry was one of the big markers of physical attraction and worthiness for mating, and Tuck had it in spades.

But Cassie still didn't get it.

'I have to go to the bathroom,' she said, turning to Gina. 'Try not to get into a fight with him while I'm gone. Remember, Reese is counting on us.'

'I'll be on my best behaviour,' Gina assured her.

If Cassie had been better at picking up sarcasm she wouldn't have been assured one iota, but she nodded, satisfied.

'Here—reapply,' Gina said, reaching into her clutch purse

and pulling out the deep mulberry lipstick she'd slathered on Cassie's mouth earlier.

Cassie frowned. 'Why?'

'Because.' Gina sighed. 'That's the price of wearing lippy.' She waggled the item at her friend, who was looking at it as if it were a foreign object she'd never seen before. 'Beauty is pain.'

Cassie smiled at the old catchphrase. *Beauty is pain.* She'd learned many things about being a woman under Gina's tutelage. Gina could wear a pair of killer stilettos out clubbing all night without a single wince. Cassie had pretty much forgotten everything in the intervening decade, but she'd never forgotten how Gina had taken her under her wing—as if she were an Antipodean Eliza Doolittle.

Of course Cassie had failed 'Female 101' resoundingly, but Gina had been sweet and patient and there was just something about her vibrant personality that drew people. Cassie and Gina had stayed in contact despite the wedge that had been driven between the Awesome Foursome after Gina had thrown her one-night stand with Carter in Marnie's face that fateful last night together ten years ago.

And now, a decade down the track, Gina was still looking out for her in the fashion stakes. Gina had taken one look at the shapeless maxi-dress Cassie had been going to wear and declared it an unnatural disaster. Before Cassie had known it she was swathed in soft grape fabric with no sleeves, a plunging crossover neckline, a ruched form-fitting waist and an A-line skirt, the hem of which fluttered just below her knees.

Her straight brown hair had been freed from its regulation floral scrunchie and loosely curled. Sparkly, strappy kitten heels had been supplied. A subtle hand had seen to eyeshadow and mascara. Lipstick had been brandished with gusto.

'Reapply,' Gina repeated.

Bowing to a greater knowledge, Cassie took the lipstick as instructed and departed.

Tuck pulled up at the table he'd been allocated a minute later. His knee ached but he ignored it in deference to the sultry sex goddess with raven hair. She was dressed in something red and clingy, sitting there looking up at him with a smile on her full mouth. A connoisseur of women from way back, he liked what he saw.

He shot her one of his killer smiles. He knew they were killer because an article about him in *Cosmo* had spent an entire paragraph talking about the sheer wickedness of his smile.

'Well this here may just be my lucky night,' he drawled, deliberately dragging out his vowels, plying her with all his Southern charm. His accent had been blunted over the years, with travel and living far from his Texan roots, but he could still pull it out when required.

According to the magazines, women just loved all that Southern country-boy charisma.

Gina quirked an elegantly arched eyebrow. 'Oh, yes? Do tell,' she murmured.

'Ah, you're the Brit.' He grinned. 'Gina, right?'

She nodded. 'And you're the quarterback.'

Tuck checked the closest handwritten place card on the table, disappointed to see that he was sitting directly opposite this sexy Englishwoman. He held it up and looked at her. 'What say we switch this one for whoever's supposed to be sitting next to you?'

'Hmm…' Gina placed her elbows on the table, propping her chin on one palm, pretending to think. 'I think Reese meant to keep you and I apart.'

Tuck shot her his best wounded look. 'And why would she want to do that?'

'I think she was afraid you and I might come to blows.'

He continued his *faux* outrage. 'Over what?'

'Over her recent…shall we say…split from the groom. *Your* best friend?'

'Ah. Well, now, if Dylan's unconcerned then there's no good in me holding a grudge, is there? Besides,' Tuck said, pulling out his chair and sitting, his knee protesting at the movement, 'I can flirt just as well from this side.'

Gina laughed. She couldn't help herself. The big blond quarterback had an ego the size of North America. 'You're *that* good, huh?'

'Darlin', I am *the* best.'

Gina spied Cassie in the distance, making her way back to the table. She flicked her gaze to Tuck. It would be good to see him brought down a notch or two. 'Works every time, huh?'

Tuck grinned at the sudden sparkle of light he could see in her eyes. '*Every* time.'

'No one's immune to your charm?'

Tuck shook his head. 'Women love me. If they're female and breathing…' He shrugged, then dazzled her with another wide smile. 'What can I say? I have a gift.'

Gina smiled back. He really was an exceedingly good-looking man, and his cast-iron confidence only added to his allure. It was a shame she wasn't in the right frame of mind for a dalliance because she had an idea a night in bed with Tuck would be a great way to forget how badly she'd stuffed up all those years ago.

But her heart wasn't in it.

Just then the DJ played his first number for the night and Tuck pressed home the advantage. 'Ah, they're playing our song,' he teased. 'How about we knock off the pretence and you just dance with me, Gina?'

Gina considered him a moment, aware of Cassie drawing closer all the time behind Tuck's head. 'Nah, getting me to dance would be too easy. Care to take a little wager?'

Tuck smiled at her. A woman who liked to gamble—better and better. He leaned forward. 'I'm all ears.'

'I bet you can't get her—' Gina nodded her head to indicate Cassie '—to dance.'

Tuck turned in his chair to see who Gina had in mind for him. A woman about the same age as Gina in some kind of purple dress was walking towards them. She had long dark brown hair arranged in loose ringlets that fell forward over nice bare shoulders. She had a cute nose, pretty eyes and an interesting mouth, and she was walking along seemingly oblivious to her surroundings, a slight frown marring her forehead as if her thoughts were somewhere else.

She was no English sex kitten, that was for sure.

She didn't look like the average gridiron groupie either. Still, she was female, and Tuck had always liked a challenge. He turned back and smiled at Gina. 'Piece of cake.'

Gina laughed. 'Oh, this is going to be good.'

Tuck raised an eyebrow. 'What do I get? When I win?'

Gina smiled. 'The pleasure of Cassie's company, of course.'

Tuck inclined his head. 'Of course.'

Despite her earlier concerns about leaving Gina and Tuck together, Cassie had given it little thought in the fifteen minutes she'd been away. Her brain had been mulling over the findings of an astronomy research paper she'd read last night. She'd even applied the lipstick as ordered by Gina without conscious thought as she recalled the fascinating data.

She was surprised for a moment when she arrived back at the table to find Tuck Whats-his-name sitting there with Gina, apparently getting along just fine. She slotted the research into a file in her head and shut it down with a mental mouse click.

'Everything okay here?' she asked.

Tuck took a deep breath, then stood and used one of his very best *hey-baby* smiles on Cassie. 'Hi,' he said. 'I'm Reese's cousin, Tuck.' He stuck out his hand. 'It's mighty fine to meet you, ma'am.'

Cassie blinked up at him as he towered over her. Two things struck her at once. The man smelled incredible. Her nostrils flared as her senses filled up with him. And it wasn't his cologne, because she was pretty sure she couldn't smell anything artificial at all. Maybe a hint of soap or deodorant.

This was much rawer. More primal. Powerful. Overpowering, even. It made her want to press her nose to his shirt and inhale him. It *demanded* that she do so and she had to actually put her hands on the chair-back to stop herself.

So this was pheromones.

Scientists had known of their existence for decades, and perfume companies around the world had been trying to perfect them for just as long, but this man exuded it in hot, sticky waves.

Her salivary glands went into hyper-drive and she swallowed as she grappled with the urge to sniff him.

The second thing was his eyes. They were an intense, startling blue. The exact shade of an exploding star she'd once seen through the lens of a deep space telescope. They were out of this world. They were cosmic. Captivating.

Tuck looked into Cassie's upturned face. She was staring at him, her lips slightly parted, the sound of her breath husky in his ears. He glanced at Gina and grinned.

Piece of cake.

'Ma'am?'

Cassie dragged herself back from the universe she could see in his eyes, his intoxicating scent still singing to her like a Siren from the rocks. 'Oh, yes…sorry.' She shook her head. What had he said? Name. He'd introduced himself. 'I'm Cassie,' she said. 'Cassiopeia.'

And then she made the mistake of slipping her hand into his and his pheromones tugged at her—hard.

'So you're the geek,' he said softly, smiling at her.

Another dizzying wave of male animal wafted over her and it took a moment for Cassie's brain to clear the fog.

Yes, she was the geek. And he was the jock. She had him by a good sixty IQ points—probably more. She didn't get stupid around men. She didn't get stupid, period!

So start acting like it!

She pulled her hand from his abruptly. 'And you're the *jock,*' she said, as much to remind herself as a statement of fact.

Tuck refused to be offended. He shot Gina a *faux* insulted look. 'Why do I get the feeling that Cassie isn't fond of jocks?'

Gina lifted a shoulder. 'Don't take it personally. Cassie's not fond of men generally.' He shot her a look and she cut him off before he gave voice to what she knew he was thinking. 'Not women, either.'

Tuck grinned, then turned his attention back to Cassie. Okay, so he had his work cut out for him. His momma always said things came too damn easy to him anyway. Her eyes were even prettier up close. A grey-blue, like a misty lake, with subtle charcoal and silver eyeshadow bringing out both colours perfectly.

He nodded at her place card on the table next to his and said, 'Looks like I have the whole night to change your mind.' Then he pulled out her chair and smiled at her.

Cassie didn't move for a moment. She simply stared at him as the deep modulation of his voice joined forces with his heady scent to drench every cell in her body with a sexual malaise. Her nipples beading against the fabric of the flimsy dress Gina had loaned her snapped her out of it.

'I usually require several pieces of evidence from trusted sources before I change my mind about anything,' she said primly, taking the seat.

'Noted,' Tuck murmured, stifling a grin as he took his seat. He lounged back in it, regarding Cassie as she fiddled with her cutlery. 'So, you don't sound like you're from around these here parts,' he said.

'No.' Cassie refused to elaborate. Just because Reese thought it was a good idea to sit them together, it didn't mean she had to be agreeable.

Gina rolled her eyes and took pity on Tuck. 'Cassie's Australian.'

'Ah. Whereabouts? Sydney? That's one pretty little city you have there,' he said.

'Canberra,' Cassie said as she ran her finger up and down the flat of her knife. 'It's the capital,' she added. A lot of people didn't realise that.

And he *was* a jock.

'Well, now,' he said, leaning forward in his chair, his gaze acknowledging Gina before returning to Cassie, 'we can have us a meeting of the United Nations.'

'Hardly,' Cassie said, desperately trying to sit as far back in her chair as possible and remember that he was a jock— a *footballer*—even if he did have pheromones so potent he should be being studied at the Smithsonian. Or milked and sold to the highest-bidding perfume manufacturer.

'There are one hundred and ninety-three member states in the United Nations. And they meet in Geneva.' She looked at Tuck. Jocks weren't very good with geography. 'That's in Switzerland.'

Tuck raised an eyebrow. He was used to people making assumptions about his intelligence. Truth be told, he played up to them mostly—because calling people on their ignorance was usually an amusing way to pass the time.

It looked as if he was going to have a whole lot of fun with Cassie. 'That's just north of Ireland, right?'

Cassie pursed her lips. 'It's in Europe.'

'Europe? *Dang*,' Tuck said, broadening his accent. 'I'm always getting them muddled up.'

'Of course if you're talking about the Security Council,' Cassie plunged on, as the deep twang in his accent twanged some invisible strings low down inside her she'd never known existed, 'that's in New York. And you'd be in luck as Australia has just scored a seat on the Security Council.'

Tuck shot a look at Gina, who winked and grinned, clearly enjoying herself. Tuck was about to say something like, *They wear those funny blue helmets at the Security Council, right?* But the imperious tones of his and Reese's Great-Aunt Ada interrupted.

'Samuel Tucker,' she said in her brash, booming New York accent. 'How'd you sneak in here undetected?'

Tuck stood and smiled down at the self-appointed matriarch of the family. A died-in-the-wool Yankee, she liked to pretend that the Southern branch didn't exist most of the time, but he had a soft spot for the sharp-tongued octogenarian.

'Aunt Ada,' he said, sweeping her up in his arms for a hearty hug. 'Still as pretty as a picture, I see.'

Cassie felt herself sag a little as Tuck and his overwhelming masculinity gave her some breathing space.

'Don't sweet-talk me, young man. What are you doing all the way over here?'

Tuck gestured to the table. 'I'm keeping Reese's friends company.'

'Reese…' Ada tutted. 'Running off after that Marine… That girl hasn't got the sense she was born with…lucky she's my favourite.'

'Now, come on, Aunt Ada,' Tuck teased. 'I thought *I* was your favourite.' Ada gave him a playful pat on the shoulder, then lifted one gnarled old hand and squeezed his cheek.

Gina's mobile rang and she almost ignored it. She couldn't decide what was more fascinating—the big blond quarterback sweet-talking an old lady or Cassie's deer-in-the-headlights face. But it rang insistently, and Ada turned to her, looking imperiously down her nose.

'Well, girl, are you going to answer that or not?'

Gina, recognising authority when she saw it, picked it up immediately. The screen display flashed a familiar number. 'It's Reese,' she announced.

'Reese.' Ada tutted again. 'Tell her to get back here. This non-wedding party was *her* hare-brained idea.'

Gina laughed, but as she answered the phone Ada's interest had already wandered.

Cassie felt her shrewd gaze next.

'This your girl?' she said, turning to Tuck.

'Absolutely not,' Cassie said indignantly.

Then Tuck undid his jacket button and it fell open, wafting a heady dose of pheromones her way. She shut her eyes briefly as her pulse spiked in primal response.

'She's not your usual type,' Ada said, ignoring Cassie's denial.

'I am *not* his girl,' Cassie repeated, even though she could practically hear every cell calling his name.

'It's okay,' Ada assured her. 'I hate his usual type. Too... fussy.'

Tuck looked down at Cassie. She was frowning at him, her eyebrows weren't plucked, and she wasn't wearing a single scrap of jewellery. No one in the world would have described her as fussy. And yet there was something rather intriguing about her...

'We are *not* together,' Cassie reiterated. The thought was utterly preposterous.

'Reese says she and Mason aren't coming back tonight,' Gina announced as she terminated the phone call, interrupting the conversation.

'Right, then,' Ada said. 'Looks like we have a show to be getting on with. Samuel, go and tell that dreadful DJ to announce dinner. I'll get the wait staff to start serving.'

The three of them watched her sweep away. 'Wow,' Gina said. 'She's scary.'

Tuck grinned. 'Hell, yeah. Excuse me, Gina, Cassiopeia.' He dropped his voice an octave, then bowed at her slightly, finding and holding her gaze. 'Keep my seat warm, darlin', I won't be long.'

Cassie gaped as his cosmic blue eyes pierced her to the spot and his voice washed over her in tidal wave of heat.

Gina's low throaty laughter barely registered.

Two hours later Cassie was strung so tight every muscle was screaming at her. Tuck was holding court at the table, charming all and sundry.

Big, warm-blooded, male and there.

A giant sex gland, emitting a chemical compound her body was, *apparently,* biologically programmed to crave.

Him. A *jock.* Why *him?*

Every time their arms brushed or his thigh pressed briefly along hers her pulse spiked, her hands shook a little. And when he laughed in that whole body way of his, which he did frequently, throwing his head back, baring the heavy thud of his jugular to her gaze, her nostrils flared and filled with the thick, luscious scent of him.

An insistent voice whispered through her head, pounded through her blood. *Smell him. Lick him. Touch him.* With every tick of the clock, every beat of her heart, it grew louder.

It was insane. Madness.

This sort of thing didn't happen to her. Hormones. Primal imperatives. She was above bodily urges. Her head always—*always*—ruled her body.

But here she was, just like the rest of the human race, at the mercy of biology.

It just didn't compute.

The man was as dumb as a rock. He'd thought they were talking about food when she'd mentioned Pi. He'd called a truly amazing piece of equipment unlocking the secrets of the universe the *Hobble* telescope. He didn't even know the Vice-President of his own country.

He was a Neanderthal.

But still every nerve in her body twitched in a state of complete excitement.

Cassie desperately tried to recall the aurora research waiting in her room—the research she'd been looking forward to getting back to at the end of the night. When was the last time she'd gone two hours without thinking about it? She'd been working on the project for five years. She ate, slept, breathed it.

And for two whole hours it had been the *furthest* thing from her mind.

Marnie laughed at something Tuck said, dragging Cassie's attention back to the big blond caveman by her side. She checked her watch—was it too early to leave? She wasn't used to feeling this out of her depth. Sure, social situations weren't her forte but this was plain torture. If she could get back to her room and the comfort of the familiar Tuck and the awful persistent thrum in her blood would surely fade to black.

She glanced up at Gina, who shook her head and mouthed, 'Don't even think of it.'

Cassie sighed, resigned to her fate, as the raunchy strains of

Sweet Home Alabama blasted around them. Marnie whooped and leapt up to dance along with a few others from the table.

Tuck looked across at Gina and winked. He stood and looked down at the woman who had sat beside him for two hours as if she was afraid his particular brand of stupid was contagious. Didn't she *know* he was God's gift to women?

He grinned as he held out his hand towards her. 'What do you say, Cassiopeia? Fancy a dance?'

Cassie stared at his hand. It was big, and she swore she could see waves of whatever the hell he was emitting undulating seductively from his palm. 'Oh, no.' She shook her head. 'I don't dance.'

Tuck hadn't got to where he was today by giving up at the first hurdle. He kept his hand where it was. 'It's not hard, darlin',' he murmured. 'Just hang on and follow my lead.'

Cassie swallowed. That was what she was afraid of. She had a very bad feeling she'd follow that intoxicating scent anywhere. She shook her head again and looked at him. A bad move as his cosmic gaze sucked her in closer to his orbit.

'I'm a terrible dancer,' she said. She dragged her gaze from him. 'Isn't that right, Gina?'

Gina nodded. Cassie had no rhythm at all. 'She speaks the truth. But...' She looked at Tuck, then at Cassie. Her Antipodean friend looked as if she'd rather face a firing squad then dance with Tuck. *Interesting.* She'd never seen Cassie so ruffled and, bet or no bet, she wanted to see where this went.

'I think every woman should dance with a star quarterback once in her life,' Gina said.

Tuck raised an eyebrow at her as Gina conceded the bet to him.

'Ex,' Cassie said. And when Gina looked at her enquiringly she clarified, 'He's an ex...quarterback.'

Gina drummed her fingers on the table. 'You know, it *is*

customary at weddings for the bridesmaids to dance with the groomsmen,' she pointed out.

Gina had taken it upon herself to be Cassie's social guru during the year they'd roomed together, and Cassie had learned a lot about social mores that no textbook could ever have taught her. But she was big on survival instincts, and Cassie was pretty sure staying away from Tuck was the smart thing to do.

And she was very smart.

Even if she was rapidly dropping IQ points every time she looked at him.

'But this is the wedding-that-wasn't,' she pointed out, striving for the brisk logic she was known for. 'We are the bridal-party-that-wasn't. Surely that cancels out societal expectations?'

Tuck waggled the fingers of his still outstretched hand at her. 'I think it's important to keep up appearances, though,' he said. 'These Park Avenue types are big on that.'

Cassie looked away from the lure of those fingers at Gina, who nodded at her and said, 'He's right. You wouldn't want to embarrass Reese, would you? It's okay,' she assured her. 'Tuck looks like he knows what he's doing.'

Tuck grinned, but he didn't take his eyes off Cassie. 'Yes, ma'am.'

Cassie glanced back at him, towering over her in all his intoxicating temptation. Maybe a dance would help. Maybe if she got the chance to sniff him a little this unnatural craving taking over her body, infecting her brain like a plague of boils, would be satisfied. That seemed logical.

Cassie slipped her hand into his.

And her cells roared to life.

CHAPTER TWO

BY THE TIME they got to the dance floor the last notes of *Sweet Home Alabama* had died out and the music had changed to a slow Righteous Brothers' melody. All the couples that had been boogying energetically melted into each other and the singles left the floor. Cassie turned to go as well, but Tuck grabbed her hand and pulled her in close, grinning at her.

'Where are you going, darlin'?'

Cassie's breath felt like thick fog in her throat. 'I…can't waltz.'

She found it hard enough co-ordinating her hands and feet with some space between her and her dancing partners. She was going to do some damage to his feet for sure.

And she did not trust herself too close to him.

'Sure you can. Just hold on,' he said, taking her resisting hands and placing them on his pecs, 'and shuffle your feet a little. There ain't no dance police here tonight.'

Cassie didn't hear his crack about dance police. Her palms were filled with hard firm muscle as the fabric seemed to melt away. The music melted away too—as did the people crowding around them.

She couldn't take her eyes off the sight of her hands on his chest.

Tuck smiled to himself. 'There you go—see.' He took a step closer, his chin brushing the top of her head. He slipped his hands lightly onto her waist. There was definite curve there and he snuggled his palm into it. 'I don't bite.'

Cassie fought through the fog, dragging her eyes away from how small her hands looked in comparison to his broadness. She looked up. Way up. He was tall. And close. A handwidth away, she guessed.

Before tonight she would have been able to assess the distance accurately, but she simply couldn't think straight at the moment. He was radiating heat and energy and those damn pheromones, totally scrambling her usual focus. His hands at her waist were burning a tract right down to her middle.

He smiled at her, his starburst eyes showering their effervescence all over her. She looked down, but that was a mistake also as his chest filled her vision, the knot of his tie swaying hypnotically in front of her with every movement of his body. And all the time an insistent whisper played in her head, swarmed through her blood in time with the swing of him.

Smell him, lick him, touch him.

She dragged her gaze upwards, desperate to stop the pull of the hypnotic rhythm. It snagged on the slow, steady bound of his carotid, his growth of whiskers not able to conceal the thick thud of it. She wondered what he'd smell like there. What he'd taste like.

Her nostrils flared. Her breath grew thick. She dug her fingers into the flat of his chest as she battled the urge to take a step closer.

Dear God, she was growing dumber by the second.

Shocked and dazed, she dragged her gaze down. Way down. Down to their feet. Down to the hole she wished would open up.

Tuck also looked down, frowning at how rigid she felt in his arms. As if she was going to shatter at any moment. Or going to bolt at any second. No woman had ever been so reluctant to be in his company. Or so keen to be away from it.

She could give a man a complex.

One thing was for sure. She needed to relax or she was going to have a seizure. 'So...Cassiopeia? That's not a name you hear every day. Is that a family tradition?'

Cassie looked up. His eyes flashed at her and she lost her breath for a moment. Were they closer? He seemed nearer. More potent. His chest was closer.

'Cassie?'

She blinked. What? Oh, yes. Talking. That was good. She was good at talking. Usually...

'My mum...she named me. After the constellation.' She paused. Did he even know what that was? 'That's a group of stars,' she clarified.

Tuck chuckled. This woman was going to give him a complex. Who'd have thought he'd be interested in such a little snob? The endearing thing was she seemed oblivious to it all. 'Like the Zodiac?' he enquired, purposefully broadening his accent again.

Cassie gaped at him. How could she possibly want to lick the neck of a man with a pea-sized intellect?

There was just no accounting for biology.

'No, *not* like the Zodiac.'

He feigned a frown. 'Ain't you into astrology?'

'Astronomy,' she said, gritting her teeth. *'A-stron-omy.'*

'So, that's not like...Sagittarius and stuff?'

'No,' she said primly. 'It's the study of celestial objects. It's *science*. Not voodoo.'

Tuck laughed again. He liked it when she got all passionate and fired up. There was a spark in those blue-grey eyes, a glitter. Would they get like that when she was all passionate and fired up in bed?

Suddenly it seemed like something he wouldn't mind knowing.

The song ended and the pace picked up a little. A couple behind them bumped into Cassie and she stumbled and stood on his foot. 'Oh, God, sorry,' she gasped, pulling away as her front collided with his.

His broad, muscular front.

'Hey, there, it's okay,' Tuck said, steadying her under her elbows, holding on as she tried to pull away, keeping her close. Their bodies were almost—but not quite—touching. 'No harm done,' he said, smiling at her. 'Why don't you just lay your head here on my chest and stay awhile longer?'

She should tell him to go to hell. But her nostrils flared again as something primal inside her recognised him as male. And he smelled so damn good.

A whisper ran through her head. *Do it.*

Lay your head down. Shut your eyes. Press your nose into his chest.

Cassie fought against the powerful urge as long as she could but she was losing fast. Each sway of his body bathed her in his *eau-du*-male scent and before she knew it her cheek had brushed against the fabric of his jacket and was angled slightly, her nose pressed into his lapel.

She inhaled. Deep and long. Every cell was filled with him. Every tastebud went into rapture. Every brain synapse went into a frenzy.

It was so damn good she never wanted to exhale.

It was only the dizzying approach of hypoxia that forced her hand. She quickly breathed out, then took in another huge greedy gulp of him. His scent seduced her senses, stroked along her belly, unfurled through her bloodstream.

She pressed herself a little closer and her eyes rolled back in her head as his heat flooded all round her.

Tuck was surprised when Cassie's body moved flush

against his after her standoffishness. But he liked the way she fitted, her body moulding against his, her head tucked in under his chin nicely. And she let him lead, which was a novelty. Most women he danced with weren't so passive in his arms.

They danced all flirty and dirty and sexy.

Not that Tuck had anything against *flirty, dirty* or *sexy*. He was all for them. But too often it felt like an act. As if the women he dated felt they *had* to gyrate and shimmy and generally carry on like a B-grade porn star to attract or keep his attention.

Okay, he'd never had a reputation for longevity—his two-year marriage was a sure sign of that—but he was, at his most basic, a guy. And just being *female* was enough to keep his attention.

Ever since his divorce he'd gone back to his partying ways—living the dream, a different woman every night—the ultimate male fantasy. But he'd forgotten how good this felt, how nice it was to slow-dance, to hold a woman and enjoy the feeling of her all relaxed against him.

Even if she did think he was dumb as a rock.

'I think you've got this dancing thing down pat, darlin',' he murmured against her hair.

Cassie just heard him through the trancelike state she'd entered. Each breath she drew in fogged her head a little more, stroking along nerve-endings and leadening her bones. She was pretty sure she was drooling on his jacket.

But he had her in his thrall.

His hands felt big and male on her hips, and hot—very hot. She was aware of every part of her body. It was alive with the scent of him.

His chin rubbed the top of her head and she glanced up. Her gaze fell on the heavy thud of his carotid again, pulsing just above his collar beside the hard ridge of his trachea. Her mouth watered a little more and Cassie sucked in a breath.

'Well, *hey,* y'all!'

Cassie dragged herself back from the impulse to push her nose into Tuck's neck, grateful for Marnie's interruption. She looked at her friend, who was dancing with a preppy-looking guy, still a little dazed.

'It's getting hot in here,' Marnie said, then winked as her partner danced her away.

Cassie blinked at her retreating back and then glanced at Tuck, who was looking intently at her with his intense extra-terrestrial gaze.

What was she thinking?

She searched her brain for an answer. How great he smelled. How great he might taste. But more than that. She'd been thinking how small and feminine she felt tucked in under his chin, his hands shaping her hips.

How female.

She blinked, shocked by her thoughts. Since when had she cared about that? But her gaze was filled with his perfect symmetrical features and it all became fuzzy again. Why couldn't he have a prominent forehead and squinty eyes and a crooked nose? He was a footballer, for crying out loud, didn't they break noses regularly?

Why didn't she feel like this about Len, her fellow researcher-cum-occasional-lover? She'd never once had to quell the urge to sniff *him.* They worked together every day, occasionally accompanied each other to university functions, and every once in a while he got antsy and irritable and they had sex, so he could concentrate on what was really important—astronomy.

She'd never slow-danced with Len. Nor did she want to.

She'd never wanted to crawl inside his skin.

It was a scary thought, and Cassie tried to pull away as another slow song started up, but Tuck held her fast and her damn body capitulated readily. Too readily. It was obvious biology was going to win out over intellect and logic tonight and that just wasn't acceptable.

She needed to defuse the situation, to distract herself from the dizzying power of him.

'So,' she said, reaching for a safe, easy topic of conversation, 'Tuck isn't your real name?'

It was hardly Mensa level, and they weren't about to unlock the secrets of dark matter, but at least it would give her back some control.

Mind over body.

And he looked like a guy who liked to talk about himself.

'No.' Tuck shook his head. 'My Christian name is Samuel. Samuel Tucker. But no one calls me that. Except my mother.'

Even his wife had called him Tuck.

'And Great-Aunt Ada,' Cassie reminded him.

Tuck smiled. 'And Great-Aunt Ada.'

Cassie frowned. 'Why not be called by the name you were given?'

Tuck shrugged. 'It's a nickname.' He looked down into her genuinely perplexed face. 'Don't they have nicknames in Australia? You're called Cassie instead of Cassiopeia.'

Cassie shook her head. 'No. Cassie is an *abbreviation* of my Christian name, not a nickname. If that were the case for you, you'd be known as Sam.'

Tuck waited for her to spell *abbreviation* for his poor addled brain. If she hadn't felt a hundred kinds of right, all smooshed up and slow dancing against him, he'd be getting kind of ticked off by her attitude towards his mental prowess.

Instead he was prepared to humour her.

'Except Tuck sounds cooler.'

Cassie frowned. '*Cooler?* Who says?'

Tuck liked the way her brows drew together, showcasing her grey-blue eyes to perfection. 'Tens of thousands of football fans, screaming my name across every state in this great land for a decade.'

Not to mention quite a few more of the female variety also screaming it out loud in hotel beds across every state for just as long.

'Oh.' Cassie thought about it for a moment, but she'd never understood the dynamics of hero-worship regarding something as frivolous as sport. 'Sorry, I don't get that.'

He shrugged. 'It's a guy thing.'

Cassie suspected it was probably a *jock* thing, but she tucked it away anyway to ask Len about when they next spoke.

Thankfully the song ended and, feeling more in control of her recalcitrant hormones, she took the opportunity to step firmly away from him. 'I'm done now,' she said, and was proud of how strong her voice sounded when her body was howling to be nearer to him.

Tuck smiled and bowed slightly, ever the gentleman, as he gestured for her to precede him. It didn't stop him from perving on her ass the whole way back to the table, though.

Almost two hours later everyone had left and Marnie, Gina and Cassie, under the direction of Great-Aunt Ada, had seen all the guests off and organised the removal of the gifts that had been left despite Reese insisting that no one bring any.

Tuck and his pheromones had also insisted on helping.

Cassie was getting twitchy. She had a paper to get back to. She didn't have time for a big, blond ex-quarterback who'd obviously fallen out of the stupid tree. And hit every branch on the way down.

No matter how nice he smelled.

But somehow he was accompanying them back inside the grand entrance to the Bellington Estate, and then he was walking up the ornate stone staircase next to her, his arm occasionally brushing hers. When Marnie and Gina turned left at the top Cassie hoped that Tuck would do so too.

No such luck.

He smiled at her as he turned right. 'After you,' he said.

Cassie looked over her shoulder at Gina and Marnie, who had stopped and were looking at her with bemused expressions.

Gina waved her fingers and said, 'Need someone to *tuck* you in?'

Marnie seemed to have trouble keeping a straight face and Cassie frowned at her.

'I think she's got that covered,' Marnie said. 'Night, Cassie. Night, Tuck. Sweet dreams.'

Cassie glanced at Tuck, who was also smiling.

'Good night, ladies. See you in the morning.'

Before Cassie could make further comment her 'friends' had turned away and she was watching their backs retreat. She hoped that Marnie and Gina would use the time to talk, because it had been awkward between them at the table tonight. Although if the distance between them as they walked was anything to go by it didn't look like they were ready to bury the hatchet just yet.

She looked at Tuck, and even though he was a good two metres away his aroma wafted her way and she instantly forgot about the animosity between her friends. Her belly tightened and then looped the loop.

'What's your room number? I'll see you to your door.'

The last thing Cassie wanted was to have Tuck anywhere near her room. In fact she'd be perfectly happy never to be anywhere near him again. She was unsettled. Confused.

She was never unsettled. Never confused. And she didn't like it. Not one bit.

'I don't need you to accompany me to my room,' she said, taking care as she passed him to keep her distance.

Tuck watched the swing of her ass again for a moment or two, then called after her, 'My momma would tan my hide if I didn't see my date to her door.'

Cassie stopped mid-stride and turned to face him. 'I am *not* your date.'

'You sure danced like I was your date.'

Heat flooded her cheeks as she remembered how she'd clung and buried her nose in his clothes, as if he was her own personal scratch-and-sniff jock. Cassiopeia Barclay did *not* blush—ever! Curious at the strange phenomenon, she brought her palms up to cradle her face.

She cleared her throat. 'It was…crowded,' she said defensively, dropping her hands and folding her arms primly.

Tuck's gaze dropped. Her folded arms had pushed her breasts up and together, exposing a nice curve of bare flesh at the criss-cross front of her dress for his viewing pleasure. Tuck had seen a lot bigger. He'd also seen smaller. Cassie's looked just about right to him. A perky B cup, he'd hazard a guess.

Tuck grinned. 'Come on, darlin', it's late. Let's get you to bed.'

Cassie shoved her hands on her hips, determined not to let an image of him sprawled in her big hotel bed derail her thoughts. 'Don't call me *darlin'*.' She mimicked his slow, easy Southern drawl to perfection. 'And I'm perfectly capable of finding my way to my room. *I* can count.'

Tuck's grin broadened. 'Well, maybe you can help me find my room?' He scratched his head in the most perplexed manner he could muster. 'There's a lot of wings in this place and it does get kind of confusin' after a hundred, don't it?'

Cassie rolled her eyes. The man was living proof that evolution could go in reverse. 'How on earth do you count all those millions that kicking a stupid ball around earned you?'

Tuck shoved his hands in his pockets. 'Got me some bean-counters for that.'

Cassie couldn't believe what she was hearing. He was going to be one of those has-been sports stars whose money was all gone in a matter of years because he had a little too much yardage between the goalposts to keep track of it himself. And he trusted too easily.

'Follow me,' she said huffily as she headed down the long grand hallway.

Tuck's gaze ran over the contours of her back and settled on how her dress swung and fluttered with each movement. 'Your wish is my command,' he murmured under his breath.

Tuck deliberately took his time, stopping to examine old paintings hanging on the stonework, suits of armour and the antique vases that dotted the magnificent corridor. He kept up a running commentary for Cassie's sake, purely because it seemed to annoy her.

'*Will* you hurry up?' she said impatiently, looking over her shoulder for the tenth time as he stopped to read the name of the artist of a particularly austere portrait. 'I have a paper to get to.'

Tuck looked up. 'You brought work?' He shook his head at her and tsked as he meandered closer. 'All work and no play makes Cassiopeia a dull girl.'

Cassie glared at him as they got underway again. 'Not that I expect you to understand this, but there is nothing dull about auroras on Jupiter.'

'Auroras?'

'Yes—you know, like the Aurora Borealis?' His blank look didn't seem promising. 'The Northern Lights?' she clarified.

Tuck had witnessed the Aurora Borealis in Scandinavia on two separate occasions, but he wasn't about to disappoint Cassie's assumptions. 'Isn't she some mermaid?'

Cassie sighed. There really *was* no grain in his silo. He

was an empty vessel. 'No. It's a *real* thing. It's why I'm here. I'm completing my PhD studies at Cornell so next year I can go on a research trip to Antarctica. And Aurora was Sleeping Beauty. *Ariel* was the Little Mermaid.'

Tuck shrugged. 'Well, it sounds like a mermaid if you ask me.' And then he shot her his best goofy grin for good measure.

Thankfully her room approached, and Cassie all but leapt at the ornate doorknob. 'This is me,' she said. 'What did you say your room number was again?'

She'd barely been able to concentrate on anything he'd said. When he wasn't wandering off like a distracted child or lagging behind to look at things he was right there beside her, weaving his heady scent all around her.

Like he was now.

Tuck smiled. 'Three hundred and twenty three,' he said, and watched the fact that he would be sleeping directly opposite her dawn slowly on her face. 'Howdy, neighbour.'

'Oh.' Cassie looked at the door opposite. Too close for comfort. Her highly developed sense of fight or flight kicked in as another dose of his masculinity wafted over her.

'Right, then,' she said, fishing in Gina's glittery clutch purse for her room key and locating it with shaking hands.

The adrenaline. It had to be the adrenaline.

'Goodnight,' she said, barely looking at him as she turned away and reached for the door handle, hastily swiping the plastic card through the electronic strip.

The light turned red and she swiped it again, her hands even shakier. Another red light elicited a frustrated little growl from the back of her throat. She needed to get inside her room. Inside was work and logic and focus and sanity.

Out here with Tuck's quiet presence behind her was insanity. *And damnation.*

She could feel it pulling at her body with sticky tentacles, drugging her with its perfume, wrapping her up in its heady thrall.

She swiped one more time. *Red light.*

'Allow me.'

Cassie's fingers stilled as Tuck's hand slid over them. His body moved in behind hers and she was instantly cocooned in his intoxicating aroma. She shut her eyes as her nipples responded to the blatant cue. She could feel his breath in her hair, the warm press of his chest against her back, the power of his thighs behind hers.

She leant her forehead against the door, desperately reaching for logic. 'I spend all day probing the outer depths of our solar system through a massive telescope,' she said. 'I'm pretty sure I can open a damn door.'

'Shh,' Tuck said, easing the key out of her unresisting fingers. 'Some things don't need big brains,' he murmured. He took the plastic. 'Some things need a slow hand...an easy touch.'

He slid the card through the strip with deliberate slowness. The lock whirred, the light turned green and he smiled as he turned the handle and pushed the door open a fraction.

'Easy.'

Cassie practically whimpered at the low, deep sound of his Southern accent. It weaved around her like the melodic notes of a snake charmer, trapping her. The door was right there. It was open. All she needed to do was move. But she couldn't.

'Cassie?'

Tuck could feel her trembling and a surge of desire crested in his belly. His groin tightened. His blood slowed to a thick, primal bound. He laid a gentle hand on her shoulder and, to his surprise, she turned. Only a whisper separated them as heat flashed like a solar flare between them.

Her eyes looked all misty and dazed, her pupils large in the grey-blue depths. They seemed to shimmer up at him and he fell headlong into them. Her mouth was slightly parted and it drew his gaze. He picked up a long dark ringlet draped forward over her shoulder and wound it around his finger. 'Has anyone ever told you you're quite beautiful?'

Cassie's throat was dry as a sandpit as she shut her eyes against the seduction in his. No one had ever told her that. And she'd never cared. 'I've never aspired to be beautiful,' she dismissed. She was more comfortable with brainy.

He waited for her lashes to flutter open again before saying, 'Well, you've failed.'

Tuck only intended to give her the briefest of kisses as he slid his palm onto her cheek. Just a little taste of her mouth. The mouth that had dissed him all night. Just to show her how pretty damn clever he could be.

And to leave her wanting more.

But the second his mouth touched hers and she opened to him as if he was water and she was dying of thirst it all went flying out of the window.

Cassie mewed as his lips brushed hers and her senses filled up with him. There was no thought or logic or analysis in play any longer as she overdosed on his intoxicating scent, sucking him in, drenching her cells in his pheromones. Her body had completely taken over and left her brain out of the equation.

She raised herself up on tiptoes. Her hands slid around his neck. Her mouth parted of its own accord. She moaned and dragged him closer as hot, scalding lust lashed her insides and flayed her flesh with the driving need for more.

It didn't make any sense. Not when she swiped her tongue across his lips, or pushed it inside, or stroked it against his. Not when she moaned. Not when she gasped. Not when she grabbed his lapels to press herself closer.

She'd never been kissed like this.

She'd never *kissed* like this.

And still she was full of him. Her head buzzed with the

essence of him. Her mouth was on fire. Her belly was tight. The heat between her legs tingled and burned.

Tuck barely managed to hold onto her as Cassie kissed him as if she was an evil genius intent on wicked things and he was her latest experiment. He might not be dumb as a rock but he was certainly as hard as one now as her deep, sexy kisses, body-squirming and desperate little whimpers stroked all his hot spots.

She even kissed differently from other women. No mouth gymnastics, no hands down his pants in seconds, no theatrical panting, no *Oh, baby, baby.* Just a scorching one hundred percent, full-throttle touchdown of a kiss. Her lips on his lips. Open and going for it.

He pushed her hard against the door, wanting to get closer, to kiss her deeper. But he'd forgotten it was already slightly open and she stumbled backwards. Their mouths tore apart.

He grabbed for her, finding her elbow, dropping it once she'd stabilised. And then they stood staring at each other, breathing hard, not moving for a moment, neither sure which way to jump.

Tuck knew enough about women to know that look in Cassie's eyes. He knew he could pick her up, stride into her room and lay her on the bed and she'd follow wherever he took her. And enjoy every single second of it.

But he saw a whole bunch of other stuff in her eyes too. Most of it he couldn't decipher. But he could see her confusion quite clearly. Obviously that kiss just did not compute for Cassie.

She looked as if she needed some time to wrap her head around it. Hell, *he* sure as hell did!

'Are you okay?'

Cassie nodded automatically *but* she doubted she'd ever be okay again. *What the hell had just happened?* She felt as if she'd just had a lobotomy. Could a kiss render you stupid?

'I think I should go now. Unless...' He dropped his gaze to her swollen mouth.

Cassie shook her head and took a step back. *No 'unless'. Go, yes. Just go.* He'd turned her into a dunce.

Tuck smiled at her dazed look. It was nice to have left an impression on Little-Miss-Know-It-All, even if he *was* going to go to bed with a hard-on the size of Texas. 'Goodnight, Cassiopeia.'

Cassie was incapable of answering him. She feared she'd been struck mute. As well as dumb. She watched him swagger to his room opposite, slot his key in, open his door. He turned as he stepped into his room.

'I'll be right over here. If you need a cup of *shhu-gar*.'

Cassie had no pithy comeback as his door clicked quietly shut.

CHAPTER THREE

AFTER TOSSING AND turning for most of the night—not something that was good for her sanity—Cassie woke at nine a.m. and the first thing she thought about was Tuck. She dragged a pillow over her head and bellowed a loud, furious denial.

She *always* woke at six. And most certainly *never* thought about a man.

Cassie's brain was engaged the moment her eyes flicked open after her regulation eight hours' sleep. For the last several years her waking thoughts had centred on her aurora research and she'd spring out of bed and head straight for her computer.

This morning her head was full of Tuck and *the kiss.*

Her computer, the research, *her will to live*—all lost in a sea of oestrogen.

She yanked the pillow off her head and turned on her side. Her baggy T-shirt was twisted around her torso and the movement pulled it taut against her breasts. Her nipples responded to the brush of fabric, her belly clamped, and a red-hot tingle took up residence at the juncture of her thighs.

Cassie dragged some deep breaths in and out, trying to conjure up the latest deep-space images she'd seen yesterday. But it was no use—she could still smell him in her nostrils and taste him on her mouth.

The phone rang and she snatched it up immediately, grateful for something else to do, to think about.

'Hello?'

'Cassie, get off that computer and get your heiny down here now,' Marnie demanded. 'Reese is back and we're having breakfast.'

Her friend's Southern accent reminded her of Tuck's lazy Texan drawl and Cassie almost groaned out loud. 'I'll be there in ten.'

Anything—*anything*—to take her mind off the annoying jock.

Cassie entered the grand dining room exactly ten minutes later, completely oblivious to the eyebrows her rather informal attire was raising. She'd thrown on a pair of loose leggings and a baggy T-shirt with a slogan that said *'Back in my day we had nine planets'*—one of the many geek-themed shirts Gina, Marnie and Reese had sent her over the years.

She hadn't even bothered to brush her hair—just pulled it back into her regulation low ponytail, with her regulation floral scrunchie, and pushed one of her many-toothed Alice bands into it, ensuring it stayed scraped back off her forehead. There really was nothing more annoying than hair getting in the way when she was in the middle of something.

Actually, there was now. And its name was *Tuck.*

Unlike the rest of the people in the dining room, dressed in their country club pasteles, her friends didn't bat an eyelid as Cassie scurried their way, then plonked herself in one of the three empty seats at the round table. They'd have been shocked had Cassie dressed in any other way.

Cassie forced a smile to her face as she looked at a glowing Reese, radiating the same kind of happiness she had a decade ago when she and her Marine had first met. 'When did you get back? Where's Mason?'

'An hour ago.' Reese grinned, sipping at some coffee. 'He's taking care of some business.'

Cassie barely registered Reese's reply but nodded anyway. A waiter interrupted and Cassie, ignoring the piles of pancakes the others were tucking into, ordered the same thing she had every morning for breakfast—yoghurt and muesli and two slices of grain toast with Vegemite. When he informed her they didn't have Vegemite she ordered jam.

'You okay?' Reese frowned. 'You look kind of tired.'

'I didn't sleep very well,' Cassie said.

Marnie looked at Gina, and Gina narrowed her eyes at Cassie. 'Since when doesn't Little-Miss-Eight-Hours not sleep well?'

Cassie looked at her friends all watching her with curiosity. She shrugged. She didn't know what to tell them because she'd *never* not slept well.

Gina lounged back in her chair, her arms crossed, her fingers tapping against her arms. 'This hasn't got anything to do with a certain quarterback, has it?'

Marnie sat forward, her blonde hair neat as a pin in a high ponytail that was one hundred percent more cute and perky than Cassie's. 'It does, doesn't it?'

Reese frowned at both her friends. 'Tuck?'

'Tuck and Cassie danced last night,' Gina said.

'Real close,' Marnie added.

Reese blinked at her. 'Cassie?'

Cassie had decided on her way down to the dining room that she wasn't going to tell a soul about the strange feelings coursing through her body, but she felt herself sag under the scrutiny of three sets of eyes. She'd always been a great believer in solving problems by seeking out experts in the field. And, having lived with these three women and been through all their relationship ups and downs, she had to admit she had a panel of experts in front of her.

What better people to confide in?

'I don't know what's happening,' she murmured. 'I couldn't sleep last night. I *always* sleep. I *need* to sleep. It's vitally important that I do. I take *specific* medication to switch off my brain so I can sleep. And it never fails. I'm out like a light. Usually... And this morning I didn't wake until nine... I'm always up at six. *Always*.'

'Well, you were tired,' Marnie reasoned.

'And do you know what my first waking thought was about?' Cassie continued, ignoring Marnie.

'I'm guessing it was about something a little closer to the earth than usual?' Gina said.

Cassie sighed in disgust. 'It was him. *The jock*.' She looked at her friends for answers. 'I don't understand what's happening to me.'

Her friends didn't say anything for a moment, as if they were waiting for her to say more or to clarify something. Then, one by one, the three women opposite her broke into broad grins.

She frowned. 'What?'

Her friends had the audacity to laugh then, looking at each other as they cracked up. Cassie glared at them. 'This is not funny.'

'No, of course not,' Reese soothed as she struggled to regain her composure. 'Falling in love is never funny.'

Cassie gaped at Reese. 'Don't be ridiculous,' she spluttered.

'Aww...' Marnie purred, ignoring Cassie's protest. 'Our little girl is all grown up now,' she teased.

'And to think,' Reese continued, 'we voted you the girl least likely to ever fall for a man.'

Cassie crossed her arms across her chest and waited for their frivolity to wane. She would not entertain such unscientific mumbo-jumbo. Love was a fiction perpetuated by romance novels and Hollywood.

'It's not love,' she said frostily when the last smile had fallen beneath her uncompromising glare. 'Just because you're seeing the world through rose-coloured glasses, Reese, does not mean I've taken leave of *my* senses. You know I don't believe in that voodoo. It's his pheromones—that's all. The man smells *incredible*...'

Cassie could still smell him on her, and she shut her eyes for a moment to savour it.

'It was dizzying,' she said, eyes still closed. 'Truly sensational. Like it was all I could do to stop myself sniffing and sniffing and sniffing him all night.'

Cassie's eyelids fluttered open and she found her friends staring at her with varying degrees of perplexity. She cleared her throat and straightened in her chair. 'Anyway...it's obviously a scent I'm biologically programmed to respond to. It's just...biochemistry. Nothing more.'

The waiter arrived and conversation stopped as he placed Cassie's breakfast in front of her. When he left Cassie looked at Gina. 'Surely there's a lay word for that other than *love?* When your body overrules your brain?'

Gina nodded. 'Yep. We call it horny.'

Cassie shook her head. 'No.' She was a scientist. *She refused to be horny.*

Gina nodded again. 'Totally gagging for it.'

Cassie wasn't sure what that meant exactly, but it sounded like something they'd say in the locker room on an American cop show. 'Absolutely not.'

'Libido?' Reese supplied.

Cassie paused. She liked that word best. It was backed up by science—the non-Freudian kind. It could be proved—the area of the brain responsible for libido had been studied extensively.

'Yes,' Gina agreed. 'It's your libido knocking.'

'Okay, I can buy that,' Cassie conceded. 'But my libido has never been an issue before, so why is it knocking now?'

'Well, that's easy,' Gina said. 'When was the last time you had sex?'

Cassie thought about it for a moment. It had been Len's birthday request. 'Seven months ago.'

Gina blinked. 'Seven *months?*' She looked at Reese and Marnie, who were also staring at Cassie's admission. 'Well, in that case it's *definitely* your libido.'

'Who's the guy?' Marnie asked.

'His name is Len. He's another astronomer at the university. We've been working on the same project for the last five years. We have a regular hook-up.'

'Every *seven* months?' Gina interjected.

'It varies,' Cassie said, oblivious to the palpable incredulity around the table. 'Usually whenever he starts to get cranky. I've found that it improves his focus.'

'Okay...' Gina said, shaking her head. 'So this last time— was it...you know...good?'

Cassie shrugged. Personally she'd never got the big deal about sex. 'It was satisfactory.'

Gina looked at Reese for back-up. 'I think what Gina means,' Reese continued, 'is did you...you know...' she lowered her voice '...orgasm?'

'Oh, no,' Cassie said, unfazed by the conversation. When they'd all lived together Cassie had been privy to many girly chats about all kinds of sex-related issues. She'd learned a great deal of stuff in that house that a bunch of lectures and books had never taught her. 'I've never had an orgasm.'

Had Cassie been one to find humour in awkward situations she would have found the total disbelief on her friends' faces completely hilarious. They'd all stopped eating and were staring at her.

'What…*never?*' Marnie asked after a stunned silence.

Cassie shook her head. 'No.'

'Not even…by yourself?' Reese asked.

'Or with a vibrator?' added Gina, last to recover.

Cassie looked from one to the other. 'I've never masturbated and I don't own, nor have I ever, a vibrator.'

More silence followed, finally broken by Gina's, 'Well, that's just *unnatural.* Going without sex is one thing, but there is no excuse for not indulging in a little self-love, Cassiopeia. It's perfectly healthy. *Normal,* actually. Didn't I teach you anything?'

Cassie put down her spoon. 'No, it's fine. Some people don't need sex.' She shrugged. 'I'm one of them.'

'It's *not* fine,' Reese interjected. 'I don't know who this Len is that you've been having sex with…very, *very* infrequently…but he's definitely doing it all wrong.'

'No, it's not his fault.'

'Oh, I think it is,' Marnie said.

'No, really.' Cassie looked at her friends' concerned faces. 'The medication I take to sleep…one of its side-effects is libido suppression and difficulty achieving orgasm.'

Gina shuddered. 'I think I'd rather stay awake for the rest of my life.' She looked at Cassie. 'Are you sure you need it?'

Cassie nodded. 'Without it my brain doesn't switch off and I can't sleep. And that's extremely detrimental to my health. I start to get a little OCD without sleep. And one stay in the psych ward as a teenager was more than enough.' Cassie vividly remembered the chaos her mind had descended into—how she'd quickly spiralled out of control. 'Trust me, that's an experience I never want to repeat.'

Gina, Reese and Marnie didn't even know what to say to *that* revelation. They were still stuck back at the no-orgasm thing.

'I still think Len could try a little harder,' Marnie said after the silence had gone on for a while.

'Oh, he tried in the beginning. A couple of times. But it wasn't happening and it was taking for ever and I really don't have time for all that carry-on. It was never really for my benefit anyway, so now we don't bother about me.'

Gina gaped. 'Do you...kiss? Is there foreplay?'

Cassie shook her head. 'Not really. I prefer it when he cuts to the chase. It's quicker that way.'

Gina looked at Reese. 'Where did we go wrong with her?'

Reese shook her head. 'I have no idea.'

'Right,' Gina said, picking up her coffee cup and taking a sip. 'Let's deal with the most pressing issue and hopefully the other problem will sort itself out. What we have here is you suffering from a libido that has suddenly roared to life—which is probably due to a combination of lack of sexual satisfaction for the *entirety* of your life and the fact that you're almost thirty. Women's sex drives peak around thirty. That's a well-known scientific fact, right? Or it is according to women's magazines.'

Cassie nodded. 'Correct.'

'And Tuck has come along at this crossroads of sexual frustration and the natural peaking of your sex drive and it's like he's...tripped a switch.'

Cassie was pretty sure it could be put more scientifically, but she liked Gina's logic. And logic was beautiful. 'Good. Okay. So what do I do about it?'

Gina shrugged, putting her coffee cup back in its saucer. 'Easy. You bonk Tuck's brains out until that libido of yours stops bitching.'

Reese choked on a mouthful of pancake. When she'd finished coughing she said to Gina, 'I don't think that's a good idea. I love my cousin. He's hot and sweet, and from what I read in the tabloids he may well be God's gift to the female of the species, but he's not exactly the settling down type.'

'I'm not suggesting she *marry* the man,' Gina said. 'Not *everyone* needs to get married, Reese.' She turned to look at Cassie. 'I think she should just use him for sex—get him out of her system. He doesn't look like the kind of man who'd object to being used as a scratching post for a horny thirty-year-old genius.'

Cassie felt something tighten low and deep inside her at the mere thought of being horizontal with Tuck. 'Maybe I could just up my meds? Suppress my libido chemically?'

Marnie reached out her hand and placed it over top of Cassie's. 'There could be worse ways to iron out a few kinks, Cass. He's a mighty fine-looking man. Very sexy.'

Cassie was pretty sure there weren't. Why did her body want *him?* Mighty fine or not, the man had clearly forgotten to pay his brain bill. What on earth were they going to talk about while they were *doing* it? She and Len discussed their research. What could she talk to *him* about?

'Yeah, but I'm not sure I want to be naked in front of a guy who doesn't know what Pi is... Why couldn't he be a geek? Smart men are my kind of sexy.'

Reese shook her head. 'He played dumb, didn't he?' she said to Gina.

'Yep. To be fair, though,' Gina said, 'Cassie *was* speaking to him slowly and using very simple words.'

Reese sighed. 'Yeah, he does that when people make assumptions.' She looked at Cassie. 'Well, you better hold on to your hat, Cassiopeia, because Tuck's brain is about as big as his ego. He graduated *summa cum laude* in pure math and he's currently working with a young start-up company in California developing a stats app for the NFL. He's no savant, but he's no dummy either.'

It was Cassie's turn to blink. 'Maths?' She *loved* maths.

Reese nodded. 'Not just a pretty face.'

Marnie straightened up. 'Speaking of pretty faces....'

Gina and Reese also straightened. 'What?' Cassie turned to look behind her. Not that she really needed to. She could already feel his pull.

She sucked in a breath as Tuck swaggered towards them, once again greeting his fans with casual aplomb. Was it his broad chest and narrow hips, beautifully showcased in dark trousers and a pale lemon shirt unbuttoned at the throat, that flared her nostrils and set her mouth watering? Or maybe it was his short crinkly blond locks that would surely curl with any kind of length?

Or was it just his big beautiful brain that made her want to lick him all over? *Dear God, she was turning into an animal!*

Cassie quickly turned back, her brain already shutting down. Reese glanced at Gina and Marnie, who were both watching Cassie's reaction with bemused expressions. They'd seen their friend flustered before—but never over a man.

'Morning, ladies,' Tuck said as he drew within a metre of the table. 'Cassiopeia,' he murmured as he pulled up the chair beside her and sat down.

He turned to smile at her. Except Cassie this morning was very different from the one last night. Her hair was straight and ruthlessly pushed off her face, her make-up was non-existent, and she was wearing something baggy and voluminous that totally obscured the body she'd been showing off last night.

She was no swan this morning, that was for sure.

But her pretty grey-blue eyes still looked at him with that compelling mix of intelligence and confusion and he liked that he was still rattling her.

'You turn into a pumpkin, darlin'?'

'Tuck!' Reese gasped.

'What?' he protested, looking at his cousin completely unabashed. 'I'm just saying Cassie's looking a little...different this morning.'

Cassie wasn't remotely insulted by the observation. How she looked or didn't look had never mattered. What concerned her was the riot going on inside her body as his scent, now encoded into her DNA, pulled her into its orbit. The sudden leap in her pulse, the flare of her nostrils, the gush of saliva coating a mouth as dry as stardust.

He smelled different this morning, but the same. There was a hint of something sweet, a tang masking the earthy smell of male, but it only added to his allure. It tickled at her nose with each inhalation. It wafted over her in sticky waves. It undulated through her breasts and belly.

She could see the hollow at the base of his throat, the steady bound of his pulse, and it took all her willpower to stop herself leaning into him and burying her nose right there.

Dear God—he might not be as stupid as she'd thought, but she was losing IQ points fast.

Everyone was looking at her. *Say something, damn it!*

'Why, when you have a maths degree, did you lead me to believe you were dumb?'

Tuck shot a look at his cousin. 'Aww, Reese,' he said, putting on his best yokel accent, 'you done went and spoiled all my fun.'

'Knock it off, Tuck.' Reese tutted. 'You shouldn't bait people. It's not nice.'

Cassie frowned, ignoring them. 'I don't understand why you would underestimate your intelligence.'

Tuck supposed Cassie wouldn't, in her world of logic and reason, so there was no point trying to explain how crazy being treated like a dumb jock made him. She hadn't been deliberately obtuse, like so many others, just clueless, so he was prepared to cut her some slack.

'Would you have let me kiss you some more last night if you'd known I was smarter?'

Cassie suspected she very much would have. Brains and pheromones were apparently a dangerous combination. Hell, the man could kiss her right now, in front of a dining room full of people, and she'd be powerless to resist.

'Some more?' Gina said, her eyebrows practically hitting her hairline.

'He kissed you!' Marnie spluttered.

'You kissed her?' Reese demanded.

Tuck looked at the three fierce women opposite him and then at the silent one beside him, her gaze roving over his throat like a vampire deciding where to make her first bite. It branded him like a physical caress and streaked heat to his groin where things stirred with the same potency they'd had last night.

'Cassie?' Marnie prompted.

Cassie dragged her eyes off Tuck's neck. 'Oh, yeah. I left that bit out, didn't I?'

'Er, *yeah,*' Marnie said.

Cassie looked at her friends, all looking at her expectantly, waiting for more. Tuck was watching her too. And all the while his pheromones battered and pulled at her, weakening her resistance. She had to get away from them.

From him.

She stood. 'I have work to do.'

'Oh, no—wait, Cassie,' Marnie said. 'You can't spend all your time at a luxury estate holed up in your room on your laptop.'

Tuck couldn't agree more. Being holed up in her room with her on his lap, making Little-Miss-Know-It-All come undone, sounded much preferable.

'Marnie's right,' Gina said. 'We're going to the spa for the day. Why don't you join us?'

Cassie was surprised that Marnie and Gina were voluntarily spending time in each other's company. Although was that a desperate *please come* look in Gina's eyes? Normally she would have agreed to be their buffer zone, but a day where their deflection would land squarely on her and, by association, Tuck, was not something she wanted to volunteer for.

Gina might be convinced that *bonking* Tuck was the solution, but Cassie wasn't ready to allow hormones and libido to conquer brainpower.

She just needed to get absorbed in her work again.

'Stars wait for no woman,' she said, glancing at Tuck for good measure, to send him a message too—*she wouldn't be derailed by biology.*

And she fell into his cosmic blue eyes, temporarily forgetting her own name.

Tuck smiled at her, raising an eyebrow slightly at her defiant expression. But she wasn't fooling him. He could see other things in her gaze as well, like the hunger from last night. Maybe he could convince her about the beauty of a different kind of star. The kind that popped and exploded behind shut lids as she rode the tail of a stratospheric orgasm.

'Join us later for something to eat.'

Cassie dragged her gaze from Tuck's, grateful to Gina for the interruption. He looked at her as if he knew exactly what she was thinking and it was unsettling. 'I'll see,' she evaded as Gina's desperation not to be alone with Marnie was confirmed. 'I have a lot of stuff to get through before I start at Cornell next week. I'll probably get room service.'

She might not be looking at him but she could still feel his eyes on her. His words from last night came back to her. *All work and no play make Cassie a dull girl.* She'd never been tempted to ditch her work before, but his hot gaze made her want to do a lot of things she hadn't done.

'We'll call you when we're done,' Marnie said.

Cassie nodded. She stood awkwardly for a moment or two, conscious of all eyes on her, then bade them goodbye.

The four remaining occupants of the table watched her walk away. Tuck shuddered as her shapeless shirt hung like a bag on her frame.

'Now, why would a woman want to hide such a damn fine figure?' he asked as he turned back to face the table.

Three sets of female eyes were trained firmly upon him and he shifted uncomfortably. He was a man used to female attention—but not like this.

'What?' he said warily.

'Don't play with her, Tuck,' Reese warned. 'She's not like your other women.'

Tuck kind of liked that the most about Cassie, but he cocked an eyebrow and tried to look a little insulted. 'My other women?'

'You know what I mean,' Reese said reproachfully. 'She's not a player.'

'She's pretty sheltered,' Marnie added.

Tuck looked at Cassie's three musketeers. 'She's a big girl. Surely she can look after herself?'

'She's not experienced with guys like you,' Gina explained.

'Guys like me?'

Gina shot him a silky smile. 'Man-whore guys.'

Tuck faked a hurt look and shot it his cousin's way. 'Reese, honey, your friends are being mean to me.'

Reese snorted. 'Tuck. Listen to me. I know your career ending in injury the way it did was hard, and that you've been a little aimless since your divorce and have been…enjoying the spoils of being God's gift to women…but I'm asking you to *not* choose Cassie as your next form of denial.'

It was Tuck's turn to snort. His career ending, his impulsive marriage crumbling, his infertility—all had been body-blows over the last couple of years. Separately they would have been challenging to any man's ego, but together they'd been an enormous whammy. So what if he'd been trying to prove he was still *the man?*

But Reese was right, Cassie wasn't his type. He dated women who knew the ropes. And he didn't need a PhD in relationships to know that Cassie did not.

He put up his hands in surrender. 'Okay. I won't go near her. I promise.'

Reese patted his hand. 'Atta-boy.'

By ten o'clock Cassie was ready to weep with frustration. She'd achieved exactly nothing all day. Instead of auroras and how they affected weather patterns on Jupiter she'd doodled Tuck's name on a writing pad all day. Every web search she'd conducted, every paper she'd picked up, every image she'd looked at, Tuck and his smell and his accent and his lazy grin had hijacked her thoughts.

Her whole body ached with trying to deny the surge of hormones that had her in their thrall. Two cold showers hadn't helped—she still felt hot and feverish, as if she was craving a drug. She'd tried to work through it, she really had, but everything got back to Tuck.

One night—that was all she had to do. She just had to get through this night and then she'd be gone in the morning, and far away from him and his pheromones, and she could get her brain back. Her focus.

She stared at her door for the thousandth time. Just through it and across the hallway was the cause of all her angst. Cassie took a step towards it. *No!* She forced herself to stop, turn around. She snatched up the phone instead and dialled Gina.

'I need you to talk me off the ledge.'

'Well, hello to you too,' Gina said.

'I mean it. I can't stop thinking about him.'

'If you rang me to talk you out of it, you rang the wrong

friend—should have chosen Marnie. I absolutely think you should go for it.'

Cassie gripped the phone. Suddenly she *was* ready for hormones and libido to trump brainpower. 'Tell me more about your theory.'

'What...the bonk Tuck theory?'

'Yes.'

'It's simple, really. You're the one who's always telling us we're biological creatures at heart, with primal needs, right?'

'Uh-huh.'

'So isn't it logical, then, to follow that biological imperative?'

Cassie liked logic—a lot. And she couldn't fault Gina's. She'd just never imagined that *she'd* be at the mercy of biology.

'Look upon it as an experiment to prove the theory,' Gina continued. 'You scientists are big on that, right? You have a problem. Tuck could be the solution. But there's only one way to find out for sure, right?'

'So like a...a sexual experiment?'

'Yes,' Gina said enthusiastically. 'Exactly.'

'I guess I could submit to a one-off experiment,' Cassie mused, chewing her lip, her heart pounding at the thought. 'To test the theory.'

'Er...it might take more than a one-off, Cass.'

Cassie considered that for a moment. 'I don't think so. I don't think I'm wired for more than one-offs...and it's about biology after all, right? So, theoretically, the act of copulation should be enough to satisfy.'

'I think you're going to get more than *copulation* from Tuck. Just saying...'

Cassie nodded, ignoring the warning as her brain moved on to logistics. 'So, what...? I should just go up and say *How about it?*'

Gina laughed. 'Just knock on his door and tell him you want him. Trust me, he'll take it from there.'

Tuck glanced at the clock when a knock sounded on his door. It was almost eleven. He was sprawled on his king-size bed, in his hotel robe, watching a game with the lights and the sound turned low.

And he knew it was her.

He drained the last of his beer before sauntering towards the door, a grin on his face. He turned the handle and pulled it partially open, his hand sliding up the frame to rest somewhere above his head.

Cassie stood there looking up at him. 'Can I come in?'

Tuck felt her quiet request grab hold of his gut and squeeze. No sexy posturing. No batting of her eyelids. 'What do you want, Cassiopeia?'

Cassie swallowed, not even sure if she could get the word out around her parched throat. 'You,' she croaked.

Tuck's breath stuttered to a halt for a moment and his grip on the door tightened. She was grim-faced and serious, and sporting scraped-back hair and terrible clothes, yet his body surged to attention. He'd promised he wouldn't go near her, but he hadn't made any promises in regards to her coming to *him*.

He pulled the door open further and fell back, gesturing her inside.

CHAPTER FOUR

CASSIE SHUT HER eyes as she brushed past him, her nostrils flaring at his scent, her dry mouth suddenly inundated with saliva. She walked to the centre of the room, her heart rate ratcheting off the charts. She turned to face him. He was lounging against the door, and in the dim light he looked all broad and brooding and watchful.

Now what?

She'd kind of hoped he'd take over from here. Gina had assured her he would. But clearly he wasn't going to make it easy.

'Are you going to stand over there?' she asked.

Her voice sounded weird in the air-conditioned bubble of the silent hotel room. High and breathy. She swallowed again.

'For the moment,' Tuck said, crossing his arms.

Cassie wished he wouldn't. She wanted him to come closer. To bring his height and his breadth and his perfectly symmetrical features and his incredibly male smell right over, close to her. And take the lead.

Computing the wind speed across auroras on giant gas planets, she could do—asking a man to have sex with her, not so much.

She opened her mouth, took a tentative step towards him, then stopped. Shut her mouth. This should be easy. A cinch.

She had a giant brain and an excellent vocabulary. But once again she felt as if she was wearing the dunce's cap.

Tuck took pity on her. He'd never known a woman to be alone in a room with him and *not* know what to do. Especially when he was in nothing but a robe and his underwear. It was strangely erotic.

'So, does *"you"* mean what I think it means?' he asked.

Cassie's brain came back online at the verbal prompt. He was giving her a way in—a conversation-starter. And she snatched at it like the last molecule of oxygen on earth.

'Yes,' she said, then cleared her throat because it sounded sappy and weak again. 'I'm not very good at this—'

'Boy,' Tuck interrupted with a smile, 'how'd that one go down? Couldn't have been easy to admit. I imagine you're good at most things.'

Cassie glared at his interruption—didn't he know how hard this was? 'I'm good at *everything*...except this.'

'And *this* is...?'

Cassie took a deep breath. 'This is me asking you to have sex. With me.'

It was blunt and gauche and totally unsexy—and Tuck had never been more turned on in his life.

'This is purely scientific, you understand?' Cassie clarified as Tuck continued to watch her with his blue eyes. 'I seem to have developed a...thing for your pheromones.'

Tuck raised an eyebrow. 'My pheromones?'

'Yes. They're chemicals the body emits—'

Tuck chuckled, interrupting her. 'I know what pheromones are, Cassiopeia.'

'Oh, right...yes, sorry. Well, I don't know if you know this or not, but you do smell pretty amazing.'

Tuck smiled. 'I have been told that a time or two before.'

Cassie absorbed that information, missing the nuance in her bid to get to the point. 'Anyway...I find myself unable to concentrate on my work, and Gina suggested that, because I'm a female in my sexual prime, my libido is demanding to be…serviced…and that a spot of…copulation…might be the solution to my problem.'

Tuck felt his erection swell further. He should *not* be turned on by a woman in shapeless clothes talking about servicing and copulation. Pretty, perky women with enhanced assets and bold use of four-letter words were his staple turn-ons.

And yet he was very turned on. 'Copulation?'

She nodded. 'It's all very logical, really.'

Tuck made his way towards her, keeping his pace slow and lazy. 'So this is you *seducing* me?'

Cassie took a step back as his masculine scent drew her into his wild pheromone cloud. 'I…guess.'

Tuck stopped when he was an arm's length from her. He dropped his gaze and took a slow tour of her body. It didn't take long—there wasn't a lot he could make out. Her breasts, which he remembered very well from her criss-cross dress last night, were vaguely discernible beneath a voluminous T-shirt that proclaimed *'Come to the nerd side. We have Pi'*.

He smiled at the logo as he lifted a hand and fingered the sleeve. '*This* is what you wear to a seduction?'

Cassie looked down. It hadn't even occurred to her to change her clothes. She'd got into her pyjamas an hour ago, after her second cold shower. Gina would have a fit if she knew. 'Oh. Yes. Guess it's not very—' she swallowed '—sexy.'

Tuck shrugged. 'Funny can be sexy.'

'It's a tradition,' she explained as his gaze roved all over her shirt. It suddenly felt like it was on fire. 'Gina, Reese and Marnie send me geek T-shirts as a…it's a joke…' She petered out as she realised she was babbling. 'Sorry. Like I say, I'm not very good at this.'

Tuck disagreed. Cassie's unique approach was being very much appreciated by one particular part of his body. 'So,' he murmured, his fingers dropping from Cassie's sleeve to stroke up and down her arm, 'would you like the standard copulation package or one of the many variations I offer?'

Cassie pulled her arm away as an army of goose bumps marched across her skin and a seductive waft of Tuck flared her nostrils. 'Oh, I think the standard will be fine.' Her voice was husky again and she cleared it. 'I still have a paper to get back to. No time for variations.'

Tuck smiled. A man with a less robust ego might have been intimidated by her haste to be done with it. But he was not one to go for *'copulation'* by the clock. And she'd given him a goal now—to wipe that research paper from her head for the rest of the night.

Or die trying.

'Okay,' he said, stepping in closer to her, until her body was a hand-touch away, 'long, sweet, slow loving it is.'

Cassie swayed as her senses were engulfed in a wave of him, drenching every cell in a primal urge. She felt his hand warm on her waist, steadying her, and her eyes pinged open, her gaze snared in the brilliant blue of his.

'That's your *standard?*' she asked, her voice squeaky.

Tuck shrugged. 'I have high standards.'

He brought his free hand up to cradle her jaw. Her pupils were large and dilated, the sound of her breath was rough in his ears, her nostrils were flaring, her mouth was parted. Tuck knew all the signs of an aroused woman. And any other woman would be plastered all over him by now, eager to fulfil his every whim.

The fact that she wasn't was sweet and quaint and endearing. And vaguely thrilling.

Not that he had any issues with sexually aggressive women. He loved confidence and strength in and out of bed. But this—having a woman waiting for *his* move for a change—was, strangely, a real turn-on.

Cassie swore she could hear the sluggish grind of gears as time seemed to slow right down. Her head spun with the smell of him and she wanted him to kiss her so badly she didn't even recognise the woman she'd suddenly become.

'Tuck...' The word spilled from her lips on a desperate whisper she had no conscious control over.

Tuck sucked in a breath. The volume of want in her voice was lashing him with an identical desire. His fingers speared into her hair, his thumb brushing her temple. 'What do you want, Cassie?' he asked, his lips slowly descending towards hers.

Cassie was reeling. She could barely think through the fog of pheromones addling her senses, intoxicating her. 'I want you to kiss me,' she whispered, the words flowing thick and heavy like syrup from her throat.

Tuck didn't need it. He swooped the last few centimetres and crushed his mouth against hers. Her lips opened on a whimper that speared straight to his groin, and when her tongue tentatively touched, his heat traced its way there too. He groaned as her mouth opened more and her arms slid around his neck. He pulled her closer, until not even his platinum credit card could have been slipped between them. His hand dropped to her shoulder, skimmed her breast, moulded her hip, and then both his hands moved in unison to the cheeks of her butt hidden beneath layers of fabric.

He pulled her hips in hard, grinding his erection against her. She broke away, gasping, but his lips refused to let her retreat, following and claiming hers again in another hot lashing of lust which she opened to on a tiny little whimper that lit fires in all his erogenous zones.

His hand slid under her shirt, his palm fitting into the small of her back, then moving up the contours of her spine. Up, up, up. Her skin was hot and smooth to touch. The arch of her back, the dip of her ribs, the absence of bra strap fuelled the fever thrumming in his blood. Lust jabbed him in the solar plexus and he jerked her harder against him.

He needed her naked. He needed her laid out on his bed. He needed her calling his name and scratching her nails down his back. He dragged his mouth from hers.

Cassie swayed at the sudden loss of her anchor. The mewing noise coming from somewhere in her throat was totally foreign to her ears. His scent filled her head and drummed against her body like fat drops of sweet, sticky rain.

She couldn't think. All she could do was feel as her senses took over. Taste, touch, hearing, sight, smell.

Dear God, the addictive scent of him.

She blinked up at him. 'Wha…?'

Tuck's groin surged at her bewildered look, at the arousal dilating her pupils with undiluted desire. 'Bed,' he said, his hands sliding down her arms, his fingers linking through hers as he tugged on them gently, pulling her forward as he walked backwards.

The backs of his calves hit the mattress and he stopped. The soft downlights over the bed glowed across her flushed cheeks and glittered in her lust-drunk eyes. Some of her hair had loosened from its ponytail and she looked a little wild. Her ravaged lips and the way they were parted in silent invitation pushed her into wanton territory.

She looked one hundred percent into him and he couldn't remember the last time a woman had looked at him like that—for what he could give her in that moment as opposed to the rest of her life. Not even his ex-wife April had done that. There was no agenda, no artifice. Just a woman who wanted him—Samuel Tucker the man. Not the star quarterback.

Not his money. Not his ring. Not his babies.

Just him.

Frankly, he'd never been more attracted to a woman in his

life. He smiled at her as he drew her close, his hands cupping her face again. 'You're very beautiful,' he said.

The words flowed right over Cassie. She didn't care about that. Beauty was superfluous when the attraction was chemical. She didn't need it. She just needed the smell of his skin, the thud of his pulse, the primal act of joining.

He dipped his head and pressed a kiss to her eye, to her cheek, to her temple, his hands dropping by his sides. Cassie turned her face, her cheek brushing the roughness of his. A gust of his earthy male essence fanned over her like a hot dry wind. He kissed down her neck and her nose brushed the angle of his jaw. His aroma intensified. She pushed it against his skin and breathed in long and deep.

Her belly clenched and she groaned out loud. 'You smell so good,' she muttered.

Tuck lifted his head. Her pupils looked even more dilated than before. She was really getting off on those pheromones. He grinned. 'You smell pretty good yourself.' And he dropped his head again to claim her mouth.

But Cassie was suddenly overwhelmed by the urge to smell him. All over. To push her nose into the fat pounding pulse in his throat, to sniff at his temple, to smell his hair. To explore lower—to know the scent of his chest and his belly and his thighs.

To suck in great, big, dizzying lungfuls of him.

She evaded his mouth as it descended, her nose finding the steady beat pulsing along the hard ridge of his throat. It was warm, and his whiskers prickled her skin, smelling sweet yet somehow utterly male. She sucked in big deep breaths, each one washing over her in hot, satisfying waves. But it wasn't enough. She moved up, following the dips of his trachea to the pulse that beat where throat met jaw.

She inhaled deeply there too, dragging in his essence, feeling it lighten her head and tighten her belly. She meandered left along the line of his jaw, breathing him deep into her lungs as she went, and when she reached where the angle of his jaw met his ear she moaned involuntarily as heat bloomed through her pelvis.

Tuck's hands tightened on Cassie's waist as her moan filled his head. His eyes had shut as she'd explored his neck. Her nose and lips buzzing up his throat had sent heat to far-flung areas of his body. He pulled away from her, his heart pounding in his chest, the need to kiss her, to taste her mouth again, too powerful to resist.

For a second they just looked at each other, only the sound of their uneven breath between them. Then her nostrils flared, and her tongue darted out to swipe across her bottom lip, and lust kicked Tuck hard in his gut.

'Cassie,' he muttered, his head swooping down to claim her mouth again.

But Cassie evaded its trajectory, her head filled with one blinding imperative. *His scent.*

'Cassie?'

'I'm sorry,' she said, her chest rising and falling with difficulty, as if every oxygen molecule inside her was drenched in the sticky seduction of his pheromones. 'Can I just…sniff you for a while?'

Tuck laughed, but it died a quick death when he realised she was serious. The woman was definitely getting off on the smell of him. It was such a completely innocent thing to want amidst the carnal lure of lust surrounding them. And God knew it was a lot more satisfying than the women who got off on his fame, or the idea they were going to be the next Mrs Samuel Tucker.

She was looking at him with uncertainty clouding her blue-grey eyes and he wanted the breathy, needy Cassie back. He put his hands up in surrender. Cassie obviously had some kind of itch she wanted to scratch—he was just pleased she'd chosen him to relieve it.

'Whatever floats your boat, darlin'.'

Cassie didn't hesitate. His heady aroma was drawing her back to him with all the power of a magnetic force. She pushed her nose back into his neck, greedily refamiliarising herself with his thick, luscious tang.

'Yes,' she whispered as she moved down this time. 'Yes.'

Tuck swallowed as her breath licked heat down to the hollow at the base of his throat, her moan as she inhaled there fanning his arousal. She lingered for a moment or two, then travelled lower, her nose invading the soft towelling of his robe, moving it sideways as she followed the hard ridge of his collarbone. She reached for the belt of his robe and tugged. When the robe gaped open his erection bucked against the confines of his underwear and he grasped her hips for stability as a wave of red-hot lust almost brought him to his knees.

He hung on silently and waited, his erection aching as she stared at his chest, her nostrils flaring. Then she lifted her hands and pushed the robe off his shoulders. He shrugged them and it fell to the ground, and when she buried her face in the centre of his chest it took all his willpower not to envelop her with his arms, to remember this was *her* show.

After what seemed an age she lifted her head and said, 'Back,' as she pushed on his chest.

Tuck let her push him onto the bed and sat on the mattress looking up at her as she stood between his spread thighs, looking down. Her cheeks were flushed and something base glittered in her eyes.

'All the way,' she muttered, and he obediently fell back against the mattress, his feet still firmly planted on the floor.

He didn't care that he was in nothing but his underwear, with a monster erection threatening to bust free. She was staring at his body with carnal intent and he was totally in her thrall.

'Take your hair down,' he murmured.

Much to his surprise she did it without argument, obviously automatically, with her mind on other things. She was blissfully unaware of how sexy it was, cascading around her shoulders. He smiled at the economy of movement. Other women would have given it a sexy little shake, or piled it up high on their heads and let if drift down as they shimmied about seductively.

But not this one.

Cassie didn't even know where to start as she stared down at him. She was blind to the dips and hollows, the planes and angles, the magnificence of him on anything other than a primal level. How biologically defined he was to hunt and protect. To mate. To procreate. Not even the erection straining his underwear registered on anything other than a scientific level.

She couldn't think past the scent of him—as if it was made specifically for her DNA to recognise and she was the only one who could smell it. Respond to it. His chest pounded with the thump of his heart and his belly bounded to the corresponding pump of his aorta.

Her nostrils flared. *There*. Right there.

She nudged her knee on the bed between his legs and barely registered his sharp intake of breath as she bent over his belly and nuzzled the firm flesh covering the jump of his abdominal pulse. She moaned as her senses filled with him.

And then it wasn't enough. She needed more. She needed to know all of him. She drifted up the centre of his belly, meandering her nose and mouth across his nipples and then drifting further, pushing them into the clean scent of his armpits, feeling the light caress of downy hair against her face.

He smelled like soap and deodorant and the scent she was recognising as pure Tuck, and her breasts tingled in response.

She moved up to his throat and jaw again, brushing his temple, rubbing her face in his hair, where something fresh and woodsy flared her nostrils and undulated along her pelvic floor.

Then it was time to head south again. Her nose brushed his, his husky breathing in time with hers, she buzzed his mouth and smelled beer, and felt the rush of air and heat as a low moan slipped from his lips. She went lower, back down his throat, his chest, his belly. It clenched beneath her ministrations and she looked up at him. His eyes were closed, his mouth parted, his fingers clenched in the sheet beside him.

Her chin brushed material as she looked down at the final frontier. She wanted to know what he smelled like *there*. She stood back on her feet and reached for the band of his underwear.

Tuck's eyes flew open as he grabbed her hand. 'Oh, no, you don't,' he said, looking at her through a haze of lust. 'I'm down to my underwear and you're still fully clothed. Time to level the playing field, don't you think?'

Cassie blinked. Tuck's Texan drawl seemed even more pronounced now it was all husky to boot. She looked down at herself. Her state of dress had been the furthest thing from her mind. 'Right,' she said.

Another woman would have felt shy about getting naked before a man for the first time, but Cassie didn't have a problem with it. Hers was just another female body, after all. Just like every other woman's on earth.

Just biology.

She quickly shrugged out of her shirt and shimmied out of her leggings with Tuck watching every move. When his breath hissed out she looked up to find him staring at her, his gaze firmly fixed on her naked breasts. Her nipples beaded beneath his scrutiny and muscles deep inside her clenched hard.

His gaze drifted lower, to her underwear, and the juncture of her thighs burned and tingled as if he'd blasted her with a hot blue laser beam. She struggled to rein in her choppy breath.

His hoot of laughter was quite unexpected.

'"*Talk nerdy to me*"?' he asked.

Cassie looked down at the logo on her underwear. Again, not something she'd thought about changing. Not that she'd brought anything sexy to change into. Not that she owned anything sexy in the underwear department.

'Let me guess. Gina?'

Cassie shook her head. 'Actually, these are from Reese.'

Tuck laughed again, letting his head fall back against the mattress. Which was all the invitation Cassie needed. He'd wanted a level playing field—he'd got it. Now she wanted her pound of flesh. She looked down at his underwear, her gaze snagging on the erection, and her mouth watered.

She placed one hand on the bed beside him and used the other to reach for the band of his underwear. He sucked in a loud breath and lifted his head off the mattress. Their gazes meshed. They didn't say a word, but he lifted his hips and Cassie stripped his underwear away, pulling it off his feet before coming close again, looking down at him.

Cassie had seen her fair share of penises in her life. She'd known a few intimately. Although none had managed to produce anywhere near the screeching level of arousal that Tuck's had—especially from sight alone! And she'd seen them in all their variation in hundreds of textbooks over the years. She'd never found them particularly attractive, and had pretty much felt that one wasn't that much different from another.

Which just went to show what kind of a freaking genius she was!

Tuck's was the most beautiful specimen she'd ever seen. Long and thick, nestled in light curls, and lying hard and potent against his belly. A fat vein ran up the middle, and once again her mouth watered.

She dropped to her knees without thinking, kneeling between his as she pushed her face against it, running her nose up and down the length of the vein, inhaling its essence. Musk and man.

Tuck's groan, his hand in her hair, his strangled, 'Cassie...' drove her on.

She shifted from the rampant thrust of him to the flat of his belly beneath, and further afield to the heat of his groin, dragging the scent of him inside her as she went. But it was inevitable that she'd return to his erection—as if that was the source of his pheromones, the mother lode—and she inhaled deeply as her lips brushed his girth. She followed it all the way to the head, marvelling at how the skin could feel soft like a rose petal but the core as strong as steel.

A bead of fluid at the tip wafted more musk her way and without conscious thought her tongue dipped into it, savouring its tang as it joined the heady mix intoxicating her senses.

Tuck reared up, cursing. 'Okay—no,' he said, dragging her up his body and falling back with her, rolling so he pinned her to the bed.

A man could only take so much.

'Enough,' he growled. 'My turn.'

And he flayed her mouth with a kiss full of heat and want and something else he wasn't familiar with and didn't care to know about.

Cassie just held on as his kiss spun her onto another plane. Heat swept through her body and she welcomed it. Yes. *This* was what her body was craving. *This.*

Primitive. Base. Primal.

His hands pushed at her knickers and she helped him, wriggling and kicking until she was free of them, desperate to have him inside her, to quell her hormones for once and for all.

'Yes,' she said against his mouth. 'Now.'

Time to do it. To do what she'd come to do. To get it over with. She'd had her fill of his pheromones. Now it was time for more.

To couple. To mate. To copulate.

Tuck's mind was spinning into a quagmire of lust and desire he could barely find his way out of. He had to slow it down or he was going to explode.

'Slow down, there,' he murmured as he eased a hand between her legs.

Cassie froze. *No!* This wasn't what this was about. It was about exorcising the power of her hormones, satisfying her libido and then moving on. Getting it out of her system. Her hormones had demanded she mate—she was mating.

It was biochemistry. Biology.

It was business. Not pleasure.

Not that pleasure had ever been a possibility for her. And she sure as hell wasn't going to open herself to that dry old argument when she had a paper to get back to.

'No,' she gasped against his mouth, pushing his hand aside as she grabbed his erection. 'I need you in me now.'

She did. She really did. She needed to shut her hormones up for once and all!

'But I want to—'

Cassie cut him off with her mouth, slamming a kiss on his lips that left them dizzy and clinging to each other. *Who knew she could kiss like that?*

'Damn it, Tuck,' she said, breaking away as her hormones screamed at her for fulfilment. *'Now!'*

Tuck was too far gone. Her kiss, and her brand of innocent seduction, and most especially her hand kneading his erection were too, too much—and her whimper when he broke away was a potent aphrodisiac.

'Tuck,' she moaned, grabbing for him.

'Condom,' he said, reaching over the side of the mattress into his bag, locating one in the side zip pocket and quickly donning it.

And then he was back, and Cassie was reaching for him, opening her legs and lifting her hips in invitation, and he took what she was offering, so utterly free of any agenda, and drove himself into her in one easy thrust.

Cassie's gasp was loud in his ears and he stopped abruptly. 'Are you okay?' he asked, looking down at her. Her face was scrunched up.

She wasn't a virgin, was she?

Cassie could feel the hot length of him hard inside her and doubted she'd ever been filled so completely. It hurt so damn good she swore she could hear her libido sigh.

Yes. *Ahh.* Yes. That was it. *This* was what she needed.

'Yes,' she said.

Yes, yes, yes. It would be over in a minute—two at the outside if Len was any litmus test—and then she'd be free to get on with her life, with her pesky libido back in its box.

She shifted restlessly beneath him. 'Don't stop.'

Tuck obliged, rising up on his elbows, looming over her as he began a slow, teasing thrust guaranteed to satisfy. Arousal streaked hot fingers into his thighs and buttocks as her tightness massaged and squeezed the length of him, and he knew he was going to need all his staying power to hold out for her.

Cassie moaned. She might never have found sex to be personally fulfilling, but she'd always enjoyed the feel of a man inside her and got satisfaction from the pleasure her partner derived from it. As if she'd engineered a successful experiment. And she was determined that today would be no different. Tuck would find his release soon and she could bask in the happy glow of a job well done.

And so, damn it, could her libido.

Of course it was hard to concentrate on the end game when Tuck insisted on such slow, rhythmic thrusts. She didn't like the feeling of pressure building in her pelvis. She'd been there before and knew it never amounted to anything—that it only ever got so far and no more.

Tuck adjusted the angle of his thrust as Cassie lay passively in his arms. He smiled down at the look of concentration on her face. 'Stop thinking,' he growled, leaning in to press a hard kiss on her mouth. It was satisfying to see when he pulled away that he'd kissed the lust back. 'Stop thinking,' he reiterated.

Cassie shut her eyes briefly as he picked up the pace and something stirred deep inside her. Something she didn't like. Something that she knew intuitively she'd never be able to contain.

And that just wasn't part of the world she lived in.

It reminded her too much of a time during her teenage years when her grip on the world had loosened and things had rapidly spiralled out of her control.

A place she never wanted to revisit.

'Don't wait for me,' she dismissed. 'I may take for ever.'

Tuck grinned. 'We've got all night. And I'm not going without you, darlin'.'"

Cassie knew with sudden clarity that he was telling the truth, and a surge of dread rose in her chest. For some strange reason she didn't want to appear sexually inadequate before him. But just thinking about the impossibility of it all made her instantly tense.

Tuck groaned, dropping his head to her neck. 'God, you feel so tight,' he muttered, dropping kisses on her throat.

Cassie sighed. There was only one thing for it—and she thanked Gina and Marnie and Reese for making her watch that movie where the actress faked an orgasm in a coffee shop, because at least she had some clue how to go about it.

She shut her eyes and started to moan, softly at first, then picking up, adding in some panting—and didn't she remember seeing another film with the Awesome Foursome where the actress dug her nails into the actor's back a lot, even scratched them down? She threw that in for good measure.

Tuck felt the bite of Cassie's nails right down to his groin, and cried out as her moans and pants pushed him closer to the edge. He picked up the pace, dropping his forehead against hers as their orgasms built and built. Cassie's cries got louder, and when she reached for his buttocks and squeezed tight his orgasm hit warp speed.

'Yes, Tuck, yes,' Cassie croaked in his ear, knowing he was close and gasping her pleasure, no matter how fake, right into his ear.

She was too busy concentrating on faking it to be in tune with the buzz going on inside her, but that was okay. If Tuck's big hard body pounding into hers hadn't satisfied her libido than nothing would.

'Tuck,' she cried. 'Tuck. I'm… I'm…'

Tuck's belly pulled taut and red-hot pleasure eddied and swirled just out of his reach as his orgasm bubbled to the surface. 'Yes, Cassie, yes. Let go. I'll come with you.'

Cassie cried out in what she hoped was a fairly accurate rendition of an orgasming woman. It certainly seemed to convince Tuck, who groaned her name as he thrust and thrust and thrust, causing a little more tension to gather in her pelvis.

Cassie let her cries die down in pace with his as he collapsed on top of her. She might not have been satisfied in the strictest sense of the word, but there was something very primitive and sating about being possessed so utterly.

Something carnal. Hormonal.

Tuck stirred, kissing Cassie's neck, her collarbone. He rolled off her onto his back with a long contented groan, his heart still pounding like a train, his head spinning from one of the most forceful orgasms he'd ever had. For long moments he couldn't even move.

When he was capable of stirring he rolled up onto his elbow and looked down into her face, needing to know that it had been as good for her. To see that look he knew so well. That *Paper? What paper?* look.

Instead she smiled at him and patted his biceps. 'That was nice,' she chirped.

Nice? Tuck eyed her suspiciously. There were three things he was good at in life—football, math and sex.

And there was nothing *nice* about his brand of sex.

He'd slept with a lot of women—which wasn't necessarily something to be proud of, but he knew for a damn fact not one of them had left his bed anything other than one hundred percent satisfied. He was satisfaction *guaranteed.* And as such he knew the signs. Could read it in their eyes.

Hell, he could pick a sated woman out of a line-up at fifty paces.

He would not have picked Cassie out of a line-up.

'Oh, my God,' he murmured. 'You faked it.'

CHAPTER FIVE

TUCK FLOPPED ON to his back. No one had ever—*ever*—faked it with him. That wasn't arrogance or conceit—it was the damn plain truth of it.

It was ironic that he'd just had one of those *oh-my-god* moments and she was lying there all *that-was-nice.* He stared at the ceiling, trying to decide whether he should be insulted, but he found himself laughing instead.

Somehow it seemed par for the course for this very bizarre seduction.

Cassie felt his low laughter stroke deep inside her to muscles and tissues that still seemed tense and excitable. She frowned. They weren't supposed to be like that—they were supposed to be loose, limber.

Done. Content. Over.

Gina's warning that once might not be enough came back to haunt her. *Well, too bad!* She'd given in to the insanity of her libido and now she wanted her brain back!

Tuck shook his head, still contemplating the ceiling. 'I can't believe you faked it.' And he laughed again.

'Look, it's okay,' Cassie assured him, eyes also firmly trained on the ceiling as she went into the familiar patter. Len had required a lot of reassurance in the beginning too. 'It's not your fault. It's me… I'm just not physically capable of climaxing. It has nothing to do with your technique…or your speed—'

Tuck laughed harder, interrupting her clueless critique. He rolled up on his elbow again. 'Darlin', you are hard on a man's ego.'

Cassie blinked and her nostrils flared as a heady dose of pheromones engulfed her. Those muscles inside her snapped to attention, pulling taut and sizzling with tension.

No. *No, no, no.*

Concentrate. Soothe the man's ego and then take your libido far, far away. Take it to Cornell and bury it in a PhD.

'Sorry, I didn't mean… Look, it just doesn't happen for me. It's a…a thing.'

Tuck saw her pupils dilating again. *Interesting.* 'Like a medical condition?' he asked innocently as he nuzzled her ear.

Cassie swallowed, her eyelids fluttering closed. 'Kind of.'

He dropped a kiss on her temple. 'Sounds awful,' he murmured.

'Oh, no, it's fine,' Cassie said, shaking her head, trying to clear the fog filling it as his scent wrapped her up in seductive thread. 'I don't need it.'

Tuck smiled against her hair line. If anyone needed an orgasm it was Cassiopeia. 'Honey,' he said as his mouth zeroed in on hers, '*everyone* needs a little bit of *it* sometimes.'

Cassie opened her eyes to deny his statement just as his mouth made contact with hers, and a wave of longing for *it* crashed over her. It was impossible. How could she crave something she'd never had? Miss something she didn't know? Want something she didn't need?

Where was the logic in that?

But his kiss laid her bare, plundering her mouth, flaying her with heat and pheromones, demanding that she kiss him back with equal vigour. And she did—clinging to him, twisting her arms around his neck, attacking his mouth with a savagery utterly foreign to her.

A sense of falling gripped her when he finally pulled away, and Cassie was grateful for being horizontal and anchored to him.

Tuck looked down into her flushed face. She was breathing hard. They both were. They were going again—and this time she was coming with him.

He pulled away. 'I'll be back in a moment,' he said.

Cassie watched him climb out of the bed in a stupor, her head spinning from the kiss and the dizzying essence of him spinning her in its web. She struggled against it, her brain urging her to be sensible.

She levered herself on her elbows. 'I should go.'

'Oh, no, you don't,' Tuck said as he strode towards the bathroom to rid himself of the condom. 'I haven't finished with you yet.'

Go! her brain screamed. *Go now!*

Her brain willed her muscles to move. But her muscles said no. Every cell in her body, drenched in sex, leadened by his command to stay, said no. And then he was back, striding towards her, gloriously naked, stopping to snag some foil packets from his bag and throwing them on the bedside table. And then he was pushing her back, stroking his hands down her body, finger-painting his pheromones all over her. Stupid took over.

Okay, she accepted as she welcomed the heat of his mouth on hers. *Slight change of plan.* They were going again. She could do that. Obviously another coupling was what her body was craving. She could do it. She could go twice.

And then get back to her paper.

Tuck had no idea what Cassie was thinking as his mouth left hers for parts further south. He was too caught up in being so rampantly hard again, considering what had happened not even ten minutes ago, and he was determined not to waste it. This time it would be about her. No taking.

No faking.

He'd followed the same game plan he always followed when he was with a woman, but had let Cassie's wild urgings and amazing aptitude for acting distract him from his goal. She was going to be singing the *Hallelujah Chorus* tonight if it killed him.

Cassie's head spun and she shut her eyes as Tuck's hot tongue traced a pathway down her throat. What was he *doing?* She was ready. *He* was most definitely ready. Why wasn't he inside her already? She shifted restlessly against him, spreading her legs to accommodate him, lifting her hips.

Tuck smiled, ignoring her blatant invitation. No way— not this time. He ran his tongue up and over the swell of a breast, and when he reached the nipple he swiped his tongue over it, then sucked it inside, smiling as it leapt to attention in his mouth.

Cassie's eyes flew open as a jolt of sensation pinged along muscle fibres and nerve-endings already at snapping point. Her nipples were extraordinarily sensitive, and having them fondled during sex had always been irritating. She tried to sit up, to tell him to stop, that it wasn't necessary, but his mouth closed over her other nipple and she fell back against the mattress on a whimper.

Tuck was obviously determined to go where no man had ever been—the O zone.

'You know,' she panted, her eyes shut, her back arching off the bed as his teeth grazed and taunted her nipple—which strangely didn't feel irritating at all when he did it. 'You really don't have to do this. To try. I won't think any less of you.'

Tuck ignored her. 'Is that so?' He sucked on her nipple hard, satisfied to hear a strange gurgly noise at the back of her throat.

Cassie resolutely held on to her sanity—no matter how tenuous it suddenly appeared. 'It's really not going to happen, so you might as well just...' she swallowed as his tongue flicked back and forth over the taut peak he was toying with '...get down to business.'

Tuck withdrew his mouth and looked up at her. He could see the moist, puckered stance of her nipple in his peripheral vision, and it was deeply satisfying to know that she was viewing him through the evidence of her own arousal.

'Wanna bet?' He smiled, then returned his attention to the nipple, hungry for the satisfying hardness of it against his palate.

Cassie shut her eyes. 'Is not about chance,' she said, her breath choppy. 'It's statistics. You must understand that, right?' She raised her head to look at him and was hit by a surge of lust at the sight of his blond head bowed over her breast. She flopped back down, pushing it ruthlessly away.

Where was she again?

'I know I'm statistically unlikely to achieve orgasm simply because I never have.'

'Uh-huh,' Tuck said, her nipple slipping from his mouth as he left for more southern destinations.

His hand followed, brushing light strokes down her ribcage to her hip, across the flat of her belly and fluttering down her thighs. His mouth found her belly button and he lapped wet circles around it, dipping in and out as he went.

Cassie felt every muscle fibre beneath shudder in anticipation. She'd never felt this much tension in her belly before. It was heavy—screeching with it.

'It's not you.' She pressed on, for her sanity's sake if nothing else, as he caressed her inner thigh and she felt it all the way to her centre. 'I take this medication. It helps me sleep. But it...' She panted as his tongue moved lower. 'It suppresses certain other...' A strangled gasp rose in her throat as she felt a finger brush over the place where everything felt slick and wet and tingly. She gulped for air. 'Other processes...'

Tuck raised his head to look at her. He could smell her arousal, and his erection kicked at the thought of tasting her.

He made sure their gazes were locked when he said, 'It just means I have to work a little harder.' He slipped a finger inside her. Her swift intake of breath and the way her hands bunched in the sheet punched him hard in the gut. 'I'm not afraid of hard work.'

Cassie couldn't look away from the compelling determination in his star blue eyes. There were things inside them that she didn't understand—and didn't want to either. She shut her eyes, blocked him out. Blocked out the heaviness in her breasts, the tension in her belly, the hard probe of his finger buried inside her.

'Yes, but how good can it really—?' Another finger slid inside her and she gasped at its intrusion. It took a few moments for her to lamely add, 'Be?'

Sensation swamped her, momentarily drowning out the yammering of her brain before she clawed it back.

'I've seen comet trails,' she panted as he pulled his fingers out and pushed them in again. 'And exploding stars.' More pushing and pulling and panting. 'The birth of universes. Nothing can beat that.'

Tuck looked up from her belly, where he was doodling wet circles with his tongue, withdrawing his fingers. 'Oh, honey, just you lie back,' he murmured. 'Let me teach you some things they don't rate at Mensa.'

And he settled between her legs, pushing them wide with his shoulders, feasting his eyes on the end game. Her arousal wafted towards him and he salivated at the thought of tasting her. A surge of red-hot lust enveloped him at seeing the thatch of dark hair reminding him she was all woman.

Cassie's eyes widened as Tuck lowered his head and his

intent became clear. 'Oh, no,' she said, placing her hand over herself, barring his way. 'No, no, *no*. You definitely don't have to do *that*.'

Tuck looked up. From this vantage point he could see her still erect nipples, standing proud and puckered, and smell her musky scent. He flared his nostrils. It filled his head and it took all his willpower not to bury his face in her. 'I know. But I want to.'

Cassie shook her head. 'Nothing works,' she reiterated. Why wasn't he listening to her?

Tuck's hands slid up her body to stroke her breasts, his fingers smoothing over the taut peaks of her nipples. 'Trust me,' he murmured.

Cassie gasped as his touch bloomed and tingled at the juncture of her thighs, just below where his face hovered. It burned and ached. 'I've never...'

'It's okay.' He grinned. 'I'm an expert.'

And then he lowered his head, nudging her hand aside, just nuzzling her at first, brushing his closed mouth along her sex, familiarising himself with the contours, filling his senses up with her.

Then he let his tongue do some exploring. He swiped it against the centre of her and grunted in satisfaction when she gasped and bucked against him. He inhaled then, deep and long, and his head roared with a surge of lust and male possession and he opened his mouth over her, needing more, wanting all of her.

Cassie felt a jolt of something hot and hard slam into her belly and she shut her eyes against the urgency of it. Tuck's tongue licked and probed and sucked as his fingers spread their own joy, stroking and teasing and rubbing her nipples to a state of almost painful arousal, and she gasped and squirmed beneath the relentless attack.

She lifted her head to look at him, and the sight of his

blond head between her legs flushed like a drug through her system. When his tongue found the hard nub that she'd never really bothered to explore for herself and flicked it she just about lifted off the bed.

'Tuck!' she cried out as sensations she'd never experienced before catapulted her into a whole new realm.

Tuck's hand moved down from her breast to splay low and wide on her belly, clamping her to the mattress, holding her earthbound as she bucked and writhed beneath the onslaught of his tongue. He was holding her right where she was, taunting her with all he had, tasting her, determined to make her so rattled she wouldn't know which solar system she was in.

And all the time a primal beat thrummed through his head and streaked hot urgency through the muscles of his belly and buttocks. He was torn between the overriding urge to drive into her, to plunge himself into all that tight heat and feel her around him again, and the need to suck up every last morsel of her, to feast on her, to propel her to a place she'd never been.

A place more cosmic than she'd ever seen.

Cassie didn't know what was happening to her as heat and pressure built everywhere, but she was suddenly terrified. She hadn't felt anything like this before but she knew with a disturbing clarity that she wanted it—bad.

And that was the most frightening thing of all.

The only thing she'd ever wanted this badly was to go to Antarctica on a research mission, and now even that seemed to pale in comparison to the tidal force of lust and seething need consuming her body.

Her life dealt in certainties. Fact and logic and common sense were her true north. She depended on them. She needed them. And this…whatever it was…was making a mockery of them.

If this was the power of an orgasm she could do without.

'No,' she muttered, her head tossing from side to side, her eyes shut fast. She didn't want this. 'No.'

'Yes,' Tuck said, sensing that most of the battle was inside Cassie's head. He held her fast and sucked down hard on her clitoris. 'Stop fighting it, Cassie,' he said when he finally lifted his head.

Cassie shook her head. 'No,' she muttered as sensations rose and she pushed them back.

Tuck grimaced. He knew she was there, that she was on the edge, so close. *Goddamn it,* he'd never met a woman so averse to a good time in his life.

'Yes,' he said, shifting his hand off her belly and using it in tandem with his tongue, stroking his index finger up and down her centre as his other hand ministered to the tight pucker of her nipples.

She didn't need to have this in her life—to change everything she'd thought she knew. She knew what she wanted. And it wasn't the total consuming vortex of sex.

Tuck urged her on, pushing a finger inside all her tight, slick heat. And then another.

Cassie gaped at the invasion. Something started to pool and ripple, down low and deep, and hot urgent fingers dug into her buttocks and thighs. But she clamped down hard against it, pushing it back. Her heels drummed against the mattress. Her head rocked from side to side.

Tuck looked up at her. Her head was thrown back, her mouth open, gasping with every thrust of his fingers. 'I can show you some stars, darlin', like you've never seen before,' he murmured. 'You just gotta let go.'

Cassie whimpered. *Let go?* What did that mean? She didn't know *how* to let go.

'Relax, let it take you,' Tuck soothed as she cried out in obvious conflict.

Cassie sobbed as the effort to push back the looming tide

threatened to overwhelm her. Nothing was familiar. Nothing was the same. Everything was coming apart around her as a swirling, sucking sensation deep in her core obliterated all thought and consciousness and finally pulled her into its abyss.

Tuck felt her clamp tight around his fingers and knew she was finally there. He dropped his head and lashed his tongue back and forward over the nub that had grown impossibly hard. Her back arched off the bed and he squeezed her nipple between his fingers.

Cassie cried out as her mind left her body and flew. Tuck had promised her stars, and as deep, unremitting pleasure drenched her she floated through a cosmos of colours, with a kaleidoscope of shooting stars bursting around her like fireworks. She was actually amongst them—not just observing them from afar. Reaching out for them. Basking in their heat and absorbing their incandescence into her soul.

Tuck did not let up, feasting greedily until Cassie's muscles stopped contracting around him and the cries and the wild bucking of her hips started to settle. He gently withdrew his fingers from her, propping his chin on her belly as he watched them die to a hush, waiting for the moment that she opened her eyes.

And he wasn't disappointed. When she finally lay spent and still on the mattress, and her eyes eventually fluttered open, the blue-grey was practically slate with drunken satisfaction, her pupils big and black, her focus obviously not quite twenty-twenty as she blinked at him rapidly.

'Tuck?'

Now he could pick her out of a line-up.

Now she didn't even look as if she could *spell* the word *paper*.

'I... I...'

Tuck smiled at her utter bewilderment, but it grabbed a big

handful of his gut and squeezed hard. He grinned, crawling up her body, dropping a kiss on her belly, and one between her breasts and the hollow at the base of her throat, before lashing her mouth with a deep, wet kiss, his erection surging as it pressed into her thigh.

'Hold on, darlin',' he muttered against her mouth as he reached for a foil packet, 'we're not done yet.'

Cassie watched, still in a daze, as he tore at the packet with his teeth. There weren't a lot of coherent thoughts in her head, but her stomach clenched at the sight of him, hard and ready, and once again her brain went on vacation as her body responded to the primal cue to mate.

And then he was over her, and in her, his mouth drugging her with kisses that took her back to that place amongst the stars, and his erection was stroking inside her, reviving tissues that were already in a dangerously excitable state. And she was flying again, but it was better this time because he was with her, and she held on to him tight as they astral-planed through the cosmos, revelling in the shake and the shudder of him, his guttural cries in her ear ratcheting the pleasure up, taking her higher and higher and higher.

Cassie didn't know how long they were gone for. Or how long it took to come back down to earth. Time ceased to exist and the awareness of her surroundings crept back very slowly. The mattress beneath her. The weight of his body on hers. The sound of their breath as they lay together, gasping.

All these years and *that* was what she'd been missing out on?

At some stage Tuck rolled off her, getting up to dispose of the condom, then rejoined her, lying down next to her as she stared at the ceiling, contemplating the magic that had just happened.

When she finally got her breath back she said, 'Please tell me you can do that again.'

Obviously her brain was still missing in action.

Tuck rolled his head to look at her and laughed. It looked as if one round of good sex had turned Little-Miss-Brainiac into Little-Miss-Nymphomaniac. 'I may need a moment or two.'

Cassie was pretty sure she was going to need some recovery time too. She turned on her side, her gaze roving over his face. 'Is it…is it always like that?'

Tuck nodded, but he knew that wasn't true. What they'd just had wasn't like anything else he'd ever experienced. Sex had always been good, but never like this. Not even with April, whom he'd thought he'd loved. Or tried to anyway.

The knowledge was unsettling.

He rolled his head back to stare at the ceiling again. 'It is with me, darlin',' he said, keeping up his usual patter.

Cassie got goose bumps as the low, slow drawl of Tuck's accent whispered across her skin and stroked those muscles inside her that didn't seem to be able to get enough of him. Her gaze was drawn to the rise and fall of his chest and she actually reached out and trailed her fingers down it—something, prior to yesterday, she would have thought she'd need a frontal lobotomy to do.

Her cheek rested on his biceps and his scent tickled her senses again. She pressed her nose into the warm bulk and inhaled him deep inside her body. A blast of his natural essence invaded her cells again and stirred the embers of her orgasm.

Tuck smiled. 'I could bottle some of those pheromones, if you like?'

Cassie dragged herself away. Why bottle it when it was right here? In the flesh? Gina *was* right. Maybe she needed a little time? Like a whole night?

She was leaving in the morning—hopefully with her brain returned—why deprive herself?

'Direct from the source is always best,' she said, trying to sound scientific and factual when she felt tongue-tied and unsure of herself.

Tuck grinned as he looked down at her. 'Don't you have a paper to get back to?'

Cassie nodded. She did. She really did. But she was pretty sure even simple words were beyond her at the moment, let alone complex analysis of weather patterns on Jupiter. Not to mention the fact that for the first time in her life she actually didn't *care* about the complex weather systems of Jupiter.

'I'm not sure I'll understand it. I think I just lost a hundred IQ points.'

Tuck chuckled. 'Welcome to being average. I hope you enjoy your stay.'

If this was how average people passed their time Cassie was beginning to think that being a genius was the dumbest thing anyone could be.

'I'm leaving for Cornell in the morning,' she said. She had no idea where it had come from, but there was obviously still one functioning brain cell somewhere that seemed to remember what had been *the most important thing in her life* until half an hour ago.

Tuck rolled up in one swift movement, settling himself into the cradle of her hips. 'So tonight we'll just play dumb. How's it been so far?'

Cassie blinked. 'Very…educational.'

'Oh, so you approve of my copulation techniques?' he teased. 'Your libido has been adequately serviced?'

Cassie might have been clueless about a lot of things but, having read a lot of textbooks and seen a lot of nature shows, even *she* was aware that what they'd just shared was nothing to do with the slaking of a biological imperative.

'Well, I have minimal comparative data, and no blind studies to—'

Tuck's mouth cut her off and she lost her mind for a while as his scent filled her up with heady need. When he pulled back they were both a little out of breath.

'I'll take that as a no,' he said. 'It's okay. I'll try harder. They don't call me Mr-Satisfaction-Guaranteed for nothing. Libido servicing is right up my alley. Are you hungry?'

'It's almost midnight,' she murmured. Cassie never ate after seven o'clock. It wasn't good for the digestion.

Tuck shrugged. 'So?'

Cassie blinked as a huge belly rumble echoed in the space between them and she realised she was starving. She'd become a truly primitive woman—utterly biological. 'I could go for some toast.'

Tuck smiled as he dropped a hard kiss on her mouth and reached over and snatched up the phone. 'Trust me—you'll like what I can do with strawberries and cream much better.'

Cassie woke wrapped spoon-like in Tuck's arms at eight the next morning. It was the second morning in a row she'd woken late. The second morning in a row she'd woken thinking about him. The second morning in a row she'd woken with Jupiter as far from her brain as the actual planet itself.

And the first morning ever she'd woken with a man rubbing all his rampant male hardness against her. Tuck's hand was at her breast, and his essence filled her waking senses with sex and surrender, giving her brain no chance to switch on.

Tuck sensed the moment she came awake and his hand tightened around the swell of her breast, his fingers rolling over her nipple. When she moaned and arched her back he dragged her closer, kissing her neck.

'When do you have to leave?' he muttered in her ear.

Leave? Cassie thought hard through the fog of pheromones

and the heavy scent of sex clouding her senses. 'Whenever I can get a train,' she said.

Tuck licked a path from her ear to the slope where her shoulder met her throat as his hand slipped between her legs. 'When do you *need* to be at Cornell?'

Cassie shut her eyes as his fingers stroked against her centre. 'Day...after...tomorrow...' she murmured, easing her legs apart to give him better access.

'So you could stay another night?' he said, his finger sinking into the slick heat of her. 'Just to make sure your libido is well and truly serviced. I'd hate for that to get in the way of your very important studies.'

Cassie thought he made a very good point—just as he found the spot that was screaming for his touch. She gasped. 'Yes. That would be awful. I need to focus at Cornell.' She needed her libido back in its box. 'I could do one more night.'

Tuck was too far gone to acknowledge his triumph. All he could feel was the wet heat of her as he slid his erection up and down the length of her slick entrance—close, so close.

'Do you have any condoms in your room?' he asked.

Cassie squirmed against him, tilting her pelvis, desperately needing him inside her, not taunting her from the outside. 'Why would *I* have condoms?'

Tuck groaned, trying to wrestle back control. 'We're out.' And a place as posh as the Bellington wasn't likely to have a condom vending machine. '*Somebody* was insatiable last night.'

Cassie blushed. She'd lost count of the number of orgasms she'd had. They'd all just blurred together into one long brain-incapacitating event.

Tuck pulled away from her with difficulty. Even knowing he couldn't get any woman pregnant, he'd always been a stickler for safe sex. He reached for the telephone. 'I'll ring the concierge.'

Cassie dragged in gulps of air, trying to clear the sexual fog, but as per usual all she did was drag in more of him and her belly tightened. She rolled onto her back, her head turning towards him. 'The concierge will get you condoms?'

'The concierge will get a star quarterback whatever the hell he likes.'

'Even an *ex?*' she asked, trying to imagine a famous astronomer—*real* stars, in her opinion—getting the same treatment.

Tuck flinched slightly at the *ex.* For well over a decade he'd defined himself by the magic he'd made on the field. It still cut deep that it had all been snatched away. But he pushed it aside. 'Yup.'

Cassie tried to fathom the celebrity paradigm, but even that was too much with her brain gone walkabout. 'Wait,' she said as he went to dial. 'I'll ring Gina.'

Tuck frowned. 'Why not the concierge?'

'Because Gina already knows we're doing it.'

And the fewer people who knew she'd lost her mind the better.

CHAPTER SIX

CASSIE AND TUCK stayed another *two* nights. Just to be sure her libido was well and truly serviced. They rose late on the third morning, had a dirty shower and, unable to avoid the phone calls and text messages from her gal pals any longer, Cassie joined them in the dining room for a late breakfast.

'Well, well, well,' Gina drawled as Cassie sat down. 'Never thought I'd see the day. Cassiopeia Barclay all loved up.'

Cassie snorted. 'Don't be ridiculous. Love is a romantic construct—'

'Perpetrated by romance novels and Hollywood with no sound scientific basis,' Gina finished.

Cassie shot her a sheepish look. 'Exactly.' She fiddled with her cutlery. 'Tuck and I are just—'

'Copulating?' Reese said, winking at Gina.

Cassie nodded, even though she knew they'd moved far beyond copulation. Beyond scratching a biological itch. Her libido had been well and truly satisfied after the first twenty-four hours—it was just being plain greedy now. 'Yes.'

'And has Tuck copulated his way through my box of condoms yet?' Gina asked.

Cassie almost said he'd copulated her brains out as she thought about how many of those condoms they had used. Their wet, slippery shower sex this morning stirred her olfactory centre and she blushed under the scrutiny of three sets of eyes. She'd blushed more in the last three days than she had her entire life.

Three things she didn't do was blush, swoon or cry, and she was two out of three at the moment. It was just as well she was leaving today and could get back to being someone she recognised.

'Not quite,' she said.

'I can't believe you and Tuck…' Reese shook her head. 'I thought for sure he was bound to date blonde airheads for the rest of his life.'

'April wasn't blonde,' Marnie said. 'Or an airhead. She was a nurse, wasn't she?'

Reese nodded. 'They met while he was having his knee reconstruction. She was nice…sweet. But they were married for less than *two years*. And now he's back to dating surgically enhanced pneumatic blondes again.'

'Except for Cassie,' Gina mused, and all three women looked at her again, sitting at the dining table in a baggy T-shirt proclaiming *'Geek is the new sexy'*, her long straight dark brown hair scraped back in a low ponytail and Alice band, her messy eyebrows knitted together.

'We're not dating,' Cassie reiterated. 'We're—'

'Copulating,' her friends said in unison, then laughed.

Cassie smiled at their infectious happiness. 'Well, we're not even doing that any more. I'm leaving today, and nothing is more important to me now than finishing my PhD and being on that plane to Antarctica next year.'

'Good for you,' Marnie said.

'Make sure you talk to me before you go. A designer friend of mine is making a huge splash in sexy thermalwear,' Gina said, raising her coffee cup.

Cassie blinked. 'I think they issue us with thermals.'

Gina shuddered. 'I can just imagine what *they'd* be like.'

Reese laughed at the blank look on Cassie's face. 'How are you getting to Cornell?'

'Tuck's giving me a lift to New York and I'll get a bus to Ithica from there.'

Reese raised an eyebrow. Mr Love-'em-and-Leave-'em, who'd told her a few days ago he was staying on at the Hamptons at a friend's place for a week, was dropping his plans and heading back to New York?

Interesting. Very interesting…

In the end Tuck insisted on driving her all the way to Cornell in his big black BMW. She'd protested about the distance, but he'd just shrugged and said he enjoyed a road trip. It took five hours from the Hamptons, and there wasn't one minute of it when Cassie wasn't aware of the length and breadth of him, of his heat, of his scent.

The aroma she'd come to recognise as pure Tuck—*to respond to like Pavlov's dog*—filled the inside of the cab, completely obliterating the luxury car smell and enveloping her in a hormonal fugue all the way to Ithica. She vaguely remembered them talking about her study and about his app, but the details were fuzzy.

It was late afternoon when they arrived—not that the long summer day gave any indication of the hour. The campus was surprisingly bustling for the mid-year break. Young people were laughing and smiling in groups, carrying books and laptops, or sitting on the grass under shady trees, engrossed in their phones or other electronic gadgets.

It took them an hour to locate her accommodation block and check in. Tuck helped her up with her bags. The corridors were buzzing with what Tuck soon found out to be high school students when he was recognised. He stopped for a chat and posed for pictures while he signed autographs for some very excited kids.

Cassie watched on, bemused, as Tuck high-fived and talked about football and retirement and his knee. The students—from Wisconsin—were doing Summer College, studying entomology, and he talked to them about the importance of getting an education. They buzzed around him like the insects they were studying, and she began to wonder if everything with a pulse was attracted to his seriously addictive pheromones.

Eventually they let him leave and she found her room, unlocking the door and pushing it open. Tuck carried her bag through. 'I can't believe,' he said as he set her suitcase on the single bed, 'you've come here for three months *from Australia* and that's all you brought. Most women I know take a suitcase that size away for the weekend. For their make-up.'

She shrugged as she looked round the small but functional room. 'I don't care much for clothes.'

Tuck looked her up and down and chuckled at the understatement. He'd always appreciated women's packaging, but after three days in bed with Cassie he was never judging a book by its cover again.

'I agree,' he said as he thought about all the delight hidden beneath her voluminous shirts and how long it had been since he'd seen it. The shower seemed a very long time ago. 'I think they're highly overrated.'

Cassie felt the drop in his voice's pitch undulate through the muscles deep inside her that had already received such an athletic workout back in the Hamptons. She glanced at him. He had his hands shoved in the pockets of the trendy three-quarter chinos he wore with a polo shirt sporting some kind of NFL logo, and a surge of pheromones hit her square between the eyes.

She looked away, her glance falling on the only horizontal surface in the room—the bed. She looked back at him. She'd spent practically every waking and sleeping hour of the last three days in bed with the man looking at her now as if he was calculating how quickly he could get her out of her clothes.

A shout in the corridor, followed by some heavy footsteps, yanked her back from the ledge.

Tuck dragged his eyes off Cassie, raking his hand through his hair. Unfortunately they found the bed. The narrow single bed—staple of the college dorm all over the country. He'd spent a lot of his college life on a bed just like it. Or beds just like it, anyway. And he knew from experience they weren't made for long, lazy sessions with a woman.

They were made for haste, not finesse, and paper-thin walls didn't guarantee ambience *or* privacy. At eighteen that hadn't been an issue, but at thirty-three, with a bad knee and various other aches and pains, he was way too old to fold himself into a bed not fit for an athlete.

No matter how tempting it was to yank her into his arms and go hunting for that body he knew was under all those layers. He looked around the tiny room and thanked God he never had to live like this again.

'Why are you here? Doesn't a place as esteemed as Cornell have some better digs for its PhD students?'

Cassie nodded. 'Sure. But this is cheap—which is important when you've been a professional uni student for over a decade. These dorms become vacant over the summer break, so they're keen to fill them and the price is right.'

Tuck's gaze drifted back to the bed as he absorbed her words. It had been a long time since he'd had to give any thought to the cost of living. He had more than enough money from his decade-long career, and enough continuing endorsements never to have to worry about money again. And the app project promised to be another winner.

There was more yahooing in the corridor, and Tuck turned slightly in the direction of a *thunk* as someone obviously hit the wall. A burst of laughter sounded and he turned back to face her. 'Won't that interfere with your study?'

'No. I'll be spending most of my time at the Space Sciences Building or the observatory,' she said. 'It's just a place to sleep.'

Tuck's gaze was once again drawn to the bed at her mention of sleep. A vision of her on it, with him, most definitely *not* sleeping, filled his head. His groin tightened and he looked at her, the same time she looked at him, and the room seemed to shrink even further.

'It's not a very big bed,' he murmured.

Cassie shrugged. 'There's just me.'

Tuck felt the sudden urge to puff his chest and say something macho like, *Damn straight, there'll just be you!* But then that conjured thoughts of her on this bed by herself, maybe naked, maybe touching herself while she thought about him. *Not that she probably did that.* But the thought stirred the tightening in his groin to a full-blown erection.

His gaze dropped to her mouth and he took a step towards her. Noticed the flare of her nostrils, the dilation of her pupils, her chest rising and falling with the same agitated rhythm as the night of their first kiss.

Cassie shut her eyes briefly as her body swayed towards the chemical cloud she seemed programmed to obey. And she almost took a step too. But the shrill ring of a phone pierced the sound and yanked her back from his hypnotic pull.

She looked around, hindered for a moment by sluggish brain cells and the unfamiliar ring—it wasn't her mobile and nor was it Tuck's.

'Your desk,' Tuck said, stepping back.

Cassie looked at the desk, pushed into a nook not far from the foot of the bed. She identified a slimline black telephone and took the three paces required to snatch it up, grateful for a little distance from Tuck. It was Professor Judy Walsh, who would be working with her on the completion of her PhD, welcoming her to the campus and checking she was good to go in the morning. They had a brief conversation, which Cassie barely took in, conscious as she was of Tuck prowling back and forth behind her like a caged animal.

Every *cell* in her body, every *hair* covering her body vibrated with his physical presence.

When she hung up she was angry. With Tuck. But mostly with herself. Studying at Cornell, the university that had nurtured the genius of greats like Carl Sagan, had been a lifelong dream and she was letting some weird aberration derail her pursuit of her goals.

It was a good thing that Professor Walsh had rung when she had. Exactly what Cassie had needed to refocus. Because the way things had been heading prior to the interruption had precious little to do with astronomy.

Focus, Cassiopeia.

She turned to face Tuck, staying right where she was. The room was small, so distance wasn't an option, but she'd take whatever space she could get. 'Thanks for the lift,' she said. 'But if you don't mind I really have to get settled in. Set up my computer, unpack. Etcetera.'

Tuck regarded her for a moment. Considering the size of her suitcase, and the fact she owned a laptop, he doubted it would take her ten minutes to do all of it. So there was only one conclusion to draw.

She was blowing him off.

He was so stunned for a moment he didn't say anything. Then he threw back his head and laughed. First she faked it and now she was blowing him off. Two things *no* woman had ever done to him. She wasn't just hell on a man's ego—she was death to it.

He had thought of taking her out for a bite to eat, but she'd obviously scratched her itch and was ready to move on. No long drawn-out goodbye, no clinging to him and begging him to call from Little Miss Mensa.

'So this is goodbye, huh?'

Cassie nodded. 'Yes.'

She often felt socially awkward, but this was a whole other level. She'd never been in the position of having to bid farewell to a man who had spent a fair portion of three days camped out between her legs. What did one say in such circumstances?

'Thank you for...'

For what? For the orgasms? For the copulation? For the pheromones? For an experiment she'd never forget as long as she lived?

'Everything,' she ended lamely.

Tuck grinned as he easily read every thought that flitted through her mind. 'Don't ever play poker, Cassiopeia,' he murmured.

He reached into his pocket for his wallet and pulled out a card. His real card, with his real phone number—not the one he gave to hard-to-shake groupies. 'You could always call me if your libido starts getting a little antsy again.'

He held it out and she looked at it as if it was a vial of poison. His grin broadened. Most women in this situation would have begged him for it. Hell, having his phone number in their hot little hands would probably be a story they'd tell to the end of their days.

Cassie stood her ground by the desk. 'It won't. My brain is firmly back in charge. And there's no room for...that.'

Tuck raised an eyebrow at the finality in her words. He had no doubt she meant it in all those higher functioning areas, of which she had many. She didn't strike him as a woman who let anything ruin her focus—especially now her libido was in check. But it was that little hesitation coming from somewhere deeper that gave him pause.

He strode the three paces that separated them and placed his card on her desk. 'Goodbye, Cassiopeia. It was fun.'

He didn't wait for a response, just turned and walked out through the door. It wasn't until he reached his car that Tuck realised it *had* been fun.

Not fun in the yee-ha, laugh-out-loud, usual way. It hadn't been gambling in Vegas with a pocketful of green and a blonde on his arm, or partying in Paris, or hearing the roar of the crowd coming out at him from under the Thursday night lights. Those had been the things that had defined fun for him until now—especially since his career slump and his marriage breakdown. But they felt kind of empty in comparison. Like an act. A façade. Something that Tuck-the-jock did to ensure he was the toast of the town, the life of the party.

But three days in bed with Cassie had made him reassess his definition. Okay, there hadn't been a lot of talking, but neither had there been a lot of sexual gymnastics. Mostly they'd just explored each other's bodies. Just touching and stroking and joining together, then drifting to sleep and starting all over again.

But it was the first time he could remember he'd been himself in a long time. Stripped back to the man, not the quarterback, because Cassie didn't have a clue who the footballer was nor did she give a damn. He'd been anonymous for a change.

And *that* had been fun.

Cassie stood very still for a long time after Tuck left, staring at the closed door. *Fun.* No one had ever told her she was fun. Not even as a child. The kids at school had called her brainiac and geek. Her doctor had called her a smart little cookie. Her teachers had said she was a whizz-kid. The university chancellor had called her a once-in-a-generation mind.

She'd never been anyone's *fun* before.

She picked up his card, his scent enveloping her as she brushed it against her mouth. It took all her willpower to toss it in the empty rubbish bin.

Three days later Cassie realised she'd created a monster—or fed one anyway—because her libido was back at full bitch again. The first day had been good. She'd felt focused and invigorated, springing from bed, eager to live the dream. But the next morning her thoughts had returned to the carnal, and slowly things had started to slide until her concentration was shot, her ability to analyse simple data non-existent and her interest had hit an all-time low.

And *everything* reminded her of Tuck. Passing the students hanging out in the hallway. Pulling one of her geek logo shirts over her head. Looking at the images from deep-space telescopes and seeing a pair of starburst-blue eyes.

Her professor had asked her earlier today if everything was okay. *Actually enquired if she was homesick.* As if she was one of the fifteen-year-olds currently running around campus instead of an almost thirty-year-old astronomer with a Mensa-rated IQ studying auroras on Jupiter.

Even now, at nine o'clock at night, sitting at her desk, she looked down at the paper she was reading to find she'd been doodling a certain name in the margins. *Like a teenager!* Not that she'd ever been *that* kind of a teenager.

Cassie squirmed in her chair in disgust, throwing her pen down. But that didn't help as her body was hell-bent on betraying her too. The movement stirred internal muscles that were still hypersensitive and sensation rolled through the pit of her belly. The brush of her arms against her nipples had them hard and aching. The same type of ache that had taken up semi-permanent residence between her legs and woke her in the middle of the night.

Cassie reached for the phone to dial Gina. She'd know

what to say, what to do. But she withdrew her hand at the last moment, not sure she really wanted to hear her friend's recommendations or—worse—advice about needing to collect more data from Tuck for her libido experiment.

She was a freaking genius, for crying out loud! Her head *would* rule her body.

She threw the paper down and opened her laptop, looking at the latest images they'd received today. Jupiter's auroras were particularly vibrant, and usually just the sheer enormity and random beauty of the solar system was enough to lift her beyond any of the mundane issues of earth. But it wasn't tonight.

Half an hour later she closed the laptop lid, knowing there was really only one solution to her problem. She could feel herself sliding towards an abyss she was all too familiar with and, whether she liked it or not, *the jock* seemed to be her way out.

Okay, she'd told him her brain was back. And it was. She'd told him her libido wouldn't be out of control again. And it wasn't. It just needed one more night.

Maybe he'd be open to one more night?

Mind made up, she scrambled frantically through her wastebasket, her fingers snatching at the card sitting at the very bottom, automatically bringing it to her nose for a long, deep sniff. His lingering pheromones catapulted through her system like a shooting star and any arguments her brain might have made got lost in a sea of stupid.

Her fingers trembled as she rang the number. Her heart thundered as it rang once, twice, three times. Her breath caught in her throat when he picked up and said, 'This is Tuck.'

His voice sounded deep and sexy and deliciously Texan and her brain powered down. She opened her mouth to say something, anything, but nothing came out.

'Hello?'

Cassie tried again and failed. For crying out loud, she could recite the Magna Carta, the American Declaration of Independence and every single one of Winston Churchill's war speeches word for word and she couldn't say a simple hello?

'Cassiopeia...is that you?'

Still she couldn't get the words to come.

'Cassie!'

His sharp enquiry snapped her out of her daze. 'T...Tuck... I...'

'Cassie? Are you okay?'

There was concern in his voice and she hastened to assure him she was fine. 'Yes, I'm good...fine... I just... I...'

Now she was talking to him she didn't know how to say it. She'd already asked him for sex once—it should be easy. But it wasn't. There was a silence at his end now too, that seemed to stretch interminably.

'Don't move,' he said in her ear. 'I'm coming.' And the receiver clicked.

Cassie was lying awake when the soft knock sounded on her door at exactly one-thirty. She'd spent the last four hours convincing herself he didn't really mean he was coming for her straight away—*tonight*. And how could he possibly get inside the locked dorm? But she didn't know anyone else who would be knocking on her door in the middle of the night.

She padded across the floor, her pulse thrumming so loudly in her head she was afraid she was going to wake the whole dorm. She took a steadying breath as she flipped the lock and turned the knob—to reveal one ex-quarterback standing on her doorstep, oozing pheromones in loose running pants and a T-shirt with some sports logo that stretched nicely over every muscle in his chest.

'Tuck,' she murmured. 'How'd you get in?'

'The RA at the front desk is a Texan,' he muttered, his gaze zeroing in on her mouth. He'd been daydreaming about kissing her like some lovelorn Romeo for the last three days and talk just wasn't on his agenda.

He reached for her, yanking her into his arms, his lips swooping to claim hers as he kicked the door shut behind him. Her mouth opened on a frantic little whimper and she tasted like toothpaste and desperation. He sucked it all in, hauling her up his body, gratified to feel the press of her breasts and the wrap of her legs tight around his waist as he ploughed a path straight to her bed.

And then they were falling back on to it and they were stripping away each other's clothes. Her shirt hit the floor and his followed. Her underwear joined the pile. His running pants and cotton briefs seemed to melt away, and then they were skin on skin, licking and sucking and sniffing and kissing and stroking and stoking until they'd built to a fever-pitch where only the strong, thick thrust of him pounding inside her was enough to satisfy the primal roar in their heads and the even more primal demands of their bodies.

Tuck collapsed on top of her as they both lay spent in the aftermath. For a moment he couldn't even move. It had been that intense. Then he rolled off her, groaning his bone-deep satisfaction. He hit his head against the wall and then banged his perpetually sore knee as he tried to adjust his too-big frame. He cursed as it twinged painfully.

'You really need a bigger bed,' he panted as he shifted to dispose of the condom, then scooped her up and pulled her half on top of him to accommodate both of them within the narrow confines of the mattress.

Cassie gurgled something unintelligible in response as her body seemed to levitate in the afterglow. When she could string enough words together to make a sentence she raised her head and looked down at him through half-lowered lids. 'You came,' she murmured as a strange sort of peace suffused her.

Tuck grinned. 'So did you.'

She rolled her sleepy eyes at him, then snuggled her cheek against his nearest pec as if he were her own personal pillow.

He smiled and stroked her hair, his own eyes shutting as long sleepless nights combined with a potent sexual malaise drifted them both into a deep slumber.

CHAPTER SEVEN

EVERYTHING ACHED WHEN Tuck woke at six the next morning. His back was stiff from the wafer-thin mattress, his knee throbbed, his neck was at an awkward angle and his ankles were sore from his feet hanging over the end of the bed.

But Cassie was warm and pliant, snuggled along the length of him, her hair streaming over his chest, her leg bent at the knee, trapping his thigh, her hand splayed on his abdomen, dangerously close to a part of his anatomy that had been *up* for a while.

Tuck smiled. *Atta-boy.*

Unfortunately he didn't have time this morning to do it justice. He had to get up, get going. He had a meeting with some execs in New York at eleven about the app. But, despite the aches and pains from a night in a bed made for an Oompa-loompa aggravating his injuries from a decade of being regularly slammed for sport, he was reluctant to move.

Soon. He'd go soon.

His gaze drifted around a room quite unlike any other female dorm room he'd ever been in—his jock status had pretty much seen to it that he could judge from personal experience. Hell, it was unlike *any* female bedroom he'd ever been in. No personalised curtains. No pretty rugs. No flowers or multiple soft stuffed toys or brightly coloured cushions or throws littering surfaces. No pinks, no purples, no pastels. No ornaments, no lava lamps, no photographs of friends or lovers.

It was about as girly as a jail cell.

Still, there were some touches to break up the starkness of the room. A couple of star charts were posted above the desk. Some blown-up photographs of who knew what were stuck to the walls. Stars? Black holes? Galaxies far, far away? Whatever they were, they were captivatingly beautiful in their majesty, and Tuck couldn't think of anything more awesome than having the solar system as your office.

A poster of an eerie green glow being cast over a landscape of white was stuck to one wardrobe door, and on the other what appeared to be a planet with a wispy ring of electric blue light at its pole. Auroras, perhaps?

But it was the large poster taking up the entire back of her door that drew his attention. It was of Barringer Crater in Arizona. He knew that because he'd been obsessed by the fifty-thousand-year-old hole in the ground since he'd been a kid and had been there several times. It was a big brown pockmark in the middle of nowhere, and it seemed an odd, even ugly earthbound addition compared to the beauty of the other celestial decorations.

She stirred and Tuck looked down at her. Her hand on his stomach curled into a light fist, dragging its fingernails deliciously against his skin, and he shut his eyes for a moment enjoying the sensation. As did his erection.

'Morning, sleepyhead,' he said, opening his eyes and dropping a kiss on her hair. He really, really had to get going.

Cassie woke to solid warmth and her nostrils full of Tuck. No thoughts of anything *but* Tuck in her head. 'Hmmm,' she murmured, stretching against him, her eyes slowly drifting open. She smiled as her bird's-eye view down the flat of his stomach ended in the delicious outline of his erection.

'Hmmm,' she said again as her hand slid down his belly and reached for it.

Tuck shut his eyes as her hand closed around him and talons of need clawed deep into his buttocks. He reached down and placed a stilling hand on hers. 'I can't stay. I have a meeting at eleven that I can't get out of.'

'Uh-huh,' Cassie said as she gave his girth a squeeze, her thumb running over its firm head.

Tuck dragged her hand away—that was *not* helping. 'Why,' he asked in an effort to distract her, him and his erection, 'do you have a poster of Barringer Crater on your door?'

Cassie dragged her gaze from his fascinating anatomy and glanced up at him, resting her chin on his pec for a moment. He didn't look as if he was going to be easily dissuaded, and the fact that he knew its actual name rather than calling it Meteor Crater, as it was popularly known, piqued her interest. She sighed, then turned her head towards the door, resting her other cheek on his chest.

'I've always wanted to go there,' she said, eyeing the poster. 'There's one like it in Australia, called Wolfe Creek. My mother took me when I was little so it's a bit of a fascination of mine. The girls and I were going to stop in and visit it on our road trip a decade ago, but then...then there was "the great falling out" and it never happened.'

She turned her head back, resting her chin on his chest again, looking straight into his starburst eyes. Tuck's hand absently stroked the small of her back. There wasn't a lot of room in her single bed and he seemed to take it all up. Her position close to the edge was precarious and his hand at the base of her spine was the only thing anchoring her.

'So I promised myself this time around I'd go and see it. It's my reward for when I complete my three months at Cornell.'

Tuck chuckled. 'Sounds much more sensible than getting wasted at Daytona Beach.'

Cassie nodded, not remotely concerned about being thought of as sensible. She *was* sensible. She never did anything rash or ill-considered.

Except this.

Tuck was the very definition of rash and ill-considered. But surely one blip in almost thirty years was allowable? 'I take it you've been?' she said. 'To Barringer?'

Tuck nodded. 'A few times, actually. The stars out there are amazing.'

'Well, they would be,' Cassie said. 'It's the middle of the dessert. No ambient light. No pollution.'

'Yeah.' Tuck smiled as she got all scientific on him. He picked up a lock of her hair and let it sift through his fingers. 'So…about last night…'

Cassie dropped her forehead to his chest. 'I'm sorry,' she said, her voice muffled against his pec. She looked up. 'I think my libido went into some kind of…withdrawal situation. I just needed…*it* just needed another night.'

Tuck grinned. 'Another hit, huh?'

Cassie didn't like the idea that she might be addicted to Tuck. She was far too highly evolved for that—even if evidence to the contrary had not been forthcoming of late.

She had to stay in charge of this thing.

'Libido is influenced by a variety of factors often not under conscious control,' she said, trying to give herself an out for her inexplicable behaviour.

'So you may require my *services* again?' Tuck tried to decide whether he cared about being used by a horny PhD student who cared even less about his celebrity status than she did about football. *He didn't.*

Cassie's nipples beaded against his chest at the suggestion, as if it was made from a block of ice instead of hot, pliant muscle. She looked down at his still present erection. Her nostrils flared. Lust surged through her belly.

'Possibly,' she murmured, entranced by the pure masculinity of it, her synapses shorting out as her hand slid down.

'Oh, no, you don't,' Tuck said, grabbing her fingers before they could wreak havoc at their destination. 'I really have to go.'

Cassie glanced at him. 'I'll be quick,' she said, and shimmied down his body, kissing his ribs, his belly button, his hip on her way down.

Tuck shut his eyes as the heat of her mouth closed over him. 'Oh, God, I've created a monster,' he groaned, his eyes shutting as his resistance ebbed beneath her onslaught. He threaded his hands through her hair and surrendered to the pleasure, his appointment forgotten.

When she called him two nights later, asking for just one more night, Tuck hired a helicopter, grateful that his money and celebrity meant he didn't have to endure another eight-hour round trip in his car.

Two nights later he did the same thing. But she hadn't instigated the trip this time, so he was a little nervous when he knocked on her door at ten o'clock.

'One more?' he asked when she opened it.

Her shirt said 'Never drink and derive', and she looked all smart and serious and cute and nerdy, with a pencil tucked behind her ear, and he wanted her so damn bad he didn't even wait for an answer before yanking her into his arms, swivelling her around and using their combined body weight to shut the door, pressing her hard against it as he plundered every millimetre of her mouth.

Hell, they didn't even make it to the bed.

He sure as hell had no idea what delightful underwear logo awaited him, because he just tore it right off in his haste to be inside her. And nothing mattered after that except the crazy, blind, driving need that seemed to grow more desperate every day.

Tuck woke the next morning, every bone, muscle and joint protesting, knowing he would never survive another night on Cassie's mattress.

He was just too old and injured for dorm beds.

Cassie wasn't with him and he raised his head, expecting to see her sitting at her desk or standing by her wardrobe getting dressed. But the room was empty. He looked at his watch. Eight o'clock. Given how late it had been when they'd eventually gone to sleep, he wasn't surprised he'd slept in.

But when had she left?

Tuck unfolded himself from the bed, his body aching as he stood slowly and headed to the pile of clothes by the door that he didn't even remember losing last night. He bent over and both knees twinged. He climbed into his shorts and pulled his T-shirt over his head. A scrap of fabric remained on the floor and he picked it up, grinning at what was left of Cassie's underwear and its amusing logo: *Vacancy: Rocket Scientists need only apply.*

He walked to her desk and tossed them in the bin. And that was when he saw the note propped up by a couple of textbooks. He opened it, and the first line jumped out at him.

We can't keep doing this, Tuck.

Well, she was damn right about that. Her bed just wasn't made for two.

I'm getting nothing done. I can't concentrate. And all I do is think about you. I think it's best if I go cold turkey. I know that with hard work, focus and medication my libido will have to eventually submit to the dictates of a higher power. It has been my dream to come to Cornell, a much desired step in a grander plan, and I ask that you not derail that. Or, given that you are so much more practised at this than I, let me derail it either. If I call, please ignore me. No one's ever died from sexual deprivation and I don't expect I'll be the first. It has, as you say, been fun, but it's over.

Tuck read the note several times. Even the way she wrote, so precise and matter-of-fact, cracked him up, and he found his grin getting broader with each read-through.

She was right, of course. What they were doing was utterly distracting and not very productive. He had some work backed up on the app that he'd been neglecting. So ending it—whatever the hell *it* was—would be one solution. But suddenly he had a much better one. He scrunched up the note and threw it in the bin.

He had a busy day ahead of him. He needed breakfast and a plan.

Two hours later he was sitting in the very posh offices of a property rental agency, talking to a very attractive woman about finding him an upmarket serviced apartment in Ithica for him to move into immediately.

Of course he could have done it himself—got a phone book and rung around. But in his experience it was best to outsource these things to an expert who knew the local market and had an eye for class.

The brassy blonde called Abigail fitted the docket perfectly. It helped that she knew who he was, although she was careful not to fawn, which told him she was used to dealing with the higher end of the market. Even so he was more than aware from her subtle body language that she'd be first in line to volunteer should he need company in his bed whilst in Ithica.

The problem was she just didn't do it for him. She should have. She was exactly his type—blonde, well put together, and a cougar to boot. Tuck liked cougars. They weren't usually out for anything other than a good time and a few hours of action between the sheets. If they could bag a celebrity that was just the cherry on the cake for them.

But, surprisingly, over the course of a week his type had changed.

Her eyes were artfully made up, with perfectly arched brows, but they didn't glitter with intelligence or hold the secrets of the universe. Her hair fell in a fluffy cloud around her head and shoulders and reeked of a posh salon, but he'd bet his last dime she couldn't go three hours without brushing it, let alone three whole days full of head-banging, style-destroying sex.

And then there were her...assets. They were nicely on display and, hell, Tuck had always appreciated a nice rack—but he realised there was a certain degree of titillation in having to check things out thoroughly to find the good stuff.

And he knew just the woman who fitted the bill. His new type. And it wasn't Abigail.

She was, however, exceedingly efficient, and within an hour she had located the perfect place for him in a quiet tree-lined neighbourhood a ten-minute walk from campus. Tuck took a taxi to the posh low-rise and spent all afternoon making phone calls to set himself up for the next three months.

Even if Cassie was resistant to moving in with him—and

he had to admit it seemed kind of crazy after only a week—he'd slept his last night in that god-awful dorm bed. She could stay on campus if she really wanted, but if she called in the middle of the night again, wanting him, he'd be sending a car for her.

From now on any and all naked action would be taking place on the cloud-like comfort of a pillow-top mattress.

At six o'clock his wardrobe and his home office, which his PA had packed up and put on an Ithica-bound chopper, arrived, and he spent the next hour setting up. He unpacked the suitcases of clothes and set up his office in the spare bedroom, leaving the desk area in the master bedroom for Cassie's stuff.

Relocating his life was no big deal when the constraints of the everyday—like a job and a budget—were non-existent, and for that Tuck was grateful. It didn't matter where he was—he could do what he did anywhere. As long as he had access to Cassie.

It was just after seven when he was done. He knew Cassie often didn't get back to the dorm until after eight, so he jumped in the car he'd rented and bought enough groceries to fill the fridge. Lucky for Cassie he was an awesome cook, and he whipped up a quick pasta meal for them both before girding his loins and heading back to the dorm.

Cassie recognised Tuck's voice as soon as she entered the dorm, holding court as he was in the lounge area to a group of rapt teenagers. No big surprise, really. She was beginning to think she would recognise his voice underwater amidst a pod of whales.

Her pulse skipped a little. Hadn't he got her note? She couldn't decide whether the feeling in the pit of her stomach was anger or relief. Whether she was mad at him or likely to tear all his clothes off in front of impressionable teenagers.

God knew, she'd thought about nothing else all day.

She shook her head. Just over a week ago she hadn't had any indecision about her emotions. Her life, her feelings— should she have had any—had been completely cut and dry. And then along came Tuck. And her brain had gone into hiding!

She felt a momentary quiver of something that felt a lot like anxiety. She recognised it from those troubled teen years, before medication had helped her control a brain that sped constantly ahead.

She pushed it away on a hard swallow.

'Cassie.' Tuck stood as he spotted her. 'Okay, guys.' He apologised as he prepared to leave, despite the protests. 'Gotta go now.'

He caught up with Cassie outside her door, searching through her bag for her key. 'Evening, ma'am,' he murmured near her ear, low and drawn-out, just as he knew she liked. The falter in her brisk activity was satisfying.

'I left you a note,' Cassie said as his pheromones embraced her and she shut her eyes to resist them. She fitted her key in the lock and opened the door.

Tuck followed her into her room. 'I got it,' he said.

Cassie folded her arms, because they were aching for him and she just didn't trust her body when she no longer understood it. She glared at him. 'This is not cold turkey.'

Tuck smiled at her cranky face. Her eyebrows were drawn together and she was looking at him like mould under a microscope. But he could see the telltale signs giving her away. The flutter of the pulse in the hollow of her throat, the slight flare of her nostrils, the beading of her nipples which, thanks to her folded arms, he could see clearly.

'I had a better idea.'

'It doesn't look like it from where I'm standing,' she said.

'I rented an apartment. It's ten minutes' walk from here and I think you should move in with me.'

Cassie blinked. Had she heard right or had he finally dumbed her down enough that she'd surpassed stupid and slipped right on to crazy?

'Just think about it,' Tuck said, jumping into the silence, holding up his hands as if he was expecting her to attack at any minute. 'It's logical, really.'

Yeah, he knew that was a low blow, considering the plan was three-quarters insane. But he knew he had to make a logical argument.

'You said in your note that you couldn't concentrate. And that all you could think about was me. I'm proposing that living with me will give you the best of both worlds. No need for cold turkey. If I was here all the time, if you had access to me all the time, you wouldn't have to spend all day thinking about *not* having access to me. You'd know I was here to come home to.'

Cassie, who had been girding her loins to throw him out—preferably without ravishing him first—considered what he was saying.

'Part of the problem the last week has been that you've been denying your urges until they've built up and up and your libido is at screaming point. If I was here all the time they wouldn't have to build. Your libido could calm down.'

Cassie remembered the days when her libido had been non-existent. *The good old days.* 'I was hoping that my libido might have…had its fill by now.'

'Well, libidos can be tricky things. Sometimes these things can take a while to burn out.'

Wasn't that just what Gina had said? 'How long's a while?' she demanded. 'Define it.'

Tuck shook his head solemnly. 'Well, that's not easily definable—there are too many variables.' Tuck wasn't above a bit of geek-talk to sway her his way. 'It could be a week. It could be your entire three months at Cornell. That's a long time with shot concentration.' Tuck shoved his hands into the pockets of his track pants. '*Very* unproductive.'

Cassie didn't like the sound of that. Maybe a 'calm' libido was the best she could hope for while this thing *burnt itself out,* as Tuck had put it. It certainly wasn't showing any sign of abating yet if the very powerful urge to kiss him currently playing havoc with her willpower was anything to go by.

'Why not give it a trial run?' he suggested. 'I think you'll find it beneficial to your concentration, but if you don't...' Tuck shrugged. 'You can always come back here.'

Cassie had to admit it did sound logical. A trial. Another experiment. She had no doubt that he was manipulating her lifelong obsession with logic, but that didn't mean he wasn't right. And, more than ever, she needed logic in her life.

Cassie nodded. 'Okay. Agreed. Can you get my suitcase down from the top of the wardrobe?'

It was Tuck's turn to blink. He'd thought it was going to be much more difficult than that. He had arguments stacked up that he'd been rehearsing for hours.

'Well?' Cassie said as she looked at a stationary Tuck. 'Are we going or not?'

Tuck grinned. 'Yes, ma'am.'

And it worked brilliantly. Tuck had been right. Knowing he was there to come home to freed up all her head space and she was finally able to get into her work. Sure, she got a little spacey towards the end of the day, when her libido was obviously starting to run a little low on its Tuck hit, but Cassie was so productive she was almost delirious with it.

Having a constant supply of sex also meant more sleep, which Cassie knew was a major requirement of her overactive brain. Instead of days of famine which had kept her awake and hungry, followed by a night of feasting which had kept her awake and sated, she had a constant source of fuel and something more potent than sleeping tablets to get her off to sleep.

Not that she would ever stop taking them. She might be on top, but the memories of a time when she hadn't been still burned brightly and she relied on the pills to help her maintain her mental balance.

Still, things were good. Way better than Cassie would have ever thought possible. And if every now and then the thought that she was *living with a man* confused her logic she put it in the 'too hard' basket along with her libido and concentrated on her work.

Their first Sunday morning together threw up the first potential hurdle, and it came from out of the blue. Tuck had been out after an early round of sex and bought every paper he could lay his hands on. It was a bit of a Sunday morning ritual for him, and Cassie was content to sit with him, eating the omelette he'd made, and work her way through the papers too.

'Why'd you get this one?' she asked, holding up a tabloid well known for bizarre stories on alien life and other things belonging in the realm of the wild and whacky.

Tuck looked up from a sports section. 'Force of habit. It's amazing how much you find out about yourself in the pages of a tabloid.'

Cassie raised an eyebrow. 'I think that's called narcissism,' she said as she flicked to the second page.

Tuck grinned. 'No. It's called protecting my reputation.' He turned his attention back to the college ball scores as he said, 'Plus I know who to sic my lawyer on.'

Cassie shook her head, her gaze falling on a particularly startling headline. 'Do you mean like this?' she asked, holding it up for him to see. '"Tuck is my Baby Daddy"'.

Tuck's head snapped up as the blazing bold headline jumped out at him. His NFL official photograph was there, along with a picture of a vaguely familiar busty blonde woman with a toddler on her hip. 'What the...?' he said as he stood and headed to her side of the table.

'Do you know someone called Jenny Jones?' Cassie asked as she scanned the article.

Tuck leaned on Cassie's chair, rage building inside him as he read over her shoulder. Sure, he remembered Jenny. He'd spent two nights with her in Vegas just after his divorce was final.

'Yeah.' Tuck's jaw clenched. 'I know her.' He reached for his phone and stalked to the bay windows that looked down onto the street.

'Who are you ringing?' she asked.

'My lawyer.'

It went to voicemail and Tuck left a terse message about the amount of money he was paying him and how he expected to hear from him in the next ten minutes.

'It's a lie,' he said, turning to face Cassie. He couldn't believe the bare-faced audacity of the paper to print such a wild, unsubstantiated claim. Generally his management would have been asked for comment, given a heads-up, but sometimes rags like this didn't bother with clarification.

He was going to sue their goddamned asses off. They were going to be sorry they'd *ever* screwed with him.

Cassie blinked at Tuck's vehemence. He started to pace,

his fists curled, his face stony. 'So you don't know her?' she said, tracking his restless prowl. 'You didn't sleep with her?'

'Oh, I know her,' Tuck said, abruptly halting his pacing. 'And I slept with her. Exactly as she claims in the article.'

'So...you *could* be the father?' Cassie said. It seemed logical to her.

Tuck shook his head emphatically. 'No.'

Cassie frowned. 'You used condoms?'

'Yes, we did. I *always* use condoms.'

'You know they only have a ninety-nine percent accuracy, right? Statistically it is still possible—'

'It's not possible,' Tuck interrupted.

'Well, there is a one percent—'

'No,' Tuck interrupted again. 'It's *not* possible.' He shoved his hand through his hair. 'I'm infertile. Probably have been most of my life. "Idiopathic", they call it. Which just means they don't know what the hell's caused it. But they suspect it was a virus that laid me low when I was eighteen...totally screwed up my season too. Trust me—I can tell you, for sure that I couldn't get a woman pregnant if she was the most fertile female on the planet. Which is kind of ironic, considering the number of paternity tests I've faced over the years.'

'How long have you known?' she asked.

'I found out when April and I tried to get pregnant.'

It had been a particularly nasty whammy, on top of the recurrent knee injury screwing with his career. Nothing like being a dud at everything—quarterback, husband, man.

Cassie didn't know what to say. With absolutely no desire to have children herself, she didn't understand the drive. But she could see that Tuck was gutted by it. 'I'm...sorry,' she said.

The phone rang then, and Tuck answered immediately. Cassie listened to the one-sided conversation. Although perhaps *rant* was a better word. Tuck was steamed, and she wasn't sure she'd ever heard that many four-letter words.

Tuck ended the call and threw the phone on the table in disgust.

'I take it this happens a lot?'

He nodded. 'This will be the eighth paternity claim against me.' He raked a hand through his hair. 'Sorry, you probably don't need this. But I can assure you it's not true.'

Cassie frowned. 'No need to apologise. Nothing to do with me.'

Tuck blinked. He'd been with women in the past when these accusations had come at him and they'd been spitting mad. Cassie just sat there, looking at him all nonplussed, and he couldn't help but laugh. 'You're the only woman I know that wouldn't have a hissy fit over this.'

'It's not really my business, is it?' She shrugged.

'Well, most women in your position would think it *was* their business.'

'They would?'

Tuck nodded. 'They'd be kind of pissed.'

'Because of the jealousy thing?' Cassie asked.

Tuck laughed again. 'Ahh…yup. Most women want me to marry *them* and give *them* lots of little quarterbacks. They'd be *more* than annoyed that someone else was trying to claim that place in my life.'

Cassie thought about that for a moment. She supposed human jealousy and other less evolved emotions might come into play here—but not with her.

'But I don't want to marry you,' she said. 'And I don't want to have your babies. I'm here for three months, then I'm going back to Australia, and next year I'm going to Antarctica. And all of the years after that are going to be dedicated to my career which, as my mother could tell you, is not family-friendly. This is just a libido thing, remember?'

Bloody hell—she was hard on a man's ego. An ego that had already suffered a few hard years with the triple blow of a tanking career, a crumbling marriage and infertility. And just when he was on the up Jenny came along to sink in the boot.

The fact that Cassie wanted nothing from him other than a little libido-taming sounded damn good to him. And most of all it was honest. She was the only woman who had ever been straight with him about what she wanted—not even April had been honest about that.

And *damn* if that didn't feel good.

CHAPTER EIGHT

THE FOLLOWING WEEK Reese called as Cassie walked to the apartment after a full day at the Earth Sciences building. The campus was a virtual ghost town, with most of the summer students heading home for the looming Fourth of July celebrations. Cassie understood the importance of the holiday to Americans, but it was annoying to be losing a day at the university when she was finally back on track with her studies.

After some preliminary chit-chat about Cornell and the PhD, and Reese and Mason's state of bliss, Reese said, 'So, Mason and I are having a big Fourth thing here, and we were hoping you could hop on a bus tomorrow and come join us.'

Ordinarily Cassie would have said yes. She'd missed Reese, and although she had kept in touch over the years it was a novelty for them to be in the same country!

'Can't,' she said. 'Tuck has plans for me.'

'Tuck?'

'Yes,' Cassie said. 'Some big surprise he's arranged.'

'*My* Tuck?' Reese clarified. 'You're...still seeing each other?'

'Uh-huh.' There was silence at the end of the line for a moment, and Cassie realised maybe this news was the type of thing that *gal pals* shared with each other. 'Sort of.'

'Sort of?'

'Well, it's not like that. I mean, it *is*…but… It's just a libido thing. It's just…sex. I only moved in with him for the sex.'

'You *moved in* with him?'

Cassie held the phone away from her ear as Reese's squeak reverberated loudly around her ear canal.

'Okay,' Reese said. 'Whoever this is, stop goofing around and put my friend Cassie on. My friend Cassie with a mega-brain, who lives and breathes astronomy and *does not* shack up with a man she met not even a month ago. Who doesn't *shack up* period!'

'Funny,' Cassie murmured, holding the phone slightly away from her ear as Reese's voice became more and more shrill.

'Cassie…honey…this is completely out of character for you…'

'I know that,' Cassie said. 'But my work was suffering. All I could do was think about him…it was so…*dumb!* Then Tuck got a place at Ithica and suggested how logical it was that I move in—'

Reese snorted. 'I bet he did.'

Cassie shook her head vehemently. 'No, he was right. This way I get to satisfy my brain *and* my libido.'

'Win-win,' Reese said.

'Exactly,' Cassie agreed.

There was some more silence before Reese spoke again. 'Honey…Tuck's my cousin, and I love him, but…he can be a bit of a…hound dog. Just look at this latest news about that woman in Vegas.'

'It's not his baby, Reese.'

'Oh…are the paternity results in already?'

'He doesn't need them,' Cassie said. 'He's infertile. He found out when he and April were trying to get pregnant.'

'Oh, no,' Reese gasped. 'Poor Tuck. I didn't know that.

I knew he was going through a hard time a few years back, but I didn't realise...'

Cassie stopped and waited at a pedestrian light. 'He's fine,' she dismissed.

'Are you sure? Tuck's always had a pretty big ego, and most men's identities *are* wrapped up in things like their jobs and their virility. To have someone popping up and throwing his inabilities in his face... I don't know. It has to be a blow...'

The light changed and Cassie crossed the road. 'Well, he sicced his lawyer on to it with great delight and hasn't mentioned it since, so...'

'Men don't, though...they brood and bury it. Just look at how screwed up Mason was. It's not very healthy. Have you asked him about it?'

'No.' Cassie felt a pang. Was Reese right? *Was* Tuck bothered by this more than he was letting on? 'Should I have?'

Was *she* supposed to do something about it?

This was why she preferred science. It made sense. She knew what do with it.

'No, no...' Reese assured her. 'Anyway, I have to go, but maybe Mason and I could come to Ithica next weekend for a visit? I'll have probably wrapped my head around the whole Cassie-living-with-a-man thing by then. Maybe we can all get together? I'll see what Gina and Marnie are doing.'

Cassie hung up a minute later, the apartment in her sights. But for the first time in three weeks the spring in her step was missing.

'You're quiet,' Tuck said an hour later as he picked up their plates and headed for the kitchen.

Normally Cassie was full of the day's developments, where she was at with the project, or the latest thing of beauty a telescope had captured somewhere in outer space. But tonight she'd eaten and let him do most of the talking.

Cassie opened her mouth to deny it, but then she realised he was right. She'd been preoccupied with what Reese had said and trying to puzzle out what was expected of her. If this whole thing with Jenny had suddenly brought Tuck's infertility to the fore and he was feeling somehow less...*masculine,* was it her role to restore his sense of worth?

Was she supposed to get him talking about it? Give him an avenue for discussion? Did he need his hand held? His ego stroked?

Should she have asked him about it?

Argh! She'd never felt this inept in her life. Where was Gina when she needed her?

'Reese thinks that this paternity thing may be magnifying a sense of injured masculinity stemming from your infertility and that you may be brooding and burying your feelings in an unhealthy way,' she blurted out.

Tuck blinked. 'You told Reese about my infertility?'

Cassie shrugged. 'I assumed she already knew,' she said matter-of-factly. She missed the tightening at the angle of his jaw as she ploughed on. 'Is she right?'

Tuck turned to face the sink and flicked the hot water tap on. 'Reese should mind her own damn business.'

Cassie stared at Tuck's back. Right, then. That seemed a fairly definitive *stay-out-of-it* to her. Except she knew enough about social interaction to know that words and actions could often contradict.

She stood and headed towards him. 'If she is, I was thinking maybe I could...help you through it.' *Somehow...* 'Like the way you're helping *me* with my libido issues.'

Tuck turned back and smiled at her, a gleam in his eyes. 'Oh, you're helping.'

'I am?'

'Sure—nothing like a steady supply of great sex to soothe a man's ego.'

So his ego *was* bent out of shape? She pulled up at the other side of the bench. 'I think that might be the unhealthy part.'

Tuck leaned his butt against the sink. 'I don't know about you, but I've never felt more healthy.'

Cassie had to admit, as every cell in her body purred beneath the blast of sexual energy arcing between them, that the man made a good point. But this hadn't exactly been the easiest thing for her to do, and she wouldn't let him, or her libido, derail her from her objective.

'Tuck. I'm trying to…to be sensitive to your…issues…'

Tuck was momentarily stunned, and then he laughed. 'Well, look at you,' he teased. 'Going all Dr Feelgood on me.'

'Tuck.'

He sobered. 'I'm fine.' He turned back to the sink. 'I was married, my career tanked, we couldn't have a baby and then I wasn't married any more.'

'Two years isn't very long,' she said to his beautiful broad back. Even her parents, who lived in a strange kind of separate togetherness, had managed thirty years.

Tuck shrugged. 'I doubt anyone was surprised. We'd only known each other for a few months before we got hitched.'

Cassie tried to absorb the enormity of such an impulsive act. It seemed as crazy as Reese falling for Mason in a week all those years ago. Or Gina sleeping with the betrothed Carter.

And just as unfathomable.

'That seems a little rash,' she said.

Tuck stared at the suds covering his hands. It *had* been rash, but at the time it had seemed so damn right. He turned again, shoving one soapy hand on his hip. Cassie was looking at him cluelessly, her eyebrows scrunched together in a frown, a pencil behind her ear. He doubted she'd understand his state of absolute desperation in her world of crystal-clear logic.

But he suddenly wanted her to.

'She was a nurse where I was having my physical therapy. I'd been through several operations and my career was stalled, she was young and sweet and adorable, and I felt old and clapped-out and impotent. She believed in me in a way that wasn't fake like so many others around me and I *needed* that. Football was all I had. It was all I knew.'

He raked a hand through his hair, angry at himself still for taking all her youth and sweetness and sucking it out of her as his career spiralled downwards.

'When she wanted a baby it seemed like the one thing I *could* give her—because the glamorous life of an athlete's wife hadn't exactly been rainbows and unicorns. And, even though part of me knew that bringing a kid into the crumbling mix of our marriage would be stupid, she loved me and I was *trying* to hold on to that. To have one part of my life going right. It seemed like a way to hold us together.'

Cassie frowned. 'For a smart man that was a really dumb move.'

Tuck gave a short, sharp laugh. Trust Cassie to tell it like it was. 'I don't know… It might have been okay if I'd loved her like she'd loved me, if we'd got pregnant. But we couldn't… and when we found out that it was me…it was my fault…it hit me worse than the tackle that gave me a concussion during my first Super Bowl. I mean, I was the *QB,* I was *the man*…and then I wasn't. I couldn't be a father and I couldn't play football either, so what was I?'

Cassie could hear the anguish twisting his words and knew it was her turn to say something. Her role to make it better. Her social awkwardness closed in around her. 'I don't think your…ability to father a child defines you any more than your ability to kick a football around.'

Tuck crossed his arms. 'It sure didn't feel like it at the time. I think I spent a lot of time *defining* myself as a right SOB for a while there.'

'And now? With football and babies off the table?' she asked.

'Not much point wanting something you can't have, is there? Football is over, and I've come to terms with that. And to be honest I'm not really sure I want a kid anyway.' He shrugged. 'I've moved on.'

'For what it's worth, I don't much care about having kids either.'

Tuck chuckled. 'And that's what I like about you. So you can assure Reese I'm just fine. That my *masculinity*...' he dropped his gaze to her breasts '...is just fine.'

Cassie swallowed. *Oh, yes, indeed it was.*

Tuck's mobile rang later that night, just as he finished Skyping with a software engineer about the app. If it had been anyone else other than Dylan he wouldn't have answered. The shower had just been turned on and a wet, naked Cassie was exactly what he needed after a day of dealing with lawyer crap—and their conversation earlier had roused old hurts.

But he'd spoken so little to his best friend since Reese had jilted him a month ago he knew he had to take the call. They chatted for a while about the wash-up from the wedding-that-wasn't, and Tuck was satisfied that Dylan really seemed okay, and they chatted about the most recent paternity allegations against Tuck.

'So...' Dylan said. 'Reese called me earlier.'

'Ah,' Tuck said. His meddling cousin *had* been a busy little beaver, hadn't she? 'Don't you think it's odd to be taking phone calls from the woman who so recently jilted you?'

'Nice try at deflection, buddy. But you know Reese is worried that Cassie will get hurt.'

Tuck frowned. So this wasn't about him and his masculinity. It was about Cassie. And Reese was sending her ex-fiancé to do her dirty work. 'Reese should know that Cassie is not the kind to emotionally invest. She's just having fun. Blowing off some steam. We both are.'

'Right...but maybe you want to think about not getting involved for a while? Let the dust settle from this Jenny thing? Trust me, you don't die from celibacy.'

'It's fine, Dylan,' Tuck assured him. 'It's the perfect relationship. She's not some groupie. She doesn't want to marry me *or* have my babies. Which is just as well, considering...'

Tuck had tried not to make that sound bitter, but Dylan was the only person other than April, a couple of doctors and apparently now Reese who knew the truth, and this week in particular his infertility had come back to haunt him.

'She's here for three months, bro, and I'm her drug of choice,' he hastened to add. 'It's a temporary thing. It's... symbiotic.'

Dylan laughed. 'Symbiotic? She turning you into a scientist too?'

Tuck laughed too. 'Just getting my geek on.'

'She doesn't really strike me as your...type.'

Tuck shrugged. 'I think I'm getting myself a new type.'

'Okay...'

'No, I mean it,' Tuck said. 'She's amazing, you know. She has all this serious geek thing going on, and she walks around with this pencil behind her ear all the time, and it's so damn cute. But underneath it all she's incredibly passionate. And she doesn't do any of that clingy, needy stuff—'

'I thought,' Dylan butted in, 'you *liked* them clingy?'

Tuck had to admit that up until now that had been true. He'd liked being the *big man,* squiring around his women, treating them like princesses no matter how brief their acquaintance. But that had been the role his celebrity, a string of eager women and examples from his peers had forced him into early in his dating career, setting up an unhealthy pattern.

Cassie's independence had been a breath of fresh air.

Tuck grinned. 'Apparently not.'

There was silence for a moment or two, then Dylan said, 'Are you…are you *serious* about her?'

'Nah.' Tuck laughed, pushing the feeling that Cassie was already under his skin aside. 'It's just fun, Dylan. She's using me. I'm letting her. Win-win.'

'Just…be careful, okay? And by that I mean look out for you too.'

'Aww, buddy, are we going to hug now?'

'Okay. I'm going to hang up.'

'Good, I have a naked woman in a shower waiting for me.'

Dylan snorted. 'Celibacy rocks. You should try it.'

Tuck laughed. 'Whatever gets you through the night.'

One minute later he'd shed his clothes, stepped into the cubicle, and his hands were sliding onto Cassie's wet hips and heading north.

Celibacy rocks, his ass.

Cassie looked down at the arid landscape far below. Tuck's Gulf Stream had been flying since six a.m. and it was now midday.

'When are you going to tell me where we're going?' she asked Tuck as he placed a tray with a selection of gourmet subs cut into small portions on the table between them.

Tuck sat opposite her and grinned. 'You'll know when we get there.'

Cassie didn't like surprises. There was no logic to them at all. 'Fine,' she said as she selected the closest portion. 'Can you tell me how much longer we'll be flying?'

'Another hour or so,' he said, then bit into his sub.

As Cassie had no idea in which direction they were flying—although it was obviously some kind of west—the ETA didn't really help to ascertain their whereabouts, but at least she had a timeframe in her head. She liked to *know* things. When she set out every day for work she already knew in her head what the day would be like. It didn't mean she couldn't be flexible, should something crop up out of the blue, it was just logical and time-effective to have a systematic plan.

They ate quietly for a few minutes, with Tuck's gaze never leaving her face. His eyes kept dropping to her mouth, and it was disconcerting that something so mundane could kick her libido into overdrive.

She was beginning to think this thing would *never* burn itself out!

'So,' she said, looking around the plane's interior, desperate for some conversation to divert the blood pooling between her thighs back to her brain. 'I guess this means you're seriously rich, huh?'

Tuck stopped chewing for a moment at her bald statement. Then he laughed, and then coughed as he almost inhaled his lunch. Most women had *that* sized up within a few minutes and then spent the entire time trying to spend as much of his money as possible. It was a novelty to be with someone who didn't seem to care. In fact, by the look on her face, it would seem this was the first time his wealth had actually sunk in.

'I've done all right for myself,' he said, after she'd passed him a bottle of water and he'd gulped down a couple of mouthfuls.

Tuck waited for her to ask him to clarify how well he'd done, or to ask how much the plane had cost. Instead she said, 'I've never been in a plane this small.'

Tuck shook his head and chuckled.

Cassie frowned. 'What?'

'Nothing...I've just never met a woman like you.'

'I'd be surprised if you had,' she said. 'Female astronomers with a genius IQ are pretty thin on the ground.'

He laughed again. 'No...I mean so oblivious to material things.'

Cassie shrugged. 'Human beings really only have five basic requirements. The rest is just...*stuff.*'

'Makes you kind of hard to impress,' he joked.

Cassie raised an eyebrow at him. 'I think your ability to give me screaming orgasms every night, night after night, is pretty impressive.'

Her words, delivered in that non-flirty, matter-of-fact tone of hers, crawled right inside his pants and stroked. He was used to being appreciated for his 'stuff' and it was a turn-on to be appreciated for his innate talents. He felt as if he was standing under the lights again, football in hand, listening to the crowd screaming his name.

The last few years had been generally emasculating—Cassie's unconditional presence in his life made him feel virile and potent again.

'You make a hell of an argument.' He smiled. 'But I think you need to prepare yourself to be pretty damn impressed when this plane lands. And I'm going to do it without even touching you.'

Cassie stood in the open doorway of the Gulf Stream an hour later, looking out into the glare of a hot dry day for a clue as to their location. Then she saw the sign proclaiming their destination—Flagstaff, Arizona. Her heart skipped a beat. She turned to look at Tuck, who loomed behind her.

'We're going to Barringer?'

Tuck grinned. 'Yup.'

Cassie was momentarily speechless. She'd had no idea when Tuck had asked her to pack an overnight bag last night where they'd end up, but this would have been her very last guess. She turned back to look at the sign again.

It was perfect. He couldn't have picked a more perfect destination to bring her to.

'I...I don't know what to say.' She looked back at him. 'Thank you, Tuck. Thank you so much. This is totally...'

She didn't have words. And it was hard to speak anyway as a bloom of heat in her chest travelled upwards, threatening to close off her throat.

'Impressive?' he supplied.

Cassie nodded. He looked so cocky and sure of himself, knowing how very much it meant to her, and all scruffy and casual. His pheromones oozed all over her and that heat spread everywhere. *He was sexy when he was right.*

She launched herself into his arms, her mouth seeking his, wanting to smell him, taste him, absorb him into her. Her tongue sought his and he groaned against her mouth, his hands splaying low on the small of her back, holding her steady, anchoring them together as ardour swayed them both in the narrow doorway.

'Wow—that impressive, huh?' he teased when she finally let go of him. Her spontaneity was as sexy as hell for someone who didn't really *do* spontaneity.

Cassie felt a little light-headed for a moment, clinging to his biceps all warm and bulky in her palms. 'You did good.'

He smiled and gestured for her to precede him. 'Well, let's get going, then.'

After that the afternoon flew by. Despite it being a holiday, a vintage Cadillac Deville convertible was waiting for them at the airport, because apparently an American road trip called for an American classic even if it only took them twenty minutes to arrive at their destination.

Cassie felt a little trill of happiness as she bounded out of the car. It increased when she looked at Tuck. The only thing he could have done that was more perfect was fly her to the moon, but she guessed even Tuck had his limitations.

Not to mention those nights when he'd taken her closer to the stars than any deep-space telescope ever had...

There were quite a few visitors bustling in and out of the Visitor Center, and Cassie hurried quickly in its direction, impatient to see the crater. She wasn't disappointed. The site of the massive hole in the earth, four thousand feet across, stopped her in its tracks. It was simply awe-inspiring, and Cassie just stood and stared at it, her astronomer's heart just about bursting out of her chest, trying to wrap her head around the circumstances of its creation.

'You're excited, right?' Tuck murmured low in her ear.

Cassie dug him in the ribs, but her face felt flushed, her pulse tripped, she was hyperaware—it *was* a tiny bit sexual. 'I wish you'd told me,' she said, turning to face him. 'I don't have my camera with me.'

Tuck held up a bag that held a very expensive piece of photographic gear that he'd figured would impress even a woman who had access to kick-ass telescopes on a daily basis.

Cassie grabbed him by his shirt and smacked a brief, hard kiss on his mouth. 'You are outdoing yourself today.'

Tuck grinned. 'Oh, there's more where that came from, baby.'

But Cassie barely heard him, distracted as she was by the path skirting the rim of the crater. If she'd been allowed, she would have jumped over the edge and dashed to the bottom. It looked like a lunar surface, hallowed ground, and to walk where the Apollo astronauts had trained would be a dream come true.

'There's a rim tour starting in ten minutes,' Tuck said.

'We'll catch the next one,' she said, because she was impatient but also because she didn't want to hear someone else's patter first. She just wanted to absorb everything and match it with the reams of knowledge teeming in her head.

Tuck chuckled. 'Okay, lead on.'

They spent two hours in the blazing sun, stopping and starting and reading information boards and taking pictures. Cassie talked geek stuff about asteroids and took pictures, and Tuck enjoyed her breadth of knowledge mixed with her infectious excitement. He'd never seen her so animated and he liked it.

Then they joined a tour for another go around the rim, which wasn't anywhere near as exciting—mainly because it took the group of twenty only about two minutes to recognise Tuck, and he spent a lot of time as they went around talking about himself to a bunch of fans and not next to Cassie as he'd wanted.

They stopped at one of the viewing areas and Cassie looked over at Tuck, talking to a couple of teenagers. He shot her an apologetic shrug and she just smiled and rolled her eyes. The guide was talking about the make-up of the asteroid that had slammed into the earth and Cassie separated herself slightly to snap another picture down into the crater.

A man holding a camera sidled up beside her and said, 'Magnificent, isn't it?'

Cassie looked away from the viewfinder. 'Oh, yes,' she breathed. 'Truly amazing.' She looked through the lens again.

'You're with Tuck, yes?' he asked casually. 'You his...?' He looked her up and down. 'Girlfriend?'

Cassie glanced at him. The guy was looking at her as if he was trying to figure out what genus and species she belonged to. He had a huge gold ring on his finger and a heavy gold chain around his neck. And a very large, expensive-looking camera with a gigantic lens. Tuck would have said he was compensating for something.

'Not really.'

What else could she say? *No, he's just my libido's drug of choice?* Hardly something you'd tell a stranger, even if it was the very startling truth. Plus, after today she wasn't sure what she felt about him. It suddenly seemed more than just sex between them. But maybe that was just the crater talking?

The guy was still watching her closely, and Cassie glanced over to see Tuck signing another autograph. She turned her attention back to the camera, snapping off more pictures.

'You're not his usual...type.'

Cassie's finger faltered on the button. She was wearing a pair of roomy gym shorts that allowed a good flow of air in the stifling heat and her usual three-sizes-too-big T-shirt that said *'Higgs Boson Gives Me a Hadron'*. Tuck had bought her a baseball cap from the gift shop and squashed it down on her head before the tour had started. Her dark brown hair hung down her back in its usual low ponytail, held fast by a floral scrunchie.

Her cheeks were flushed pink from the heat and she had sweat on her upper lip and forehead. She looked at the man over the top of the camera.

'They usually wear...' he looked over her outfit again, as if he was some Parisian designer who did not like what he saw '...less. And have more...make-up.'

Cassie frowned at the completely impractical observation. 'Who wears make-up in this heat?'

Then a little boy ran up to him, saying, 'Daddy, Daddy.'

'Hey, Zack,' he said.

'Look, I got Tuck's autograph.'

And then the guide moved them on and the conversation was over as the guy was dragged back to his family and Tuck headed her way.

'More pictures?' Tuck asked.

His hand slid onto her neck under the knot of her ponytail and Cassie smiled up at him. 'Can't wait to see these on my laptop,' she said.

Tuck kissed the tip of her nose and they moved on with the rest of the tour.

They stayed until the crater closed at five, and then drove into Flagstaff and wandered about the town centre, enjoying the Fourth of July celebrations. Tuck regaled Cassie with stories of his family's legendary Texan celebrations.

'Oh, look, they've got fireworks later,' Cassie said as she bit into an enormous stick of fairy floss—or cotton candy, as Tuck had told her.

'Oh, no. I have plans for you,' Tuck said, his arm around her waist, drawing her close into his side as they walked around amidst the crowds. He'd commandeered her baseball cap and pulled it down low, managing to stay inconspicuous in these much bigger crowds.

Cassie's belly clenched at the low, husky note in his voice. This whole venture had put her libido on high alert. 'But I *like* fireworks,' she said. As a young child Cassie had literally felt transported to the stars amidst all the pop and dazzle.

Tuck grinned. 'Oh, there'll be fireworks. Don't you worry about that.'

Cassie looked at him and could see another night of heaven in his arms. 'Where are we staying tonight?' she asked.

'Ah...' He grinned. 'That's the best bit.' He ducked his head and swiped a mouthful of cotton candy that melted on his tongue. 'Come on—eat that and I'll show you.'

They drove out of Flagstaff with the Cadillac's top down and headed towards the crater again. A lot of women would have been impressed by the romance, the fifties movie feel—an open-top, a man who could have graced any screen, the open road—but Cassie simply let her head loll back against the headrest and watched the stars float above her.

They passed the road to the crater they'd taken earlier today and some lights could be seen shining from the crater's RV park.

Tuck drove another minute and started to slow. 'I reckon this is as good a spot as any,' he said as he left the road and drove into the desert wilderness, the headlights illuminating an expanse of rocky, arid nothing.

They bumped over some rocks and low vegetation before Tuck turned off the engine and killed the lights, plunging them into the still, inky blackness of a desert night. They hadn't travelled far from the highway and behind them the RV park seemed reasonably close.

'What are you doing?' Cassie asked.

'I want an astronomy lesson,' he said. 'And it just so happens that I'm sleeping with a world-class astronomer. I thought a night under the stars would be kind of cool.'

Cassie looked up again. Millions of stars winked down at her through the obsidian dome of the night sky. It had been so long since she'd looked at them—really looked at them— with the *human eye*. She'd been studying the cosmos for over a decade, and with the advantage of deep-space telescopes and the miracles of modern imaging it was easy to forget the sense of wonder and insignificance she'd used to feel when looking up.

It crowded in on her now, and she took a deep unsteady breath.

'I have luxury bedding in the trunk,' Tuck said. 'I thought we could sleep on the hood of the Caddy.'

Cassie, her head resting back against the leather headrest, rolled her head to the side. It was dark, the one-quarter moon still low in the sky, but she could see Tuck's eyes shining with the same sort of wonder that Marnie's used to hold when she'd begged for an impromptu astronomy session.

'Unless you'd rather check into a hotel?'

Cassie slowly shook her head. It was an ideal night for some star-gazing. 'I can't think of any place more perfect than this,' she murmured. 'Or anyone I'd rather be with.'

Cassie blinked as the words slipped from her lips. Obviously her libido was mouthy, but even she could recognise how the words resonated with her on a much deeper level. She'd found something with Tuck that it had never occurred to her to seek out. And she liked it.

Tuck was taken aback by the spontaneous declaration, and the sincerity in Cassie's gaze. It had been a novelty, being with a woman who didn't cling and wasn't emotionally needy, but it wasn't until this moment that he realised it was also nice to hear her acknowledge that whatever it was they had, she was into it too.

To acknowledge that maybe she needed him as much as he was growing to need her.

'I'll get the stuff,' he said. Because, frankly, he didn't know what to say to such utter honesty. He was so used to *the game* he didn't know how to react when someone played it straight.

Cassie nodded as Tuck climbed out of the car. Another woman might have been puzzled about Tuck's non-reaction to her statement, but Cassie was as eager as Tuck to get flat on her back. And mind-games just weren't her forte.

As it turned out they didn't end up flat on their backs. Tuck adjusted a double sleeping bag with a thick foam mattress on the hood, but when they got inside he propped his back against the windshield and she nestled between his legs, her back to his front, her head on his shoulder, with the entire Arizonan sky stretched like a sheath of black satin above them.

'Do you suppose we'll see a shooting star?' Tuck asked.

His breath stirred the hair at her temple and Cassie momentarily shut her eyes. 'Absolutely,' she said, her eyelids opening. 'If we watch long enough. Although statistically we are more likely to see one after midnight. But you know they're not technically stars, right? They're meteors.'

Tuck lay back and listened to Cassie chatter about a subject on which she obviously knew a great deal. He liked listening to her, and her Australian accent, so obvious most of the time, became less distinct as her voice took on a generic wonder.

She pointed out all the constellations, including Cassiopeia, and was full of facts and figures and interesting anecdotes. The night was perfect, their location even more so, and they did indeed see several shooting stars over the two hours they sat with their faces turned upwards.

'I suppose you've known all this since you could talk?' Tuck murmured as she regaled him with some ancient Greek myths about the constellations.

Cassie nodded. 'I used to spend hours under the stars with Mum as a little girl. I used to complain about going to bed and wish we had a glass roof, so I could sleep under the stars. Then she bought me these glow-in-the-dark star stickers for my ceiling. There were planets as well. We mapped the whole solar system out—all geographically correct, with the constellations accurately represented—and I got to sleep under the stars every night.'

Tuck stroked his fingers up and down Cassie's arm. The desert night air was getting cool now, and he felt gooseflesh beneath the pads of his fingers. 'You sound like you're close to your mother?' he said as he pulled the bedding up around them.

Cassie shrugged. Her relationship with her mother had always been hard to define. 'Yes and no.'

Tuck heard the wistfulness in her voice. 'Oh?'

Cassie didn't know how to explain it. 'I was the child that interrupted her astronomy career. Put a stop to her grand plans of a great discovery that would forever change the world and a subsequent Nobel Prize. Don't get me wrong, I fully understand, and she pushed me to go on and do what she hadn't been able to, but…I don't know… I think there's part of her that has always resented the intrusion of a child…of *me*. She loved having me around to teach me things about the stars, but outside of that there's just this part of her that I never seem to be able to reach…like the stars, I guess.'

Cassie wasn't sure where the calm insights had come from. She'd never given them voice before. Never thought about them too much. But there was a whole lot going on with her emotionally lately that she'd never thought possible. And somehow, cocooned in this warm dark night with Tuck, it seemed right to talk about it.

'What about your dad?' Tuck asked.

'He adores her…but he's never really understood her. Her brilliance. And certainly not why she chose him. He sure as hell doesn't get *me*. So he does his thing, and she does hers, and I do mine and we all live in a kind of oblivious co-existence. I don't know…it works, but I don't think they're happy.'

Tuck thought about the fiery, passionate relationship of his own parents and couldn't even begin to imagine them just *co-existing*. He thought about how passionate his relationship with Cassie was, and the vibrancy of their in-between times too.

Their conversations.

He knew he would never survive in a relationship where everyone *co-existed* and nobody lived.

Cassie shifted against him and heat traced through his groin with all the urgency of a meteor shower. 'Well, I guess it takes all types, honey,' he said as he let his hand drift from her arm to her side, under her shirt and up her ribs to the smooth rise of breast.

Cassie shut her eyes and moaned as his thumb taunted the

stiffening peak of her nipple. The stars were forgotten as her nose brushed against his neck, inhaling a mega-dose of pheromones and suddenly her desires went from cosmic to carnal.

She turned in his arms, crawling up his body until she was straddling him. His erection nudged the apex of her thighs and she ground down a little. The harsh suck of his breath was loud in the eerie Arizonian desert and when she lowered her mouth to his their passion ignited.

Before she could blink her shirt was up and off her head and her breasts were bared to the cool night air and to him, and they were kissing and pulling at each other's clothes, and then he was inside her and they were making out on the hood of the car, oblivious to their exposure, driven by the intangible force of nature all around them and their own innate drive to be one.

And Cassie did indeed see fireworks as she came, hard and fast, her head thrown back, her gaze open wide to the stars as they blended in a kaleidoscope of colour and came showering down around her.

CHAPTER NINE

IT FELT LIKE hours later that Cassie stirred from her post-coital doze, but it was probably less than thirty minutes. The cool air was caressing her exposed skin and she needed to take her medication.

'Where are you going?' Tuck murmured as her warmth left his side. He reached for her as she sat up and tugged on her T-shirt.

'Just taking my tablet,' she said as she shrugged into the warmth of the fabric and eased down off the side of the car.

She delved into her handbag, located on the passenger seat. Cold air nipped at her bare legs and crept icy fingers beneath her hem and onto her naked butt as she opened the internal zipper where she'd placed her tablets that morning. She pushed out a small blue pill into her palm and washed it down using the bottle of water that Tuck had bought at Barringer.

She hurried back to Tuck and his big warm body, spread on the hood so invitingly. She dived in beside him and sighed as he gathered her into his chest and pulled the covers up over them.

'I wouldn't have thought you'd need that to sleep any more,' he said, kissing the top of her head. Her hair was cold against his face. 'I thought *I* was your drug of choice?'

Cassie smiled. 'You are. But I still need the other one.'

Tuck stroked his fingers up and down her arm as he gazed

absently at the stars. 'Sounds like addiction to me.' He tsked, his voice low, teasing. 'You might have to go cold turkey.'

Cassie tensed against him. *She needed it.* Going off it just wasn't an option.

'I know just the thing you can use as a substitute,' he murmured, his hand stroking lower, moving onto her naked hip.

Cassie didn't even feel the light brush of his fingers as her brain vehemently rejected his suggestion. She pushed herself away, coming up onto her elbow. 'No. I can never go off them. *Never.*'

Tuck blinked at her. Her face was scrunched into a fierce frown, the stars behind her forming a crown. 'O...kay...'

'I *need* them. They keep my brain from racing. They shut it down so I can sleep.'

He grinned again, picking up a lock of hair that had escaped her scrunchie and fallen forward over a bare shoulder. 'That's exactly what an orgasm does. Best sleeping pill there is.'

Cassie sat, pulling her knees up, tucking them against her chest. 'I mean it. The pills and I are a package deal. I learned the hard way a long time ago that my sanity depends on them.'

Tuck paused. Cassie was rocking slightly, and she looked all wild-eyed beneath the moonlight. 'Hey,' he said, dragging himself up into a sitting position too, 'it's okay. I was just teasing.'

'It's not funny.'

Tuck put his arm around Cassie's shoulders and felt her resist for a moment or two before relaxing against him. He could feel a slight tremble running through her and he didn't think it was from the cold. 'What happened?' he asked, his palm running up and down her arm, warming her.

Cassie didn't say anything for a while. She hadn't really told anyone about that time in any detail. Not because it was a secret, but because she hadn't been close enough to anyone to share it. Apart from that reference to it at the breakfast table at the Bellington Estate, she hadn't even told her college girlfriends.

'I was fourteen. I wasn't a typical teenager. I never really slept a lot—my brain was always busy—but I became convinced there was an error in a textbook that I'd been studying. I became obsessed with it—up all night on the computer trying to cross-reference, e-mailing hundreds of experts in the field trying to prove I was right, e-mailing the publishers, constantly harassing them to have it fixed. My brain was full of it. My schoolwork was ignored and I couldn't sleep. I was surviving on less and less each night until I wasn't even getting an hour's respite.'

Cassie stopped. With the benefit of time and clearer thought-processes she could see how trivial it had been, and how fanatical and irrational she'd become, but it had felt like a matter of national importance at the time.

'It was all I talked about, all I thought about. I barely ate. I couldn't sit still long enough to eat. Eventually I was admitted to hospital with dehydration. But I was rambling about it...*raving,* I suppose is a better word. And from there I was admitted to a psych unit.'

Tuck's hold on her tightened as her voice, husky in the silence of the night, gave away the turmoil not evidenced in her dispassionate words. He guessed this kind of thing was the flipside of genius.

'They drugged me up. I lost days...weeks...where I was this zombie. Where I had no say or control over my life. I couldn't think. My mind was blank. I could barely feed myself.' She shuddered. 'Eventually they got my medication right and I came out of the fog. It was scary.' She looked at him. 'And I never want to go there again.'

'Shh,' Tuck said, kissing her forehead, amazed at what

she'd been through. At how susceptible her genius had made her. 'I understand. The medication gives you control.'

Cassie nodded. 'More than anything, I learned that my brain needs sleep to be healthy, to perform at its highest level. *To be me.* And if that means I have to swallow one little pill every night for the rest of my life, even if I have to wake up to do it, then that's what I'm going to do. Because the alternative…'

Tuck felt her shudder again and pulled her harder against him, wrapping both his arms around her shoulders. This was the first time he'd ever seen her vulnerable and he couldn't help but feel that they'd taken a major step forward.

'Is unacceptable,' he finished for her. 'I know,' he agreed. 'I know.'

The distant rumble of an engine from the direction of the RV park woke Cassie at six the next morning. She was snuggled into Tuck's side, her head on his shoulder, all warm and cosy despite the cool air on her face. She stretched and rolled on her back. The inky obsidian of last night had morphed into a crystal-clear desert dawn, with a slight blush of pink tingeing the pale blue arc that stretched endlessly to the distant horizon.

She smiled as Tuck rolled towards her, his big arm clamping around her waist, his lips nuzzling her neck.

'We have to get going,' he murmured into her hair, reluctant as all hell to leave their deliciously warm cocoon. He felt closer to her this morning after her revelation last night than he'd ever felt. But they had a Gulf Stream to catch. 'The plane leaves in an hour.'

Cassie nodded. Ordinarily she would have sprung up and been keen to get back home. To Cornell. She was essentially losing two days out of her academic schedule by taking this time out. But she wouldn't have missed this in a million years.

Being here, seeing Barringer, having a truly magical night under the stars…

And all because of Tuck.

Lying here, in his arms, she was grateful that she'd have this amazing memory to take back home with her. But more than that she was beginning to think that maybe there might be more to life than twenty-four-seven study.

And, surprisingly, it *didn't* scare the hell out of her.

A minute later Tuck kissed her neck. 'Come on—time to shake a tail feather.' And he hauled himself up into a sitting position.

'I don't know where my clothes are.' Cassie yawned. She'd lost her shirt again not long after her confession to him last night.

Tuck threw back the covers and looked down at her naked body, stretched before him. It had a predictable effect on him and his body snapped to instant awareness.

'Clothes are overrated,' he said as he trailed a hand down her body from the hollow of her throat to her pubic bone. He eased himself back on his elbow, leaned in and kissed her neck, his hand easing back up her body to cup a breast.

Cassie shivered as the cool morning breeze sizzled across her heated skin. She stretched her neck to give him better access, and when his hand travelled south again and slipped between her legs they opened eagerly. When the pad of his thumb stroked against her centre she moaned. When one finger probed, then slipped inside, she arched her back. When another joined it she called his name. And when his head followed the path of his hands and settled between her legs Cassie surrendered to the maelstrom.

She built quickly, the speed and strength of her orgasm multiplying as visual data from all around bombarded her senses. The perfect arc of blue sky, the vast flatness rolling all the way out to the horizon, the eerie quiet broken only by her delirious cries, the cool breeze, and Tuck's blond head between her legs doing that thing he did that pushed her over the edge *every single time.*

The overpowering visuals coalesced and ripples of release fanned through her belly. She lifted her hips as they became hard and unrelenting. She cried out, jack-knifing up as they flung her into space and her whole world threatened to collapse in on her. She thrust her hand into his hair, holding him fast, riding the wave and the hard edge of his tongue until her body shattered and fell and twirled back to earth. She collapsed back against the hood, shamelessly spread before him and the sky above like some pagan sacrifice, overwhelmingly sated.

Another engine noise caused her to stir a little while later and she opened her eyes. Tuck was kissing his way back up her body. 'We really *do* have to go,' he said against her neck as he dropped her shirt on her belly.

Cassie was fairly incapable of speech. She could see the highway not far away, and the first RV of the day turning on to it, heading in their direction.

Tuck lay down beside her, lifting his hips as he eased his shorts up. 'I think I'll need to investigate the bottom of the sleeping bag a little more thoroughly to find the rest of our clothes,' he said.

The RV pulled to the side of the road, in their direct line of sight, but still probably a hundred or so metres from them. Tuck looked up, frowning at the intrusion into their private little bubble.

'Come on then, Cassiopeia,' he said as he heard a car door open and close. 'If these people are stopping to ask us if we're okay we'd better be dressed.' He swung his legs off the hood and jumped to the ground. 'Of course...' his gaze fanned over her again '...if you just want to stay here for ever like that with me then I'm sure I could arrange that too.'

Cassie shook herself out of her post-coital daze at Tuck's reminder that there was a world for them to get back to. That Cornell was waiting. She pulled her shirt over her head and Tuck held out his hand to help her down.

The wind caught her shirt and it billowed out as Tuck lifted her down. Cassie felt the breeze cool places that were still quite overheated, but was thankful that she favoured baggy shirts—she didn't fancy giving the man at the side of the road an eyeful, no matter how distant.

She stumbled against Tuck as her feet hit the dirt and one of them found a sharp little rock. 'Ow!' She cursed, screwing up her face at the jab of pain.

'You okay?' Tuck asked, grabbing her by the arms to steady her.

Cassie nodded as she breathed through the pain. 'Fine,' she said on a sucked-in breath.

Tuck grinned down at her. 'You're kind of cute when you cuss.'

She glared at him, but his hand was sliding onto her jaw and his mouth was descending and his kiss swept the indignation, the pain and every IQ point she owned into the ether. His pheromones filled her head and Cassie clung to his naked chest as they made her dizzy.

Tuck pulled away, groaning against her mouth. 'We *have* to go.'

A minute later the RV left, and ten minutes after that they were on the road back to Flagstaff. Within the hour they were wheels up and winging their way back to Ithica.

Two nights later Cassie shut the lid of her laptop around ten. Tuck was sitting up in bed, his long, muscular legs crossed at the ankles, watching a Thursday night game on the massive big screen television that dominated the wall opposite their bed. He had the sound turned down low for her benefit, but he really needn't have bothered. Cassie easily became consumed in her work to the exclusion of everything else. The street could have exploded and she'd have been oblivious.

He gave her a goofy grin, one of several he'd given her since she'd come home, and she frowned. He'd been mysterious about his day too. 'You're up to something,' she said.

Tuck feigned a hurt look. 'Not me.'

Cassie smiled at his obvious lie. 'I'm having a shower.'

'I'll be here waiting for you when you get back,' he said.

Cassie eyed him suspiciously as she headed for the bathroom. She was tired. *Good* tired. Ready to go to sleep tired. She'd never felt tired prior to meeting Tuck. She'd always been a little on the wired side and her need for that one little pill had never been questioned. But Tuck was right. Sexual satisfaction was a powerful sedative—a pity they couldn't bottle it.

Cassie was in and out of the shower in ten minutes, padding back into the room in just her underwear, her hair in its regulation ponytail. She could feel his eyes leave the television and follow her every movement as she went through the drawers searching for a shirt.

'You shouldn't bother with a shirt,' Tuck said, eyeing the swing of her breasts, football game forgotten.

Cassie turned to face him, her nipples responding to the blatant strain of sex in his voice. 'Oh?'

Tuck laughed at the slogan on her underwear. It had a Pi sign and read 'I speak geek'. He held out his hand. 'Come to bed *just* like that.'

Tuck was wearing a pair of boxer briefs and nothing else and Cassie was drawn across the room, his voice wrapping silky strands around her waist and slowly tugging. She detoured around to her side of the bed and peeled the sheet back as she climbed in. Tuck flicked the TV off with the remote and Cassie reached out to snap off the lights, plunging the room into darkness.

Except there wasn't complete darkness. An eerie green glow lit the ceiling and Cassie gasped as she looked up and saw hundreds of glow-in-the-dark stars covering the huge expanse of ceiling in the very large room.

She looked at Tuck. 'You did this today?'

He nodded. 'I paid one of the astronomy majors to do me an exact replica of our solar system. You like?'

Cassie squirmed down until she was lying on her back. 'Cassiopeia,' she said, pointing to the constellation as familiar to her as her own name.

Tuck lay down beside her and they star-gazed as they had that other night in Arizona, except indoors this time.

'Are you even allowed to do this?' she asked, glancing at him as they exhausted the solar system. 'Defacing a rental apartment?'

Tuck shrugged. 'I'll pay to have them removed and the ceiling returned to all its boring plainness if they want when we're done here.'

'Yes, it *was* kind of boring, wasn't it?' she murmured as the stars glowed down at her. 'But not any more.'

Tuck nodded. Just like his life. It had been boring and pre-dictable before Cassie. He knew that sounded ungrateful, that plenty of people had lives that were barely tolerable and that his life had been very good. There'd been many years when he'd enjoyed it and the perks that came with it. But being on the celebrity treadmill, going through the motions, was about as appealing now as a plain white ceiling.

If he wasn't careful he'd forget that they had an expiry date.

'And the best part is,' Tuck said, rolling up onto his elbow, looking down at her, 'I literally get to make you see stars every night.'

Cassie shut her eyes as his scent wafted over her and breathed him deep into her lungs. The primal urge to feel him inside her bloomed deep and low.

'But I think it's only fair that you get to see them first.' She pushed on his chest. When he fell back against the bed she rolled on top of him.

Tuck smiled up at her as she straddled him, naked but for her underwear, just like that night in the desert. 'Okay...' he said, his palms sliding up her torso, finding her breasts. 'If you insist.'

But his hands soon fell away as her intent became clear, and when she kissed her way down his body and right into his boxer briefs he felt as if he'd snatched a little piece of heaven from off the ceiling.

The next morning the bubble they'd been living in, tucked away in Ithica, away from the rest of the world, well and truly burst. It was a phone call from Marnie that alerted Cassie to the looming disaster.

'How you doin', hon? Are you okay?' Marnie asked.

Cassie stopped looking at the data on her computer screen and frowned. There was something in Marnie's Southern twang that put her on high alert. 'Er...yes...sure... Why wouldn't I be?'

'Oh. You haven't seen it, then?' she asked.

'Seen what?'

'The tabloid article?'

Cassie went back to her work. 'About the paternity stuff? That's old news.'

'No, not that. Same tabloid but...it's about *you* and Tuck. There's some not very flattering pics, and the headline...it's pretty awful.'

It was sweet of Marnie to alert her, but Cassie just didn't

care about celebrity gossip or the weird obsession people had with it. 'I'm sure I'll survive,' she said dryly.

'Okay…just don't… Ignore it, okay? Anyone who knows you knows how beautiful you are—inside and out.'

Cassie frowned at the odd parting remark, but was quickly absorbed in her work again.

Gina phoned next, followed by Reese. She assured both of them that she was fine and had better things to do with her time than worry about tabloid gossip. And she put it out of her mind.

Until she arrived home at seven and Tuck was pacing in front of the large windows, yelling into his phone.

'I don't just want an apology. I want a price put on that pap's head. I want him dead or alive. I want the whole freaking paper shut down. I want to tie them up in the world's most expensive legal case until they're haemorrhaging money. They think they can mess with me after the Jenny thing? They just made me their worst freaking enemy!'

Cassie jumped as Tuck hurled his phone at the glass. It bounced off and crashed to the ground. He raked a hand through his hair, ignoring the felled piece of expensive technology.

'Hi,' she said.

Tuck turned and saw her standing there. He took half a dozen long strides and swept her into his arms. He didn't say anything, but she could tell from the fierceness of his hug that he was still angry.

Tuck pulled back and looked into Cassie's blue-grey eyes. They'd become such a part of his life he couldn't begin to imagine a time when she wouldn't be here, all calm and thoughtful. And that made him even crazier—their time together was definitely finite!

'There's something I have to tell you,' he said.

'Is this about the tabloid article?' she asked.

Tuck gaped. When his PA had first alerted him that morning he hadn't thought that Cassie would want her day interrupted—plus he hadn't wanted to tell her over the phone. So he'd left informing her in preference to jumping on as many heads as he possibly could before she got home.

'You've *seen* it?'

'No,' she said. 'But I've had phone calls from Reese, Gina and Marnie about it.'

Damn! He hadn't thought about them. 'It's okay. By the time I'm through with them they'll think the Jenny debacle was a freaking Sunday school picnic.'

Cassie stepped out of his arms. This seemed a lot of fuss about some dumb tabloid article. 'For goodness' sake, what does it say?'

'Oh. They didn't tell you?'

'No, I was busy doing *important* things, like my PhD research at the very place where *Carl Sagan* himself studied. Now, what the hell does it say that has everyone in such a tizz? Have you got a copy?'

Tuck looked behind him at the pile of newspapers he'd bought from practically every newsstand in Ithica. 'One or two,' he said.

Cassie blinked at the stacks that littered the formal dining table and the nearby floor. She marched over, picked one off the top and opened it. The glaring headline on page three jumped out at her—*'Tuck's Ugly Duck'*.

There were several pictures. One was of them at Barringer Crater, where she looked all hot and bedraggled, and three more had been taken the next morning. One was a shot of the wind billowing under her T-shirt, so she looked like the Michelin man, another was of her face all screwed up when that rock had jabbed into her, and the last was their passionate kiss just after that, with Tuck all bare-chested.

They were a little fuzzy, but it was definitely them.

The article speculated as to who she was and how unlike Tuck's usual glamorous consorts she was. It seemed to be drawing a parallel between the fading of his star and his luck in the lady stakes. Cassie rolled her eyes and threw the paper down in disgust.

'It was that bastard in the RV,' Tuck said, resuming his pacing. 'He has to have been paparazzi too—not just some visitor wanting to cash in on an unexpected opportunity. You'd need a serious camera to get those images of us.'

Cassie thought about it for a moment. 'It was the guy with the big gold jewellery,' she said.

Tuck stopped pacing. 'What? Why didn't you tell me there was a pap around?'

She shrugged. 'I didn't realise he was at the time.'

'Well, what makes you think it was him now?'

'He kind of hung around a bit. He asked me if you were my boyfriend. He commented that I wasn't your usual type. He looked kind of puzzled as to why we were together. He had a little boy with him...Zack...you signed an autograph for him.'

Tuck nodded. He remembered. The man hadn't been familiar—and Tuck had got to know most of the paps over the years.

'Good,' he said, stalking over and picking his phone up off the floor. He hit the last call button.

Cassie listened to the one-sided conversation as Tuck relayed the details to his lawyer and they discussed ways to access Barringer Crater's records of who had come through that day. Tuck paced again as he spoke, and even though his anger seemed less palpable she could sense frustration surging off him in waves, much the same way she'd always been sensitive to his pheromones.

Tuck hung up the phone and turned to face Cassie. 'I'm sorry. I'm so, so sorry,' he said, trying to gauge how Cassie was feeling about the article. 'I won't let them get away with this.'

Cassie shrugged. 'Get away with what? Who cares what they think?'

Tuck blinked. Any other woman he knew would be *outraged* at that headline. 'But they've insulted you,' he said.

Cassie snorted. 'You think I'm *insulted*? You think how *beautiful* you are counts when you're up for a Nobel Prize? Those things don't go to the *prettiest* candidate, Tuck. You think *science* cares about what you look like? You think they select people to go to Antarctica based on their *attractiveness?* I really don't think you realise how very, very little this matters to me.'

'They don't have the right to say such horribly hurtful things in a national newspaper about you,' Tuck said, his anger once again exploding to the surface at Cassie's calm acceptance. 'About *any* woman.' Didn't she realise how beautiful she was?

Cassie shook her head, amazed at how angry he seemed to be. But then she supposed it *was* a bit of a slap in the face for Tuck, who was used to accolades, to being known for his beautiful women.

'Oh…I see,' she said. 'This isn't about *me*. This is about an affront to your *masculinity*. That some two-bit rag has the *audacity* to call one of *your* women ugly. Are you afraid you're not going to make the A-list any more with an ugly, brainiac *girlfriend?*' She shook her head. 'Just what the hell are you doing with me, Tuck?'

Tuck couldn't believe the words that were coming out of her mouth. Rage, white and hot, built in his gut and leeched into his bloodstream. How could she think he was so damn shallow?

'I don't *care* about that crap,' he snapped, shoving his hands on his hips. 'But I *do* care when a national newspaper calls *any* woman ugly. Who has the right to be the arbiter of that? The right to say it? And you? You are smart and sexy and warm and intelligent and beautiful and *natural* in a way beyond anything any of those *twits* with their freaking airbrushes and computer programs would know anything about, and I'm not going to sit still and let them call one of the most brilliant minds on the planet, *and the woman I love,* ugly.'

Tuck was breathing hard when he finished. In fact it took him a few seconds before he even realised what he'd said.

'What did you say?' Cassie said.

He'd said he loved her. His first instinct was to take it back. Pretend that it had been said in the heat of the moment and not meant. But, whilst it had *totally* been said in the heat of the moment, he did mean it. *He loved her.* He just hadn't realised it 'til that moment.

He'd almost spat his coffee all over the paper this morning when he'd first read the article, and his anger had been building with the ominous power and thrust of a dangerous weather front all day. He hadn't been able to articulate where the immediate irrational anger had come from when he'd first dialled his lawyer, but it had been frighteningly, utterly palpable.

And now he knew why.

He'd never felt like this about a woman. Not even April. He'd wanted to love her like this, had committed to that, but the plain truth was that he'd only ever just liked her, and she'd been there to cling to when everything was spiralling down the plughole. But it hadn't been enough, and he'd been wrong to give her hope that he could love her as she'd deserved.

As he *loved* Cassie.

'I love you,' he said. And then he said it again for good measure, weighing it up. 'I love you.'

He'd spent a lot of his life thinking those three words would mean his life was over, but it didn't feel like that—it felt as if it was just beginning. It wasn't scary and awful—it was just *right*.

Cassie blinked. 'Don't be ridiculous,' she said. 'Even if I believed that such an emotion existed, and wasn't some commercial construct to sell movies and Valentines, we've known each other for just over a month—it's preposterous.'

Tuck shook his head. 'It's not.'

Cassie couldn't believe what she was hearing. Len might never have performed oral sex on her and blown her head right off her shoulders every single night, but he would never have complicated their arrangement by falling prey to such schoolboy fancy. This was what happened when she got involved with someone who let his heart—or other parts of his body—rule his head.

Now she understood why her mother had been so determined to school her in the importance of her career and not to let distractions derail her from what was truly important.

Declarations like this could stop a person in their tracks!

But not her. She had her PhD to finish, then she was heading home to Australia, and next year she was going to Antarctica—come hell or high water. And she was *not* going to let some jock talk her out of it because he *imagined* himself in love with her.

Love was for dreamers—not thinkers. And she was most definitely a thinker.

It just wasn't *logical* that he loved her, for crying out loud!

'Well, I don't love you,' she said.

Tuck flinched at her matter-of-fact delivery. 'You're telling me you don't feel *anything* for me?'

Cassie shrugged. 'I feel sexual arousal. I feel a Pavlovian response to your pheromones. I feel a constant state of primal awareness.'

'Well, that's a start,' he said.

'I'm here because of my libido, Tuck. That's why you invited me, remember? It was never about anything other than burning off some lust.' Even as she said the words she knew they weren't one hundred percent true. 'We always had an end date.'

Tuck took a step towards her. He'd thought they'd grown closer over the last weeks, that Cassie had started to see their relationship as something more than a scratching post for her libido. Especially since their time at Barringer—since she'd told him about what had happened to her as a teenager.

'What if I don't want that any more? What if I want more?'

'More?'

'A relationship. Marriage. A family.'

It was Cassie's turn to gape. Since when had Mr-Love-Them-and-Leave-Them got so serious? Hadn't he said her complete lack of interest in weddings and babies was right up his alley?

'In a couple of months I'm going home to *Australia,* to continue my aurora research, and next year I'm going to *Antarctica* for six months. I'm not going to have *any* regrets in my life, Tuck. Not like my mother. I don't believe in love and marriage. And children aren't on my agenda. You know that.'

Tuck could feel it all slipping away. 'A career and a family don't have to be mutually exclusive.'

'You can't even *have* children, Tuck.' She saw him flinch at her blunt statement and felt conflicted by how bad it felt. *Damn it—it was the truth.* 'I didn't think you *wanted* them.'

Tuck hadn't. Not really. Not even when he'd been going through the fertility process with April. But *she* had, and it had seemed like something to bond them together even though his infertility had exacerbated his already battered sense of self.

'I do now,' he said, realising the truth of it. 'I want to have children with you.'

Cassie shook her head. 'I'll be gone for *six months,* Tuck.

And it won't be the only time my career will have me travelling. You'd be okay with that, would you?'

Tuck blanched at the thought. He missed her like crazy during her twelve-hour days at the university. Six months would seem like an eternity.

Cassie nodded at his hesitation. 'Clearly this is not working. I'll move back to the dorm.'

She headed for the bedroom. She should be calm. It was, after all, a logical decision to move on now things were not as she'd originally agreed. But her heart was thumping and there was an ache in the pit of her stomach as if she was ravenously hungry but there was nothing she wanted to eat.

Tuck took some deep breaths before he followed her in. His heart thundered and his head spun at how everything had unravelled so quickly. Cassie was throwing her clothes into her case when he joined her.

'Don't do this,' he said from the doorway.

Cassie shook her head. 'It's logical,' she said, not looking at him. 'I moved in because it was logical and now—given the way that we both feel—it's logical for me to move out.'

Tuck didn't know what he'd expected. Women he'd split with before had never been this calm. There'd been tears. Anger. Threats. It should have made a nice change, but it only made it virtually impossible to reach her. She'd reverted to her comfort zone of logic and sense and that was as far removed from gut and emotion as was possible.

He was angry and frustrated, but it seemed futile in the midst of her calm, detached packing. How could he get through to a robot? It was ironic that when he'd finally fallen in love with a woman it was with one who was incapable of returning it.

His Great-Aunt Ada would have said it was poetic justice.

'Don't,' he snapped, moving into the room. 'Stay. I'll

move. I'll go back to New York. Stay until you're done here. It's paid up for three months.'

'Don't be ridiculous,' Cassie said, automatically concentrating very hard on the job at hand instead of the growing gnaw in her gut. 'This is your place.'

Tuck reached over and slammed the drawer shut. 'I said don't,' he barked. 'You want logic? A dorm is no place for a grown woman. It makes *sense* for you stay here. Put some of those IQ points of yours to good use and *figure it out.*'

Cassie couldn't look at him as he loomed over her. His pheromones wafted off him in strong waves and despite the situation her nostrils flared. If he didn't go soon she was going to act in a very confusing and contradictory manner.

For both of them.

'Okay. Thank you,' she said.

Tuck nodded. He went to the bedside table and picked up his wallet and keys. 'I'll send for my stuff tomorrow.'

Cassie didn't acknowledge him. She didn't turn to watch him leave. She just stood by the drawers and listened to the door slam, the car start up, the garage door open, the car drive away.

And, despite knowing logically it was better this way, the pain in her gut grew bigger.

CHAPTER TEN

BAD NEWS TRAVELLED fast, and Cassie spent the next week taking phone calls from her concerned friends, assuring them that she was fine, that it was for the best. That she and Tuck had only ever been a temporary sexual thing and he'd got too emotionally involved.

And she believed it. In her head.

But the gnawing pain just didn't seem to go away, no matter how much she ate. On top of that a heaviness had taken up residence in her chest. And once again her work was shot. But this time it wasn't about her libido or her hormones, which was the most confusing thing—because even though she'd never really understood that at least she was familiar with it.

This was about something else entirely. It was about *him*. She couldn't stop thinking about *him*. Memories of their time together interrupted her days and bombarded her dreams.

Their Sunday mornings together reading the papers. Sharing an evening meal and talking about their day. Their quiet companionship every night as they worked on their projects, her at the desk in the bedroom, Tuck propped against the bedhead, a game turned on low.

And the trip to Barringer. The mystery plane ride, the open-top Cadillac, exploring the crater with him, eating candy floss, their night of stargazing, opening up to him.

And the hot, wild sex under a desert night.

Yes, okay, some of her thoughts *did* linger on their crazy, insatiable sex-life. Because she did miss the sex too. But she'd always figured that the sex would be the thing she'd miss *the most* when their relationship ended.

But it wasn't. *She missed him.* She missed him being around. Being right there. Filling up the spaces in the kitchen, the bathroom, the bedroom. Filling up the silences. She missed turning around to talk to him, to show him some miraculous cosmic image, to talk about the intricacies of her project, to ask him about his.

She hadn't realised how silent her life had been until Tuck had been there, filling it up with light and sound and noise.

It wasn't logical to feel this way. She *never* had before. It didn't make sense.

But it wouldn't go away either.

And then the weekend swung around and it was all that Cassie could do to drag herself out of bed on Saturday. She hadn't been sleeping well, despite the medication, and when she did she dreamt of Tuck. It didn't seem to matter what she did, what drug she took, how hard she worked or how late she stayed up to thoroughly exhaust herself, she couldn't switch her brain off from thinking about him.

The last thing she felt like doing was hitting the research— and she *always* felt like hitting the research. She knew it would be a distraction from her thoughts, something to help get her through another long day, but when she got there a whole batch of new images had come in overnight and she found herself thinking about Tuck even more. One of them was an ultraviolet image of a star cluster on the edge of the solar system, and it reminded her of the blue of Tuck's eyes so much she lost her breath.

She itched to ring him. To tell him about the majesty and beauty of the pictures. He'd been as fascinated by the images on her laptop as she had, and this image more than any other seemed to resonate with her.

It was like staring straight into his blue, blue gaze.

Damn it.

At three o'clock Cassie gave up trying to be productive and headed for home. The next six weeks stretched ahead interminably, and she hated that what should have been the highlight of her life had completely lost its lustre. She would forever look back on it and think not of her exciting time in one of the great cradles of learning but of Tuck.

The only consolation, as she put one foot in front of the other, was that she got to go back to the apartment instead of the dorm. At least she could be miserable in solitude.

When she got in she stripped off her leggings and fell into bed. Utter exhaustion finally took over and, as her head hit the pillow, she fell headlong into a dark and troubled sleep. Elusive images of Tuck and her mother intertwined with deep-space images so they seemed to float in a galaxy of stars, and every time she reached out to touch him, to touch her mother, they disappeared in her hand like rainbow mist.

It took the simultaneous beating on her door and the ringing of her mobile phone a few hours later to yank her out of the increasingly distressing dream. She woke with a start, her heart pounding, disorientated for a few moments. Then the noises started to filter in and she leapt from the bed, heading for the door, collecting her ringing phone on the way and answering it.

'Hello?' she said as she walked.

'It's us!' A chorus of voices reverberated through her ear.

'We're at your door,' Reese said.

'Let us in,' Gina demanded.

Cassie faltered for a moment as she neared the door, then hurried to open it, the phone still pressed to her ear.

A cheer of, 'Surprise!' and a cacophony of party horns

greeted her. Cassie hit the 'end' button on her phone just in time as her *gal pals* descended upon her, pulling her into a group hug.

'We've come to get you drunk,' Gina said, waving two bottles of champagne in the air.

Marnie, her perky blonde ponytail swinging, frowned at Gina. 'We've come to *cheer you up,*' she clarified, and Cassie guessed things were still a little cool between the two women.

'How are you, hon?' Reese said, hugging her hard again. 'My cousin's obviously been hit too many times in the head.' She pulled back. 'I could probably get Mason to send around some of his Marine buddies and rough him up a little, if you like?'

Cassie was temporarily speechless. She'd been struggling along for over a week now, pretending she was okay, but just having her oldest friends here made her feel as if she actually *was* going to be okay. That she was going to be able to survive this thing she didn't even understand.

It had never occurred to her to call them to her side, but she was so glad they were here. Tears sprang to her eyes. She blinked them away—for Pete's sake, she *never* cried!

'We have movies,' Marnie said, holding up three DVDs that looked distinctly science-fictiony.

'And we're ordering pizza,' Reese added. 'Do you have a local number? I can't believe Tuck wouldn't,' she said, wandering off to investigate the fridge for a magnet or a menu.

Gina looked around and whistled. 'Nice digs. You scored well. Did he leave anything we could trash?'

Cassie shook her head, feeling more tears threaten. 'Everything's gone.'

Gina hugged her. 'It's okay,' she said. 'We'll trash talk about him on social media instead, like all good ex-girlfriends. Now, come on—where are your glasses?'

Cassie was swept up in the noise and light that was the

Awesome Foursome and it felt good to be part of them again. To be part of their circle, to feel their love, to know that they'd slay dragons for her.

Or at least contribute to the hire of a hit-man.

And they didn't talk about Tuck—not to start with anyway. They drank champagne and toasted friendship and regaled Cassie with stories of their own recent lives while they waited for the pizza to be delivered. But as they sat at the table to eat the questioning began.

Gina went first. 'You want to talk about it?' she asked in her usual blunt manner.

Cassie didn't know. She'd certainly listened to enough tales of woe and break-up stories from her friends over the year she'd lived with them to know *talking about it* was what you were *supposed* to do. But it really hadn't been a position she'd envisaged herself in.

'Not really.'

'Was it the newspaper article?' Marnie asked, extending her hand and placing it over Cassie's forearm where it lay on the table.

Cassie shook her head. 'I don't care about some stupid headline in some stupid gossip rag.'

'No...I meant the paternity suit,' Marnie said as she gently squeezed Cassie's wrist.

'No.' Cassie withdrew her arm and reached for a slice of pepperoni pizza. 'I don't care about that either. And it's been dropped anyway.'

The women all looked at each other as Cassie bit into her pizza. 'Did he snore?' Marnie asked.

'Drop his wet towels on the floor?' Reese suggested.

'Pick his teeth at the table?' Gina said.

'I know,' Marnie said. 'He was vulgar with his money.'

Reese snorted. 'Hardly. I know... I bet he treated you like some Texan princess—a china doll.'

'Or maybe he was just lousy in bed?' Gina said.

Cassie almost choked on her pizza at the last suggestion, necessitating some back-bashing action from Gina.

Reese pushed Cassie's champagne towards her and said, 'Drink.'

When Cassie had her voice back she said, 'He did none of those things. He had perfect manners with food and his money and was well house-trained. And he most definitely was *not* lousy in bed. The man achieved the impossible with me. *Time and again.*'

Cassie's belly looped the loop at the thought of how many times Tuck had brought her to orgasm.

'Damn, I *knew* he'd be good,' Gina said wistfully.

Marnie shot her a quelling look. 'So what *did* happen?'

Cassie sighed at her well-intentioned friends gazing back at her, wanting to help. Wanting to understand so they could make things better. And who knew? Maybe they could. This was obviously a time when *EQ*, which they all had in spades, trumped IQ, which *she* had in spades but obviously meant *zip*.

'He told me he loved me.'

Marnie looked at her, puzzled. Gina and Reese exchanged an eyebrow-raise. Yep. Definitely an *EQ* thing.

'That's…it?' Reese asked.

'But…that's a good thing, Cass,' Marnie said gently.

Reese nodded. 'Most available women on this continent— hell, most of the unavailable ones too—would kill to hear those words come out of Samuel Tucker's mouth.'

Cassie threw down her half-eaten piece of pizza. 'I'm not most women. I never have been. You all know that.'

They nodded in unison. Truer words had never been spoken.

Cassie downed her champagne in one swallow. 'I don't *fall* in love. I don't *believe* in love. It's the most illogical, irrational…*thing*…in the entire universe. So much time and effort and money is wasted on it. Trying to achieve it, trying to keep it. We'd have a cure for cancer or poverty or a manned flight to Mars by now if people just channelled the same amount of energy into *important* things that they do into something as fanciful as love.'

'No such thing as love?' Marnie blanched. 'I thought you didn't believe in it like you didn't believe in God or unicorns or pots of gold at the ends of rainbows. Not that you *seriously* denied its existence.' She took a sip of her champagne. 'What about the love a mother has for her newborn baby?'

'That's evolution,' Cassie dismissed. 'Mothers are preconditioned to love. It hones their protective instincts to keep their offspring alive in the world so they can go on to continue the species. But what purpose is there for romantic love?' Cassie demanded.

'Procreation?' Marnie said.

Cassie shook her head. 'Survival of the species is maintained perfectly well without it in all species except humans.'

'Sometimes not even then,' said Gina, ever the cynic.

'How about just because it feels good?' Reese murmured.

Cassie snorted. 'Lots of things feel good.' Sex with Tuck had felt exceptionally good. 'Doesn't mean it's good *for* us. Feeling good is not a reason to do something.'

Reese blinked. 'Why not?'

'Because then we only do the things we want instead of the things we *need* to do. It's not conducive to the survival of the fittest.'

The women fell silent at an impasse they didn't seem to be able to bridge.

'Come on,' Gina said after a moment or two, filling their glasses again. 'We're not here to be downers. We're here to cheer you up. Let's go and watch some movies. We even rented the first three *Star Treks,* just for you.'

Cassie watched as the bubbles in her champagne rose to

the surface. She picked up her glass and raised it towards her friends. 'Thank you for all coming. I know this touchy-feely stuff isn't my forte, but I'm glad you're here dishing it out anyway. And I'm touched that you hired my favourite movies. I know you'd all rather stick yourself in the eye with a hot poker.'

'Cheers to that,' Gina muttered as she clinked her glass with Cassie's. 'Now, let's get this party started.'

By the time the credits had rolled on the third movie it was well after midnight, the two bottles of champagne were gone and they'd emptied two more bottles of wine Gina had discovered on a wire rack inside the pantry.

'Well, that's eight hours of my life I'm never going to get back,' Gina said as she stretched out on the bed.

They'd all piled into the king-sized bed to watch the DVDs on the big screen.

'Feeling better now?' Marnie asked as she glanced at Cassie.

Cassie nodded. 'Yes. Thank you.' And she did. A night with her *gal pals* had taken her mind off Tuck. She'd even laughed through Gina and Reese's alternative running commentary of the movie. 'Thank you for coming.'

She felt as if she'd gained some perspective, having her friends around. There was no need to feel so overwhelmed by things she didn't understand when she had such great women in her life—at the end of a telephone.

'I was feeling sorry for myself. But not any more.'

'You look better,' Marnie said.

'I feel much stronger,' Cassie agreed.

'Good. Our work here is done.' Reese smiled, settling down onto her pillow. 'Now, turn the lights out and let's get some sleep. We've got a long drive back to New York in the morning and none of us are nineteen any more.'

Cassie reached out and flipped off the lights and was greeted by a chorus of gasps. She looked up at hundreds of stars glowing down at her.

'Wow,' Gina said.

'Cassie,' Marnie whispered. 'It's beautiful. Did you do that?'

Cassie felt her eyes fill with tears and the stars grew halos, then they danced and twisted as they refracted through the rapidly building moisture.

'No,' she said, her voice wobbly. 'Tuck did.'

Suddenly the pain in her stomach reached excruciating levels, and then it exploded with such force it took her breath away. A sob rose in her throat and she choked on it as her lungs fought for space inside a chest welling with sensation. Another sob rose, and then another, until she was full-on crying.

So much for feeling stronger.

Reese sat up. 'Cassie?'

The others followed suit. Marnie reached over and flicked the light back on. They stared at their friend, not sure what to do or say. They'd never seen Cassie cry. It had only been to-night they'd seen her in any kind of emotional quandary at all.

'Cassie?' Gina said, hauling Cassie upright and pulling her into a big hug, stroking her hair.

'What's wrong, honey?' Reese murmured, rubbing Cassie's back.

'I don't know what's wrong with me,' Cassie howled into Gina's neck. But it was scaring the hell out of her. This loss of control was eerily similar to that torrid time in her teens, and she was frightened she was losing her mind. 'I don't cry. I *never* cry. I want it to stop.'

'It's okay,' Marnie added. 'You cry all you want. Crying's good. It's natural in this sort of situation. Trust me, I know it's not big in geek land, but sometimes, as a woman, there's nothing that beats a good old-fashioned howl.'

This was natural? Cassie couldn't believe that something so preposterous could be true. But none of her friends was looking at her as if she was going crazy, and nor did she seem to be able to stop.

'Really?' she sobbed.

Everyone nodded, and somehow she felt reassured that this was part and parcel of whatever the hell was happening to her, not a spiral into something deep and dark, so she just kept her head on Gina's shoulder and let every single tear fall free.

Twenty minutes later the tears had settled to some hiccoughy sighs, and Cassie pulled herself off Gina's shoulder. Reese handed her a wad of tissues. 'Thanks,' Cassie said. 'I seriously don't know what's come over me lately.'

'Have you ever thought,' Gina said, approaching the subject gently, 'maybe you love him?'

Reese and Marnie looked at each other, stunned that such a thought had come from Gina, who had declared herself pretty much divorced from the emotion herself.

Cassie shook her head again. 'No. I told you I don't believe in love.'

'Well, sometimes that doesn't really matter,' Reese said, jumping in. God knew, she'd been whammied by love at a most inconvenient time. 'Some of the world's most sane and sensible women have fallen under its influence.'

'No,' Cassie repeated. 'I've barely known him a month.'

'I knew with Mason after a week,' Reese said gently.

Cassie snorted—what a debacle *that* had been. 'No,' she said again.

'Okay, then,' Reese said. 'Tell me what you're feeling right now. Tell me what you were feeling just before you cried for twenty minutes. What you've been feeling since Tuck left.'

'Well, it sure as hell isn't *love*,' Cassie said indignantly. 'I feel...'

She petered out. Cassie didn't usually do this sort of thing—talk about her feelings. Her feelings were generally pretty clear-cut. She didn't even know where to start.

'Go on,' Marnie encouraged, moving closer.

'I can't concentrate, and there's this pain in my...gut. I keep having these memories of our time together that won't stop. I can...*smell* him when he's not around. I can't sleep—and I really, really need to sleep. I eat, but I can't taste the food. I'm not interested in my research. I...I can't even think straight any more.'

Gina, Reese and Marnie looked at each other. Gina winked. Reese grinned. Marnie got the giggles. Then they all laughed.

Cassie glared at them. 'What?' she demanded.

'That *is* love, silly,' Reese said.

Cassie blinked at the utterly ridiculous statement. 'No.' She shook her head.

No one had ever called her silly in her life, and she certainly wasn't going to let Reese get away with it when she'd just made possibly the most absurd statement she'd ever heard.

'I've just rattled off a list that sounds more indicative of a *brain tumour* than anything else and you tell me it's *love? That's* silly.'

She looked at Gina and Marnie, who were nodding their heads in agreement with Reese.

'You have all the symptoms,' Marnie agreed.

'Which you'd know, if you spent more time reading fiction and watching romcoms instead of reading astronomy textbooks and watching science fiction,' Gina added.

They were serious. Deadly serious. And she believed them. If there were three better experts on the subject anywhere in the world she'd be surprised, and they'd never steered her wrong before.

'*This* is love? I thought love was supposed to be *wonderful?* This doesn't feel wonderful,' she said, looking earnestly at each of her friends, wanting them to tell her they'd made a mistake. 'It feels awful. It...*sucks.*'

Reese laughed. 'That it does.'

'So I'm not going crazy?' she asked, still shaky over her loss of control.

'Nope,' Reese assured her.

Cassie's chest felt tight both in relief and dread. What the hell was she going to do now? Her mother had pretty much spent her life regretting falling in love with her father.

'How do I stop it?' she asked.

Reese shook her head. 'I'm afraid it's terminal. But it *is* manageable. And I promise you can live to a ripe old productive age.'

Marnie hummed 'The Wedding March' and Cassie stared at her. 'I have to *marry* him?' she squeaked. 'That didn't work out so well for my parents. They barely speak to each other.'

'No.' Gina sighed, glaring at Marnie. 'Just...*be* with him. In whatever way that works for you both.'

'Compromise,' Reese agreed. 'You're two smart cookies. You'll work it out. Just listen to your heart.'

'But I...' Cassie's head was spinning. First she'd been sideswiped by her libido and now a foreign emotion was taking over her sensibilities. 'I'm ruled by my head. I'm not ruled by my heart.'

'You are now, hon,' Reese said. 'You are now.'

The next morning Cassie found herself ensconced in Reese's car, heading for New York. She had no idea what she was going to say to Tuck when she got there. She just knew she'd lain awake going over and over it in her head.

The thought that it could really be love she felt for Tuck was still a foreign notion, but her friends were right. Whether she accepted the premise or not, the answer to her conundrum seemed to be Tuck. *Being with Tuck.*

And it was only *logical* to do something about it. To put that part right so her life could fall back into the order she liked and respected.

Reese chatted about her plans for the future with Mason and other inane topics, for which Cassie was thankful, and eventually the miles were gone and Reese had weaved through the New York traffic to deposit Cassie outside her cousin's apartment.

Reese pulled up and dialled Tuck's apartment number on her phone. His gruff. 'What?' confirmed he was inside.

'Good—you're home. I'll be there in a sec,' Reese said pleasantly, and hung up. She turned to face Cassie. 'You're up,' she said, then dragged her in for a big hug. 'Remember,' she said, 'three little words will get you everywhere, okay?'

Cassie nodded, even though she still couldn't quite believe this horrible affliction was *love.* But then they were out of the car and Reese had sweet-talked Cassie past Tuck's doorman, whom she seemed to know quite well, and Cassie was in the lift to the penthouse apartment before she could blink.

Tuck was standing on the other side of it, waiting for the lift doors to open. If Reese thought she could come to his place and blast him over some imagined slight to one of her closest friends—well, she could just turn around and walk away again.

Cassiopeia Barclay had made it more than clear she didn't want him in her life.

The lift dinged, the doors started to slide open and he opened his mouth to let loose his tirade. But it died on his lips as Cassie stood before him.

'Cassie?'

She looked just as he remembered. Terrible fashion sense, carelessly tied back hair, no bra, dark frowny eyebrows, small serious face.

And his heart leapt, hungry at the sight of her.

Cassie didn't move for a while and the lift doors started to slide shut again. Tuck took two strides, slamming his hand up high on either side of the shutting doors, wedging his body in between.

He looked big and blond and scruffy, and his pheromones filled the lift—as lethal to her system as cyanide gas. Her chest filled with the same pain and fullness she hadn't been able to define until Reese had given it a label.

Love.

So it was true. She did love him. Her cells recognised it— they practically buzzed with it. She was suffering a terminal condition and the worst part was the cause was the only cure.

The lift doors succumbed to Tuck's unrelenting hold and jerked open again. 'What do you want?' he asked.

She gulped at the hardness in his voice. 'I'd like to…talk to you.'

'If you're here because you're all horny again, you can forget it. I'm not your own personal plaything.'

Tuck walked away from the lift because he knew he was being a hypocrite. If she so much as looked at him with sex in her eyes he knew she could use him six ways to Sunday and he'd be more than a willing partner.

Just thinking about it gave him a raging hard-on.

Cassie's legs sparked into action as the lift doors started to close again, and she walked into a spacious apartment dominated by the light filtering through massive windows at the far end through which she could see the Manhattan skyline.

'No. I haven't come for…' She faltered. It seemed so bald to speak it aloud. 'It's about something else.'

Tuck headed for his kitchen. He grabbed a heavy glass

tumbler from a cupboard and held it beneath the spout of the fridge's ice dispenser. Three cubes made a satisfying clinking noise. The bottle of Scotch which had copped a fair amount of misuse this last week sat on his kitchen bench, almost empty, and it was satisfying to pour the last of its contents over the ice.

He threw back half of it immediately, the burn sucking his breath away. But it was preferable to the burn that had taken up permanent residence in his gut. 'You want a drink?' he asked.

Cassie shook her head. 'No. Thank you.'

They looked at each other across the room. 'Well?' Tuck said eventually as the silence stretched.

'I came to tell you...' She stopped. Those three little words seemed pretty bald, given the way they'd parted, but Reese did know her *love* stuff. 'To tell you that I love you.'

Tuck almost choked on his next, more measured sip of Scotch. They were the words he'd longed to hear a week ago, but the lack of emotion behind them was startling.

'You love me?' he said. 'Just like that?'

'Well, no,' Cassie said, taking a few more steps further into the apartment. 'I'm not good at this. I didn't know that was what it was...this thing. But Reese said—'

Tuck's short, bitter laugh interrupted her. 'Ah, Reese—all loved up and eager to see everyone else loved up as well.'

Cassie frowned. 'No. That's not how it is.'

'Well, how *is* it, then?'

'I can't think or concentrate any more. My research means nothing to me...'

Tuck shrugged. 'So this is about *your* work? Thinking about me interrupts your work? Which brings us back to that libido of yours again. All right, then,' he said, slamming his glass down on the counter, reaching for his belt, undoing it, slipping it through the loops. 'Let's go. Can't have your sex-drive getting in the way of important cosmic research.'

Cassie stepped back, horrified at his suggestion. 'No. I'm trying to tell you...' Tuck pulled his shirt over his head. 'I'm not very good at this stuff.'

His hand was on his zip. The teeth parting seemed loud in the building silence between them. Cassie covered the distance between them, placing her hand on his to halt any further attempts at stripping.

'Please,' she said. 'I'm trying to do this logically, to keep this all straight in my head, and you're not helping.'

Tuck could see desperation shimmering in her blue-grey eyes. It wasn't something he was used to seeing. Could she be telling the truth? *No matter how badly?* Dared he even hope?

'I don't care what's in your head,' he said, poking his index finger at her forehead. 'I don't give a crap about logic.' He needed to know she *felt* something. 'I only care what's in your heart.' He jabbed the same finger into the centre of her chest.

The jab wasn't hard, but Cassie felt it right down to her spine. It stirred unfamiliar feelings. Helplessness. Inadequacy. She wasn't used to feeling like that. Tears welled in her eyes.

'I don't know,' she said, shaking her head as the first tear spilled over. Her nose started to itch and her throat felt as if it was being strangled from the inside. 'I don't *know* what's in it.' A sob came from deep in her chest and more tears fell. 'I've never felt anything inside it before so I don't know how it works.'

Two heaving sobs joined the first, squeezing through her rib-cage, and she tried to breathe and talk but for once in her life she didn't seem able to do two things at once. 'All I know is it's big and deep and messy.' Her face was screwed up, and her words were forced out between sobs. She wasn't sure she was being remotely intelligible. 'And murky. And it threatens to derail everything I know about me and the world around me—'

She stopped then, because she was crying too hard to talk and breathe, but she fought for control because whatever the words that were spewing out of her mouth in an inarticulate mess she needed to say them.

'And it scares the hell out of me because it's something I don't seem to have any control over. And you know how much I need to have control. I feel like I'm going cr…cr…crazy.' She sobbed-hiccoughed. 'And I can't go there again…'

She broke down for a moment, emotion overwhelming her.

'And now I'm cr…cr…crying, and I *never* cry. I've tried to make my head rule my heart…like it always has…but my heart's just not listening any more. It wants what it w-wants, and none of the other stuff m-matters. It's only you that matters.'

Cassie collapsed against his chest, dissolving into more tears. She'd said it. She'd said what was in her heart. She had no idea if it had made any sense—hell, she'd hadn't had a clue her heart had so damn much to say—but it was out now.

Tuck pulled her close as she cried, his heart flying in his chest. 'Shh,' he soothed. 'Shh.'

But it seemed to go on unabated, and he just stood there and held her and let her cry. For a woman who didn't cry she was giving it a good whirl.

But then she had years to make up for.

When it seemed to settle he smiled down at her. Her eyes were red, her neck was all blotchy and she was sniffling. She'd never been more beautiful. He kissed her hard on the mouth.

'Now, *that* was from the heart,' he said as he pulled away.

Cassie wasn't sure if it was a compliment or not, but he was grinning down at her, and when he said, 'I love you too,' she finally relaxed.

'You're not going crazy,' he said, looking down into her tearstained face, because he understood how much that prospect terrified her. 'You're just getting in touch with your emotional side.'

'I don't like my emotional side,' she said, and sniffed.

Tuck chuckled. 'That's okay, because I love it.' He kissed her again. 'We're getting married,' he said. 'Soon.'

Cassie blinked. *That* she hadn't expected. 'Why?'

'Because that's the next *logical* move when you're in love,' he said, dropping a kiss on her nose.

'Isn't that a little rushed, though?'

'Sure—for some. But I reckon we both know what we want, and after years of not knowing, I don't want to waste any more time.'

'But there's so much we need to talk about,' she said. 'What about Antarctica? What about that family you want?'

'Cassiopeia, I'm not going to stop you from going to Antarctica or pursuing any part of your career.'

Cassie's heart leapt at his words. 'But…you seemed hesitant about it last time…at the apartment…the night you left.'

'Of course.' He smiled, his hands cradling her cheeks. 'Six months is a long time. I'm going to miss you like crazy. But I'll survive.' He kissed her long and slow to punctuate his commitment.

When he was finished he dropped his hands.

'As for a family—I don't mean we have to have one straight away. We're young. We've got time. And it doesn't have to be a traditional family. We can adopt. We can foster a kid from the system. We can get a surrogate. And you don't have to give up work. You have me, and I'm going to make a freaking great dad. My job is portable and we have the means.'

Cassie's head spun. 'You have this all worked out, don't you?'

Tuck nodded. 'I do. All you have to say is *I do* too and we'll work it out. When it makes sense to be together, why delay?'

Cassie couldn't fault his logic. And logic she understood. 'I do,' she said.

Tuck grinned and swept her in his arms, crushing a kiss against her mouth that had her clinging and moaning for more as her senses filled with his wild Tuck pheromones.

'Damn straight you do,' Tuck muttered against her mouth, before swinging her up into his arms and introducing her to his bedroom.

* * * * *

REUNITED WITH THE REBEL BILLIONAIRE

CATHERINE MANN

To Dannielle – a strong, proactive survivor with one of the most generous hearts I've ever encountered. You inspire me.

One

Fiona Harper-Reynaud was married to *American Sports* magazine's "Hottest Athlete of the Year" for two years running.

She hadn't married the New Orleans Hurricanes' star quarterback for his looks. In fact, she'd always been drawn to the academic sort more than the jock type. But when that jock happened to be visiting an art gallery fund-raiser she'd been hosting for her father, she'd been intrigued. When Henri Reynaud had shown an appreciation and understanding of the nuances of botanic versus scenic art, she'd fallen hook, line and sinker into those dreamy, intelligent dark eyes of his. His eyes were the color of coffee and carried just as strong a jolt.

Still, she'd held back because of her own history with relationships, and yes, two broken engagements.

Held back for all of a couple of weeks. And ever since then her life hadn't stopped spiraling out of control.

Sure, they'd eloped because they'd thought she was pregnant. But she'd loved him so intensely, so passionately, reason scattered like petals from a windswept azalea. They hadn't realized until it was too late they had no substantive foundation in their marriage when difficult times came their way. And what little base they'd built upon had crumbled quickly.

Especially right now.

In two short hours, Fiona would be greeting the elite community of New Orleans for her latest fund-raiser, purely in a volunteer capacity. Any time a foundation offered to pay, she donated the funds back to the charity. She believed deeply in the causes she supported and was grateful to have the wealth and time to help.

But the pressure of the high-glitz affair wasn't what rattled her. The doctor visit today had her scared, and more determined than ever she couldn't continue a marriage built on anything but love. Certainly not built only on obligation.

She switched her phone to speaker and placed it on the antique dresser, one of many beautiful pieces in the home she shared with Henri in New Orleans's gracious and historic Garden District. Her eyes lingered on the crystal-framed photograph of her with Henri from a trip they'd taken to Paris a few years back. Their smiles caught her off guard.

Had her life ever been that happy? The version of herself in the photograph felt like a stranger now.

She'd been so focused on the photograph, she almost forgot she was on the phone with Adelaide, her future sister-in-law and longtime personal assistant to Henri's half brother Dempsey. At long last the two were engaged. Their love had taken longer to bloom, unlike Henri's impulsive proposal to Fiona.

Blinking, Fiona shifted her attention back to the conversation. To her family. She internally laughed at that thought. Family implied closeness and solidarity. Instead of that, she felt numbingly alone and isolated.

And there was no reason for that. The Reynaud family was large and the majority of them resided right here in New Orleans. Two of her husband's brothers lived in a private compound of homes on Lake Pontchartrain. And they'd be at that compound tonight for the fund-raiser.

Star athletes, celebrities and politicians would gather and mingle for Fiona's newest cause. Conversation would fill the air. And if her past events were any indication, she would raise the funds necessary to open up the new animal shelter.

She perched on the delicate Victorian settee at the end of her four-poster bed. She pulled on one thigh-high stocking as she listened to her future sister-in-law rattle off the wines, liquors and other beverages delivered.

Still caught in the past, when she'd fallen hard for Henri Reynaud, she rolled the silk socking up her other leg. Henri had chased her relentlessly until she'd begun to believe him when he said he adored her mind every bit as much as her body.

Her body.

Hands shaking, she tugged the band on her thigh into place. She couldn't afford to think about those days before their marriage turned rocky, only to have him stay with her because of her health. She respected his honor, even as it hurt her to the core to lose his love. But she couldn't accept anything less than honest emotion.

Which meant she had to keep her secret. She tugged a wrinkle from her stocking and continued her phone conversation with Adelaide. "I can't thank you enough for helping me out with tonight's fund-raiser."

"Glad to lend my help. I wish you would ask more often."

"I didn't want to impose or make you feel pressured before when Dempsey was your boss." She'd known Adelaide for years, but only recently had they all learned of her romance with Dempsey Reynaud.

"But now that we're going to be sisters-in-law, I'm fair game?"

"Oh, um, I'm sorry." Her mind was so jumbled today. "I didn't mean that the way it came out."

"No need to apologize," Adelaide said, laughing softly. "Truly. I was just teasing. I'm really glad to lend a hand. It's a great cause. You do so much for charity—it's an inspiration."

"Well, I would have been an inspiring failure if not for your help today setting up the party at the compound." The main family compound on Lake Pontchartrain was larger and more ornate than Fiona and Henri's personal getaway. They'd purchased the place for privacy, a space she could decorate in her own antique, airy style in contrast to the palatial Greek Revival and Italianate mansions that made up the bulk of the family compound. She was grateful for the privacy right now as she readied herself for the party and steadied her nerves.

"Emergencies crop up for everyone. Did you sort

things out with your car?" Traces of concern laced Adelaide's voice.

Fiona winced. She didn't like lying to people, but if she admitted to seeing the doctor today that would trigger questions she was still too shaken to answer. After years of fertility treatments, she was used to keeping her medical history and heartbreak secret. "All is well, Adelaide. Thank you."

Or at least she hoped all was well. The doctor told her she shouldn't worry.

Easier said than done after all she had been through. Worrying had become her natural state, her automatic reflex lately.

"Glad to hear it. I emailed you the changes made to the menu so you can cross-check with the receipts."

"Changes?" Anxiety coiled in Fiona's chest. Normally she rolled with last-minute changes. They presented her with an opportunity to become more creative in the execution of the event. Every event she'd ever run had called for an adjustment or two. But her mind was elsewhere and her deeply introspective state made dealing with these external changes difficult.

"There were some last-minute problems with getting fresh mushrooms, so I made substitutions. Do you want me to go over them now?" Keys clicked in the background.

"Of course not. I trust your taste and experience." And she did.

"If you need my help with anything else, let me know." Adelaide hesitated until the sound of someone else speaking then leaving the room faded. "I'm comfortable in my work world, but my future role and responsibilities as a Reynaud spouse will be new territory to me."

And Fiona's time as a Reynaud wife was drawing to an end, even if the family didn't know it yet. Her heart sank. "You are a professional at this. You could take any event to a whole new level. Just make sure to find what you want your niche to be. The men in this family can steamroll right over a person." The words tumbled out of her mouth, and her cool, collected front began to crumble.

"Fiona…" Concern tinged her voice. "Are you okay?"

"Don't mind me. I'm fine. I'll see you soon. I need to get changed." She couldn't attend the event in stockings, a thong and a bra. No matter how fine the imported Italian lace. "Thanks again." She disconnected and slid her sapphire-blue gown from the end of the bed.

She stepped into the floor-length dress, the silk chiffon a cool glide over her skin, the dress and underwear strategically designed. The fabric fit snugly in a swathe around her breasts and hips, with a looser pleated skirt grazing her ankles. A sequin-studded belt complemented her glinting diamond chandelier earrings.

No one would see her scars. No one other than her husband and doctors knew.

Double mastectomy.

Reconstruction.

Prophylactic—preventative. In hopes of evading the disease that had claimed her mother, her aunt and her grandmother.

Fiona had never had breast cancer. But with her genetics, she couldn't afford to take the risk. She pressed the dress to her chest and tried not to think of the doctor's words today about a suspicious reading on her breast MRI that could be nothing. The doctor said the lump was almost certainly benign fat necrosis. But just to be safe he wanted to biopsy...

The creaking of the opening door startled her. Her dress slid down and she grabbed it by the embellished straps, pressing it back to her chest even though she knew only one person would walk in unannounced.

Her husband.

America's hottest athlete for two years running.

And the man she hadn't slept with since her surgery six months ago.

Henri's hands fell to rest on her shoulders, his breath caressing her neck. "Need help with the zipper?"

Henri took risks in his job on a regular basis. Sure, his teammates worked their asses off to prevent a hard tackle from his blind side, but he understood and accepted that every time he stepped onto the field, he could suffer a career-ending injury.

Fans called him brave. Sports analysts sometimes labeled him reckless. The press branded him fearless.

They were all wrong.

He'd been scared as hell every day since the doctors declared Fiona had inherited her family's cancer gene. It didn't matter that their marriage had been on the rocks. He'd been rocked to his foundation. Still was.

Henri clenched her shoulders so his hands wouldn't shake. Even the smallest touch between them was filled with tension. And not in the way that made him weak in the knees. "Your zipper?"

With a will of their own, his eyes took in the long exposed line of her neck, her deep brown hair corralled by a thin braid so that lengthy, loose curls cascaded in a narrow path down her back. He looked farther down her spine to the small of her back that called to him to touch, to kiss in a lingering, familiar way. But he'd lost the right. She'd made that clear when he'd tried to reconcile after the doctor's prognosis.

"Thank you. Yes, please," she said, glancing over her shoulder nervously and pulling her hair aside, the strands so dark they almost appeared black at night. He hated seeing that sort of distance in her amber-colored eyes. "I'm running late because of, um, a last-minute snafu with the caterer."

"Adelaide said you were having trouble with your car, so I came home early. But I see it's in the garage. What was wrong?"

Whipping her head away from his gaze, she muttered, "Doesn't matter."

It was becoming her trademark response. It didn't matter.

That was a lie. He could tell by the way her mouth thinned as she spoke.

He let out a deep sigh as his gaze traced over their room. Or should he say—their *former* room. He'd taken to sleeping in the guest bedroom of the restored home. Away from her. They'd even lost the ability to lie next to each other at night. To show up for each other in that simple way.

In front of him was the first gift he'd ever bought Fiona. It was a handsome jewelry armoire that doubled as a full-length mirror. It was a one-of-a-kind antique piece. Whimsical and light. Just like Fiona in her jewel-colored dress. Looking at the gilded mirror framing the reflection of his exquisite wife reminded him of how far they'd fallen. Damn.

This whole room was a mausoleum to what had been.

He wanted her to lean on him. Even if it was just a little bit. This wasn't what he wanted. "Anything else I can do to help?"

"I've got it under control." Finality colored her words.

"You always do." It came out harsher than he intended. But dammit, he was trying. Couldn't she see that?

She spun around to face him, her petite frame filling with rigid rage as the silk of her gown whirled against his shins. Raising her chin and her brow, she pressed her lips tight, primly. "No need to be snarky."

Sticking his hands in his pants pockets, he shrugged, his Brioni tuxedo jacket sliding along his shoulders. "I am completely serious."

Fiona's sherry eyes softened, the amber depths intoxicating. She took a deep breath and stared at him. A breeze stirred the stale air of the room, filtering through the window with the sounds of foot traffic and car horns. It was a grounding sound, reminding him of when they'd first bought this house—when they'd been a team. They'd spent months working together on every detail of restoring the historic Victorian home, a celebrated building that had once been a schoolhouse, then a convent.

And they'd done it together. They'd transformed this deteriorating five-thousand-square-foot house into a home.

"Sorry, I didn't mean to start a fight. Adelaide was

a huge help during a really long day. Let's just get through the evening. It's harder and harder to pretend there's nothing wrong between us."

Something was off with her today, but he couldn't tell what. It was clear enough, though, that she was trying to pick a fight with him.

"I don't want to fight with you, either." He didn't know what the hell he wanted anymore other than to have things the way they were.

"You used to love a good argument with me. Only me. You get along with everyone else. I never understood that."

"We had fire, you and I." It had been a sizzling love. One that warmed him to his damn core. And he knew there was still a spark in the embers. He couldn't believe it was all gone.

"Had, Henri. That's my point. It's over, and you need to quit making excuses to delay the final step." Ferocity returned to her fairylike features. A warrior in blue silk and sequins.

"Not excuses. You needed to recover. Then we agreed we wouldn't do anything that would disrupt the start of the season. Then with my brother's wedding on the horizon—"

"Excuses. Divorce isn't the end of the world." She pinned up a curl that had escaped the confines of the delicate braid binding the others into place.

Everything about her these days was carefully put together so that no one saw a hint of the turmoil beneath. For months he'd respected that. Understood she was the one calling the shots with her health issues. But how could she deny herself any help? Ever? She'd made it clear he didn't know how to be the least bit of assistance.

And now, divorce was the recurring refrain.

"Our family is in the spotlight. A split between us would eat up positive oxygen in the press." He needed her to take a deep breath. They needed to figure out everything. He needed to stall.

She turned back around, using the mirror to smooth her dress. "No one is going to think poorly of you for leaving me. I will make it clear I'm the one who asked for the divorce."

Anger boiled, heating his cheeks. "I don't give a damn what people think about me."

"But you do care about your team. I understand." He picked up on the implication of her words. That he didn't care about *her*. And that couldn't be farther off base. She was still trying to pick a fight. To widen the gap between them.

"We're going to be late." The tone of his voice was soft. Almost like a whisper. He wanted to calm her down, to stop this from turning into an unnecessary fight. Something was upsetting her. Something major.

As much as he wanted to understand her, he couldn't. The party was about to start and he didn't have the time to unwrap the subtle meaning of all her words.

All he wanted was to have their old life back instead of silently cohabitating and putting on a front for the world. He longed for her to look at him the way she used to, with that smile that said as much as she enjoyed the party, she savored their time alone together even more. He ached for their relationship to be as uncomplicated as it once was when they traveled the country for the season, traveled the world in the off-season. They both enjoyed history and art. Sightseeing on hikes, whether to see Stonehenge or the Great Wall of China.

Tapping the back of her dress, he met her gaze in the mirror, holding her tawny eyes and reveling in the way her pupils widened with unmistakable desire. Settling his hands back on her shoulders, he breathed against her ear and neck. "Unless you would like me to take the zipper back down again."

Her lashes fluttered shut for a second and a softness entered her normally clenched jaw. In that brief moment, he thought this might be how they closed the gap.

Instead, her eyelids flew open and she shimmied out from underneath his hands. "No, thank you. I have a fund-raiser to oversee. And then make no mistake, we need to set a firm date to see our attorney and end the marriage."

Two

Fiona picked at sequins on her dress as Henri steered their Maserati through the gates and toward the huge Greek Revival mansion on the hill. She'd lived just down the road from that house once, she and Henri in their wing and his youngest brother, Jean-Pierre, in another. Both wings were large enough for privacy. Both easily big enough to fit four of the homes she'd grown up in, and her family had been wealthy enough to impress, with her father owning a midsize accounting firm.

But once her honeymoon phase had worn off with Henri and she'd realized she wasn't pregnant, they'd begun trying for a baby in earnest. That mammoth mansion had grown more claustrophobic with each failed attempt. Then with each fertility treatment. There'd been miscarriages they hadn't even told the family about. So many more health heartaches they hadn't shared with his family.

After her very public miscarriage in her second trimester, he'd bought them the house in the Garden District to give them both space from the Reynaud fishbowl lifestyle. Their emotions had been bubbling over far too often, in good and bad ways.

Living here? It was just too difficult. Spanish moss trailed like bridal veils from live oak trees on either side of the private driveway leading into the Reynaud estate on Lake Pontchartrain. It was in an exclusive section of Metairie, Louisiana, west of the city. Pontoon boats were moored in shallow waters while long docks stretched into the low-lying mist that often settled on the surface, sea grass spiking through and hiding local creatures. The gardens were lush and verdant, the ground fertile. Gardeners had to work overtime to hold back the Louisiana undergrowth that could take over in no time. The place was large, looming—alive.

She glanced at her too-damn-handsome husband as he steered their sports car up the winding drive toward the original home on the family complex, the place where Henri and his brothers had spent time in their youth. Gervais, the oldest brother, and his fiancée lived here now, and the couple had allowed Fiona to host her event on the property.

Henri's tailored Brioni tuxedo fit his hard, muscled body well. His square jaw was cleanly shaved, his handsome face the kind that could have graced a *GQ* cover. Her attraction to him hadn't changed, but so much had shifted between them since their impulsive elopement three years ago. While she didn't care about missing out on a large wedding, she did wonder if things might have turned out differently if they'd waited longer, gotten to know each other better before the stress piled on.

Now they would never know.

He bypassed the valet and opted to park in the family garage. The steel door slid open to reveal a black Range Rover and a Ferrari facing forward, shiny with polish, grills glistening. He backed into an open space, the massive garage stretching off to the side filled with recreational vehicles. The boats and Jet Skis were down in the boathouse at the dock. This family loved their toys. They played hard. Lived large. And loved full-out.

Losing Henri already left a hole in her life. Losing this family would leave another.

She swallowed down a lump as the garage door slid closed and he shut off the vehicle.

"Fiona?" He thumbed the top of the steering wheel. "Thank you for keeping up the happy couple act in public. I know things haven't been easy between us."

"This fund-raiser means a lot to me."

"Of course it does." His mouth went tight and she realized she'd hurt him.

How could they be so certain things were over and still have the power to hurt each other with a stray word? "I appreciate that your connections make this possible."

He glanced at her, smoothing his lapel. "You throw a great party that wins over a crowd not easily wowed."

"I owe Adelaide for her help today."

"When your car broke down."

She nodded tightly, the lie sticking in her throat.

He reached out to touch a curl and let it loosely wrap

around his finger as if with a will of its own. "You look incredible tonight. Gorgeous."

"Thank you."

"Any chance you're interested in indulging in some make-up sex, even if only temporary?"

The offer was tempting, mouthwateringly so, as she took in the sight of her husband's broad shoulders, was seduced by the gentle touch of his fingers rubbing just one curl.

"We need to get inside."

His mocha-colored eyes lingered on her mouth as tangibly as any kiss, setting her senses on fire. "Of course. Just know the offer stands."

He winked before smoothly sliding out of the car and moving around to the passenger side with the speed and grace that served him well on the ball field. Her skin still tingled from the thought of having sex with him again. They'd been so very good together in bed, with a chemistry that was off the charts.

Would that change because of her surgery? It was a risk she'd never been able to bring herself to take.

Just the thought had her gut knotting with nerves. But the next thing she knew, her silver Jimmy Choo heels were clicking along to the side entrance and across the foyer's marble floors. The space was filled with people from corner to corner, chatter and music from the grand piano echoing up to the high ceiling. The party was in full swing. The place was packed, people standing so close together they were pushed up against walls with hand-painted murals depicting a fox hunt.

Once upon a time she'd lived for these parties. But right now, she wanted to grab the banister and run up the huge staircase with a landing so large it fit a small sofa for casual chitchat in the corner.

Her hand tucked in Henri's arm, she went on autopilot party mode, nodding and answering people's greetings. She and Henri had played this game often, fooling others. She had to admit that while women chased him unabashedly, his gaze never strayed. He was a man of honor. His father's infidelities had left a mark on him. Henri had made it clear he would never cheat—even when the love had left their marriage.

No, she couldn't let her thoughts go there. To the end of love and of them. At least, not while they were in public. Too many people were counting on her. While planning this fund-raiser had served as a distraction from the widening gap between her and Henri, the whole event still had to be properly executed.

Time to investigate her handiwork. Excusing herself, Fiona walked over to the favor table. Turquoise boxes with silver calligraphic font reading "Love at First Woof" lined the table. Laughing inwardly, she picked up one of the boxes. This one was wrapped in a white ribbon. She opened the box, pleased to find the pewter dog earrings staring back at her. Satisfied, she retied the bow, set the box on the table, and picked up a box wrapped with black ribbon. To her relief, the pewter paw tie tacks were in there, as well. Good. The favors were even cuter than she had remembered.

Fiona's gaze flicked to the service dogs from a rescue organization. They sat at attention, eyes watchful and warm. Glancing over her shoulder, she saw the plates of food in the dining room. People were gathered around the food, scooping crab cakes and chicken skewers onto their plates.

Convinced that everything was more than in order, she surveyed further, walking into a more casual family space with an entertainment bar and Palladian windows overlooking the pool and grounds.

No detail had been missed thanks to the highly efficient catering staff she'd hired and Adelaide had overseen. Smiling faintly, Fiona peered outside at the twinkling doghouse situated just beyond the luxurious in-ground pool. The doghouse was a scale replica of the Reynaud mansion, and it was going to the shelter after tonight. But for now, it lit the grounds and housed hand-painted water bowls for the shelter dogs. Four of the shelter dogs walked around the pool, enjoying all the attention and affection from the guests.

People were spread out. Laughter floated on the breeze, and so did snippets of conversation. A small Jack Russell terrier was lazily stretched on Mrs. Daniza's lap. A fuzzy white dog was curled up, fast asleep, beneath Jack Rani's chair. The dogs were winning over friends with deep pockets.

Everything appeared to be in order. But then again, Fiona knew firsthand the difference between appearances and actual reality.

Sadness washed over her. Grabbing a glass of water from a nearby beverage station, she continued on as Henri went to speak to his brothers. Movement was good. Movement was necessary. The busier she stayed, the less her emotions would sting through her veins.

And it was as if the world knew she needed a distraction. As she slipped out onto the pool deck, she saw two of her favorite Hurricanes' players—wide receiver "Wild Card" Wade and "Freight Train" Freddy. Not only did they inspire her with how much of their time they donated to worthwhile causes, the two men always made her laugh.

It seemed that tonight would be no exception. Freight Train was in a black suit, but his tie had dog butts all over it and his belt buckle was a silver paw print. He and Wild Card were posing for pictures with two of the shelter dogs. Their energy was contagious.

Directly across from Freight Train and Wild Card were the Texas branch of the Reynaud clan. When fund-raisers or troubles arose, despite the complicated and sometimes strained relationships, they jumped in. The two Texas boys were sipping wine and talking to a Louisiana senator. The cousins were supporting their relative who played for the Hurricanes. Brant Reynaud wore his ever-present small yellow rosebud on his lapel.

Everyone was out in full force to support her latest cause. She would miss this sense of family.

Landscape lighting highlighted ornamental plantings and statues. She checked the outdoor kitchen to one side of the pool to make sure all was in order. The hearth area was unmistakably popular, a fire already ablaze in the stone surround. Built-in stone seating was covered with thick cushions and protected by a pergola with a casual wrought-iron framework. The Reynaud brothers were there. Well, at least two of them. Fiona watched as Gervais waved Henri over.

One of the things that amused Fiona was the sheer amount of posturing the boys did when they were around each other. They loved each other—there was no doubt about that. But the brothers were all driven and natural-born competitors.

They were all tall, with athletic builds, dark eyes

and even darker hair, thick and lush. While Gervais, Henri and Jean-Pierre were full brothers, Dempsey was the result of one of their father's affairs. The brothers had each gotten their mother's hair coloring, while their father had donated his size and strength.

The semicircle of the Reynaud clan was an elegant one. Gervais, the most refined of the brothers, was at ease in his role as oldest, leader of the pack. Erika, his fiancée, laid a gentle hand on Gervais's forearm as she leaned into the conversation. The light from the hearth caught on her silver rings and cushion-cut diamond engagement ring. One would likely never guess Erika had served in her home country's military, although her princess bearing was entirely clear.

To Gervais's immediate left stood Dempsey, ever-present football pin on the lapel of his tuxedo, with lovely, efficient Adelaide at his side.

Fiona told herself that she was lucky not to have to work. That she made a positive impact in the world with her volunteer philanthropic efforts. Not holding down a regular job outside the home also enabled her to travel with her husband. She helped organize outings for the other family members who traveled with the Hurricanes, as well. Keeping the players and their families happy kept the team focused and out of trouble.

She looked around at the packed event, a total success. Anyone would think she had a full life.

Except she couldn't bring herself to have sex with her husband. She'd been so certain the surgery was the right decision. She'd gone to counseling before and after. Her husband had been completely supportive.

And still the distance between them had grown wider and wider these past months, emphasizing how little they knew about each other. They'd married because of infatuation, great sex, a shared love of art and a pregnancy scare that sped up the wedding date.

Now that the initial glow of infatuation had passed and they didn't even have sex to carry them through the rough patches, a common love for gallery showings wasn't enough to hold them together. Their marriage was floundering. Badly. She needed to keep in mind how dangerous it would be to let her guard down around a man who had worked hard to take care of her through her decision.

And with a cancer scare looming over her today, she couldn't bear the thought that he would stay with her out of sympathy.

Henri wasn't in much of a party mood, no matter how much his brothers elbowed him and teased him about his latest fumble. His Texas cousins weren't cutting him any slack, either.

He'd been thinking about the divorce his wife insisted on pursuing.

While the love had left their marriage, he'd heard plenty say that marriage had ups and downs. He wasn't a quitter. And damn it all, he still burned to have her.

His gaze skimmed the guests around the pool, landing on his wife. Her trailing curls and slim curves called to him, reminding him of the enticing feel of her back as he'd tugged her zipper up.

She smiled at whomever she spoke to—a man with his back to the rest of the crowd—and nodded as she walked away. The man turned and Henri's breath froze in his chest. He knew the man well. Dr. Carlson was a partner in the practice Fiona used to see before they'd transferred her to another physician for the surgery.

Fear jelling in his gut, Henri charged away from his brothers and cousins, shouldering through the crowd to his wife.

"Henri—"

He grasped her arm and guided her toward the shore of Lake Pontchartrain. "In a moment. When no one can overhear us."

Lights from yachts and boats dotted the distance. Along the shoreline, couples walked hand in hand. Henri opened the boathouse door and stepped inside. Moonlight streaked through the windows, across Fiona's face. Confusion and frustration stamped her lovely features.

He angled them beneath a pontoon boat on a lift. The boat was still wet from use, and water tapped the ground in a rhythm that almost matched his pounding heart. Inhaling deeply, he caught the musty scent of the boathouse mixed with the cinnamon notes of Fiona's perfume. He'd bought it for her on a trip to France before all of these difficulties had really gotten out of control.

"Enough already, Henri. Would you please tell me why we're out here?"

He clasped both of her shoulders. "Are you okay?"

"What do you mean?"

"I saw you talking to Dr. Carlson." He looked in her sherry-colored eyes, trying to read her. Something flickered there, something he could have sworn was fear, but then she looked away, her lashes shielding her expression.

Staring at the floor, she chewed her bottom lip for

an instant before answering, "We were discussing a fund-raiser and party for the pediatric oncology ward. The planner had a heart attack and they need someone to step in and help."

Okay, but why was she looking away? "You're sure that's all?"

She hesitated a second too long. "What do you mean?"

Fear exploded inside him. "Are you feeling all right?" He clasped her shoulders. "Physically. Is there something wrong? If so, you know I'm here for you. Whatever you need, just tell me."

She squeezed her eyes closed, shaking her head, tears sliding free.

He reached to sketch his knuckles along her cheeks and capture the tears, hands shaking. "Oh, God, Fiona, is it…" His throat moved in a long swallow. "Do you have…"

She touched his mouth. "You don't have to worry about me. I'm fine. Thank you, but you have no reason to feel obligated."

"Obligated?" He kissed her fingertips. "You are my wife, my responsibility—"

"Please, Henri." She took his hands from her face and clasped them briefly before letting go. "You are a good man. I've never doubted that. This is an emotional time for both of us, and let's not make it worse with confrontations. Let's just return to the party."

He wouldn't be dismissed so easily. "What were you laughing so hysterically about?" Anger edged through the fear. "And would you like to clue me in on the joke? Because right now I could use something to lighten the mood."

"No joke," she said with a sigh, meeting his gaze. "Just so ironic."

"Then what are you hiding?"

"Henri." She chewed her bottom lip again, her gaze skipping around evasively before she continued. "Um, he asked me out for a drink to discuss the fund-raiser."

Henri saw red. Pure red. "He asked you out for a drink? As in a date? Not because of the fund-raiser?"

"Because of the fund-raiser, but yes, he clearly meant a date, as well." She pulled at her curls, color mounting in her cheeks.

Henri had to stay calm. Had to make it through this conversation. "And what did you say?"

"I told him I'm still married, of course." Gaze narrowing, she launched the words at him like daggers.

"Clearly that wasn't a problem for him, since you are wearing my ring."

She shrugged her shoulders, chandelier earrings swaying. "That didn't bother him in the least."

Henri turned toward the door, ready to return to the party and deck the guy straight into the pool.

Fiona placed a hand on his shoulder. "Stop, Henri. He mentioned hearing we're splitting up. He thought I was available."

"How would he have heard such a thing?" His mind went back to the original concern. "Were you at the doctor's office where he's a partner?"

She swallowed hard. "You seem to have forgotten his brother is our lawyer."

"Not anymore."

"I was thinking the same thing, actually." She picked at her French manicure. "We should get separate attorneys."

Dammit. This conversation was not going the way he intended. He just wanted to pull her into his arms and take her here. Now. To say to hell with the past and future. No more jealousy or discussion about…hell.

He just wanted her. "This is not the time or the place to talk about lawyers. Enjoy your party and your success." He cupped her face in his hands, his thumbs stroking along her cheeks as he stepped closer, the heat of her lithe body reaching to him. "You've raised enough seed money for the shelter tonight. They can start their capital campaign for a whole new building. Let's celebrate."

She swayed toward him for an instant, as if she too was caught in that same web of desire. Her gaze fell away from his for a moment, roving his broad-shouldered body, then returned to meet his hungry gaze. There was something there still. He could feel it in the way her lips, slightly parted, seemed to call him to her.

Stepping back abruptly, she grasped the door latch. "Enjoy?" She shook her head, a curl sliding forward over her shoulder. "I don't think that's possible. There's too much left unsettled for me to think about anything but getting my life in order."

In a swirl of French perfume, she walked out the door and raced along the dock back to the party. The forcefulness of her reaction left him wondering what he was missing, but the speed of her departure closed the door on finding out.

She couldn't go back to the party. Not with her emotions in such a turmoil. She hadn't expected the brief conversation with Tom Carlson to lead to a showdown with her husband. But Tom had seen her come through the office earlier…and he had asked her for a drink. She'd shut him down hard. Even if she weren't married, she was not in a place emotionally to be in a relationship right now.

Life was getting too complicated. She longed for simpler times again.

Peace.

Family.

So she sought out the last remnants. She loaded a plate of party food onto a tray with two glasses of mint iced tea and went upstairs to Grandpa Leon's suite. His Alzheimer's had progressed to the point that he required a round-the-clock nurse to keep watch over him so he didn't wander off. His nighttime nurse's aide sat in the study area off his bedroom, reading on her phone. A brunette in her midthirties, she had a warm expression on her face at all times. The perfect temperament for at-home care.

She looked up quickly and set her phone beside her. "Good evening, Mrs. Reynaud. Mr. Leon is on the balcony enjoying the stars over the lake."

They'd glassed in the balcony so the temperature could be regulated year-round, and he could safely sit outside without fear of him falling—or climbing down as he'd tried to do one evening.

"Thank you," Fiona said. "Please do feel free to join the party while I visit with Gramps."

"That sounds lovely. Thank you. I'll step downstairs for a snack. I'll be back in a half hour, if that's all right?"

"Absolutely. Take your time." Fiona loved her grandfather-in-law and treasured this time with him.

His disease was stealing him away and she would soon be gone. Her heart squeezed tighter as she stepped through the open French doors leading to the enclosed balcony.

"Grandpa Leon," she said softly, adjusting the tray and settling it on the wrought-iron table between two chairs. "I've brought you a bite to eat."

The older man turned, his shock of gray hair whiter every day as if each lost memory stole more of his youth along with the color in the once dark strands. "They don't like me going to parties anymore. I believe they're afraid of what I might say."

"Everyone loves having you there. I'm sorry you feel that way, though." The family was just trying to protect him from embarrassment.

"It's not your fault my memory's failing. The boys are just trying to protect me and my pride." Spearing a bit of shrimp scampi on his fork, he looked up at her gratefully. "This is good, especially for party food. Filling. Not a bunch of those frilly little canapés."

"We have plenty of those, too. I just know your preference."

"And I appreciate that. My tastes are the only thing not failing in my mind. But I imagine you knew that. You were always a perceptive girl. I am going to miss you."

Her head jerked up. What did he know? He couldn't possibly have guessed about the divorce. "Grandpa Leon, I'm not sure what you mean."

He tapped his temple. "When my illness takes over. Even in my fog, I feel the sense of loss. I feel it here." He tapped his chest. "The people who should be a part of my life. But I can't recall who belongs to me and who doesn't."

Fiona didn't even know what to say, so she covered his hand with hers and squeezed. "I do love you and I won't forget you."

"And I love you, too, sister dear."

She blinked away a tear. She shouldn't be surprised any longer at these moments he mistook her for someone else. Still… She shoved to her feet and started for the door.

Turning to look back at the man who soon wouldn't be her grandfather anymore, Fiona said, "Do you want seconds on anything?"

He stared back at her, a confused look in his java-brown eyes. "Seconds?" He stared down at his empty plate. "What did the chef make for dinner? I can't seem to recall."

She struggled for what to say and then realized specifics didn't matter so much as peace. "Tonight's menu included your very favorite."

He smiled, passing his plate to her. "Of course, my favorite. I would like more. And dessert—pie with ice cream."

"Of course."

Would he even remember he'd asked for it when she returned? She would bring it all the same and savor her last moments as part of this wonderful family.

Would she still be welcome here to visit him after the split became known to the rest of the family? Would she even be able to come here without losing her mind? The pain would be…intense. Especially at first. And later? She could barely think into the future. She'd been so afraid to dream years ahead for fear there were no years for her.

Today had reminded her all too well of those fears.

Three

Always hungry—which was the fate of an athlete—Henri pulled open the door to the Sub-Zero fridge, rummaging around shelves big enough to park a car—his personal choice in the kitchen remodel. It was three in the morning and no way would he make it until dawn. Though the food at the party had been decadent, he needed to put proper fuel into his system. In season, he put his body through the wringer and there was a helluva lot at stake.

He pulled out a carton of eggs and placed them on the granite counter. Running a hand through his hair, his mind drifted back to the fund-raiser.

From an outside perspective, the event was a complete success. Seven figures had been raised, more than enough seed money to launch a capital campaign to build a new shelter. His wife's fund-raising goal had been surpassed. And he was damn proud of her. Even if things were difficult right now, he admired her spirit. He'd practically had to drag her out of the fundraiser as the cleanup crews arrived. Fiona had wanted to make sure that everything was perfect, that things were easy on the housekeeping staff.

Of course, by the time they'd returned to their house, she'd bolted from his company and retreated to her room. Par for the course these days.

Opening a cabinet drawer, he pulled out a frying pan and sprayed it with olive oil. He switched on the gas of the massive gourmet cooktop and adjusted the flame. Once the pan began to hiss to life, he cracked two eggs, reveling in the sound and the promise of protein.

Cooking was one of the things that he actually liked to do for himself. And for Fiona. He'd made them delicious, flavorful and healthy meals. That was one of the reasons they'd spent so much time restoring this kitchen. It had been a space where they had bonded.

They had jointly picked the decorations in the room, visiting high-end antiques stores in the French Quarter and finding beautiful pieces. Like the big turn-of-the-century clock that occupied a prominent spot on the south wall. The clock was an intricate work of angles and loops. The antique vibe of the wrought iron had reminded them both of Ireland, which was one of the first places they'd traveled to together.

The room contained an eclectic mix of items—nothing matched, but the pieces complemented each other, pulling the room together.

With a sigh, he slid the eggs out of the pan and onto a plate. After he'd fumbled in the drawer for a fork, he grabbed the plate and made his way to the large window in the dining room. He sat at the head of the long cherrywood table, bought for entertaining the whole family. A gilded mirror hung over the sideboard laden with Fiona's well-polished silver. Even though they'd built this haven together, if they split, he would be booted out on his ass and moving back to the family compound with his brothers. He loved his family, but this place was home now, deep in the heart of New Orleans.

The thought of leaving made it too damn hard to sit at this table—their table. Pushing his plate of half-eaten eggs away, he shot to his feet and wandered to the window.

Sometimes the contrasts of this city just struck him, the historic buildings jutting up against contemporary trends. It was a place between worlds and cultures. The New Orleans moon hung in the late night sky, just peeking through sullen clouds that covered the stars. He'd always enjoyed the moodiness of this place, his new home after growing up in Texas. This fit his personality, his temperament. He'd thought he had his life together when he met Fiona. Perfect wife. Dream career. Jazz music that could wake the dead and reach a cold man's soul.

His brothers would laugh at him for saying stuff like that, call him a sensitive wuss, but Fiona had understood the side of him that enjoyed art and music. It cut him deep that she said they didn't know each other, that they had no foundation and nothing in common.

She minimized what they'd built together, and that sliced him to the core. It hadn't helped one bit that men were hitting on her at the party, already sensing a divorce in the wind even if they hadn't announced it to a soul.

He was used to men approaching his wife. She was drop-dead gorgeous in a chic and timeless way that would draw attention for the rest of her life. But tonight had been different. He spent so much time on the road and she usually traveled with him. But even when they weren't together, they'd always trusted each other. The thought of her moving on, of her with another man, shredded him inside. He didn't consider himself the jealous type, but he damn well wasn't ready to call it quits and watch her move on with someone—anyone—else.

Without his realizing it, his feet carried him past the window, past the living room. And suddenly, he was upstairs outside Fiona's room.

Her door was wide open. That was the first thing that jarred him. He'd become so accustomed to seeing that closed door when he passed by her room at night. Fiona had literally shut him out.

So why was it open tonight?

Not that he was going to miss the opportunity to approach her.

The soft, warm light from her bedroom bathed the hall in a yellow glow. Curiosity tugged at him, and he peered into the room.

She was curled up in a tight ball on the settee at the foot of the bed, her sequined waistband expanding and contracting with her slow, determined breaths. He was surprised to see her still in her party clothes. Even with disheveled, wavy hair she was damn breathtaking. Her shoes were casually and chaotically tossed to the side.

For a moment, he thought she was asleep, and then he realized...

Fiona was crying.

A rush of protectiveness pulsed through his body. Fiona had been so calculating and logical these days that this spilling of emotion overwhelmed him. Damn, he didn't want to see her like this. He *never* wanted to see her like this. It made him feel helpless, and that was a feeling he'd never handled well.

Once when Henri was younger, he'd walked into his mother's room to find her crying. Tears had streaked her face, mascara marring her normally perfect complexion. She had been crying over the death of her career as a model. And his father's infidelity. She'd been so shattered, and all Henri could do was watch from the sidelines.

She hadn't been the most attentive or involved parent, but she'd been his mother and he'd wanted to make the world right for her.

He'd felt every bit as useless then as he felt now.

"Fiona?" He stepped tentatively into the room.

Startled, she sat up, dragging her wrist across her tears and smudging mascara into her hairline. "Henri, I don't need help with my zipper."

"I was on my way to my room and I heard you." He stepped deeper into the room, tuxedo jacket hooked on one finger and slung over his shoulder. "Are you okay?"

"No, I'm not," she said in a shaky voice, swinging her bare feet to the floor and digging her toes into the wool Persian rug they'd chosen together at an estate auction.

Something was different about her today. She was

showing a vulnerability around him, an openness, he hadn't seen in nearly a year. And that meant there was still something salvageable between them.

For the first time in a long time, they were actually talking, and he wasn't giving up that window of opportunity to figure out what was going on in her mind. He didn't know where they were going, but he sure as hell wasn't willing to just write off what they'd had. "It's tougher and tougher to be together in front of people and pretend. I get that. Totally. That's what you're upset about, isn't it?"

"Of course," she answered too quickly.

"Why am I having trouble believing you?" He draped his jacket over a wing-back chair by the restored fireplace. "We didn't have trouble with trust before."

"It's easy to trust when you don't know each other well, when we kept our life superficial." The words came out of her mouth almost like lines from a play. Too calculated, too rehearsed.

He leaned back against the marble mantel. "You're going to have to explain that to me, because I'm still bemused as hell as to where we went wrong."

Sighing, she smoothed the silk dress over her knees. "We forgot to talk about the important things, like what would happen if we couldn't have kids. What we would have bonding us besides having lots of sex and procreating."

Sifting through her explanation, he tried to make sense of her conflicting signals, her words and body language and nervous twitches all at odds. "You only saw sex between us as about having children? Is that why you've been pushing me away since your mastectomy and hysterectomy?" Because of the genetic testing, the doctor had recommended both, and Henri hadn't been able to deny the grief they'd both felt over the end to any chance of conceiving a child together. But the bottom line was, he'd cared most about keeping his wife alive. "You know I'm here for you, no matter what. I'm not going to leave you when you need me."

Her expression was shuttered, her emotions hidden again. "We've discussed this. Without kids, we have nothing holding us together."

Nothing except for their passion, their shared interests. Their shared life. She couldn't be willing to discount that so quickly.

"And you're still against adoption?" He was stumped about that, considering her father was adopted. But she'd closed down when he brought up the subject.

"I'm against a man staying with me for the children or out of sympathy because he thinks I'm going to die." She shot to her feet, a coolness edging her features. "Could we please stop this discussion, dammit?"

Was that what she thought? That he had only stayed because of her cancer gene? They'd discussed divorce before then, but only briefly. After? She'd dug in her heels about the split.

He couldn't deny he wouldn't have left a woman facing the possibility of a terminal illness, but their relationship was more complex than that. He shoved away from the fireplace strewn with Wedgwood knickknacks, strode toward her and stopped just short of the settee.

He clasped her shoulders. "You said we never talked enough. So let's talk. Tell me."

Henri needed her to talk. To figure this out. Because

even now, even with the smudged makeup and tousled brown hair, she was damn beautiful. The heat of her skin beneath his hands was familiar and intoxicating.

He still wanted her. Cancer or no cancer. Kids or no kids. Though his hands stayed steady on her shoulders, he wanted to send them traveling on her body. To push her back on the bed.

Their bed—before she'd sent him to his own room after they'd returned from her surgery overseas. She'd said the surgery left her in too much pain to risk being bumped in the night. And somehow over time, she'd kept the separate rooms edict in place. He didn't know how so much time had slipped away, but day by day, he'd been so damn afraid he would say or do the wrong thing when she was in such a fragile state. He'd gone along with her request for space until the next thing he'd known their lawyer was drawing up papers.

He was done waiting around. He was a man of action.

After a moment of hesitation, she shrugged off his hands. "Talking now won't change us splitting up. You have to understand that."

"Then let's talk to give each other peace when we walk away." If he could keep her talking, they were still together. She wouldn't be closing the door in his face.

She chewed her bottom lip before releasing it slowly, then nodding. "Speak then."

He sat on the settee and held her hand, tugging gently. She held back for a moment before surrendering to sit beside him. He shuffled at the last instant so she landed on his lap.

"That's not playing fair."

"Then move."

Indecision shifted across her heart-shaped face, then a spark of something. Pure Fiona spunk. She wriggled once, causing a throbbing ache in his groin an instant before she settled.

He raised an eyebrow. "Now *that's* not playing fair."

"I thought you wanted to talk."

"I did. Now it's tough to think." He tapped her lips. "But I'm trying. We could start with you telling me what really made you cry."

She avoided his gaze as she said, "I had a long talk with your grandfather this evening. Seeing him fading away made me sad." Resting her head on Henri's chest, she took a ragged breath. Grandpa Leon and Fiona had always been close.

"I understand that feeling well. It's hard to watch, hard to think about. I miss him already." Pulling her closer, Henri softened as she wrapped her arms around him. Lifting a hand, he stroked her dark brown hair, releasing the braid that confined her curls. This was what he missed. Being close like this. Feeling her against him. "Are you really prepared to walk away from this family? My brothers, Adelaide…everyone?"

Fiona stayed against his chest, fingers twirling around the back of his neck. Shocks of electric energy tingled along his spine. His hand slid down the side of her body, gingerly touching the silky fabric of her dress, making him itch for more. The light smell of her perfume worked his nerves. It had grown silent between them. The only audible noise was the click-click-click of the ceiling fan.

"Perhaps they will still like me afterward." The words came out like a whisper.

"Of course they will." It was impossible not to like her.

"But I understand it could be awkward for everyone, especially for you when you move on." Again, she cut into his core.

"You already have me in a relationship with someone else? That's cold." He hadn't had eyes for anyone but her since they'd met. He'd been head over heels for her from the get-go.

"I imagine the women will be flocking to you the instant they hear you're free."

Fiona's face was close to his now. Her mouth inches from his. The breath from her words warmed his lips.

"But I only want you." He tilted his head, touched the bottom of her chin and kissed her fully, his tongue meeting and sweeping against hers.

The familiar texture of her lips, the taste of her, awakened a deep need in him. They knew each other's bodies and needs. He knew just where to stroke behind her ears to make her purr.

Fiona kissed him back, wrapping her arms around him, pulling him close against her. Her fingers slid into his hair, caressing along his scalp and grazing lower, her nails lightly trailing along his neck, then digging into his shoulders with need.

His hands roved down her back, the ridge of her zipper reminding him of earlier when he'd slid it up, link by link. Every time, touching her set him on fire. The silk of her dress was every bit as soft as her skin.

And he had once made it his personal mission to learn the terrain of every inch of that skin.

His fingers played down to her hips, digging in as he tugged her even closer on his lap. The curve of her ass pressed against the swelling ache of his erection, making him throb even harder. He nipped along her ear, then soothed the love bite with the tip of his tongue. Her head fell back and her lips parted with a breathy sigh that prompted his growl of approval in response. He kissed down her neck, to the sweet curve of her shoulder. His hand skimmed up her side—

And just as quickly as it had started, she pulled back, sliding off his lap and stumbling to her feet. Her hands shaky, she smoothed the lines in her dress.

What the hell? He struggled to pull his thoughts together but all the blood in his body was surging south hard and fast.

She stared at him, eyes full of confusion. "You need to go." Before he could speak, she made fast tracks to the door, holding it open even wider. "You *need* to go. I'll see you in the morning."

And even with the lack of blood to his brain, he knew. There was no arguing with his wife tonight.

Kicking at the cover, Fiona tossed in her king-size bed, trapped in the twilight hell between having a nightmare and being half-awake. The torture of knowing she should be able to grapple back to consciousness but unable to haul herself from the dream that felt all too real.

In the fog of her dream, Fiona pushed open the door of her childhood home, making her way across the kitchen and into the living room. Her father, a dignified-looking man with salt-and-pepper hair, sat on the overstuffed chair in the corner of the room, clutching the newspaper in his hand.

Something was wrong. She could hear it in the rattle of those papers clutched in his shaky grip. See it on his face when his gaze met hers over the top of the *New Orleans Times*.

"Dad?" The voice that puffed from her lips seemed distant. Younger.

He shook his head, his mouth tight as if holding back words was an ungodly tough effort. Panic filled her chest. She needed to find her mother.

Spinning away, she started roaming the halls of the three-story house, opening the doors. Searching for her mother. Chasing shadows that crooked their fingers, beckoning, then fading. Again and again.

At the last door, she was sure she would find her mother, a willowy woman, a society leader who stayed busy, so busy Fiona had attended boarding school during the week to be kept out of the way.

On her weekends at home, there just hadn't been enough hours to spend together. Her memories of her mom were few and far between.

Fiona opened that very last door, the one to the garden where her mother held the very best of parties. The doorknob slipped from her hand, the mahogany panel swinging wide and slamming against the wall so fast she had to jump back.

Petals swirled outside, pink from azaleas, purple from hydrangeas and white from larger magnolia blooms, all spiraling through the air so thickly they created a hurricane swirl she couldn't see through. Her mother must be beyond the storm.

Fiona pushed forward, into the whirlwind, flower petals beating at her body in silken slices that cut her skin. Left her with scars on her body and soul.

The deeper she pushed, the more the realization seeped in through those cuts. The painful truth sank in deep inside her. Her mother was gone. The cancerous hurricane had taken her mom, her grandmother, her aunt, leaving Fiona alone. The world rattled around her, the flap of petals, the crackle of newspapers, the roar of screaming denial.

Water dripped down her cheeks. Tears? Or rain? She didn't know. It didn't matter because it didn't change the ache of loss.

The garden shifted from her childhood home to the historic house she shared with Henri. Grandpa Leon sat in a wrought-iron chair, his fading memory darkening the storm clouds slowly into night. No matter how much time passed, she felt the pain of her shrinking family. The pain of so many losses. The loss of her unborn children. All of her failed attempts at stability and happiness paraded down the pathway. Losing her mother young, her aunt and grandmother, too, until there were no motherly figures left to steer her through her shaky marriage. Hopelessness pushed at her, wound her up as the darkness of the windswept garden became too oppressive. She catapulted herself forward, sitting upright in her bed.

It took a moment for Fiona to gain her bearings and to realize she was in New Orleans.

Sleep was anything but peaceful these days.

Taking a deep breath, she considered calling her father. They'd never been close and it had been a while since they'd spoken. But still, the nightmare had left her completely rattled. All of the pressures of her current situation were bubbling over.

She had to leave, sooner rather than later. She realized that even though she'd been protecting herself from the pain of having Henri stay with her out of pity, she was also protecting him from watching her fade away if the worst happened.

Her dad had never been the same after her mother died. The loss of her mother had shattered him. Though there was distance between Fiona and Henri, she still cared about him.

It was best to walk away. It was simpler to walk away than get more attached.

Morning runs had a way of clearing Henri's mind. And man, did he need some perspective after last night.

Sweat cooled on his neck as he pulled into his driveway, the muggy, verdant air mixing with the funk of his own need of a shower. He'd driven to the Hurricanes' workout facility and ran harder than he had in weeks. There was a renewed energy in his steps. Something that felt a bit like hope. Which was exactly why he was back at their restored Garden District house now. He'd been in such a rush to make it home before Fiona woke up that he hadn't even bothered with a shower. He'd simply discarded his sweaty clothes in favor of a clean T-shirt and basketball shorts.

Deep down, he knew he had to focus on the upcoming home game. It was huge for the team in a year that could net them a championship. But everything that was going on in his personal life was taking his head out of this season.

Henri shoved out of his car, waving at the security guards who were on duty. The two nondescript but well-trained men responded with a curt nod as he entered the old home through the back entrance.

As he turned the knob on the door, thoughts of Fiona filled his brain. There was something between them still. The kiss confirmed that. There had been passion on both ends of their kiss last night. Having her pressed against him felt so right. Natural. Normal. He needed to get her to see that they fit together. Bring her back to his bed, back to him.

Stepping into the kitchen, he found Fiona cooking, the scents of butter and caramel in the air. Her chocolate-brown hair was piled in a messy bun. Her sleep shorts hugged her curves, revving his interest. Glancing over her shoulder, she flashed him a small smile.

He wanted her now more than ever. But how to convince her that they needed to get back to what they had?

"You don't have to cook for me. I do want you for more than your body and awesome culinary skills." He eyed the Waterford crystal bowl of fresh blueberries next to her. An intriguing—undeniable—notion filled his mind, and he pressed himself against her as he reached for them. They'd always done best when they kept things light. That might well be the way to go with her today.

With slow deliberation, he popped a few blueberries into his mouth, eyebrows arching.

For a moment, she looked visibly riled. Damn, she was sexy.

Then she glanced away quickly and kept her focus on the task at hand. "I don't mind. I love to cook. At some point soon, I'm going to have to figure out what to do with my life."

"If you insist on going through with the divorce, you know I'll take care of you." It was all he wanted to do. To be the one to support her no matter what.

Setting a plate down on the island, she gestured for him to sit. He looked at her handiwork—a whole-wheat crepe filled with various fruits. A protein shake was already there, waiting for him.

"Eat your breakfast and stop talking before I pour cayenne pepper in your protein shake." She shook the spice at him before she carried over her own plate and the cut-crystal bowl of blueberries and sat down at the island.

Sunlight streamed into the room, filling the space with warmth.

"I'm a bad guy if I say I want to provide a generous alimony settlement?"

"I appreciate the offer. It's the verbiage about taking care of me that rubs the wrong way. Like I'm…"

"You're far from a child. Believe me, I get that." He scooped up another handful of berries, pitching one at a time into his mouth, the sweet juice bursting along his taste buds.

"I have a degree."

Henri nodded. "And you've sacrificed your career so we could travel together. I appreciate that. I thought you enjoyed our time on the road—"

She held up the cayenne.

He yanked his shake away, nudging her playfully with his shoulder. To win his way back into her bed, he needed to keep things light. "Changing the subject."

"Thank you." She set down the red pepper. "Enjoy your breakfast. I certainly intend to."

"As do I." He tapped the bowl of berries. "These are incredibly fresh."

"I haven't tried them yet." Fiona reached for the

berries, but Henri snatched them away, that devilish smile playing on his lips.

Nudging the bowl toward her, he stepped closer, closer still. He plucked up a particularly fat berry and fed it to her. Her lips nipped at his fingertips, sparking his awareness. And she seemed to be enjoying herself, as well.

"That kiss last night—"

She coughed as the food went down the wrong way. Once she cleared her throat, she asked half-jokingly, "Are you trying to choke me to death to avoid alimony?"

"That's not funny. At all."

"You're right. Bad joke born out of nerves." She looked down, her cheeks flushing with embarrassment. "Your breakfast deserves to be enjoyed."

"Thank you. We've had some incredible meals together, just us. I'm going to miss these times with you."

"You're accepting it's over?"

"You're making it tough not to." He eyed her over his fork. Frustrated. Determined. "Any chance we could have one more night together for old times' sake?"

"That's not going to happen."

He wished he understood why. The doctors had told him to give her space to process the shock of learning she carried the cancer gene, time to accept the long-term implications. They'd claimed that she would get over the self-consciousness, the grief over what she'd lost. But God, they'd spent so much of their marriage on a roller coaster of emotions. Trying for a baby. Miscarriages. Losing a baby in the second trimester. Then when the doctor pointed out how the fertility treatments could put her at risk with her maternal family's history of cancer.

Then her hysterectomy. Her double mastectomy.

So damn much to process.

He wished he had someone to talk to for understanding it from a female's perspective…but her mother and grandmother were gone, her aunt, too.

The realization dawned on him. There were women in his family. Strong, spunky women who could help him win Fiona back.

Because come hell or high water, he wasn't giving up.

Four

If Fiona had to be in the middle of a fund-raiser crisis, she'd at least found some peace that the crisis was unfolding in the sunroom of their restored Victorian home. The presence of the garden stilled her frantic heart, reminded her to breathe.

In a lot of ways, the sunroom had become her unofficial office. She came out here to think or to read old-fashioned paperback books from the library. She felt, in a manner of speaking, very turn of the century.

She let her eyes rove above the half wall, her gaze pushing past the intricate wrought iron on the windows to the garden proper. Lush trees and bushes nestled against a winding brick paver path. Taking a moment to appreciate the view, she reorganized her thoughts.

Sitting in an oversize wooden chair, she surveyed the table in front of her. It was a mess—iPads, laptops, cell phones and sticky notes littered the farm-house-style table. She was up against a deadline for the next fund-raiser to step in with emergency help for the children's oncology ward event since the other planner had had a heart attack. The concert hall she'd originally booked had backed out last minute due to a terrible fire. It hadn't seemed very likely that the hall would be fully operational again in time, so she'd made a few calls and switched the location.

Making this fund-raiser a success felt exceptionally personal. The proceeds from the event were going to cancer research. It was a cause she felt deeply about and she couldn't bear to see the children's event can-celed or even postponed. Fiona did what she did best—she threw herself into her work.

Fiona watched how Adelaide worked on the iPad, intensely focused on the screen in front of her. She was logging a lot of hours on Fiona's project. It was even more impressive because Adelaide was in the process of launching her own sportswear line.

"You have such a full plate of your own. I don't know how to thank you for your help." Fiona was truly humbled by Adelaide's support, especially on the last two events. She'd stepped in, no questions asked.

"Being a part of the Reynaud family gives great op-portunities to effect change. You know how poor I was growing up. The thought that I could improve other people's lives? I don't take that opportunity lightly. I just haven't figured out how I want to make my mark yet. So if you don't mind, I'll just hitch my philan-thropic wagon to your star for now." Turning away from the half wall, she smiled warmly at Fiona.

"Then I'll gratefully accept the help."

"Well, I trust you can help me plan my wedding. You have the best eye for things, Fiona," Adelaide said, examining the way her engagement ring caught the sunlight, sparkling with the brilliance of the ocean on the sunniest of days.

Fiona put on her best face, schooling her features into happiness, though such a task took some effort. She could feel the edges of her composure wobble under the pressure.

"It is such a lovely ring, and you will be an even more beautiful bride." Tucking a loose strand of wavy hair behind her ear, she gave her future sister-in-law the biggest smile she could manage. "Truly beautiful."

The light reflected off Adelaide's ring paled in comparison to the emotion that lit her love-struck eyes and tugged pink into her cheeks.

Her future sister-in-law began to chatter. And Fiona would have listened on, equally joyful, if she didn't notice the text message that blipped across her screen.

It was a courtesy reminder of her upcoming doctor's appointment. They had results to give her and more tests to administer.

Suddenly, despite the bright, airy nature of the sunroom, she felt claustrophobic. Anxiety wrapped her in a grip she didn't know how to shake. An acute tingling sensation rippled through her arms, and the world felt farther away from her than it ever had before. Everything—her impending divorce, her uncertain health, the loss of family—crashed into her at once.

She recognized that Adelaide was still talking, but the words were lost on her.

Fiona must have looked as bad as she felt, because her future sister-in-law stopped talking.

Setting aside her iPad, Adelaide pensively tipped her head to the side. "Is something wrong?"

"Why would you ask that?" Fiona placed her cell phone facedown on the table. It was time to focus on tangible things, to push herself back into the present moment. Concentrating on Adelaide's concerned words, Fiona let herself notice the warmth of the phone and the coolness of the table.

"You just don't seem like yourself." Adelaide held up a hand. "Never mind. Forget I asked. It's none of my business."

Fiona decided what the hell. She should dive in and be honest—or at least partially open. And yes, maybe she was acting out of fear, because Henri's kiss had rocked her resolve to move on with her life. "It's no secret in the family that Henri and I have had trouble. We've struggled with infertility. There's more to it than that."

"I'm here if you want to talk." Adelaide walked closer to her, lowering her voice, her southern accent full of earnest concern.

"What happens if I'm not part of the family anymore? Your loyalties will be here, and I understand that."

"It's that bad? You're thinking about splitting up?" An edge of surprise hitched in Adelaide's voice.

It had been a giant mistake to say that much. The last thing Fiona wanted to do was burden anyone. It was suddenly clear that she wasn't ready to discuss this, not with Adelaide. Now she had to refocus, get them back on track. Ignore the pain in her chest and move forward. That's what she was best at, anyway.

Moving forward. Stacking a few papers into perfect order, she inhaled deeply, closed her eyes and spoke.

"Let's focus on the party. I need to get through the next couple of weeks and salvage this event for the fund-raising dollars—and for the children in the hospital looking forward to their party."

"If that's what you want." Adelaide didn't seem particularly convinced, but she also didn't press her further.

"This event is important to me. More so than the others." Scrolling through a web page, she gestured at the band options. "I need it to be perfect. This disease has taken so much from so many families." Not just other families. Her family. And now it threatened her, too. In a small voice, she added, "My mother died of cancer when I was young—my grandmother and aunt, too."

"I didn't know." Adelaide reached across to squeeze Fiona's hand. "Apparently there are a lot of things I didn't know and I'm so very sorry for your pain."

"Henri and I aren't ready for people to know about the divorce until the end of the season, when the papers will be ready to be filed, but I'm thinking now we aren't going to be able to wait that long. I imagine our secrets will be out in the public soon enough if the press gets wind of things."

"The lack of privacy is difficult."

"We've worked hard to keep things private."

"Perhaps too much so, from the sound of how little the family knows of what's going on. Family can be a support system." Adelaide patted her chest. "I consider myself part of your family."

"Thank you, but if we split..." She swallowed hard.

"Most of my family is gone. I only have my father left and, well, we're not close." Since all of her friends were tied to Henri's family and the football world, that left her facing a looming void.

"Fiona, I'm here for you if you need me, regardless."

"I envy your career and independence. I need to find that for myself."

"What would you like to do with your life?"

Fiona cheeks puffed out with the force of her sigh. "I'm an art major and I throw parties. If only I had an engineering degree to tack on to the end of that, I would be a hot commodity on the job market."

Before Adelaide had a chance to respond, Princess Erika stepped into the sunroom. She was Gervais's beautiful Nordic fiancée. Her pale blond hair was gathered over one shoulder, intricately woven into a thick fishtail braid.

"Sisters," she said, rubbing her hand along her pregnant stomach. Her announcement—and engagement— had caught the whole family by surprise since the couple hadn't known each other long. But their love was clear. "I rang the bell but you didn't hear me. The cleaning lady let me in on her way out. What are we doing here and can I help? I am at loose ends until after the wedding, when I begin school. And of course newborn twins will keep me busy. The calm before the hurricane."

The hurricane? Erika had a way of twisting idioms that was endearing. Fiona would miss that and so many other things about this family she'd grown close to during her marriage.

Adelaide shook her head. "Only you would think preparing for a wedding isn't enough to keep a person busy."

The princess shrugged elegantly, wearing her impending motherhood with ease. Fiona swallowed down an ache that never quite went away. She'd had such plans for her life as a wife and mother. She'd wanted a family, a big family, unlike her solitary upbringing. Maybe Henri's large family had been part of the allure, too.

Regardless, there would be no family for her. It hurt that this woman got pregnant with twins without even trying while Fiona couldn't bear a child no matter how hard every medical professional worked to bring about a different result. But that wasn't the fault of anyone in this room.

Fiona kept her gaze firmly off Erika's stomach and on her face. "Thank you for your offer of help. We would love to have you keep us company."

"Does that mean you will share your beignets?" Erika said with a twinkle in her blue eyes. "I cannot get enough of them."

The lump in Fiona's throat became unbearable. She loved these women...but it hurt. She knew it was selfish and small, but watching them get their fairy-tale endings just served as a reminder that she was far from having that. And Erika's pregnancy was so difficult for her to watch.

Tears burned as thoughts of lost dreams threatened her ability to hold it together. And she absolutely would not lose it in front of Henri's family. Her pride was about all she had left.

Henri's body ached from practice, but he still burned to talk to Fiona. So he did the sensible thing:

he went to the sunroom. Her operation station, as he liked to call it.

He turned the corner into the sunroom, only half surprised to see Adelaide and Erika working alongside Fiona. Adelaide, iPad in hand, pointed out something on the screen to Erika.

Everything was under control. A smile tugged at his lips. It felt good to see some bit of normalcy in the house.

Not until he saw the tears welling in Fiona's sherry-colored eyes did he realize there was something truly wrong. She was on the verge of falling apart.

In one swift motion, she grabbed her phone and opened the door to the garden. It rattled behind her as she walked into what she'd often called her land-scaped haven.

Every part of him screamed to life. He should follow her. Had to follow her. Feet moving of their own volition, he started toward the door.

But something stopped him. What would he even say to her?

It was time to call in reinforcements. With a heavy sigh, he sat in the chair by the table.

"Ladies, I need your help. Adelaide, can I count on you for some assistance?"

"The party is well in hand. Your wife is a master-ful organizer." Adelaide gestured to the scattered papers on the desk. Each stack was color coordinated with sticky notes.

Tapping his fingers on the desk, he looked up at her. "My wife and I are going through, a, uh, rough patch. I could use some ideas for bringing romance back to the marriage."

"I'm very sorry to hear that," she said with undeniable sympathy. But he could see she wasn't surprised.

How had she known? Had she sensed it? Or had Fiona said something?

Erika clasped her hands. "Of course we are willing to help however we can. You and Fiona are my family too now."

"Thank you. I mean that. I'm hoping you can offer some advice, ideas."

Adelaide eyed him curiously. "What kind of time frame are you looking at?"

"I need to move quickly. Fiona is...not happy." That was an understatement. If he could just find a direction to go in. Some clue.

Erika scrutinized him with a sharp look. "Should you be speaking with her about this?"

"Never mind." He shook his head and turned on his heels. "Forget I asked."

Erika called out, "Wait. I did not mean to chase you away. I am happy to share what I can, although I do not know her well. You want your marriage to work, yes?"

"I do."

Adelaide ticked off ideas as if she was running through one of her iPad checklists. "Help her remember that you appreciate her, that you still desire her. Don't assume she knows. And remind her of the reasons you got married in the first place."

He heard her and felt as though he'd already done as much. Of course he'd put Adelaide and Erika on the spot, since they didn't really know the depth of the problems. He was asking them to shoot in the dark. But he and Fiona had guarded their privacy so intensely and now he couldn't share without making her feel betrayed.

Maybe there was a way around it without telling them everything. He and Fiona needed to get back to the early days of their marriage. Back to fun and laughter. Yes, the romance he'd mentioned. Fiona had a point that they hadn't dated long.

They'd gotten married because they thought she was pregnant, and it turned out to be a false alarm. They'd both wanted kids so much they'd focused on that goal—until suddenly surviving surgeries became their whole life. "Let's just say we've fallen into a routine and this old married man needs some concrete dating ideas."

Erika leaned forward, expression wise and intense. "That is very dear of you."

Adelaide quirked an eyebrow. "And to think America's hottest athlete is asking me for dating advice."

He spread his hands. "I'm all ears."

And he was. Because the thought of returning his marriage to the early days, before life grew complicated, had never sounded more appealing.

On her hands and knees, Fiona rooted around the flower bed, decompressing after a restless night with little sleep. Henri had locked himself in his study last night after her future sisters-in-law left. God, the man was full of mixed signals.

She carefully separated the butterfly ginger plants from the aggressive weeds that threatened them. The butterfly ginger was a sweet plant, and the invasive species that shared the flower bed threatened to snuff them out completely. She'd made a habit of maintaining balance in the garden. It provided her a sense of peace.

Especially these days.

She was so fixated on the weeds in the flower bed she barely registered the sound of footsteps on the brick pavers. Casting a glance over her right shoulder, her gaze homed right on the muscled form of Henri approaching. His lips were in a thin line, strain wearing on his face as he went underneath the ivy-wrapped arbor, passing the golden wonder tree and the forsythia sage plants. He still looked like the man she fell in love with and married three years ago.

And that was what hurt the most. She was broken, in her heart, unable to let him or anyone get close. She didn't know how to push past the icy fear.

Henri said nothing. He simply knelt next to her and started helping her. As they sat in silence, the woody scent of him filled her head with memories, each more painful than the last. Of what they were in the beginning. Of when things were good. Of how terrible things were now.

"I think it's time we surrender to the inevitable." Her heart was pounding so hard and fast, she thought it would shake her to pieces.

"What are you talking about?" he asked, his voice raspy.

"Seriously? You have to know. But if you can't bring yourself to say it, I will. Our marriage is over."

Shaking his head, he said, "You're wrong."

"Why?"

"Excuse me?"

"Tell me why I'm wrong."

"Because we got married. We said till...um, forever." He yanked a weed out of the ground.

"You can't even say the word. *Death.* I'm not dying. You don't have to feel guilty over walking away."

Frustration crept into his features, hardening his face. He tossed a weed on the ground. "Dammit, that's not at all what I said."

"But I can hear it in your voice. You feel protective, and that's not enough for us to build a life together." She shook her head. He had to see what was going on.

"We got married because we loved each other."

"We got married because we thought I was pregnant and we were infatuated with great sex. It was a whirlwind romance. We didn't know each other well enough before trouble hit. We're not okay and we never will be."

"I'll go back to the marriage counselor. I'll listen. I wasn't ready then. I am now."

"Thank you, but no. I've had enough." She couldn't stay and have her heart continually fracture and break.

"Stay until the end of the season."

"What good would that do?" Leaning back on the ground, she stared at him.

"I can't file for divorce in the middle of the season. It may be simple for you to just call it quits, but I can't walk away that easily."

"Because of the bad press." It was a low blow, but she delivered it anyway.

"Because I'm not a machine and I can't risk the stress screwing with my concentration, especially not when we have a real shot at going all the way this year. You know how much I have riding on me. How rare it is for a team to have all the right parts assembled the way the Hurricanes do this year."

The request sent her reeling. "Seriously? I'm supposed to put off my life because you want to chase a championship ring?"

"Seriously. It's not just about me, Fiona. You know that. How many people look to me to lead these guys? How can I ruin their chances at being part of a once-in-a-lifetime team? Those opportunities don't come around twice. And there are endorsements to think about, commentator jobs. So many things ride on this season."

Since she traveled with the team, she'd organized family support for the wives and kids when the guys were on the road. She couldn't deny she felt a commitment to that community. Guilt stung over throwing this at him when she knew how much those guys looked up to him. While Henri was blessed on many levels with talent and wealth, many of the guys he played with definitely weren't. The running backs could well be out of football in two years, given the short life span of their careers. Some of the linemen had been raised by hardscrabble single mothers who gave up everything to help their kids succeed.

She would be putting the season at risk… Still, she couldn't stay with him indefinitely.

"When you retire from football, you don't have to work." That was the truth. The Reynaud wealth went far beyond football and Henri played for sport, not to put food on their table. He would have enough money to be just fine if he quit tomorrow.

"Yes, I do. I'm not the type to take on pet projects. I need a full-time job. That's who I am."

Pet projects? Is that how he saw her non-paying fund-raising? It sure felt like a dig at her.

"What's wrong with a life devoted to philanthropy?" She reached for straws, pushing him hard with both hands because he'd edged closer to the truth, the hurt beneath the facade, and she felt so damn vulnerable right now. She was hanging on by a string.

"That path is one you chose, but it's not the one for me."

Indignation blinded her. "Are you calling me a dilettante? Deliberately picking a fight?"

"No." His dark eyes were clear. Focused. "But I think you might be."

Her defenses crumbled and he saw right though her. Panicking, she didn't even know what to say as he brought all that masculine appeal her way.

"You're sexy when you're riled up." He stepped closer. "No matter what we've been through. No matter how many problems we've had or how much distance, know this. I want you in my bed every bit as much as I did the first time I saw you."

Five

Anticipation sent his awareness into overdrive. Henri needed to touch her, to wrap her in his arms.

She was sexy—a tangle of tousled hair and pure fire. And in this setting—in the middle of the garden in that little muted peach dress—she looked like one of those beautiful nymphs that classical artists were always capturing.

Every bit as alluring. And every bit as elusive, too.

But he'd gotten this close to her and he could sense the answering awareness in her, a heat she'd denied too often these last months. Now, extending a hand, he trailed it along the length of her lithe arm. Gentle pressure, the kind that used to drive her wild with anticipation. She turned to face him, leaning into his light touch.

Reaching her hand, he threaded his fingers through

hers, locking them together in that one small way. He was holding on to her. To them.

He pulled her closer. Mouths inches apart. Temptation and need mounting.

Her lips parted. For a moment, things felt normal. The air was charged with palpable passion.

And then it happened. She swayed back ever so slightly. Henri could see the desire flaming in her eyes even as he spotted the *no* already forming on her lips.

So he pulled back instead, releasing her fingers to tap her on the nose. "Lady, you do tempt me."

She flattened her hands on his chest, her fingers stroking, her amber gaze conflicted. "Passion between us has never been an issue. But it will only make things more difficult when we split for good."

He tried not to take that personally, forcing himself to focus on the action over at the tall Victorian bird condominium the landscaper had installed in the garden. Taking a deep breath, he tried to haul in some calm from the backyard his contractor had promised would be a haven for years to come.

"Why do you keep talking like we're over the border and a quickie divorce is already a done deal?"

Fiona's hands clenched in his shirt with intensity. "Why won't you accept that we might as well be? Why are you making this so hard? It's not like we've even uttered the word *love* in nearly a year."

He should just say the word if that's what it took. But for some reason he couldn't push it past his lips. He was saved from a response when a squabble broke out in the birdbath nearby.

Her smile was bittersweet while she watched the little wrens fly off to leave the bath to bigger birds. "You know I'm right. People get divorced even when there aren't big issues at hand. We've been through a lot with the infertility, miscarriages, my surgery, the stress of your high-profile job, as well. It's just too much."

Did she have a point? In some ways. But at least she spoke in tangibles now, delivering more straight talk than she'd given him in a damn long time.

And in a strange way she was making sense. They had been under an immense amount of stress. He hadn't even considered that his job added to the stress of all she'd been through. He had food for thought, and even though she was still attempting to push him away, he felt a bit closer to achieving his objective of reconnecting with her.

"Fiona, I hear what you're saying now, and I understand that—"

"Please, I'm not sure you do." She rested her hand on his. "I'm sorry, Henri. I need to move on with my life."

God, she was stubborn, and that turned him on, too. "You've made that clear. We're ending our marriage after the season—"

"After my next fund-raiser. *Or now.*"

"Okay, not arguing. In fact, I'm suggesting the total opposite. We agreed we need new lawyers. That will happen after your fund-raiser so we don't taint the event. We used to have fun together. Let's use this time to relax. The pressure is off. No expectations. No doctors."

She flinched.

He hesitated. Had he missed something? Before he could ask her, she seemed to relax again.

With a slow exhale, she took a few steps toward the

simple white swing that hung from a huge old live oak that spanned most of the yard. "All right. No pressure. Explain what you mean."

Seeing his chance, he needed to proceed carefully. Not push for too much.

"Let's just be friends." The closer he was to her, the more opportunities he would have to woo his way into her bed and into her heart, back to a place where they understood each other. Where their world would still make sense. "Like we used to be. People will ask fewer questions. We can take a deep breath."

She bit her lip as she trailed a hand over the wooden scrollwork on the seat back of the swing. "But some of the family knows there are problems and the rest of the family already seems to be guessing."

Henri shrugged. He didn't care what they thought. He needed to make it right with Fiona. That was the number one priority. "Then let them unguess for now. We'll deal with the rest later."

"Don't you want their support?" She stilled, a light breeze sifting through her dark hair and teasing it along one arm.

He remembered the days when he'd just sweep her off her feet and carry her to his bed when the mood struck—which was all the damn time with her. When was the last time they'd sprinted to the bedroom to peel each other's clothes off like that?

Shaking off thoughts that would only be counterproductive in his new approach, he picked a few daisies out of the rock garden for her instead, needing to keep his hands occupied with something that wasn't her.

"I want some peace for both of us right now, and something tells me you want that, too." He gathered one simple bloom after another, hoping maybe, just maybe, this peace could bring them back together. The fact that she was considering being friends spoke volumes.

"Why would you say that?" She stepped closer to him, watching him as he wound a too-long stem around the rest of the stems to hold the flowers together.

"We've been married for three years. Call it intuition." He passed her the bouquet, remembering she far preferred simple, garden-variety flowers to anything he could have found in their hothouse.

"I didn't know men believed in intuition." An all-too-rare smile—the ghost of one, anyway—lifted the corners of her mouth.

"I do. What do you say?" He gave her his best bad-boy smile. "Wanna go play?"

The cherry-red 1965 Mustang purred as they wound through the Garden District. The midday sun loomed large, warming the leather of the seats. In the vintage pony car, she felt more alive—more aware—than she had in years.

Fiona couldn't remember the last time they'd done something spontaneous like this. Or the last time they'd chosen the Mustang over the sparkly high-end automobiles at their disposal. She was happy with the choice, though. It blended into downtown seamlessly, attracting less attention and making them seem more like a regular couple.

For now, she could forget about the suspicious lump that might or might not be anything. She could forget about the biopsy scheduled for tomorrow.

And she absolutely would not allow herself to think of the worst-case scenario.

Today, she would play with her husband.

As the car passed through the streets, Fiona gazed out the window. Sometimes she forgot how truly beautiful this place was. Old Victorian homes lined the street, boasting bright hues of red and yellow. Wrought-iron gates encircled the majority of the homes.

What she loved most about New Orleans was the way the streets and sights felt like a continuous work of art. The cultures pressed against each other, yielding brilliant statues and buildings unique to this small corner of the world.

Pulling her thoughts away from the road to downtown, she cast a sidelong glance at Henri. His head bopped to some snappy song from the 1960s. He noticed her looking at him and he flashed a small smile.

He wore a plain T-shirt, cargo shorts and aviator glasses, his dark hair gleaming in the sun. Just looking at his beard-stubbled face made her cheeks sting as if he'd already kissed her in that raspy masculine way that brought her senses to life. Today he was rugged. Rough around the edges. Hot.

And a far cry from the normally polished quarterback the press couldn't get enough of.

As he turned the car down a narrow street, she couldn't help but notice the way the muscles in his arm bunched, pressing against the T-shirt.

Anticipation bubbled in her chest. The day reminded her of when they first met—from the impromptu backyard bouquet to the impulsive drive around town. "The suspense is making me crazy. What are we doing?"

Grabbing a baseball cap from the dashboard, he

gestured to the downtown district. "We're going to play tourist today."

Wind rushed over her, stealing her cares if only for a little while.

"But I've lived here all my life." She gave a half-hearted protest.

"And sometimes the more a person lives somewhere, the more that person misses seeing what's right under their nose. There's a guy on the team who used to live at the beach and he said he hardly ever hit the waves."

"Okay, I see your point. Let's go for it. Let's 'travel' to our home city."

"I thought you'd say that." He pulled into a parking spot and was out of the car before Fiona even had a chance to unbuckle her seat belt. He opened the door, extending his hand. She took it and a surge of desire seemed to ignite in her.

What was it about those easy words of his back in their garden that had given her permission to have fun today? Without worrying about mixed signals or holding strong to her defenses around him, she felt as though maybe she could relax again. Just for a little while.

Because when was the last time they had dated each other? It had been so long, so many months ago. Her heart raced as they made their way down Bourbon Street.

Trying to see the city as a tourist forced her to approach the street differently than she ever had. She began to notice the small details—the way the air seemed spicy, alive with the Creole seasonings of the various restaurants. As she concentrated on the smells, she started to notice what stores were garnering the most attention.

The street was bustling with people. Street musicians played with such artistry she felt moved by their passion. Her hand moved toward Henri's. Giving it a quick squeeze, she breathed in the moment.

Eyeing the carriages, Henri stopped walking. "How about we do this right? Horse-drawn carriage through the city. It's the best way to see this place, after all."

"I'd like that."

"Excellent. You pick the ride that will turn this town magical."

Henri gestured to the line of horses in front of them. Fiona studied a large bay draft horse in the middle of the pack. She liked the way he stood—tall and at attention.

"That one." Fiona pointed to the bay.

"Done." Henri went to talk to the driver, and they climbed into the carriage. There wasn't a lot of room, and Fiona found herself pressed against Henri. The simple touch of their legs against each other felt electric. She wanted him to take his hand and rub her leg. Her thoughts wandered over his body as she looked at him.

The jerkiness of the carriage caused them to fold into each other. Henri was wearing an older cologne— the one he'd worn when they went abroad a while ago.

Instantly, she was transported to the UK. It had been her favorite vacation.

"Remember when we went to Stonehenge?" Fiona peered up at him through her lashes.

"You were convinced you were going to travel back in time."

Nudging him with her arm, she laughed. "Those rocks hum."

"You've been listening to too much voodoo lore and vampire stories." He tapped her nose playfully.

Laying her hand on her chest, she poured a bit of theatrical flair into her voice. "I'm a native of New Orleans. You're a transplant. Give it time."

"Hey, I'm the New Orleans golden boy."

"Because you have a golden throwing arm. It's like you fast-tracked your way into being a native."

"Then good thing I have you around to make sure I stay authentic." He stretched his arm around her, the warmth of his touch pulling on her heart. She nestled into him, leaning into his embrace. Head on his shoulder, she was content to take in the scenery and keep pretending for now the real world wasn't ready to intrude with a biopsy needle in less than twenty-four hours.

So far, the no-pressure day was going far better than he could ever have hoped for. They were connecting. It was the first time in months that they'd been so open with each other.

So honest.

Shuffling a bag of tourist trinkets to one hand, he reached into his pocket for his leather wallet. Pulling out a few crisp bills for the vendor, he nodded at the woman's child as the imp put a handmade bead necklace into the bag. The fact that these mass-produced tourist trinkets were bringing Fiona and him closer together than the diamond jewelry he'd bought amused him.

The vendor was a rangy woman with too-bright red

lipstick, but she was friendly enough. She tossed a few chili peppers in the bag. The lagniappe. It was one of the things about New Orleans he'd liked since he was a boy on vacation—the gesture of the lagniappe always made New Orleans feel like a welcoming city. Which was why he'd felt drawn to this place when he was younger.

Henri scooped up the bag along with the others as they wound their way out of the store crowded with kitschy ghost memorabilia and wax figures of famous jazz musicians. "My grandparents used to bring us here on vacation when we were kids."

"You never mentioned that before. You always talked about the jet-setting vacations."

"My family's in the boating business, after all." That was putting it mildly, really, since they'd made their billions off shipping and the cruise industry. "Gramps combined business trips with a stop here, checking out the latest route."

"That sounds like fun." She ducked under his arm as he held the door for her, bringing the scent of her hair in tantalizingly close proximity to his nose.

"It's no secret my parents weren't overly involved in our lives, so my grandparents didn't have the luxury of just playing with us. My grandfather included us in work so he could see us. I like how you've worked in the same way for the team families." Fiona's capacity to include and integrate people was something he admired about her. No one ever felt left out if Fiona was involved. She had a knack for making people feel that they mattered.

"It makes sense. The ultimate educational experience for children is to travel along. Study the world as they see it. What did you like most about New Orleans as a kid?" She flicked her ropy ponytail over her shoulder as she continued to scan the streets, drinking in the sights while the heat of the day faded along with the sinking sun.

"The music. Street music." He smiled at the memory. "I would sing along. Jean-Pierre would dance. Damn, he was good. He's always been more nimble on his feet."

"What about Gervais?"

"He just quietly tapped his foot."

She snorted. "Figures. And Dempsey?"

"Those trips had stopped by the time he joined our family." Those days had been tough, integrating their half brother into the family fold. They were tight now, and Jean-Pierre was the one who'd left. Henri shook his head and focused on the moment. "Let's get something to eat. What are you in the mood for?"

"Someplace simple in keeping with our tourist day. Somewhere open air. And someplace where you will keep talking."

"Can do." He pointed to Le Chevalier. Ivy snaked around the outside of the trellis. It was casual and intimate—the perfect combination. "How about gumbo?"

Fiona clapped her hands together. "That sounds perfect."

Her French-manicured nails looked ever so chipped. Unusual for her. As though she'd chewed the edges. He shook off the thought and focused on the moment. On her.

Henri led them to a table in the corner of the outside patio. He pushed in her chair for her and then sat beside her.

Menus in hand, the blonde waitress bustled over to them.

"Are you enjoying New Orleans?" The lilt in her accent was particularly musical.

"Oh, yes. This trip has really made us fall in love with the city." Fiona played along, clearly enjoying the feeling of anonymity as much as he did. Since they were outside, he could keep on the baseball cap and sunglasses. His disguise was intact and his wife was engaged in actual conversation with him.

"Well, that's wonderful, loves. Take your time and let me know when you need something. I'll start you with some waters."

"We'll also go ahead and order gumbo." Henri smiled, handing the menus back to the waitress.

"Excellent choice," she said, writing the order onto the pad. And then the waitress turned on her heel and walked away.

"I love that we blend in here. That there aren't hordes of people vying for our attention." Fiona rummaged through the pile of bags from their purchases.

"See? What did I tell you? It's a no-pressure date day. It does wonders for the soul."

"Mmm." Fiona nodded, piling the trinkets onto the table. A little purple jester doll stared back at him.

He surveyed the stack of souvenirs. A masquerade mask brilliantly decorated in feathers. A T-shirt for him. A bamboo cutting board in the shape of Louisiana. A cartoonish, floppy toy alligator. The necklace with bright blue beads that would look lovely against Fiona's pale skin.

"Aha." She held out the voodoo doll. "Here it is. Best purchase of the day."

"You really are such a native," Henri teased.

"Hey, now. Watch out, mister. Or you'll be under my control." She wriggled the doll at him. Then she took its right arm and made the doll tap its own head.

In a gesture of good faith, Henri tapped his own head, mirroring the doll. She gave him a wicked grin.

"Your spunk amazes me." A rolling laugh escaped his lips.

Picking up the necklace, he watched how the sunlight caught in the blue beads. The glass was cut with the intention of splaying light.

"May I?"

"You may." Lifting her hair up in one hand, she turned her back to him.

His fingers ached to touch her. Sliding the necklace over her head, he worked at fastening the tiny clasp. He rested his fingertips on her neck, enjoying the softness of her skin. Breathing in the scent of her perfume, he leaned in, pressing his lips to her neck.

But instead of leaning into him, she recoiled away. She wrapped her arms around her chest and folded into herself.

He sat back in his chair, watching her, trying to understand. "Why don't you want me to touch you? It can't be the scars, because I've seen them and you know it doesn't matter to me." Couldn't she see that he wasn't bothered by any of that superficial nonsense? It was her that he cared about.

"That time we tried to have sex, you were different. It still is between us." Her voice was low, audibly conflicted.

"Of course it's different. You had major surgery."

"But you still touch me, treat me, talk to me like I'm going to break." She picked at her manicured nails absently.

"You're the strongest woman I know. You made an incredibly difficult decision and faced it with grace. I'm so damn proud of you it blows my mind."

"Thank you." She took a sip of her water, brushing off the compliment the way she always did.

He needed to make her see that it wasn't just talk.

"I speak the truth."

"I don't feel strong. I grew up pampered and spoiled by my father, who was afraid I would die like my mother. I don't mean to sound like a spoiled brat now—a kept woman who's whining because her husband wants to baby her." She chewed her thumbnail, then quickly twisted her hands in her lap.

"I fully understand you gave up a career so we could travel together, and you fill every other waking hour doing good for people when you could be like some sports wives and spend your days at a spa. Instead you're putting together six- and seven-figure fundraisers. You're organizing family adventures and educational activities for the children who travel to see their dads play."

"Why are you saying all of this?" Suspicion edged her voice.

A long sigh escaped from his lips. "To let you know I noticed all your hard work and your thoughtfulness. Your kindness. You're an inspiration."

"Then why can't you treat me like I'm strong? Why can't you trust me that I *am* strong?"

Trust?

He was caught up on that word, turning it over in his mind like a puzzle. Why was it that he could read the nuances of a complicated defense strategy, spotting the weaknesses and potential threats with uncanny accuracy, yet he couldn't begin to interpret this simple word from his wife? He lacked the right awareness for people, the right emotional frequency. He was grasping at straws.

This stumped him. He'd felt that he'd been protecting her, not treating her as though she was delicate crystal.

Damned if he knew the answer to her question.

Six

Opening the car door, Fiona swung her legs out, her feet hitting the garage floor with a tap. Before she could thrust herself up and out of the Mustang, Henri was in front of her, offering support.

Clasping his hand, she rose, their bodies closer than she would have guessed as she straightened fully. After the distance of the last months, it was as if her measurements of personal space were all off. Their breath seemed to mingle in the space between them. A faint flush warmed her cheeks and her stomach tumbled in anticipation—and nerves.

"I just need to put the cover on the car." Henri's voice was a dull murmur as he dropped her hand.

He strode to the corner of the garage and picked up a fabric drape for the vehicle, the cover crinkling in his hand. He always had a knack for keeping things safe and secure. The need to protect was part of his nature, and one of the things that was undeniably sexy about him.

The garage windows let the last rays of the evening sun pour into the space, bathing the walls in a twinkling amber light. She'd always loved this time of year—the way the autumn colors of the trees seemed impossibly brighter and sharper as New Orleans went from summer muggy to beautifully temperate. Even from her perch leaning against a sleek tool bench, she couldn't help but appreciate the way the wind whipped through the trees, gusting and causing them to rattle.

Fall was here. The time for dead weight to trickle from branches, even in the South, time for things to change. The hair on the back of her neck stood on end, goose bumps rippling down her body.

Her marriage was going to be one of those free-falling things. A beautiful leaf cascading from a tree. Perfect, vibrant—but not built to weather the harsh winter.

Holding herself together, she forced her eyes back inside the garage. Back to Henri as he tucked the car in for the night. His dark hair curled around his ears ever so slightly. He'd set aside the sunglasses and ball cap in the car on their drive home. Now, he stood before her in his plain, somewhat faded T-shirt. Perfectly casual. He wasn't America's poster boy or the team's golden boy. He was any man. He was hers.

And he was completely sexy.

Hitching herself up onto the tool bench, her leg swaying, she took in the way his muscled arms filled the sleeves of the T-shirt to capacity. But she also noticed the faint bruises that seemed darker on his tanned skin. The result of hours on the field, training with a resolve that had always made her proud. Henri's family had done well enough that he didn't have to work. And yet he poured his soul into his team.

As he stretched the cover on the Mustang, the car let out a low hiss. A tick of the vintage automobile.

Their date had turned quiet after their deep discussion at dinner. Had it been a good idea or bad? It was certainly the kind of subject matter their former marriage counselor would have encouraged.

In the brief time they'd attended therapy, they'd both alternated between quiet and boiling angry. Then they'd ended the appointments. She drummed her fingers against the cement tool bench, wondering if they had taken more time—tried a bit harder in therapy—would they be here right now?

Meanwhile, her looming biopsy had her stomach in a turmoil. She'd thought she had until the end of football season to ease out of her marriage, but the latest health scare put a whole new timetable on their relationship. If she didn't end things soon, Henri would absolutely dig his heels in for all the wrong reasons, staying by her side to help her battle for her health. Honorable, yes. But in no way related to love as a foundation for their relationship.

So this was possibly her last night to be on somewhat even footing with Henri. Their last night to be together.

Yes, she would have to get past the awkwardness of showing him her scars, but he'd helped her dress in the hospital more than once, seen the incisions. They'd even had that one failed attempt at lovemaking. He knew the extent, and certainly the scars had faded.

The plastic surgeon had reconstructed her body, and while he'd been the best of the best, the surgery had left her feeling less than normal.

But after the day she and Henri had shared, she found none of that mattered to her tonight. She'd married a sexy, generous, caring man and she'd never stopped wanting him. Spending the day together only reminded her how much.

This would be their last night to indulge in the passion she'd been fighting for months on end. She ached to reach out and touch him, to press herself against his tanned, toned body once more. To be with him. And after tomorrow...well, things might never be the same. So she'd put this on her terms. She'd go for this now and damn the future.

Fluffing her hair over her shoulder, Fiona inhaled a sharp breath, tasting the air. The scents of falling leaves and gasoline filled her nostrils. It was now or never.

"Henri, let's walk outside, savor the sunset."

He cocked his head to the side, his forehead creased with confusion. "Sure, sounds like a nice idea."

"We're blessed to have flowers longer in the season because of the greenhouse." And their garden was her own special haven, the place she felt most at peace. "Restoring that was the most thoughtful gift you ever gave me—other than those daisies."

They began outside. She took unsure steps, wending toward the greenhouse. Brilliant oranges and yellows flamed out on the horizon. A few birds trilled in the distance, chattering over something that sounded urgent.

"I'm glad to know there are happy memories for

you." His eyes wandered over their yard. Their home. The place they'd restored with a kind of passion she wished they could have applied toward restoring *them*.

She slid her hand in his, testing the waters for seduction. "There are many happy memories. I want to treasure those."

He squeezed her hand. "Me, too."

Henri's thumb ran gently across her knuckles. Slow and deliberate.

Opening the greenhouse door with one hand, Henri led them inside. The chill in the air was replaced by temperate warmth. The scents of rosemary and sweet flowers hung heavy in the air.

It was a stark contrast from outside. The plants in here hadn't succumbed to the change of fall yet. No leaves were hanging by threads; the flowers still bloomed. All was alive with possibility in this sheltered environment.

"Mmm. Do you remember the time we went to New York City?" Her voice was open and lithe as she allowed herself to look back through their entwined history.

"I haven't thought about that trip in forever. One of the best away games of my career."

"And?" she pressed. They continued into the greenhouse, heading for the back wall where there was a small clearing and some patio furniture.

"And also one of the best art galleries I've ever stepped foot in. Then again, having a built-in guide helps that."

He sat on the lounge chair, sinking into the plush cushion. Beckoning her, he patted the space next to him.

Folding herself onto the lounge beside him, she took a deep breath. "Well, my art degree is good for things like that."

"It certainly helps. It's probably why you are brilliant at assembling fund-raisers—you approach problems with such creativity." His voice trailed off as he stroked the back of her hair.

The simple touch sent ripples of pleasure along her skin, all the more potent for how long she'd denied herself those feelings. Those touches. She wanted to tip her head back to lean more heavily against him, to demand more. But after all the times she'd pulled away from him these last months, she wanted to be clear about what she wanted.

Spinning around on the lounge, she faced him. Scooting close to him, she slung her arms around his neck, drawing closer.

"Henri, I can't deny that I want you." She saw the answering heat flash in his dark eyes, but she forced herself to continue. "Please don't read anything more into this than there is, but right now, I just want us to finish this day together. To make another memory regardless of what tomorrow holds." She hoped he understood. That he wouldn't turn her away even though she wasn't sure she deserved him on those terms. "Say something. Anything."

"You've surprised the hell out of me. I'm not sure what to say other than yes." He stroked his fingers along her cheek. "Of course, yes."

Relief eased the tension inside her for all of a moment before another feeling took hold of her. His hands stroked up her arms. Over her shoulders. As the sun set, dim lights flickered on overhead via auto sensors. The warm glow added a romantic aura to the verdant space.

His fingers found the nape of her neck. Twisting her hair in his hands, he pulled her to him, their mouths barely touching. The feeling of warm shared breath caressed her lips.

Anticipation mounted in her chest. This moment was everything. She'd almost forgotten how fast he could turn her inside out with just a look. A touch.

And then his lips met hers, his mouth sure as he molded her to him. Tension and longing filled his kiss. It was in the way he held her. How he touched her. How he *knew* her. She melted into him, her body easing into his in a manner she hadn't allowed herself in forever. His tongue explored her mouth, making her rediscover a rhythm—a way of breathing. She dragged in air scented by hothouse flowers and Henri—his skin, his sweat, his aftershave, all of it intensified in the muggy greenhouse air.

Her hands sought his back, roving over the impossible cords of muscle as the passion between them picked up in intensity, as desire developed a course of its own. She wanted him more than ever. How could she not? This was a constant between them, burning hotter than ever.

Henri pulled back. The absence of his lips shocked her for a moment, and she blinked at him. Unsure.

A small, wicked smile played along his lips.

He held her hand, pulling her into him. His breath was hot against her ear. "Let's go inside, to the bedroom."

"Let's not. Let's stay here, together." She bunched

his shirt in her eager fingers, pulling it over his head as his grin widened.

"I always have appreciated your adventurous spirit."

His hand went beneath her dress. Nimble fingers teased up her leg, setting her desire into overdrive. He caressed a spot behind one knee, lingered along the curve of her hip as he kissed her, driving her crazy for more of him and his touch. She scooted closer on the lounger until she was almost in his lap, and he finally fingered the edge of her panties and slid his hand beneath the lace. Hunger for him coiled in her belly and she pressed herself to him harder. He pulled her lace panties down, discarding them on the floor.

Her whole body hummed with anticipation.

Taking a moment to appreciate his honed body, she edged back to run light fingers over the bruises on his arms. They were purple and dark, the result of sacks he'd taken and defensive players continually trying to chop the ball out of his sure hands. She carefully avoided putting a lot of pressure on them.

She looked at his bruises, suddenly aware of her own scars again. What would he think of them? She looked up to find him staring at her. Waiting.

"No spun glass. I am strong. A survivor." She needed to remind herself even as she wanted him to know it.

"I understand that. And before we go farther, I want you to know I do know what the scars look like now. More than just seeing you. After we talked to the doctor about surgery, I asked the plastic surgeon. I wanted to understand the during, the after, the years to come."

Frustration chilled her skin and the moment. "So

you wouldn't be shocked, turned off for life after seeing me in the hospital?"

He cradled her face in his hands. "I've never been turned off. Only concerned. I wanted to support you. And sure, I didn't want to look surprised or sad for you. I didn't want to risk hurting you, especially after what you'd gone through."

Some of the tension eased. She knew he meant it. And she refused to let some superficial insecurity steal this night from her. From both of them.

She turned her cheek into his palm and gently nipped his finger. "And now what do you think?"

She'd been afraid to ask before.

He skimmed his knuckles along her cheekbone. "That I'm glad you're safe. I pray every day you'll stay that way."

She clasped his wrist, stilling his hand. "Pity? Fear? Those are *not* turn-ons."

She needed to be clear on that point.

"Caring." He palmed her breasts. "It's about caring. You know me."

Delicious shivers of awareness tingled through her, her body wakening to life.

He eased off the rest of her clothes. Slowly and deliberately. With practiced hands, he unhooked her bra. The rays from the fading sun and dim interior lights danced against her bare skin, illuminating her completely. Scars and all.

Self-consciousness whispered through her no matter how much she told herself she knew the surgical lines had faded to a pale pink, barely visible. And her breasts were, if anything, perkier than before, although she had opted for a smaller cup size, going down from D to C. But he knew that already.

And she couldn't stop her thoughts from rambling.

As he took her in with his eyes, an unmistakable heat lit his gaze and a sigh of reverence passed his lips. He swiped a flower from a nearby pot. The stem snapped easily.

"You are so beautiful." He traced her scars with the petals of the flower, the timbre of his voice lowering an octave. The silky petals tingled against her skin, sparking desire in her bones. "Every inch of you."

"You don't have to say that." She deflected compliments so often.

"Have I ever been anything but truthful?"

"Not that I know of."

"Believe me then. Trust me. I look at you and I see beauty. Even more than that, I see strength, which is so damn mesmerizing it's the greatest turn-on imaginable."

A renewed commitment to this moment surged in her. Her hands snaked toward his bare chest. With gentle pressure, she pushed him back on the lounge chair. As the light from the sun faded behind the horizon, she surveyed the way his muscles expanded. He inhaled deeply. His eyes were fixed on hers, her need mirrored in his face.

Hooking a finger in his shorts, she edged them down and off. Climbing forward, she straddled him, pressing her hips into his. Feeling more alive than she had in months.

Henri didn't have a clue what had caused her change of heart, but after more than six months of being shut out by his wife, he wasn't passing up this opportunity to be with her. To taste and love every inch of her beautiful body.

Holding back from her every day had been hell. In the early days, of course, right after her surgery, it had been easy to give her space and time to heal. But after that, once she looked as strong and healthy as ever, he'd had to employ a ruthless amount of restraint to keep his distance.

And now, by some freaking miracle he didn't even understand, she was his again. Right here. In his arms.

He cradled her breasts in his hands, stroking, caressing, savoring the feel of her every bit as much as he enjoyed the sighs of pleasure puffing from between her lips. Everything about Fiona was sexy. Her wordless demands. Her hungry sighs. Her endlessly questing hands. He'd missed those touches. Hell, he'd missed the scent of her long, dark hair against his nose when they made love.

So now, it was sensory overload having her bare skin glide over his. She restlessly wriggled against him, the moist heat of her sex rubbing along his throbbing hard-on, driving him to the edge of frenzied need after so long without her.

He didn't see the scars, not in any way that mattered. He saw her. His strong beautiful wife, a survivor, who faced life head-on with bravery and strength. He thought of her giving heart, her philanthropy and the help she always gave to the other team wives.

What would it be like to travel with her again? To have her by his side in Arizona for his next game? Even though they couldn't travel on the same aircraft since he had to fly with the team and the spouses traveled separately, being with her, really being with her on the road, was something he'd missed. Having her in his bed at night was more than just a show of support. He missed talking to her, decompressing with her, telling her about the game he was passionate about.

He'd missed all of that as much as this. But this?

He felt as if he'd won the freaking lottery by taking her out on a date tonight. She braced her hands on his chest. He cradled her hips in his hands, lifting, supporting, guiding her...

Home.

The hot clamp of her body around him threatened to send him over the edge then. She felt so good.

So right.

Every glide was perfection as she rolled her hips and he lifted her up then back down again. Damn straight, sex between them was amazing. But he hadn't even remembered how incredible. Wasn't sure something this special could be captured in a memory.

Only experienced.

Their bodies kept time with each other. They pressed together, his mouth finding her lips. Her shoulder. Her hands twined in his hair. Her breath hitching, faster and faster, let him know she was close, so very close to her release. He knew her body well and intended to use that to bring her to a shattering orgasm while holding back his own for as long as possible. No way in hell was he going without her.

His hand slid toward her and he tucked two fingers against the tight bundle of nerves between her legs. Her husky moan gusted free, her head falling back. Her hair grazed her back as she rode him harder.

Damn straight, she wasn't a fragile flower. She took

him every bit as soundly as he took her. He reveled in the sight of her, her breasts rising and falling more quickly, her gasping breath, the flush spreading over her skin until...yes...a cry of bliss flew free from her mouth, echoing through the greenhouse. A bird fluttered in the rafters and, finally, he allowed himself his own release.

He thrust upward, deeply, his orgasm hammering through him. His heart slammed against his rib cage. The power of being with her was...more than he remembered. If he could even form words or a coherent thought. He could only feel each pulse of pleasure throb through him.

Her back arching, she fell forward against his chest. Her sigh puffed over his skin, perspiration sealing them together, connecting them further even as they stayed linked, his body in hers.

This moment had been what he was trying to construct for months. A moment of connection. Something real between them. Something built on emotion and trust.

Finally, after months of confusion and frustration, he felt alive with the possibility that this might be salvageable. Their trip to Arizona for his game would be like old times.

Lying in Henri's arms on the lounger, she planned what she wanted to do to his body through the night. Of course they would have to gather their clothes first, because running through the yard naked was out of the question. Even in the privacy of their garden beyond the greenhouse, there was always the risk of the media snapping a shot with a telephoto lens.

Nothing, nothing at all, could steal this evening from her. She had to make the most of this time with him, because this was likely all they might ever have. She couldn't even go to Arizona with him because of her biopsy.

If she even dared to tell him, it would only distract him from the game. Deep down, she knew he needed to stay focused. And she didn't intend to tell him regardless, though the excuse of work made her more comfortable in her decision to withhold information.

All of which she would deal with later.

His breath caressed the top of her head. "I've missed you."

"I've missed this, too. We've been through a lot, suffered lost dreams. Maybe if things had been easier for us…"

"I'm sorry, Fiona, so sorry I couldn't make this right for you. We can have children, adopt, foster—it doesn't matter to me."

As much as his words tempted her to throw caution to the wind and dive into the promise in his eyes, she couldn't escape the specter of fear that loomed inside her.

"It wouldn't be fair to bring them into a shaky marriage, anyway."

"You didn't say no to adoption outright, though. Not initially. Did you back out because you don't trust me? The marriage?"

"It was more than us. I wouldn't be honest if I didn't admit that my genetics have scared me lately. All the women in my family have died of breast cancer or ovarian cancer. As much as I worried about dying, the thought of a child losing her mother…" She swallowed hard. "That scares me to the point where I don't know what to think. So yes, adoption is something I've thought about. I wasn't sure how you felt."

"We really didn't talk about the important things in life, did we?"

As much as she wanted to share with him now, she couldn't bring herself to tell him about her biopsy tomorrow. She understood he would expect her to travel with him this weekend, to be there for him at his game. It was going to be hard as hell to push him away.

But for better or worse, she had to do this alone.

Seven

They made love in the greenhouse, the shower, again in their old bed.

Memories of their night together slammed into Fiona as she lay beside Henri in their four-poster bed. They'd spent the night entwined with each other. They'd slept naked. Well, he'd slept naked. Sleep had eluded her. She'd pressed up against him, too full of fluctuating emotions to actually drift off.

As morning crept closer, sleep was farther from her than ever. Instead, she watched the minutes tick by. Each successive change on the clock pulled at her heart.

She'd passed the night watching the steady rise and fall of Henri's chest as he slept. His rhythmic breath was raspy, his expression relaxed while she contemplated his bed-tossed dark hair.

She felt a pang in her heart. He was so damn sexy and last night would be the final night she would ever spend with him.

Even if the biopsy turned out all right, what about the next time? Fiona wanted to freeze this moment in her mind, to carry the essence of him with her for the rest of her life. The unraveling of their marriage was painful, and while a part of her loved Henri, she knew she was doing them both a favor by leaving.

So she did the only sensible thing she could. Fiona memorized him, noting all the small details that make a person complete. She watched the unsure morning light filter into the room. The muted sunshine seemed to get caught in his stubble, highlighting his square jaw. His long, thick lashes fluttered slightly.

Guilt and anxiety tickled her stomach. When he learned that she wasn't going with him, he would be devastated. The knowledge that last night hadn't changed anything between them would rock him to his core. She hadn't meant to rattle his focus before a game, knowing too well how hard that made things for him on the field. But there was nothing to do about it. Her mind was made up.

The sheets rustled and Henri shifted beside her. His even breaths hitched and he cleared his throat as he rolled closer to her. A growl of appreciation rumbled up from his throat an instant before his eyes opened to meet hers.

He slid a hand up to cup her neck and draw her to him. He sketched a tender kiss along her cheek, his bristly face scratchy and delicious. "Good morning, sunshine."

She pressed her face to his for an instant and allowed herself to savor every last sensation. "Good morning to you, too."

His arms extended out to either side. He stretched in a way that forced her to roll onto his chest. Ending the stretch, he wrapped his muscled arms around her naked body, pulling her close. A deep sigh filled the air as he cocked his head to the side to glance at the rising sun through the part in the curtains.

"God, it's later than I thought." He patted her bottom. "We gotta get moving. I have a plane to catch. I know yours is later, but wanna grab a quick bite of breakfast before I go? I know you have to pack—"

"Henri." She cut him short, unable to let him go on any longer. "I won't be flying with the other wives to Arizona."

He sat up slowly. "You're busy stepping in at the last minute to salvage the fund-raiser. I understand."

She wanted to use the excuse he'd handed her on a silver platter, but she could see now they'd let this play out too long. "Henri, last night was incredible—" she cupped his face "—a beautiful tribute to what we shared. But it was also goodbye."

Shock, then anger, marched across his face. "I don't know what's going on with you, Fiona, but you're wrong, dammit. Last night made me more certain than ever we are not finished."

She crossed her arms, pressing the sheet to her chest. "You can believe what you want, but my mind's made up. We can put off the official announcement to the public, however, we can't keep playing the charade at home and with our families. It's not fair."

Jaw tight, he studied her silently.

It hurt so much to see him hurt, and things would

only be worse if he guessed her secret. "Henri, you're going to miss your flight."

Exhaling hard, he turned away and flung aside the sheets, striding out of her room.

And out of her life.

The Hurricanes always traveled in their team jet, but today proved to be an exception. Their usual aircraft had been grounded for maintenance. Instead, the Hurricanes made their way to Arizona in a chartered luxury jet.

Henri wasn't having much luck enjoying the plush leather seats and open floor plan that made the jet feel less like a plane and more like a living room, the quarters as nice as anything his family owned. His thoughts stayed locked on Fiona. On last night and how damn close he'd been to winning her back. Yes, he'd made it into her bed again, but as always, one night wasn't enough.

Distracted as hell, he barely registered the interactions of his teammates. Freight Train Freddy tossed a football back and forth across the seats with Wild Card Wade. They hooted and hollered, pumping up the other guys with adrenaline. Even the veterans trying to play a card game in the corner were getting in on the action, fielding passes that came their way and taunting the guys on the other side of the jet.

Normally Henri would be leading the pregame amp-up charge. But today, he sat next to Gervais, the team owner, with a few of the other front-office members. Their seats up front kept them out of the fray.

Their Texas cousin Brant Reynaud, who also played for the Hurricanes, made his way from across the cabin. His yellow rose lapel pin glinted in the warm light of the cabin. He paused briefly to lean against the cognac leather chairs by Gervais and Henri, phone in hand.

"Did you see the Twitter feed? Our fans are loving us—all those pictures from the airport are viral." He gestured to his smartphone. "Someone on the media relations staff is doing a hell of a job connecting us to the public."

Brant clapped Gervais on the shoulder before continuing toward an empty chair by Freight Train Freddy, seamlessly reeling in a one-handed catch on his way.

The words barely registered with Henri. Pointedly fixing his gaze on the intricate chandelier in the center of the cabin, he wondered what the damages were going to be to replace the thing when someone hit it with a bad throw. Gervais pulled out his own phone to investigate the latest posts.

Gervais's face hardened as he thumbed through the Hurricanes' Twitter feed. A number of fans had rushed Henri and the other Hurricanes players in the airport. These types of things were normal. Fans always wanted autographs and photographs.

Today, however, had been a little different. Gervais's eyebrows skyrocketed as he flashed the six-inch screen of the smartphone to Henri.

Henri leaned over, hands resting on his thighs. Damn. The blonde from the airport who had gotten a little handsy with Henri had posted a photograph—one that had the potential for scandal. Not that it took much these days. People's marriages and careers had been ruined over less.

The thin blonde fan was dressed in high-waisted

shorts with a sheer chiffon crop top. She'd popped her leg and planted a kiss on Henri's cheek, anchoring herself by hooking their arms together. The image, out of context, didn't show the way Henri had tried to remove her and redirect her to a more appropriate pose.

A part of him longed for simpler, less connected days. Seeing how quickly the pictures in the airport circulated on Twitter left a sour taste in his mouth. This viral information was overwhelming, even when it was good news. When things looked slightly less than legit…viral information had a way of becoming deadly.

While Gervais was largely concerned with the team's image, he also no doubt worried about his brother. "Do you think that's safe, or even wise, given the current state of your marriage?"

Stomach plummeting, Henri ran his fingers through his thick, dark hair. "I wasn't encouraging her. I was working like hell to get away."

His brother nodded, but the stern expression didn't leave his mouth. "Oh, I know that. But you're in a career that puts you in the public eye. One picture. One sound bite. That's all it takes."

"And you think I don't realize that?"

Gervais didn't know the half of it.

"Just be careful, brother. Your marriage doesn't appear steady enough to weather this kind of pressure."

"What did Erika tell you?" In that moment, Henri regretted asking Erika and Adelaide for advice.

"No one has to. I know you." Turning the screen of his phone off, Gervais folded his arms over his chest.

"All marriages go through rough patches."

"Hmm." Gervais rubbed his chin in that wise big-brother way while saying absolutely nothing in the way of big-brother help.

"Don't pull that enigmatic bull with me."

Gervais gave a quick shrug of the shoulders. "You don't act the same around each other. You don't touch each other."

"You're in that newly-in-love stage, seeing hearts and stars." Henri tried not to snarl the words, but damn. Gervais's view of his marriage hit too close to home.

"You saw hearts and stars?" Honest surprise laced Gervais's voice as he unfurled his arms, leaning forward.

Henri jutted his chin in answer to that question. But the truth? He had seen stars. God, he'd been so in love with her then. What had happened? Or better yet, how had they gotten to this point?

"We're brothers, so I'm just going to say this and if it makes you mad, then I'm sorry. But here it is. We've seen with other couples in sports how infertility can put strains on even a rock-solid marriage," Gervais said softly. Sometimes he could be so matter-of-fact, peeling back the layers most people danced around.

Infertility clearly wasn't an issue with his brother, whose fiancée was already expecting twins after one weekend encounter. And Henri couldn't deny that stung. "I'm happy for you and Erika, but honestly, brother, do you think you're the one to talk to me about the strains of infertility on a marriage?"

"Point taken. Life isn't fair."

Bitter reality pulsed in Henri's veins as he shook his head. "Don't I know it?"

"Have the two of you talked about adoption?" Gervais didn't even turn when the chandelier finally took a hit, sending the glass medallions clanking together without breaking. He stayed focused on their conversation while Dempsey, the head coach, stood to call the group to order before the next pass broke the fixture.

"It's about more than not having kids. During a round of tests after another miscarriage, she found a lump in her breast." He'd carried the weight of those secrets long enough. And clearly, he hadn't been doing a good job of it, given how much Gervais had guessed.

"Damn. Didn't her mother and grandmother—" Gervais's voice had fallen an octave lower than normal.

Henri finished the sentence for him, nerves alight and fraying. "Die of cancer? Yes. She got tested for the gene and she's a carrier."

"I'm so damn sorry."

All the pressure and secrecy from the last few months came pouring out. Once uncorked, Henri found he couldn't contain the reality of his situation anymore. Fiona wouldn't be there in Arizona. Very soon, she wouldn't be part of his life at all. And that thought...it was too damn impossible to come to terms with. "We didn't just go to Europe for a vacation six months ago. Fiona had a double mastectomy and a hysterectomy while we were over there."

"God, Henri, I am so sorry. Why didn't you tell us?"

"She didn't want to."

Gervais gripped his shoulder and squeezed. "You didn't have to bear that burden alone. I would have been there with you."

"We didn't want to run the slightest risk of the press getting wind of this. Our privacy was—is—important." Still, it meant something to have his brother's support. He knew all of them would be there for him—and for Fiona, too, if she ever allowed anyone to get that close to her.

"Your call. Your decision. But I'm here if you need me, and there's nothing wrong with needing someone. You both lost your mothers young. That's difficult as hell." One thing about Gervais that no one could question was his fierce loyalty to his family. They were his tribe.

But that didn't negate the truth. A truth that still made Henri angry as hell. "Her mother died. Mine ran off because she was mad at Dad for not keeping his pants zipped."

"Death is tragic. Betrayal hurts like hell, too, like how our mom bailed on us even though her issue was with Dad's cheating. I can see how that would make it tough for you to trust. I've wrestled with that, too, in the past."

"Fiona isn't my mother." Not by a long shot.

"But she's leaving you." He paused, tapping the screen even though the image had faded to black. "Or maybe you've pushed her away?"

"That's crap," he quickly snapped. Too quickly? "I'm working my ass off to win her back."

"If you say so." Gervais looked away, reclining his seat.

"I thought you were here to help me," he couldn't help grousing.

Scrolling through his contact list on his smartphone, Gervais stopped at Erika's entry. He waved the phone at Henri. "For this mission, I'm calling in ground support from a certain extremely efficient princess I know and adore."

And just like that, Gervais asked Erika to deliver Fiona flowers from Henri.

Maybe he did need some more help winning back his wife after all.

The pain from her biopsy had nothing on the pain in her heart. The ache that was caused by a chapter of her life ending—the end of love.

She'd taken a taxi to the appointment because she didn't want to risk having the Reynaud chauffeur telling anyone else she'd been to the doctor.

Lying on the table during the procedure, she'd wished she had someone's hand to hold—Henri's hand. Not that they would have allowed anyone in with her anyway. Possibly having him in the lobby waiting could have brought comfort...but she'd made her decision and had to stick to it.

Now Fiona had sought sanctuary in the library, amid the books and art collection. She sat in an oversize Victorian chair, curled up in a throw blanket that featured famous first lines of novels in the design. She hoped the collective power of literature and art alone would seep into her veins and make her feel whole.

Settling into the chair, she had nearly become comfortable.

Until a knock at the front door sounded. Mustering energy and some bravado, Fiona made her way to the door, brown hair piled high on her head in a messy bun.

There were a lot of things Fiona was prepared for today. Company was not one of them. Her soul ached to be alone and to mourn her wounds and losses.

When she opened the door, Fiona's face fell. Erika was in front of her, armed with a card, a bouquet of lilies and baby's breath, and a decorative box of Belgian chocolate.

"Erika, what a surprise." Fiona forced a smile.

The Nordic princess braced her grip on the flowers and candy. "May I come in? Oh, and these are from your husband." She thrust the treats into Fiona's arms. "I won't be long. I have to catch the plane with the other wives."

"Of course, right this way," Fiona mumbled, urging her inside. She appreciated the gesture but somehow she knew full well this hadn't been Henri's idea. And it also meant their problems were becoming more public.

And she felt like a wretched ingrate. Forcing a smile, she thrust her face into the flowers and inhaled. "They smell lovely. Thank you."

Fiona set the crystal vase of lilies on the entryway table beside an antique clock. "Let's have a seat and you can help me eat the chocolates. How does that sound?"

Laughing softly, Erika patted her stomach. "The babies definitely need a taste of those chocolates. And they send their thanks to Aunt Fiona."

"Then let's dig in." Fiona led the way back down the hall to the library, taking comfort in the smell of old books and vintage art. This room was a place where everything was still in order—where things didn't have the pesky habit of uprooting and shaking her world.

Fiona tugged the red satin ribbon on the box of Belgian truffles. "Erika, you're glowing."

"Thank you. Double the babies, double the glow, I guess." She plucked a raspberry-filled truffle from the box with obvious relish. "Mostly, I just want to sleep double the time and eat double the food. Not very promising for a romantic honeymoon."

Erika's self-deprecation fell flat on Fiona.

"I'm sure Gervais understands." Fiona sat in a wing-back chair, cross-legged, the chocolates in her lap.

"He does. He has been incredibly patient." Erika looked around the library, absently rubbing her stomach as she chewed her candy. The motion played on the tendrils of Fiona's heartstrings. As if she could hear the pain in Fiona's heart, Erika looked up suddenly. A pale blush colored her cheeks. "I am sorry. I do not mean to babble on about myself."

"You don't have to hold back your joy." Fiona chewed her bottom lip, studying Erika's face. "Someone told you, didn't they, about Henri's and my fertility troubles?"

"I do not mean to pry." Erika dropped into a wing-back on the other side of the fireplace.

"You aren't. It's…well, I'm working on finding my comfort zone in discussing this with others in the family. It's painful, but that doesn't mean I can't celebrate your happiness. I love children and want to enjoy them." Fiona popped a creamy truffle into her mouth, but the high-quality chocolate tasted like dust. She set the box carefully on the end table beside her chair, leaving it open for her future sister-in-law.

"Want to?" Erika tilted her head, trying to understand what she was saying.

"I do. It's been a difficult road."

"Would you like someone to listen? We are family." Erika laid a strong hand of support on Fiona's forearm.

"We may not be family much longer."

Erika frowned and leaned forward to give Fiona's

hand a quick squeeze. The grace of royalty filled her expression. She spoke deliberately, a commanding reassurance filling her words. "I am so sorry to hear that. The offer to listen does not expire."

"Thank you." She reached to clasp her hand. "I hope you and Gervais are finding time to be together in spite of the busy season. That's important. Time slips by so quickly."

"I appreciate the advice." Erika inclined her head but—thank goodness—didn't call her hypocritical.

"And I appreciate that you didn't throw it back in my face, considering I have no children and am on the brink of divorce."

"You care about my future, Gervais's, the babies'. I can see that and appreciate it."

"I do. Henri and I rushed to the altar so quickly we didn't have much time to get to know each other."

"It is not too late to change that." Erika got up and straightened the books on the shelf, peering over her shoulder.

"How can you be so sure?"

"You are still here. So there is still hope, still time. Regrets are so very sad."

Regret. It was so damn hard to live with that hanging over her head.

Fertility was only half of the issue. And maybe, just maybe, she'd get the other half off her chest once and for all. The last thing she wanted was to live with regret, without ever giving her situation the dignity of a thorough examination. She'd already confided in Erika this much. Might as well see the situation all the way through.

"How are the wedding plans going?"

"Well, very well. We have a wonderful wedding coordinator."

"Is there anything I can do for you?"

"Just enjoy the day." She rubbed the swell of her stomach. "These two babies are growing so fast I may have to choose a new wedding gown."

"You will be a lovely bride."

Erika pointed to the couch at the end of the library. Taking a seat, she patted the space next to her, staring directly at Fiona. With kind eyes and a steady voice, Erika pressed on.

"You have something else on your mind. I can see that in your eyes. Since English is not my first language I tend to read eyes and emotions more clearly these days. Please speak freely."

"It's not my business, really." Fiona sat next to Erika, avoiding direct eye contact. Instead, her gaze fell on a Victorian-era depiction of the Greek goddess Artemis. Far easier to focus on art than the reality of her situation.

"Does it have to do with your difficulties with Henri?"

"I'm not even sure how to say this." A rush of dizziness pushed at Fiona's vision. Speaking this aloud would be one of the hardest things she'd ever done.

"Simply say it." Grasping her hand, Erika held on tightly, giving her reassurance and encouragement. Fiona couldn't meet her gaze.

But the words did tumble out of her mouth. "Henri and I got married quickly because we thought I was pregnant. I may have been and had an early miscarriage—or maybe Henri already told you this?"

Erika stayed diplomatically silent, just listening, which encouraged Fiona to pour her heart out.

God, how she needed to. "Since I had the one positive pregnancy test, I assumed…well…my point is, we rushed to the altar and didn't take the time to get to know each other. We have paid a deep price for that."

"I did not know the details. I am so sorry."

"Even if you go through with the marriage as scheduled, take time to be a couple. Your children are important, but having parents with a solid marriage will reassure them."

"Are you suggesting Gervais and I should not get married?"

"That's a personal decision. I'm simply sharing my experience and wanting to make sure you are certain. That's all. I hope I haven't offended you."

"Not at all. I insisted you tell me your thoughts and they are valid. My family pushes for marriage. You are the first to present the other side of the argument." She patted Fiona's wrist. "But please be assured. I have thought this through. I am in love with Gervais. I want to be his wife for the rest of my life."

"Then I am so very happy for you." And so very heartbroken for herself.

It was going to be a long weekend before the biopsy results came back, and either way she wasn't sure how she intended to handle things.

Eight

Fiona's whole body ached, even though only her left breast had been biopsied. While she'd put on a good show for her unexpected company the day before, she couldn't deny her relief at being able to suffer in bed away from prying eyes today. In the privacy of her bed, she felt the full force of the biopsy wash over her.

Erika had left with the other wives the night before, and Fiona had been alone. Over the course of the night, the pain had grown significantly worse. She'd hardly slept, finally dozing off at dawn.

Lying on her side, she kept the pressure off her chest. Although she was grateful to lick her wounds in private, her heart was heavy from needing to lie to everyone she loved. When Erika had stopped by, a small side of Fiona wanted to share the news of the biopsy with her. This burden was hard to shoulder alone, but Fiona knew there really wasn't an option. No doubt she'd distracted Erika enough from her impending wedding and giving birth to twins without saddling her with this, too.

Blinking back tears, Fiona wondered how long it would take for the pain medicine to kick in. Desperate for relief, she needed a distraction. Immediately. Glancing at the clock, she realized the Arizona game had already started. Had she really slept in that late, dozing off and on through naps?

Clicking on the remote, Fiona channel surfed until she arrived at the Hurricanes game.

Sitting up against the headboard in a sea of pillows, she situated the oversize nightshirt. One of Henri's shirts, actually, that still carried the scent of him. She'd allowed herself this small indulgence as she watched the game. Her fingers, seemingly of their own accord, fled to the loose cotton bra and bandage combination that shielded the places where she'd been pierced by the needle. Checking. Since she'd come home, the biopsy was a constant source of anxiety.

A long rumble sounded from the deepest point in her belly and she realized she hadn't really eaten anything. Easing carefully out of the bed, her bare feet hit the soft Persian rug, then the cooler wooden floorboards. She walked gingerly downstairs and riffled through the freezer—a woman deserved ice cream on a day like this. The best medicine a girl with an ailing body and a broken heart could get. She opted for a pint-size container of plain vanilla then plopped some of the chocolates Henri had given her on top. Taking a heaping spoonful, Fiona swallowed with bliss and made her way back upstairs to her bedroom to rest.

The flat screen mounted on the wall still echoed with the game. The daisies he'd given her earlier brightened the TV-lit room. Fiona had left the lilies he'd sent yesterday downstairs in the library in an attempt to spread out the reminders of what she was about to lose.

A heaviness pressed on her chest. This particular pain had nothing to do with the biopsy needles. It had everything to do with the large part of her that wished she'd gone to Arizona.

How she wished to be there cheering with the other wives, or even just waiting for him in the hotel room. To celebrate after the game. Her mind wandered back to the way her body had somehow, after all this time, synced to his two nights ago. Fiona wanted to have sex with him again, to pretend that none of this pain and suffering was real.

Scooping another large bite of ice cream into her mouth, Fiona turned her attention back to the game. Just in time to see the camera pan to the sell-out crowd, pausing on an older couple in matching football jerseys. The fans seated around them waved signs that read *Happy Sixtieth Anniversary!* and the smiling couple turned to one another to share a tender kiss on national television before the announcers moved on to comment about Arizona's offensive drive.

But her mind was stuck on that kiss. That celebration of a lifetime of love. Her mind rushed back to the gentle way Henri had cupped her head in his hands before kissing her. She tried to remember exactly the way his lips felt against hers—that gentle pressure of their kisses. The way his tongue had explored her mouth, leaving her breathless and ready for more.

And as she thought about him, the broadcast shifted to a close-up of her quarterback husband.

Soon-to-be ex-husband, she corrected herself. More ice cream.

Her gaze raked over him in his shoulder pads and away-game jersey, his features visible even behind the bars of his face mask. He was barking orders after the huddle, waving his arms toward the strong side of the field, reading the defense and making adjustments right up until the last minute in the way only he could.

He was one of the finest in the league and this season could be his best shot at finally earning the Super Bowl ring that he deserved to wear. She regretted not being a part of that. Even more, she would regret it if their breakup distracted him from that goal in a year when Dempsey and Gervais both agreed the Hurricanes had all the right pieces to win a championship.

But this was the business of breaking up. It was painful—the undoing of a person.

Suddenly wrought with grief—for her husband as much as for herself—her soul needed some reassurance. She reached for her cell phone and thumbed through the contacts, pulling up her father's new number in his retirement beach community in Florida.

One ring. Two rings. With each successive ring, she felt more uneasy about calling her father. What if he didn't answer?

She'd almost decided to hang up and abandon her idea to reach out to him. But on the fourth ring, as her heart pounded in her chest, she heard the phone pick up.

"Daddy?" She elbowed the pillow to nudge herself up higher on the bed.

"Fiona? Is something wrong?"

"Why does it have to be bad news for me to call my father?"

The lie slipped off her tongue. For a moment, she felt bad about being so damn practiced at lying about this terribly scary aspect of her life.

"Forgive me, let's start over. Hello, dear. How are you doing?"

Not well, and of course he was 100 percent on target that she'd only called because she was upset, but she had no intention of admitting that. "I just had some time on my hands and thought I would give you a call to catch up."

"Why aren't you at the Arizona game?"

Panic gripped her. She needed a reasonable excuse. Pushing the chocolate into the ice cream, she stumbled toward a feasible explanation. "I, um, have a cold, so it was better for me not to fly. Sinuses and all." Lame excuse. But better than the truth that would undoubtedly freak her father completely out.

"The game is a close one."

"You're watching? I don't mean to keep you."

"I can hear the game playing at your house, as well. Strange time for us to talk." His gravelly voice revealed nothing. Her father had always been tight-lipped. Well, at least since her mother had passed away.

"I'm sorry, Daddy. If you need to go…"

"No. Still plenty of time left in this quarter. I can watch this part on replay. So tell me. What's the reason for the call?"

Leave it to her practical accountant father to cut right to the point. Although that had made his meltdown over her mother's illness and passing all the more difficult to take. "Dad, what did we do for vacations before Mom got sick?"

"What makes you ask that?"

She was feeling her mortality? "Her birthday is near. I've been thinking about her more than normal. But the memories are starting to fade from when I was a kid."

The sigh coursed through the phone. "We'd take you to Disney. All you wanted to do was go there when you were small. Your mom would plan the whole trip— character breakfasts and character lunches. She loved Disney because it made you glow from the inside. Your mom would always take a bag of glitter with us and she'd sprinkle it on you before we'd walk through the main gates. Called it pixie dust and told you if you believed enough, your dreams would come true."

"I barely remember that." A sad smile played on her lips as she gripped the phone with a renewed intensity.

"Fiona? I'm not good about remembering to phone, but I'm glad to hear your voice. I'll miss your mother for the rest of my life. It was nice to enjoy that memory with you."

Sometimes, Fiona was struck at the way the memory of her mother elicited so much emotion from her father. He was normally so stoic, so practical. It always caught her off guard when he fell into telling stories about his bride, who'd been called back to heaven far too young.

Fiona hung up the phone not feeling any more assured about her life. Her heart swelled with the knowledge of too many deaths and too many people who had to deal with the memory of loved ones claimed by cancer.

Rather than feeling comforted, Fiona felt a new kind of sadness settle into her veins. Hearing the strain in her dad's voice as he recalled his late wife affirmed the logical reason that she had to leave Henri. If she left now, he wouldn't be hurt the way her dad was.

But that also meant she had to face this alone. Selfishly, that scared her to her core.

Henri had a lot of reasons to feel out of sorts. The Arizona game hadn't panned out for a few reasons. Though the one that continued to be the real source of agitation was the fact that Fiona had been states away from him.

Grabbing his duffel bag, Henri left the chauffeured car and headed through the front gates and up the walkway toward their Garden District home. The old three-story Victorian loomed ahead of him, jutting against the storm clouds brewing in the background.

Clicking open the door, he was greeted by silence.

Setting his keys down on the kitchen counter, he noticed the lilies he'd sent were in the middle of the kitchen island, card askew next to the vase.

While he had no idea what he was walking into, he was certain that he had to see Fiona. The need to be there for her—no matter how hard she pushed against the idea—gave him purpose.

He took the minimal amount of texting between them as a good sign. Though they didn't talk on the phone, they had still communicated. For Henri, as long as a line of communication was still open, he harbored hope for them. Believed they could work this out.

To allow his mind to wander to the alternative was

absolutely not an option. It admitted defeat, made him a quitter. And Henri was not about to do that when it came to his wife.

Quietly, he made his way up the stairs to her room, hoping to find her lost in a good book.

Instead, when he gingerly nudged the door open, he saw she was asleep. Out cold, really.

Something about her sleeping form seemed off. She was paler than normal, wearing a loose night-shirt and couched by pillows on both sides. Her bare leg was thrown over one of the pillows, which made his thoughts wander back to their night together. How damn amazing it had been to be back in bed with her again. It had been even better than before, because now there was no way in hell he would ever take for granted the gift of being with her.

Inside her.

Except then his mind hitched on the fact that something was off in her position, the way she lay with all those pillows. Her inexplicable paleness struck him as deeply odd. It registered in his brain, but he didn't know what to do with the information. So he tucked it away, saved it for later. He was too tired to analyze that now.

Unable to pull himself away from her, he slumped into the fat wing-back chair by the fireplace. The cushions were comfortable and he relaxed. His eyes grew heavy, until he was barely able to keep his lids open. And then they closed completely, and he drifted off.

His dream took him to a memory of when they'd just met. He'd whisked her away to watch him play a game in Philadelphia. The Hurricanes had had their first major win, and all he'd wanted to do was celebrate with her.

In the hotel room postgame, the passion that had danced between them was a palpable energy.

"How about a double victory?" she'd breathed coyly into his ear, hands traveling slowly down his chest and stopping at his waistband. Her hair had been longer then, wilder. There'd been an unquenchable desire in her eyes, and he'd wanted to do his damnedest to give her everything, all of him. They were young—lives and potential sparking before them.

The next day, they'd made themselves at home in Philadelphia, ducking in and out of museums and art galleries. While most people assumed Henri was incapable of appreciating culture due to his occupation, Fiona had simply rolled with his interest. Being an art major, she could have easily made him feel inferior or assumed that he was showboating.

But Fiona would never do something like that. The appreciation of art, she'd always said, didn't take a degree—it took appreciation for the human soul. And so, they'd stolen hours in that city, getting to know each other, body and soul.

On that trip, he'd known there was something that bound them together, a passion that twined them together. Yes, there was an undeniable physical component, but that was only half of it.

They'd returned to the hotel after debating the meanings of paintings and other fine points of culture. Back in the hotel, he'd begun to learn the way she liked to be touched, exploring the fire that burned beneath her skin. He needed to capture her as she was in this moment. And so, in the dream, he began to brush paint over her, to make her immortal on canvas. And what a muse she was for a man who'd never even considered himself an artist.

But then the dream shifted, as they often did. Fiona's surety and fire had been dulled, replaced by a self-consciousness he understood but couldn't fix.

He watched her fade in his arms, become ashen. The paint he'd used to capture her beautiful lines and curves ebbed away. In their stead, her body on the canvas was covered in scars.

Sweat pooled on his brow and he woke up with a start. Eyes adjusting to reality, he came to terms with the fact that he was dreaming.

He stayed in the chair because if he moved closer he wouldn't be able to resist touching her, making the dream a reality.

Casting a glance at Fiona, he was relieved to see her there. In the moment between sleep and alertness, he'd been afraid that she might be gone, fading away even now.

She tossed to her side, facing him now. His eyes roved over her, and he wanted to reach out and hold her. There had to be something—anything—he could do to win her back. So she missed a game. In the grand scheme of things, that didn't have to make or break this.

Maybe he'd take her to the new exhibit at the art gallery.

His thoughts on the gallery were short-lived. As he studied her, he noticed something dark against the white nightshirt.

Something that looked an awful lot like blood.

* * *

Fiona found it hard to stay asleep. The pain medicine had worn off, making it impossible to find a comfortable position.

Eyes fluttering open, she blinked into focus. Out of the corner of her eyes, she noticed a man in the wing-back chair. Momentary panic flooded her mind until she was fully awake.

Henri. He was back and in their room, his face stoic and hard.

Very slowly, she sat up. Pain pulsated. Fiona did her best to hide the wince that tore through her.

"Welcome back. Congratulations on a good game."

"We lost," he said briefly, curtly.

She understood how upset he could be over a loss. She leaned back against the pillows. The pain meds had her so woozy she wasn't sure she trusted herself to walk. "Defense wasn't at their best. You can only do so much. You threw two touchdown passes and ran another. But then you don't need me to recap what happened. I'm sorry."

"Are you?" Crossing his arms, anger throbbed in his voice.

"What do you mean?" She sat against the pillows, breathing through the pain that rocked her body.

"Are you sorry?"

"Of course I'm disappointed for you. I know how much a win means to you. Just because I knew the time had come for me to stop attending, that doesn't mean I won't be following the team's progress."

"Sure." His voice was sullen and she noticed, in the half light from the lamp by the wing-back chair, that his lips had thinned into a hard line.

"Henri? What's with the clipped answers?" She was too foggy from pain meds that weren't doing enough to dull the ache to sort through these mixed signals from him. "I understand you're unhappy with my decision to not attend the game—"

"I'm not happy with your decision to keep me in the dark about the real reason you stayed in New Orleans."

How had he found out? She followed the line of his gaze and realized he was looking directly at her left breast where…

Oh, God. Her biopsy incision was leaking spots of blood.

Nine

A jumble of emotions played bumper cars in Henri's mind. The blood on her left breast…the way she tried so hard to push him away.

How could she keep this from him? Frustration—and, hell yes, fear—seized his jaw. He ground his teeth, feeling something that felt a bit like betrayal.

That she had kept him from knowing something major—and potentially life threatening—was too much to digest.

His fingers pressed into the arms of the chair as he tried stabilizing himself. Part of him wanted to run over to her side, to hold her tight against him. But knowing she was sick and in recovery, the possibility and fear of injuring her made him stay firmly planted in his chair.

Scared as hell.

"What's going on?"

"I think you've already guessed." She tugged at the white covers on the bed. But she didn't look directly at him.

A lump grew in his throat. Terrible possibilities ran through his mind. "Were you even going to tell me at all?"

She tipped her chin upward. "Not if I didn't have to. No need for both of us to worry."

They'd fallen so far apart that they didn't share something as huge as this? He'd been by her side every step of the way through medical treatments, and now she was trying to cut him out of her life. Completely. Excise him like cancer.

No. Not a chance. "Details," he demanded softly, but firmly. "I want details. We're still married. We owe each other that much."

"It's just a biopsy of a lump that's likely fatty tissue dissolving. The oncologist is almost certain it's nothing to be concerned about."

She said it as casually as someone reporting the weather. He felt the distance spread between them like an ever-collapsing sinkhole.

Oncologist? But no, it wasn't serious. "If it was nothing, you would have told me. This is why you didn't go to the game. I would have understood."

She pushed her tousled hair back, her eyes fuzzy with what appeared to be the effects of pain meds— and sure enough, a bottle rested on her bedside table. "You would have been distracted. You would have gone crazy worrying. Look at how you're reacting now."

"I am in control. Here for you, always." Why couldn't she see that?

"That's good and honorable of you to say, but it's not the reason I want you staying with me."

"So if I hadn't seen the spots of blood you wouldn't have told me at all?"

Drawing a pillow in front of her chest, she let out a small sigh. "If the worst happens, then of course you would find out. Otherwise there was no reason to upset you."

The way she discussed her health with such nonchalance rubbed him raw. As if the only reason he would care to know if she was sick was bound up in some sense of honor and duty. That did him a disservice, minimized their bond. He did not stay with her merely for appearances' sake or to come across as honorable. Dammit, why couldn't she see that?

"Did it occur to you I would want to know, to be there to support you?"

"Thank you. But you don't have to do that anymore." She smoothed a wrinkle on the pillow and gave him a pointed stare.

"I'm your husband, dammit." He reined in his temper. "I'm sorry. I didn't mean to snap at you. Could I get you something to drink? Or an ice pack for the biopsy site?"

"You know the drill." She slumped back on the pillows, her eyes sad.

"I do. Is that so wrong?"

"I don't want you feeling sorry for me."

He ignored that. Couldn't even imagine how to make her understand his desire to care for her had nothing to do with pity.

"When will you hear from the doctor?"

"Next week."

"I have one question. How long have you known?"

"Since the day of the pet rescue fund-raiser."

He inhaled sharply. He pressed his fist to his mouth—he'd hoped she had only recently found out, that it had been some sort of emergency operation. That would be much easier to swallow.

"You weren't late because your car broke down. You've been lying all week."

"I've been protecting you and protecting my privacy."

The bedroom started to become suffocating as he looked around, seeing the life they had jointly built. It all felt like a lie. Some kind of story he'd been telling himself.

More frustration piled on top of the old, building up inside him when he was already exhausted and on edge. He knew somewhere in his gut that getting out of this room was his only option. Before he said something he'd regret.

"Right." Shoving the chair out from underneath him, he sprung to his feet. From the threshold, he called over his shoulder, "I'll get you that ice pack."

With every step, Fiona drew in sharp breaths. The movement pounded in her chest, causing pain to spiderweb through her shoulder.

Of all the ways she'd envisioned Henri finding out about the biopsy, this hadn't been one of them. With slow, determined steps, she made it to the first-floor landing and caught a glimpse of her reflection in the hallway mirror.

The mirror was expansive—and Victorian. Cherubs with lutes and lyres danced down the frame, twisting and turning in endless patterns. She'd found it at a flea market years ago and fallen in love with the distressed glass.

As she examined her reflection, depression edged her vision. She was a mess. Tempest tossed. Those were her initial assessments.

Her brown hair was swept up in a high ponytail but was completely disrupted from troubled sleep. All her tossing and turning had loosened it. Her pallid complexion and tired eyes did nothing to improve matters. Pulling on the corner of her clean oversize shirt, she felt like a shadow.

Clutching her favorite Wedgwood bowl full of ice cream, she charged into the kitchen. When she rounded the corner, a wave of nausea overcame her. A by-product of the pain medicine. Taking a moment to regain her balance and calm her stomach, she eyed Henri nervously.

He was leaning against the kitchen island with his back to her. He fumbled with the ice pack, but his head was cocked to the side, examining the news story on television.

It was entertainment news, overhyped coverage of celebrity outings and gossip.

Spinning into focus was a photograph of Henri with another woman. Her body was pressed against his.

Old news. That had already popped up on Fiona's radar. She knew such a photograph didn't mean a damn thing. Fans were sometimes aggressive and pushy. Henri might be a lot of things, but a cheater? Not in his wheelhouse.

Still, sadness swept over her as her toes curled against the cool tile floor.

This photograph might not be real...but after their divorce was finalized? Well, then these types of photographs might actually be evidence of a new relationship for Henri. Her heart fell ten stories in her chest as she stared at him.

Bad enough to end a marriage and know that your ex would probably move on and find someone new. That dynamic would be much more intense for her. Henri, rising star quarterback, would be front and center in the news. She'd be forced to watch him fall in love with someone else.

The thought hit her like a ton of bricks.

He must've felt her eyes on him. He whirled around, face flushed, pointing at the screen. "That's not what—"

"I know it isn't." She steadied herself on the coffee bar.

"You do? You trust me even now?"

"I trust that you wouldn't sleep with another woman while you're still married to me." Knowing that made it all the tougher to walk away from this man. He was a good person. He deserved better from life than he'd gotten in their marriage. She knew she wasn't easy to live with and her ability to deal with stress—well, here they were.

"Thank you for trusting me." Some of the stiff tension in his shoulders eased, although she didn't think for a moment he'd forgiven her for holding back.

"I believe in your honor, your sense of fair play." That had never been a question.

"I've never wanted a woman as much as I want you, always."

Her hands wrapped her body in a protective cocoon. Tears pushed at the edge of her vision. "But I'm not the woman you married."

He stepped toward her and wrapped his hands around her waist. Pulling her into him, he whispered into her hair, breath hot on her ear, "You're every bit as beautiful. No matter what else happens between us, the attraction hasn't stopped."

"Even with the surgeries?" The words squeaked out, finding vulnerable life in the small space between them.

"I still see you." He lowered his face to hers.

Fiona wanted to believe him. Wanted things to just stop spinning out of control. But...but there was physical evidence that she could never be the same.

"But there are scars. Even with the best plastic surgeon money could buy. And there's always going to be the specter of another lump and biopsy."

"I married you for what's inside. And I'd like to think that's what you wanted me for, too." He stroked her back with warm, strong hands. "Even if there had been no reconstruction at all, I would want you. You know that."

"I do. And it makes it all the tougher to resist you."

"Then don't resist me." Tipping up her chin, he gently pressed his lips to hers.

For the briefest moment, she indulged herself in the kiss. Let herself melt into his lips and the beautiful familiarity of being in his arms, of letting the musky scent of him fill her senses. After the fear and stress of the past day, she took comfort from his strong arms and the hard wall of his chest. The steady beat of his heart was echoed by hers; they were in sync. They'd been that way once, so in tune with each other. God, she hadn't imagined all of it, had she?

She deepened the kiss, loving the taste of him and the hint of toothpaste. She gripped his T-shirt in tight fists as she nipped his bottom lip. Henri's hands fell gently to her shoulders.

"Careful, Fiona," he whispered, brushing his lips along her mouth, then her cheek.

It was a tender, lovely moment…and yet there was something off. In the way he held her, maybe? His touch was far too light.

She angled back to study his brown eyes awash with molten emotions. "Henri? What's going on? This feels suspiciously like you're treating me as if I'm some fragile glass figurine. Like spun glass. Like when I got the operations six months ago."

His eyes went so dark the ache was downright tangible. "Damn straight I'm being careful with you. You're bleeding, on pain meds, and I wasn't there with you. How the hell else am I supposed to treat you?"

His pain reached out to her until she could barely breathe from the weight of it. Images filled her mind of her father, frozen in his reading chair, newspaper upside down in his tight-fisted grip as tears streaked down his face. Her grandmother and aunt shushing her, guiding her from the room. Later helping her pack for boarding school. Then college. Then they were gone, too. The women's husbands had all stood like hollow shells at their funerals.

Oh, God, it was too much. She needed space. Air. More space. She couldn't think clearly. She was about to shatter like the glass he seemed to think she was made of. And of course he would pick up the pieces no matter how those shards stabbed at him.

Breaking contact, she laid a hand on his chest. "I think you should stay at your family's place tonight."

Lips thinning into a stoic mask, he took a deep breath. His jaw grew taut. But his emotions stayed hidden. She'd seen him do that often in the past, protect her from anything unpleasant—or anything real.

Stepping away from her, he folded his arms over his chest. "We're not divorced. And I'm not leaving you here alone when you're recovering."

She also knew that look well. An entire line from an opposing team wouldn't stand a chance of sacking the immovable force he'd become.

Fiona filled her morning with forced movement. She needed to stay busy, to bounce back from the biopsy and from the impending fracturing of her heart.

Henri had left for the gym early in the morning. She'd been awake when she heard him make his way down the stairs. Part of her wanted to crawl out of bed to talk to him. Fiona knew better, though. She had to guard her heart. He'd only briefly come to the doorway and told her he wasn't comfortable with her being alone on pain meds, so he'd arranged cleaning help for the day and a car to drive her if she wished to go anywhere.

The stony look on his face didn't leave room for argument. And he was right. She needed help and should be grateful. In her need to protect him from hurt she was still causing him pain, and she couldn't seem to work her way out of the messy maze she'd made of her life.

So she'd stayed in bed waiting until she heard his car drive away before she got up and dressed herself.

Pulling her thoughts back to the present, she tried to focus on the sensation of sun on skin. She and the other Reynaud women were lounging by the oversize pool at the main family complex on Lake Pontchartrain. Giggles surged through the air—the family was at peace. Several team wives were there as well, getting to know Erika better, which was part of the reason Fiona had felt she needed to be here. Hell, she wanted to be here.

But it was tougher than she expected, watching them joke with each other, all so happy and healthy.

All of them except for her.

Though fall was settling in, the heated pool provided sanctuary from the light, chilly breeze. Fiona watched the sunlight dance in the pool as Erika dipped a toe, testing the water.

Fiona sighed, listening to the chatter of bugs and birds as she tried to appear normal. Such a difficult ruse, especially since she'd had no choice but to make use of the chauffeur if she'd wanted to join in the outing. And she had wanted to, so very much. Still sore from the biopsy, she'd forced herself here. Determined to embrace the world.

A loose but elegant navy dress clung to her body, positioned just right to hide the scars.

Adelaide tossed her head, easing herself onto the first step of the pool. A wicked grin warmed her eyes. "We should go lingerie shopping."

"What?" The suggestion snapped Fiona back into the moment. Lingerie shopping would be pretty damn difficult in her state.

Swirling her foot in the water, Adelaide continued, "The new bride will need new lacies. We can call it an impromptu lingerie shower." She whipped out a gold credit card. "Lunch is on me."

Erika's rich peal of laughter resonated on the patio. "I am getting very big very fast. I will not be able to wear the underthings long."

Adelaide winked, emerging from the pool to sit next to Erika. "If you're doing it right, he'll tear them off your body and you'll only be able to wear them once."

A faint blush colored Erika's snow-pale skin.

One of the linebackers' wives spoke in a low rasp. Macie's gray-streaked auburn hair framed her angular face, her crow's-feet crinkling as she sipped on a bottle of water. "I wore bikini panties under my belly for the whole pregnancy."

"I wore thigh-high stockings and a cute little thong. Drove my man wild."

Adelaide nudged Erika with her shoulder. "I've got one! This isn't pregnancy related, but Dempsey goes nuts when I wear these black strappy heels. Does it every time. I'm half inclined to think they are magic."

Erika's moonlight-blond hair rippled as she laughed, and then put her hand to her stomach. "Fiona? So spill. What does that sexy man of yours like you to wear?"

Adelaide turned to face Fiona, brows raised in anticipation.

How to answer that? Sitting up, she choked on the words. Nothing came to her lips.

The stress of the past few months had taken an additional toll on Fiona. She'd unintentionally lost weight. What she hadn't realized was how much weight.

As she shrugged, attempting to brush the question off, the shoulder of her dress slipped down her arm.

Revealing the bandage from the biopsy. And the very edge of the scar just under her breast line from the mastectomy and reconstruction.

The laughter from the other wives stopped. All attention and eyes rested on her.

There was no use in pretending anymore. The charade had finally bested her. In vague horror, she watched their gazes trail from her torso to her face. Watched the transformation of pity in their eyes.

"When? How did no one know?" Erika breathed, rising to her feet. With slow, waddling movements, she made her way to Fiona's side. Sitting down with royal poise, Erika searched Fiona's face while the other team wives stayed diplomatically silent.

"We didn't want anyone to know. We just...took one of our trips and had the surgery done."

Adelaide plopped on her other side, putting a hand on Fiona's back. She ran her hand in small circles up and down her back. "But you have this whole big family here that would have wanted to be there for you. I know they would. The team family, too."

Flashes of her childhood drama and trauma scrolled through her mind. Somehow containing the pain and emotion had seemed easier this time. Had she been wrong? She didn't know. She only knew she and Henri had made the best decision they could at the time. "I'm not certain how to explain it other than to say so much of our lives was in the spotlight, we just wanted to crawl off and be alone."

"Did that help?" Leave it to Erika to be direct. But Fiona preferred that to being treated like a glass mannequin. Looking back and forth from Adelaide to Erika, Fiona noticed that they didn't seem to feel pity. Just concern.

"I thought so at the time. But now I think it could have helped Henri to talk to his brothers. Even if their advice stunk, just to lean on them. Maybe I was being selfish."

Adelaide's voice came out like a wind-tossed whisper. "How so?"

"Wanting him all to myself. I had no one else." She rubbed her temple. "I never really thought of it that way until now." Her eyes stung with tears and regret.

Giving her hands a quick squeeze and a gentle smile, Erika asked, "So you made the decision all on your own to keep it quiet?"

A dark laugh escaped Fiona's lips. "Sounds like you already know the answer to that one. Henri was emphatic about not wanting the press involved. He wanted things quietly handled."

"Even kept from family?" Adelaide asked in a quiet voice. "That was your decision to make. I'm just sorry we didn't provide the support we all would have wanted to give you both."

Fiona had been so concerned with handling this discreetly, she had never stopped to consider what Henri might have needed. So focused on her own needs, on her own wounds, she had been blinded.

In this small moment, as the afternoon sun streamed onto the pool patio, she began to understand that she had deeply hurt Henri. Which was the one thing she had been desperately trying to avoid doing.

The world started spinning. She felt distant from her surroundings. Had she really made the wrong choices?

Ten

"I owe you an apology," Fiona said softly as she stepped into Henri's room in his childhood home at the Reynaud family compound. Not the home they shared on the lake. For whatever reason, Henri had chosen to stay at Gervais's house. It had been tough to find him, but she'd tracked him down.

Now she wondered if that was wise, but there was no leaving.

She felt as if he'd put as much distance between them as he could by coming here, staying under his brother's roof instead of at their second home just up the lane. Could it have something to do with the fact they'd once lived there together? Or maybe it was the nursery they'd decorated for the child they'd lost—a room they'd never changed back. Her throat grew tight, so she blocked that thought. Maybe here was best after all.

Heart pounding, she stepped across the threshold, eyes still adjusting from the bright sun of the fall day.

Blinking slowly, she scanned the room.

The small suite, filled with trophies and photographs of her husband's high school and college careers, felt like a shrine to Henri's past. She hadn't set foot in here for a long time, but she'd always been fond of the large, gold-framed photograph of the Reynaud brothers and Grandpa Leon. The brothers had all still been in high school at the time of the photograph, and Grandpa Leon had had plenty of energy then.

The photograph pulled at her already raw heart. Refusing to become sidetracked by Grandpa Leon's state, she pressed on into the room, leaning on one of the oak poles of the four-poster bed. Henri's eyes stayed fixed on the bed where his suitcase lay open. With a sigh, he yanked another shirt from the suitcase and slung it into an open dresser drawer. Without looking at her, he asked, "How are you feeling?"

Apparently he wasn't in the mood for an apology. Sitting on the edge of the bed, she felt awkward, as if she was forcing her way into this space.

But she had to try. "A little sore but otherwise okay. I didn't even have to take a pain pill today."

"Glad to hear that. I hope you're resting enough," he said in a quiet voice, almost a monotone. Noncommittal.

"It was a biopsy. I'll be fine."

"Just be careful." For the first time since she'd walked into the room, he looked at her. His dark eyes were full of concern.

"In case I need to be prepared for something worse?"

He shrugged, leaning against the dresser. The subtle pressure caused one of his childhood baseball trophies to shift. "You're the one who said that. Not me."

He picked up an old football off the dresser. It was signed by all of his college teammates. Tossing it lightly from one hand to another, he grimaced.

Putting her fingertips to her lips, she took a moment to compose her thoughts, noting the hurt in Henri's expression.

"And that's why I'm here to say I'm sorry for not telling you about the lump and the procedure. Even though we're separated, we're still married. We share an intense history."

"Thank you for acknowledging that." As he folded his arms across his chest with the football still clutched in one hand, she noted the tension in his clenched jaw.

"You've been kind. You've been understanding. You deserve better than the way I treated you."

"You've been through a lot. I understand that." He set the ball down carefully on the dresser again.

"Please take this in the spirit intended, but it's damn hard to be married to the perfect man."

Henri let out a choked laugh, dark hair catching the glow of the lights. "I'm not sure what spirit to take that in at all—and I'm far from perfect. Just ask my brothers."

Her head to the side, she linked her hand with his. "So you'll accept my apology for not telling you about the biopsy?"

"I'm still upset, but yes, I can see that you're sorry..." His voice trailed off and he looked down.

"But?"

"But I'm certain you wouldn't do things differently. Even though you're sorry, you would still shut me out."

He held up a hand. "Don't say anything either way to agree or deny."

He hauled the suitcase off the bed, headed to the ornate closet door. Etched molding that resembled Grecian columns framed the door. Whenever she came here, the details always caught her off guard. Every visit yielded a new dimension of awareness. She'd lived in their Italianate monstrosity across the road. She should have been able to call all this home, but when had she ever taken the time to settle in?

That lack of awareness, it seemed, extended to her understanding of Henri. Now, as he put the empty suitcase in the closet, she began to understand his point of view a bit more clearly.

"We have problems. Big problems. Obviously. I just want us to find peace."

"I agree." He turned to take her by the shoulders, his whole hulking body radiating pain. "You'll be sure to tell me the second you know the results of the biopsy?"

"Of course. Right away." And she could feel how much he cared, really cared. That tore at her, left her feeling conflicted all over again. Just when she was sure she could walk away, doubts plagued her as she felt how much he cared for her. How deeply she was affected by him.

She stroked her hand over his hair, sketching her fingers along the thick, coarse strands. "I truly am sorry I hurt you. I wish our lives could have been easier. That we didn't have to face biopsies and infertility."

"Life isn't guaranteed to be easy." He leaned into her touch.

"I don't know if things would have been smoother if we were chasing a cute little toddler around now."

The tears of loss and regret stung. "A little girl with your brown eyes and feet that never stop because she loves carrying around your football."

"Fiona, you're killing me here." He put his arms around her, careful to avoid her left side.

She let herself enjoy the warmth of his embrace. She couldn't bring herself to step away. Keeping distance between them the past months had been torture and right now she couldn't recall why she had to.

Pressing her ear against his chest over the steady beat of his heart, she slid her arms around his waist. She took in the musky smell of his soap and a scent that was 100 percent Henri. Her husband. Her man.

She heard the shift in his breathing at the same time her own body kindled to life. She shouldn't be feeling this way right now. Turned on. Aching to make sweet tender love to him.

Henri nuzzled her hair. "You should rest."

Angling back, she met his gaze dead-on. "I don't want to sleep. I want you to make love to me. Here. Now. No thinking about tomorrow or what we'll say after. Let's be together—"

He kissed her silent, once, twice, holding the kiss for an instant before speaking against her mouth. "You won't hear an argument from me. I want you. Always. Anywhere, anytime."

He walked her back toward the bed, sealing his lips to hers every step of the way until her legs bumped the footboard. He angled her back onto the mattress, cradling her body with arms so strong, so gentle. She sank into the puffy comforter, reaching for Henri only to have him drop to his knees at the foot of the bed. He bunched her skirt up an inch at a time, nibbling along the inside of her left leg, stroking her other leg with his hand.

He made his way higher. Higher still. Until...

Her head pushed back into the bed as she sighed in anticipation. His breath puffed against the lacy silk of her panties, warming her.

"Lovely," he murmured.

"I went shopping."

"I was talking about you." He skimmed the panties off and his mouth found her, pressing an intimate kiss to the core of her.

She felt his hum of appreciation against her skin. She grabbed fistfuls of the blanket and twisted, pleasure sparking through her. His tongue stroked, circled, teased at the tight bundle of nerves until her head thrashed restlessly against the bed. Her heels dug into his back, anchoring him, but also anchoring herself in this oh-so-personal moment. She ached for completion. And one flick at a time he drove her to the edge of release, backed off, then brought her even closer, again and again until she demanded he finish, now, yes, now... And he listened with delicious attention to her need.

Gasps of bliss and, ah, release filled the air as ripple after ripple of pleasure shuddered through her. Her back bowed upward and her fingers slid down to comb through his hair as he eased her through the last vestiges of her orgasm.

Gently, he slid her legs from his shoulders and smoothed her dress back into place. He stretched out beside her, carrying them both up to recline against the pillows.

She traced her fingers along his T-shirt. "That was

amazing. Thank you. This may sound obvious, but it feels so good to feel good right now."

"That was my intent."

She pressed her mouth to his. "I want us both to feel good again. Make love to me."

"But you're recovering…"

"There's no reason we can't have sex as long as you're gentle." A smile tugged at her lips. "Ironic and a little funny, but I'm actually asking you to treat me like spun glass."

"I'll take you any way I can have you, lady. You're perfect, you know that, right?" He pressed kisses against the curve of her neck.

"Far from it, but thank you." She angled her head to give him easier access.

"I mean it. You're beautiful and giving and smart." His hands moved reverently over her long dark hair, skimming low, lower still and then back up again to rest on her shoulders.

"What brought this on?" She touched his face, reveling in his stubble, in his dark eyes.

"I just wanted to make sure you know. I think I get so caught up in gestures, I forget to give you the words." Gentle fingers traveled from her lips to her neck, causing shivers to run wildly down her spine. Sparks lit her nerves, the tingling then gathering at her core.

"Well, thank you for those lovely words. I appreciate it. I do understand that I am not defined by my breasts," she said.

Kissing her collarbone, he pulled her flush against him. "I'm glad you realize that."

Her heart filled again with something that felt like hope.

* * *

With Fiona asleep in his bed, he felt better than he had in weeks. Hell, better than he had in months. The scent of her on his linens was something he didn't take for granted. He'd missed this. Missed her. And looked forward to devoting even more attention to persuading her to stay right here.

But still…he felt compelled to move. To walk about the house to process the 180-degree change he saw in Fiona.

He slid out of the silk bedsheets, his feet landing on cool marble tile. On tiptoes, he made his way out of the room.

When was the last time he'd spent any time out at the lake, trying to ferret out an answer to a complex problem? He couldn't remember. He and Fiona had spent so much time trying to give themselves privacy, he'd forgotten what it was like to share space with his brothers. To ask for help.

Now, staying in this wing of his childhood home, he could see his older brother's stamp on the place. He'd made changes to personalize the home, yet he'd kept so many things from their past, too. Leaving Henri's old bedroom untouched had been a welcome surprise.

For the most part, he barely registered the mammoth house anymore. Greek Revival wasn't his style—it felt too rigid and restrictive. As he walked through the house, he found himself appreciating the quirky charm of his home in the Garden District. The eclectic Victorian space he and Fiona had reconstructed.

Needing to talk, he searched for his brother. After all, Gervais had pushed him down this path by sending his fiancée, Erika, to deliver flowers to Fiona.

Catching sight of his brother's silhouette by the pool, Henri opened the sliding glass door. Gervais stood, back to the house, on the path that led from the pool to the dock.

Gervais's shoulders were slumped. Heavy as the boughs of the live oak trees. Fragrant ginger and bushes lined the paths around the pool, next to a round fire pit surrounded by a low wall of flat rocks. A glider swing with a seat as big as a full-size bed anchored the space, which was draped in breezy white gauze threaded with a few tiny twinkly lights overhead.

His brother's hands were linked behind his back. As Henri drew closer, he could see that Gervais was squeezing his hands so tight they were turning white.

Surveying the landscape in front of them, Henri watched the dying light bathe the wooden dock in rich oranges. At the end of the dock, the pontoon boat was hoisted out of the water. They'd spent many nights out on that pontoon boat—and the yacht off to the left— when they were younger. As he looked at the pontoon boat, he felt a wave of nostalgia wash over him. Things felt simpler then. But he knew that wasn't actually true. Nothing about his family had ever been simple.

These past few months had been a strain on Henri's relationship with his family. Everything between his brothers and him had been placed on autopilot. Nods and lies became the default modes of communication.

Had those months of evading serious conversation come at the high cost of neglecting to see that his brother had been struggling? Impending marriage and managing the team were enough to test anyone, even his collected and cool older brother.

Henri tried to imagine what was on Gervais's mind:

owning the New Orleans Hurricanes, having a winning season, even what was going on with their baby brother Jean-Pierre's career as a New York quarterback.

And smack-dab in the middle of all that, Gervais was trying to plan a wedding to a princess and keep it out of the public eye, all while facing fatherhood. And Dempsey was engaged. Life was moving forward at full force.

"What are you doing down here?" Henri asked.

"Reliving the old days." Gervais's chest expanded as he breathed deeply. A football lay at his feet. He gave it a shove with his shoe.

"Do you miss it?" Henri gestured to the pigskin.

"Sure I miss playing sometimes. But I'm not you, living and breathing for the game. Honestly. I like being the brains behind the larger operation."

"Impending marriage and fatherhood has made you philosophical."

Gervais shook his head. "Practical. Focused."

"I'm so damn tired of people questioning my focus."

"People?" Cocking his head to the side, Gervais stared at his brother. It was a knowing kind of glance, one that chided him to be more specific.

"My family." He practically spat the words from his mouth.

"You *are* staring at a possible divorce." Such a blunt statement. As if Henri wasn't aware of the state of his marriage.

"So are half the guys out there playing."

"But you love your wife."

Henri stared hard at the lake, his voice growing quiet, the words feeling like ash as he spoke them. "I thought I did."

"You do, you big idiot."

Henri shoved Gervais's shoulder. "I hate it when you pull the wise big brother act."

"Then do something about it—you're the Bayou Bomber, for God's sake. You run the Hurricanes' offense from the quarterback position, slinging record-setting pass yardage with an arm destined for the Hall of Fame. You can't do better than this in your personal life?"

Henri let out a bitter laugh. "Brother, no offense. But this marriage thing is a helluva lot harder than it looks."

Gervais scooped up the football and tossed it to him. "Our family is too quick to anger and rifts."

"What are you talking about? We're tight." He stepped back, putting some distance between them before flinging the football back at his brother.

"Seriously? Are you delusional?" Gervais caught the pigskin, surprise coloring his face.

"Look at us now." Henri gestured between them and to the sprawling buildings of the family property.

"Look at our history," Gervais retorted. "Our dad didn't speak to the mother of his son for over a decade. We find out we have a brother we never knew about and Mom leaves, never to be heard from again. We have a brother in New York who barely graces our doorstep unless we're in crisis. We have one uncle who doesn't speak to us at all. And another in Texas who only shows up to support his son who plays on the team. This family doesn't have a problem cutting and running."

"I guess when you put it that way, it doesn't sound like a close-knit clan." Henri mused over his brother's words, balancing them against the security their lake-side spread had always given him. The mere presence of the Reynaud family homestead had anchored him, made him believe they were close and as stable as the Greek Revival construction. Gervais's words shook his foundation.

"Families have their problems, sure, but ours has more than a few. And I just don't want to see you fall victim to the pattern of cutting someone off rather than working through the tough stuff."

"You're referring to Fiona and me." Nodding in understanding, he tossed the football again.

"Yes, I am. You two are good together. Quite frankly, this break scares the hell out of me as I look at tying the knot myself. You two were the perfect couple."

"There's no such thing as perfect."

"Truth. So why are you expecting perfection?" Gervais lobbed more than just the football at Henri that time.

"Who says I'm the one who wants the divorce?" Gervais was out of line. Henri didn't want a divorce, didn't want things between Fiona and him to be over. His passion burned for her and her alone. Life without her… It was an impossible thought for him to even finish.

"If she's the one who wants to walk, then why aren't you fighting for her?"

"I'm giving her space." Space had been what she wanted.

"Space… Like I said, our family gives space all too easily." Gervais slammed the football to the ground, turning away from Henri to look at the compound.

His philosophical brother struck a chord in Henri. His words reverberated in his chest, stirring a renewed commitment to winning Fiona's mind, body and soul. Passion had never been a problem for him and Fiona. That burned bright and true. But this was more than getting her back into his bed. He wanted her back in his life. Full time.

He refused to be another Reynaud who cut and run.

She'd been dreaming about Henri.

In Fiona's imagination, they'd been together in Seattle, exploring the city's art district during one of the Hurricanes' trips to the West Coast. It had been the early days of their marriage, and they'd run through the rain to dart from one private studio to the next, trying to meet some of the city's up-and-coming artists just for the fun of it.

In the car on the way back to the hotel, they'd been sopping wet and laughing. Kissing. Touching with a feverish urgency. Almost as if they'd known their time together was limited and they needed to live on fast-forward.

Why hadn't she tried to slow things down? To build the bond that they'd need to get them through a lifetime instead of floating on that high of incredible physical intimacy?

Even as she thought it in her hazy dreams, she became aware of a strong hand on her hip. Stroking. Rubbing.

Alertness came to her slowly. Or maybe she just didn't mind lingering in that dreamy world between wakefulness and sleep. The real world had disappointed her enough times in the past year and a half.

She would gladly take her touches with her eyes closed for just a little while longer.

Her body hummed to life at Henri's urging, skin shivering with awareness at his caress.

"Fiona." Her husband breathed her name in a sigh that tickled along her bare neck right before he kissed her there.

Slowly. Thoroughly.

What was it about a kiss on the neck that could drive a woman wild? she wondered. Or was it only Henri's kisses that could turn her inside out like this?

Still lying on her side, she reached for him, knowing where he'd be. She palmed his rock-hard chest. He was so warm. So strong.

"Open your eyes." His soft command made her smile.

"Since when do you give orders in bed?" she teased, keeping her eyes closed.

"Since I need you to see me." His words, spoken with a starkness she hadn't expected, forced her eyes open.

"Is everything all right?" She moved her hand from his chest to his face, her eyes adjusting to the last rays of daylight filtering in through the blinds.

She'd napped for longer than she realized.

"Yes. I just needed to see you." He skimmed his hand up her side, following the curve of her waist to bring her closer to him in the bed.

"You're sure?" She crept closer still, remembering how good she'd felt in her dream. No, how good he'd made her feel just a few hours ago before she'd fallen asleep.

"Positive. I just want you to know I'm here." He dipped a kiss into the hollow behind her ear.

She sensed more at work, but she was content to lose herself in the moment. In the touches she'd denied herself for too long. No matter what the future held for her and Henri, she wanted to savor these moments in a way she hadn't known to do in the past. For too long, she'd been focused on their problems. For now, she wanted to remember the things they'd done well.

The things that made them both happy.

Threading her fingers through his hair, she sifted through to his scalp, down to his neck and over his powerful shoulders. He halted her touch midway down his arm. He gripped her hand to kiss her wrist and then continue down the inside of her forearm, surprising her with how ticklish she was there.

Their shared laughter felt like a rare gift, the moment so oddly poignant she wasn't sure if she should cry or jump him. Their eyes met. Held.

And she had her answer.

She needed this. Him. Melting into his arms, she kissed him, nipping his lower lip and stroking his tongue with growing urgency. He stripped her naked, removing every barrier between them while she poured all the longing of the last months into that kiss. His hands molded her gently, cruising over her curves and paying homage to every inch of her that wasn't in pain.

"I've missed you." He said it so softly she thought it was her own thought for a moment. "I know I've said it before, but I mean it."

"I know. Me, too," she admitted, glancing up to meet his eyes. Needing to say the words, too. "I've missed you, just being together, so much."

That's why she needed him so much right now.

He must have understood—of course he understood, since he knew her so damn well—because he shifted her thighs with his knee. He made a place for himself, gripping her hips and steering her where he wanted her. Close to him. So close.

She was ready for him, but he took his time brushing featherlight caresses up the hot, needy center of her until she had to threaten him with dire sexual payback if he didn't come inside her.

She could feel his smile against her mouth when he kissed her and the heat of him nudged inside her. His smile faded when she thrust her hips hard into his, taking all of him and holding him tight. She could feel his heart pound hard and fast against her chest on the right side where he allowed himself to make contact with her.

Arms looped around his neck, she trusted him with her body. Knew he'd be careful with her and make her feel amazing at the same time.

And oh, did he deliver.

With his powerful thrust, he could have delivered heart-stopping pleasure to her all night long. He was tireless in pursuit of her pleasure. And while normally she liked to ensure he was every bit as swept away as her, tonight she simply let the desire build. Allowed the sensations to build however he wanted. Gave herself over to him completely.

"Henri." She whispered his name more than once as he took her to one dizzying high after another.

She clung to him, raining kisses down his impossibly strong torso, savoring the shift of muscle beneath her hands with his every movement.

When he finally reached that point of no return, she met his gaze again, remembering that he wanted her to see him.

What she saw sent her crashing into blissful completion as much as any skillful touch. Wave after wave of pleasure shuddered through her, undulating over her body. She felt his release, too, not just inside her, but under her hands as his back bowed and his muscles tensed.

She held him for a long time afterward, stroking his hair and remembering every moment they'd spent together. But most of all, she thought about what she'd seen in his eyes in that shattering moment before she'd hit her peak.

Her husband still loved her. Deeply.

And she was terrified of what that meant for both of them.

Eleven

Between her jumbled feelings for Henri and waiting for her biopsy results, the past days getting ready for the fund-raiser had zipped by in a blur of emotion. She'd spent every spare moment attending to different details. Making sure the event would go off without a hitch.

Making sure she didn't have time to think about the confusing mess she'd made of her life.

The lingering aftereffects of her biopsy still caused a dull ache in her chest and throughout her shoulder. The pain didn't slow her down, though. Her recent diagnosis of the cancer gene filled Fiona with a renewed sense of commitment to the cause. This event wasn't just in memory of her mother, aunt and grandmother. No, Fiona needed this event to work—to outperform any event she'd ever done—because she needed, down to her bones, to be a part of eradicating this disease that took too much from people and their families.

So she'd spent hours on the phone, personally reaching out to all her contacts to woo them into sponsoring the event. She found creative ways to pay for a memorable gala without taking an extra penny from the client's budget. No detail was too small for her to tackle full force.

She couldn't deny that another factor contributed to her increased productivity. Henri. Her failing marriage. The reality of life without him.

The thoughts were too real, too hard for her to deal with. Fiona threw herself into the fund-raiser because it filled her with purpose and direction. Things she desperately needed in her life right now.

After another day of dogged dedication, Fiona felt suffocated by the walls of her lonely home. It was time to get some fresh air and, she did need to get some paperwork she'd left at the Reynaud compound.

Not that she was looking for an excuse to run into Henri.

A quick drive later, she arrived at the sprawling cluster of buildings...the Greek Revival main house, the Italianate home, the carriage house, the boathouse...the dock.

Her gaze snagged on a figure at the end of the dock. Gramps sat on the bench overlooking the water, and while she knew he was likely fine, she also worried about him wandering off in a fog.

She set out toward the dock and the water, each step closer filling her lungs with the familiar scents of this place that had once been her home. The lake air had a way of breathing life into her.

The Friday event would irrevocably change the course of her life. And Henri's. As much as it pained her, she knew it was time to cut the ties between them. She could not—no, she would not—be the source of pain for him anymore. He deserved more. He deserved children and a wife who wasn't so sickly. Leaving would shelter his heart from any additional pain if those results—due any time now—turned out for the worst.

Though Henri had wanted her to stay with him through the rest of the season, she couldn't put them both through that. Too much pain. Too much exposure to the electric passion that hummed between them. And after the last few days…well, she couldn't lead either of them on like that.

After the charity event on Friday, Fiona would create her own timetable for leaving Henri. One that minimized damage to both of them.

A season of difficult choices was upon her. Henri planned on attending the event on Friday before leaving Saturday for Indianapolis, where he'd play his Sunday game. The running assumption was that she'd join him, take her place in the wives' section of the stands.

But maybe…maybe the better call came in the form of a clean break after the event. Leaving him to travel alone.

Alone?

Revulsion settled in the pit of her stomach. Alone. Could she really let him be unsupported during a season that could finally be the one he deserved? A season that might allow him to achieve all his professional dreams? As he'd pointed out, it wasn't just his dreams that were on the line this year, either. So many of the Reynauds were bound up in the Hurricanes' future. Could she live with herself if she was the cause of their championship run falling apart?

Before she could explore the ramifications of her idea, she got to Grandpa Leon. He clutched a glass of juice and balanced on his lap a dinner plate that contained specks of spiced sausage and rice.

His state continued to shock Fiona. Every time she saw him, he looked less and less like himself. The disease seemed to steal more than just his mind. The effects were rendered visible on his skin, his face. Even his smile had shifted, changed.

Glancing at her, he motioned for Fiona to sit next to him. "The boys used to like boating. But I don't see them use the yacht that often. Or maybe I am forgetting that, too. It just seems everyone is so busy working."

Sitting down beside him, she laid a hand on his tissue-paper-thin skin. "You would be right about that."

"I used to work, too. A lot." Grandpa Leon's sight turned inward. Fiona wondered what he remembered in this moment. If they were real memories or imagined.

"Yes, sir, you did."

"So I guess I'm to blame." Taking a swig of his juice, he spoke into his crystal glass.

Fiona shook her head, gathering her hair in her fist and pulling it over her shoulder. Grandpa Leon had stepped up for Henri and his brothers. Set a good example about the value of hard work and family. "They're adults. We all are. We make our own choices."

Flashing her a dentureless smile, he tapped her temple. "I've always liked you. When I remember who you are, of course."

"And I adore your sense of humor in the face of what has to be... Well, I enjoy your humor."

"Thank you, dear." His gaze returned out toward the yacht. Toward the past and what had been. Swirling around the last few drops of his juice, he let out a small sigh.

"Could I get you a jacket or a pillow?" she asked just as she saw Henri walking toward them. Her stomach twisted into knots and she wanted to run into his arms, but that would mean giving him answers to questions she wasn't ready to face yet.

Gramps extended his juice glass, staring absently ahead. "Just more juice."

Springing to her feet, she grabbed the glass from him and made fast tracks for the house, racing past Henri.

So much for a conversation with Fiona. She was dodging him like the plague.

Though Henri knew Fiona was busy with her fund-raiser, he felt that her disappearing act over these past few days had more to do with what was unresolved between them.

Henri had caught sight of her from the pool patio, sitting with his grandfather, looking out on the lake. She'd always been so good with Grandpa Leon. Nurturing. Kind. And as the disease claimed more and more of his memory, Fiona never lost her temper, but took it in stride, displaying patience even saints would envy.

Making his way out to her, Henri felt anticipation quicken his steps. She'd practically run into him, glass in hand. Her face was solemn, and she was quiet as she made her way back to the house.

Grandpa Leon turned his head, looking over his shoulder at Henri. Recognition washed over his expression.

Good. These days, Grandpa Leon's ability to process who was in front of him had waned. To be recognized was a rare blessing.

Gramps clapped Henri on the back as he sat down. "Nice figure on your girlfriend there, Christophe."

Henri's stomach fell. Watching his grandfather grasp at memories would never become easy. Grandpa Leon thought he was Christophe, his father's brother.

The Texas branch of the family was deeply involved in the Reynaud shipping empire and the cruise ship business. They owned an island off Galveston that was a self-sustaining working ranch and an optional stop on many of their cruise itineraries. Guests could ride horseback on the gulf beaches or take part in one of the farm-to-table feasts that made use of the organically grown vegetables. They hadn't visited their Texas cousins in years due to a family rift. Leon had publicly cut his oldest son, Christophe, out of his will long ago, but Uncle Christophe still retained his title as a vice president of global operations and, along with his oldest son, was very much a part of the family business.

Grandpa Leon's greeting was a small slipup. It didn't mean anything. Henri coughed, stepping closer to his grandfather. He scratched the back of his neck, hoping his grandfather would recognize him now. "Um, thank you."

Leon tapped Henri's ring finger. "You're married?

Married men shouldn't have a piece on the side. It's not right."

Offering a small smile, he sat down next to his grandfather. "Grandpa, I'm Henri, and Fiona's my wife."

Fog settled on his grandfather. He pursed his lips, weighing the information. Looking down at his feet, he shook his head. "Oh, right. Of course you are, and she is. I just never expected you to go for the kind who've, um, had surgical embellishments."

"I'm not sure what you're talking about."

Grandpa Leon's eyebrows shot up. Cocking his head to the right, he gestured to his chest and lifted upward a hint.

Just in time for Fiona to come back with his re-filled juice.

Henri's voice fell low. "How do you know that?"

"I have a keen eye for the finer things in life. I just am not so sure why such an already perfect woman would alter anything about herself."

Handing the glass to Henri, Fiona leaned in to kiss Grandpa Leon's cheek. "Grandpa, you're amazing. Love you."

The older man reached up to touch the side of her face. Henri saw how the simplest movements tired his grandfather.

Dropping his hand away from Fiona, Grandpa Leon peered back and forth between Fiona and Henri. He pursed his dry lips.

Handing his grandfather the glass of juice, Henri looked at his wife, trying to ferret out what she was thinking.

Grandpa Leon took a big swig of his juice and

popped his lips. Shakily, he rose to his feet, stretching his arms out above him.

"You two kids have fun. *Jeopardy* will be on soon and I can't miss that." He winked at Henri, shuffling toward the house.

"Do you need help, Grandpa?" Henri asked earnestly.

Waving Henri off, Grandpa Leon shook his head. "No. No. You two stay here. Enjoy the sunset."

As Leon walked to the house, Fiona made her way to the dock. Sitting on the edge, she let her bare feet dangle over the water, swinging them to unheard music.

Henri strode over to join her. He was itching to speak to her. To win her back still, even though she'd been avoiding him over the last few days.

Taking a seat next to her, he remembered all the times they'd sat here when they were first married. They'd talk here for hours. About literature and art and football. Everything.

Fiona twisted her rope of long dark hair draped over her shoulder. "How strange that your grandfather knew I'd had surgery all this time and never said a word. I might have expected a man to notice if I'd opted for larger, but since I went down a cup size… I'm just surprised."

"You and I instituted the code of silence on this. Maybe he sensed that, too." His grandfather had always been intuitive, if a bit eccentric.

Leon hadn't given Henri and his brothers the most traditional upbringing once he'd stepped in to take charge of his four rowdy grandsons, but he understood boys. He'd brought a fifties-era Harley-Davidson to the Texas ranch to give them a lesson in engine rebuilding. The motorcycle had been in crates when he bought the beat-up old thing. By the end of the summer they'd reveled in seeing how fast it would race on the private ranch roads. They'd even collected a lot of bruises along the way.

Memories of his youth and his grandfather flooded him. Watching as Alzheimer's consumed Grandpa Leon's mind tore at Henri. It was as if the lines connecting the flowchart of Grandpa Leon's memories had been erased.

"All this time I thought I was the one holding back. But it's you, too. You're scared," Henri said to Fiona.

"I meet with the doctor tomorrow. I'll know one way or another. Odds really are that it's nothing."

"I want to be there..." He paused. "But I can see in your eyes I'm not welcome."

"It's not that. I'm just not sure I can..." She shook her head. "Hell, I don't know. I just need to do this on my own."

Silence pooled around them, filling the spaces between them. It cut deeper than any fight or argument they'd had.

At least when they were fighting, he felt a connection. That their relationship had a chance because there was an active struggle. This silence felt like a killing blow.

As the sun sank farther into the lake horizon, he felt the weight of their situation sink onto his shoulders. He was losing her.

Pink balloons covered the entire ceiling of the new wing of the hospital soon to open as an updated children's oncology floor. Fiona clutched a glass of champagne, taking in the mass of people that flooded the ward.

Success. Her biggest one yet. Despite the tiny budget and last-minute assignment, the event was packed. In one corner, people bid on silent auction items, which were always a strong source of donations at charity events. A few casino games provided more entertainment and allowed attendees to contribute while having fun.

But the event was mostly family oriented. Nearby, a troupe of storytellers in elaborate costumes held the attention of a glitzed-out crowd. She watched the emotions play out on the faces of the audience.

Across the room from her, Henri handed out footballs signed by the entire Hurricanes team. She watched the way the women in the crowd ogled him. A surge of jealousy sank into her veins.

The event should make her feel fulfilled. At the very least, accomplished. But as she surveyed the pianist and TV star-turned-pop singer Daisy Dani, she felt hollow. She smoothed her crepe skirt, fingers catching on the sequins that outlined a paisley pattern that managed to be elegant and bohemian at the same time. While the deep purple skirt shone with metallic highlights, the dark silk blouse on top was simple and secure. No more shoulder-baring costume mishaps for her.

Hearing Henri's laugh from across the room ignited her feet to move. Things had been strange between them over the past few days. A new sort of strain had settled between them. She'd tried texting him earlier, but phones were forbidden during practice.

The results of her biopsy had come in today. She'd

promised to let him know the results and she had. Right away.

The biopsy had revealed nothing. No cancer. Such news ought to fill her with relief and promise, but the risk of the cancer gene would always be part of her existence. Just like her scars. Permanent marks on her mind and body.

Fiona had told Henri via text that she was in the clear. Everything from the test had come back normal. No reason to worry.

As she made her way to Henri, she bumped into the doctor who had asked her out. Had that really only been a few weeks ago?

So much had changed since her last fund-raiser. Her relationship with Henri had cooled and heated...and now? Well, now it was an utter mess.

Things with the doctor were cordial, platonic. At least on her end. Avoiding a drawn-out conversation, she almost couldn't believe her eyes.

She blinked, stunned. Jean-Pierre had arrived at the party. He and Henri hadn't exchanged more than a few words in months. Things in the family had been strained since Jean-Pierre had left New Orleans. But having him show up added to the pro ball appeal of the event, and would give the fund-raising a generous boost.

As the youngest Reynaud, Jean-Pierre had inherited his love of the game from his father and his grandfather, the same as his brothers. But Jean-Pierre had gone to college playing the quarterback position, the same as Henri. And since Jean-Pierre wasn't the kind of man to play in a brother's shadow, he hadn't wanted a spot on the Hurricanes. He was a starter and an elite player. When the New York Gladiators had made him an offer, he'd taken it.

Fiona shouldered through the masses of people to her brother-in-law.

"Jean-Pierre, how did you know we could use the extra help for this? It's wonderful to see you, but why are you here?"

"Henri told me you had to salvage this event so he called me." He grinned, leaning in to give her a hug and a kiss on her cheek. "Access to the family's private plane has its perks. I had some time, so I was able to swing it."

"Thank you." She was touched. Not just by Jean-Pierre's quick flight and visit, but that Henri had thought to ask him.

Jean-Pierre acknowledged greetings from a few friends, and now the whole room was buzzing with all the star power. When his fans had shuffled past, his eyes returned to Fiona's. "Not a problem. The Gladiators' PR guy thought it was a good idea. I'm off to sign a few more autographs. Nice party. You did a great job."

She thanked him again before he melted into the crowd, moving slowly since he was signing autographs as he made his way, shaking hands and making time for everyone who wanted to see him.

With no one else vying for her attention, Fiona edged her way to Henri. He looked so handsome in his tuxedo, as he always did. But she could see the way he stiffened as she approached, as if bracing for the next hit. The tension in his jaw pulsated as she drew near. Hurt still colored his face.

Tugging at his blue shirtsleeve, she leaned into him,

her heavy sterling silver bracelet sliding down her arm. Placing her hand on his chest, she tried to memorize his scent and the way he stood. Pain ached in her joints. Everything would change after this conversation.

She just hoped she'd make it through the hardest conversation she'd ever have.

"Let's step outside. Just us." The words formed on her tongue like a prayer or a plea.

Rather than answering her, he placed his hand on the small of her back. Shivers rolled up her spine as he led them outside. Laughter and music filtered through the doors as they sat on the bench in the garden patio.

In the distance, the night hummed with the sound of expensive cars being parked by the valets. A few feet away, a water feature gurgled and multicolored lights glinted. A few patients who'd been medically cleared to attend were brought out in wheelchairs and chatted with guests. One teen in particular caught her eye, a thin girl with a party hat—a cloth jester cap—on her bald head. Streamers glittered from her chair and her mother leaned down to whisper something while her father set plates of food down on a nearby bench.

Fiona tore her gaze away before the image dragged her under, and focused her attention back on Henri. There was a buzz of activity here, but not the press of a crowd like inside. Here, they could speak privately, seated on another bench, one of the three she'd donated in memory of her mother, her grandmother and her aunt.

Henri's mouth thinned for a moment. She could see the ragged edges of his nerves, the stress she'd caused. The hurt. Her fingers clutched the edges of the stately concrete bench, sturdy, made to survive far longer than her mother had. Her breath hitched as she fought harder to tamp down the tears, the emotion.

Henri gently pried her hand free from the bench— her mother's bench—and linked fingers with her. She tried to hold onto the feel of his rough calluses from years and years of training and practice.

His wedding band glinted in the halo of patio lights. "Thank you for letting me know about the doctor visit. I'm glad the scare's over. And that you're okay."

Chewing her lip, she could only think of this party, everything surrounding her reminding her of what she needed to do no matter how much pain it caused her.

"Except the scare will never be over, Henri. There will always be a next time. You'll worry every time I go for a checkup." Words exploded from her mouth like gunshots. He needed to hear this. Needed to understand everything. "Look at you. Even when I say that now, you look like you're going to throw up."

"Because I care about you, dammit."

"I care about you, too." She couldn't deny the truth any longer. "In fact, I'm still in love with you."

"You love me? Then why the hell are you divorcing me?" he barked, confusion swimming in his dark eyes.

"Because I can see how this is tearing you apart. Even your grandfather sees me as I am. A woman with a high risk of contracting cancer one day. I pray if I do that it will be curable. But I don't know. I do know *I* can live with that possibility." She looked around her, at the patients in the wheelchairs. And she looked at their families with their haunted, exhausted and scared eyes. "But I can't live with watching how afraid it makes you."

"You were fine with us having sex and being together these past few days when you thought it was day by day." He leveled the accusation at her. His gruff voice seemed to shake the night air. "Then, once you had to think about forever, you shut me out."

"That's not fair. You're not listening."

"I am listening. I've been listening. And you know what I hear?" He turned sideways on the bench, drawing his face close to hers. Tucking a loose hair behind her ear, he breathed. "I keep hearing none of this is fair to either one of us."

Desire. Hurt. Longing. The three warring emotions beat in her chest, threatening to disrupt her course of action. But she had to focus on why she was here. To end things before either of them suffered a loss they'd never recover from. She had to be brave, to face this head-on.

Pulling away from his touch, she lowered his hand to his lap. "We shouldn't be discussing this two days before a game. You need to focus."

"Impossible." Resting his forehead on his hand, rubbing his temples, talking more to the ground than to her, he said, "There's never going to be a good time for this conversation."

"Henri, please, what are you hoping to accomplish?"

"To make you admit what we had was real." He tipped his head to look sideways at her. "But you checked out of our relationship."

Tears clogged her throat, even stinging her nose. But she wouldn't cry in front of him. She'd shed so many tears over the mess she'd made of their marriage. "Fine, you wanted this conversation now, we'll have it. I admit it. I can't deal with being married to you. I'm scared as hell, every single day when I wake up, that

I'm going to get sick, and just the thought of you grieving over me dying rips my heart out again and again."

Fiona knew how to pick a moment. Art had taught her as much. She knew what leaving looked like. Her mother, her aunt, her grandmother. Knew what it was like to be left behind, to suffer with a loss that ravaged the bones.

With tender fingers, she stroked the side of his face, tracing the faintest stubble with her fingertips. His lips parted slightly. Leaning into him, she inhaled his cologne and musk. Her lips found his. Pressed a kiss from her soul to his.

Their last kiss.

Twelve

Henri had thought football was his world. Until he met Fiona.

Love for her had slammed into him hard and fast.

As hard and fast as the Indianapolis linebacker plowing toward him—

Damn.

His body hit the ground in a crunch of shoulder pads, grunts and smack talk. Well deserved. He was losing this game for his team. His mind wasn't in the game. Hell, his heart wasn't in it.

Crisp fall air stung his lungs as he viewed the world from the ground. How damn symbolic. Dazed, he blinked into focus. Eyes scanning the crowd, he saw the disappointment on the faces of his teammates after what should have been a straightforward third-down conversion. He clenched his teeth.

This game should have been a simple win for them. The Hurricanes had a better record against better opponents. Their key players were all healthy. But instead of posting big numbers for their team and calling in some guys off the bench, they were fighting to stay in the game, and that was clearly his fault.

The world spun, but not just from the impact of the 230-pound rookie with the speed of a track star. Henri's eyes trailed to the wives' section, where he half expected to see Fiona, decked out in team colors and a scarf.

But she wasn't there. Hadn't bothered to get on the plane. She'd said she was still in love with him and for that precise reason, she needed to leave him.

Nothing made sense anymore.

He'd spent too much time knocked down lately. Pushing himself off the turf, he launched into the air, landing on his feet.

The Hurricanes fans peppered through the crowd cheered as he rose to his feet. At once believing in him and completely oblivious to the metaphorically shaky ground he stood on. They wouldn't cheer if they understood why his game was off.

Brushing the dirt from his shoulder, he started to walk toward his team. But two of the team trainers were already there, ready to help him off the field.

"I'm fine." He waved them off.

He could hear the offensive coordinator in his ear through the microphone in his helmet. "You're off the field, Henri."

"What the hell?" Henri straightened his helmet that had been knocked askew, talking to the trainers and his offensive coach at the same time. "I'm fine."

He could see his brother Dempsey, the head coach, waving him off the field from the sidelines. His backup had already sprinted to the huddle.

Benched? What in the hell would that accomplish? Henri's pride bristled. It was not as if they were punting it away. The Hurricanes were going for it on fourth down, trying to take that yardage he'd failed to grab in the last play.

"You're going to lose if you take me out." He could still recover the game. The tackle left him with new clarity.

Adjusting his ball cap, Dempsey shook his head, eyes firm and impassive as Henri reached his side. "And you're going to risk breaking your damn neck out there. I'm not ending this day with you in the hospital." He shoved his microphone aside to talk to Henri without an audience on their headsets.

Nearby, the offensive coordinator stepped up to run the show as the clock kept ticking.

"So what, I get tackled once and suddenly I'm a candidate for ICU?" Henri barked back, tugging off his helmet to keep this conversation as private as the fishbowl of a stadium would allow.

Dempsey ripped off his own headset, too, turning a shoulder to the field. Away from the inevitable cameras focused on them.

"We both know that's not what's going on here. Fiona isn't here and your rocky marriage has compromised your focus like we all damn well warned you it would. You are getting your ass handed to you out there," Dempsey said flatly.

"To hell with that. I can handle the field," he shouted back at his brother, rage coursing in his veins.

Henri's teammates nearby exchanged glances. Outbursts of emotion weren't his normal MO and no one talked back to the coach—family or not.

Dempsey leveled a glare at him. "This isn't the backyard. And you might want to think about what you say next." He slammed his headset back into place and turned his attention toward the field where the backup QB had just run for the yards they needed.

A much-needed Hurricanes first down and it hadn't come from Henri. He tried to hide his bitterness, knowing damn well a camera would be closing in on his face right about now.

Henri's cousin and Wild Card approached him, providing a wall of shoulders between him and the cameras.

"Hey, man. Just sit out a few. We'll do you proud, brother." Wild Card clapped him on the shoulder, walking out a stinger in his knee from a previous play.

"Yeah, cuz. We're a family here. Let someone else step up and take care of business. You take care of you," his cousin said with his Texas twang. No judgment, no fuss. They were good men. Good friends.

Deep down, Henri knew that. He seethed anyway.

Sitting on the bench, he watched his second family execute play after play. They moved like an extension of each other. Synced. In tune.

The longer he sat on the bench, the more Dempsey's words rang true. Dempsey had called it. Henri's performance had been poor. He'd been asking for an injury, asking to feel something other than numb.

Pulling him from the game was the right call. But then, Dempsey wasn't calling the plays because he was a novice. His older half brother had as much at stake this season as he did. More, maybe.

Henri had to get his head together for real. Because in marriage, he didn't have any backup. It was just him and he was screwing it up big-time. This was about more than football. It was about his wife. His life.

His love.

Guilt flooded through Fiona.

She should have gone to Henri's game. He'd come to her fund-raiser and, yes, the night had ended with a fight. The worst kind. The forever kind.

The longer she spent alone with her ice cream in her garden, the more she realized she needed to talk to him. She needed to shake him out of his family's habit of cutting people off—his family that had Texas cousins who mostly never spoke. And then there was the California branch that owned vineyards she'd maybe heard mentioned once. It was insane. The Reynauds had so many branches, so many healthy, thriving parts, and yet they didn't even function as a family. Didn't they know how fortunate they were?

Her phone buzzed on the wrought-iron patio table. An incoming text lit up the screen. She swiped her finger across and found a photo from the night before. A photo of the teenage cancer patient who'd worn the jester hat, her mom and dad leaning in on either side of her with matching smiles.

The text scrolled: We're making memories for a

lifetime with every moment. Thank you for an awe-some night!

A second photo came through of the girl with Henri and Jean-Pierre: So excited to meet football idols. She texted the photo to all her school friends. Thank you again.

The joy on the teen's face, on her parents' faces, blew Fiona away. They weren't just brave. Somehow they were happy in the moment. Something her family had never quite managed.

Something she'd never managed.

She'd walked away from her marriage because she didn't know if she could deal with Henri's fears. But had she even tried to manage her own? Could she honestly live with herself if she cut them both off without trying to get a handle on those fears? Her finger traced the faces—genuinely happy faces—and wondered how she'd missed that joy for herself. She kept telling Henri she was strong. But maybe she hadn't been strong enough to truly live in the moment.

It was time to quit assuming Henri would fall apart the way her father had. It was time to stop fearing she would follow her mother's path.

She'd already chosen a different path with her surgery. A hopeful path. She could embrace the day and be her own person, no matter what that future held. It was time to accept the happiness waiting for her.

Snatching up her phone and wallet, she wasn't wasting another moment. She rushed to the closest airport where the family kept their jet. She called Gervais on the way, needing to clear it with him before she used it, but he not only gave his approval, he also managed to put a pilot on site to greet her with the flight plan filed for immediate takeoff. What a godsend to have the support system of family. Why had she spent so much time pushing them away with both hands?

Fiona's stomach was a bundle of nerves as the Gulf-stream touched down in Indianapolis. She'd watched the rest of the game on the jet's television, catching the final few plays in a streaming app on her phone.

Henri had been benched even though he stood up after that hard hit in the backfield. He didn't seem to have been treated for concussion symptoms, but maybe they'd say as much in the press to dance around the fact that he simply hadn't played well.

The Hurricanes barely won, and only because the game had been put into the rest of the team's hands while the Bayou Bomber sat one out. Dempsey's strategic coaching had coaxed a win out of the backup quarterback and the rest of the starters, so she suspected Henri wasn't going to be in any kind of mood to see her and talk about their problems.

Again.

But she'd come too far now to back off. And thanks to Gervais's help again, she'd landed at the airport and hopefully would make it to meet them before they left. The jet taxied over to the parking area. She peered out the window, praying she had enough time to get to the stadium. Were any of the parked jets theirs? Surely if they'd left, Gervais would have let the pilot know their flight was in vain.

Just when she was about to grab her phone to call him and check, she caught sight of a chartered bus driving toward one of the other planes. The sort of bus the team would usually travel in collectively to the airport. Her stomach did cartwheels.

Could she have been that close to missing him? Yes, they could have spoken later, but now that she'd figured out what she'd been missing—the happiness she'd been robbing them both of—she couldn't bear the thought of waiting a second longer to see Henri.

Her jet stopped wonderfully close to the path of the bus—bless the pilot and Gervais. Eons later—or at least it felt so—the steps were in place on the Gulf-stream so she could disembark. Cautious feet found purchase on the stairway leading out of the jet. Wind gusting her hair back, she had to bring her hands to her eyes to make out the New Orleans Hurricanes team inside the bus. But then the charter bus's door opened, and the players exited one after the other.

Heart beating hard in her chest, she scanned the team for Henri. Dempsey. Wild Card. Freight Train.

They were all there. But where was Henri?

She felt far away from her body as he came into view. His broad shoulders and wind-tossed dark hair. Sunglasses that shielded his eyes even though night had fallen. Did he see her?

She couldn't wait for him to notice her. Here she was. Ready to gamble, to leap. Gathering her voice, she yelled his name.

She half tripped down the steps of the jet, her ballet flats pounding the asphalt as she ran toward him, still calling out.

"Henri? Henri!" she shouted, her feet picking up pace, her dress wrapping around her legs.

Henri's back was to her now, but his muscular frame was easy to pick out in his tailored charcoal-colored suit.

No matter what he wore, he was still as sexy as the day she'd met him.

He glanced over his shoulder. He cocked his head to the side, then as the distance closed between them she could see him raise an eyebrow. Luckily Dempsey waved away security and Henri broke ranks.

Henri's arms went wide and without hesitation she flew into them. That easy. That right. She was his. He was hers.

He looked over at his brother. "Dempsey, can we have a moment?"

Dempsey laughed. "Now you ask permission?" He gave his brother a shove in Fiona's direction.

Henri took her by the elbow and guided her back into the Reynauds' private jet. "Why are you here? Wait. Never mind. Who the hell cares? You're here."

He hauled her into his arms and kissed her. Really kissed her in a way he hadn't done in…she couldn't remember when. It was something more than the kisses of their early romance. Something more than the kisses of their newlywed days. This was the kiss of a couple tested in fire. More than the fire of passion, but the fire of life.

She eased back, sweeping her hand over his hair that curled after a fresh wash. "I'm here to say I'm sorry. To say I want to try if you'll forgive me for being afraid to face the future. Living in the day was so much…safer."

"God, I lo—"

She pressed a hand to his mouth. "I know. You've

shown me in a million ways with your patience, but I want to be the one to say it first. I love you. I want to spend every day of my life with you. I want to live for each day and focus on that. The joy, the beauty, the art. Our love. And yes, our family. I want to focus on the positive every day for however many days we have." She traced his lips. "I hope you understand that while half the fear was for me, the other half was fear of hurting you."

"Losing you these past months has hurt like hell." His arms found her waist, snaked around her hips. He pulled her closer, as if she'd blow away in the wind if he didn't. She'd missed the feel of his arms around her. Had forgotten what being together—truly together—was like.

"I'm sorry. Who would have thought dreaming of a future would be so scary?"

"I do understand, but you'll help me be strong, won't you?" His smile was light but his dark eyes were serious.

"We'll help each other. I hope there will be countless days. It's not about how much time we have, but how beautiful we can make each day together."

"Not that I'm going to tempt fate here, but I am curious. What made you change your mind? Did my family hound you? Because if they're being pushy just let me know."

"Actually, they've been incredibly helpful. Gervais even set up the plane. Looking back, I'm rethinking our decision to keep them in the dark these past months." She glanced at the window, at the bus full of players waiting patiently as the exhaust puffed into the night air. "I learned my lesson from a photo the mom of one of the patients at the party texted me. I can show you later. It's…beautiful."

"I look forward to seeing it." He brushed a kiss across her lips. "I want us to talk more, share more, spend more time together. I've decided I should quit the team."

Shock pulled at her heartstrings. She had to have misheard him. Football wasn't just a job for him. Passion for the game ran as deep as her passion for art. "What?"

"At the end of the season, I'm through."

"What about your contract?" Another gust of fall wind ripped past them, carrying the smell of oil and decomposing leaves past them.

Pushing the hair from her eyes, he kissed her forehead, his lips gentle and warm in the cool atmosphere.

"I'll buy out. Money's not an issue."

"You love the game. I don't understand." Fiona shook her head, processing the logic of his words.

"I love you more, and I'll do whatever it takes to win you back. We'll take more time to get to know each other, at home or traveling, or starting a fund-raising foundation. I'm committed to making this work. No half measures. I want you as my wife, my love, my life." He spoke in earnest. She could see that in the way a faint smile tugged at the corner of his lips and how his gaze intensified as he stared into her eyes.

But Henri without football? That didn't seem right. The game twined with his soul, his purpose. They had to reach a point where they accepted all of each other, no holding back, no reservations. They couldn't pick and choose parts to love and parts to neglect. That road had led them to ruin.

Time to begin again. To take bigger chances and risks together.

She rested her head against his chest, listening to his pounding heart. He offered her complete devotion and she appreciated the sentiment, needed to hear he'd move heaven and earth for them. But she didn't need Henri to give up his job to fix them. They'd do that together.

"Henri, you don't have to give up your job for me."

"I do if it means I could lose you again."

She repeated her thoughts from earlier out loud. "I'm yours. You're mine. When I talk about the joy of living, I mean embracing every part of who we are. I love the game, traveling, seeing you play. We can figure out the details together. If we need to, we can truly talk with the counselor rather than racing straight to the lawyer. Are you okay with that?" Communication. That's what they needed. Old-fashioned communication.

"Whatever it takes. I've made that clear." He kissed her nose. Her temple. Her neck. Her mouth. Each kiss affirming his commitment—a promise imprinted into her skin. Into her soul.

Enjoying the feel of him, she asked, "What if I say counseling and you keep playing?"

Her fingers traced designs on the back of his neck as their eyes met.

"I think you're letting me off too easily, my love."

She rolled her eyes and arched up to give him a quick kiss. "Oh, I don't think this is going to be easy at all. Not if we dig in deep with counseling."

"I can face it if we're together." He intertwined their hands. Raised their joined fists to his lips. Kissed the back of her hand while staring into her eyes.

"Together, as a team." She stepped closer, their clasped hands against her heart. "That sounds like a winning game plan to me."

* * * * *

COMING SOON!

We really hope you enjoyed reading this book.
If you're looking for more romance
be sure to head to the shops when
new books are available on

Thursday 27th March

To see which titles are coming soon, please visit
millsandboon.co.uk/nextmonth

MILLS & BOON

MILLS & BOON

THE HEART OF ROMANCE

A ROMANCE FOR EVERY READER

MODERN — Prepare to be swept off your feet by sophisticated, sexy and seductive heroes, in some of the world's most glamourous and romantic locations, where power and passion collide.

HISTORICAL — Escape with historical heroes from time gone by. Whether your passion is for wicked Regency Rakes, muscled Vikings or rugged Highlanders, awaken the romance of the past.

MEDICAL — Set your pulse racing with dedicated, delectable doctors in the high-pressure world of medicine, where emotions run high and passion, comfort and love are the best medicine.

True Love — Celebrate true love with tender stories of heartfelt romance, from the rush of falling in love to the joy a new baby can bring, and a focus on the emotional heart of a relationship.

HEROES — The excitement of a gripping thriller, with intense romance at its heart. Resourceful, true-to-life women and strong, fearless men face danger and desire - a killer combination!

 — From showing up to glowing up, these characters are on the path to leading their best lives and finding romance along the way – with plenty of sizzling spice!

To see which titles are coming soon, please visit

millsandboon.co.uk/nextmonth

LET'S TALK

Romance

For exclusive extracts, competitions
and special offers, find us online:

- **f** MillsandBoon
- **X** @MillsandBoon
- **⊙** @MillsandBoonUK
- **♪** @MillsandBoonUK

Get in touch on 01413 063 232

Afterglow Books is a trend-led, trope-filled list of books with diverse, authentic and relatable characters, a wide array of voices and representations, plus real world trials and tribulations. Featuring all the tropes you could possibly want (think small-town settings, fake relationships, grumpy vs sunshine, enemies to lovers) and all with a generous dose of spice in every story.

♪ @millsandboonuk
📷 @millsandboonuk
afterglowbooks.co.uk
#AfterglowBooks

For all the latest book news, exclusive content and giveaways scan the QR code below to sign up to the Afterglow newsletter:

SCAN ME

afterglow BOOKS

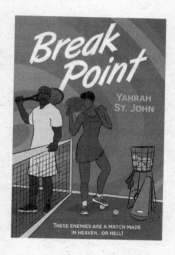

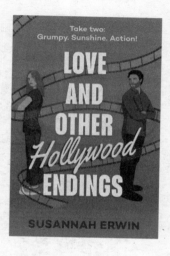

 Second chance

 Second chance

 Sports romance

 Workplace romance

 Enemies to lovers

 Grumpy/sunshine

OUT NOW

Two stories published every month. Discover more at:
Afterglowbooks.co.uk

afterglow BOOKS

Looking for more Afterglow Books?

Try the perfect subscription for spicy romance lovers and save 50% on your first parcel.

PLUS receive these additional benefits when you subscribe:

- **FREE** delivery direct to your door
- **EXCLUSIVE** offers every month
- **SAVE** up to 30% on pre-paid subscriptions

SUBSCRIBE AND SAVE

millsandboon.co.uk/Subscribe

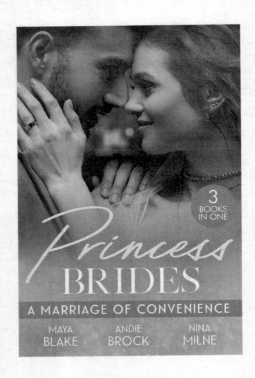

MILLS & BOON
A ROMANCE FOR EVERY READER

- **FREE** delivery direct to your door
- **EXCLUSIVE** offers every month
- **SAVE** up to 30% on pre-paid subscriptions

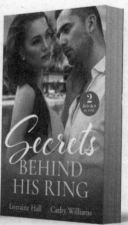

SUBSCRIBE AND SAVE

millsandboon.co.uk/Subscribe